C000195203

IN THE CITY OF THE DEAD

The wraith, barely seen, moved forward and raised one spectral, skeletal hand. It held a knife that glittered blood red and obsidian black, and shimmered in and out of reality just as the hand that held it. Ziv bared his teeth and threw his own knife; it passed harmlessly through the apparition and landed with a metallic clink against a stalagmite. The wraith ignored him, advancing on Astrid, who backed hastily away. The others were engaged in battling off zombies — even Brion, who was using his plain steel sword with awkward, desperate strokes. The zombies made a horrible, ululating wail that echoed continuously around the rock walls.

One by one, they burst into ravening flame, even the fallen, writhing pieces. That was Tyes' doing, as he dropped his guard and spent his store of power in a reckless pyrotechnic display. He staggered, and Pelk caught him.

"Go!" Tyes yelled, pushing his assistant toward the unguarded doorway. Pelk ran, then turned back at the entrance. Brion was coming, and Iarsang — Astrid and Ziv seemed frozen where they were. Tyes started towards them, but the wraith lunged with sudden, bitter speed.

It seemed impossible that anyone could move faster than the apparition, but Ziv twisted himself into the thing's path. The knife slid easily into his shoulder; the Changramai's returning cut went harmlessly through the creature's robes. Ziv staggered backwards; the knife was still pulsing strangely in his shoulder, and he reached up to tear it out. The hilt came away in his hand, but the red-and-black blade was gone.

His wound did not bleed.

› STORMRIDERS ›

A

SHADOW WORLD

NOVEL

BY

ROXANNE LONGSTREET

Copyright © 1990 Iron Crown Enterprises, Inc.
P.O. Box 1605, Charlottesville, VA 22902 USA

Shadow World and the Shadow World logo
are trademarks of Iron Crown Enterprises

ISBN 1-55806-138-X   STOCK # 6200

Cover Illustration: David Dorman

No part of this book may be reproduced, stored in a retrieval system, or
transmitted, in any form or by means, mechanical, electronic or otherwise,
without prior permission of the publishers, except that brief passages may
be quoted for reviews.

All characters and events portrayed in this book are fictional, and any
resemblance to real people or incidents is purely coincidental.

First Printing: 1990
Printed in USA

DEDICATION

To my father and mother, for believing in me (which is
important) and for loving me (which is more important).

ACKNOWLEDGMENTS

This work is the product of a lot of faith and support from many,
many people, most of whom will have to go unacknowledged until my
next book (if they ever let me do this again). In particular, though, I owe
Ed Andrews, who steered me into Shadow World and may never be
able to pry me out again; my readers — Ruth McNiel, Linda
Witherspoon, Brit Ledbetter, Leslie Womack, Jenny Womack, J
Womack, and Denise Jahraus — who were as liberal with criticism as
they were with praise; the entire staff of Cheerleader Supply Company
and all its divisions, who asks me every day how things are going; the
National Accounts Division at ADP, who gave me time to do this by
their enormous efficiency; and the Greater Dallas Writers Association.

Thanks to George Tinsley, Andrew Sealy, Andrea Redcay, Mona
Fluitt, Rachel Scarbrough, Marcia McNiel, and James (I Feel Good)
Brown, for being great friends, and to Ken and George, the moving
trolls, for helping me get settled in a crisis.

Most especially, thanks to James Alan Hanna, for being sentimental.

MAP OF JAIMAN

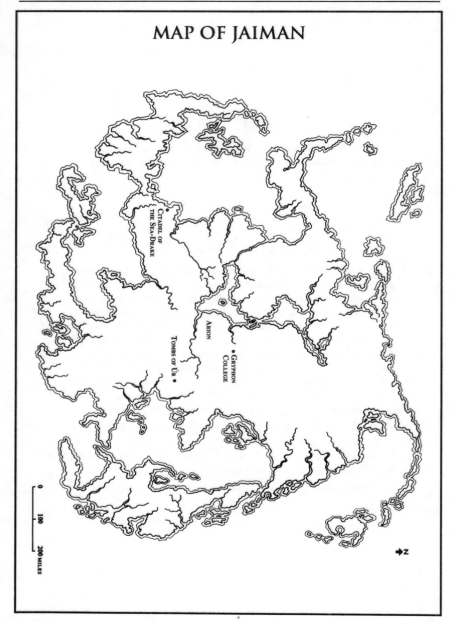

MAP OF QUELLBOURNE

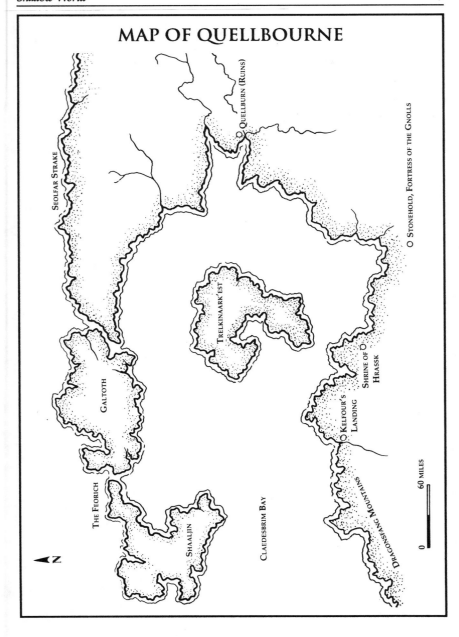

QUELLBURN (RUINS)

STONEHOLD, FORTRESS OF THE GNOLLS

SEOLFAR STRAKE

TRELKINAARK 'EST

SHRINE OF HRASSK

GALTOTH

KELFOUR'S LANDING

THE FEORICH

SHAALJIN

CLAEDESBRIM BAY

DRAGONSFANG MOUNTAINS

0　　　60 MILES

N

' STORMRIDERS '

◗ PROLOGUE ◖

The sorcerer threw open his precious chest of memories and searched through it again. He hoarded these things, things that on first sight had sparked some vague suggestion of a past life. Every day, sometimes every hour, he rooted through the untidy pile and tried to hold to those memories for long enough to piece them together.

Nothing. He let a huge opal ring fall back into the chest with a clatter, then swept his fingers across the broken strings of a harp. Broken strings, broken mind. He'd been whole, once. He'd be whole again.

Something rolled out of the chest and caught the faint candlelight; a ring, again, this one dotted with rubies and made to fit a woman's small finger. The sorcerer rubbed it possessively against his tattered robe and crooned to it, a sing-song of broken little prayers. Nothing came back except a vague scent of perfume and a shattering, tactile memory of rage beyond sanity —

He stood, suddenly, holding to the rage, and walked across the hall. A door there, long shut, he swung open. This room, especially, invoked faint stirrings in him, but nothing he could identify. The floor was of polished marble, but there was an eerily complex pattern set in the white tiles. The pattern drew the eye, soothed the mind; he'd almost set foot on it many times only to turn away in some last, unexplained sense of dread.

Today, though — today there was only the brilliant, diamond-like memory of rage, and nothing to hold him back. He put one foot on the first tile of the maze, and then the other. There was a cold, menacing sensation that stroked the back of his neck, but he held to the rage.

The rage was his. He remembered the woman, too: a slender, dark-haired woman in middle years, stern but beautiful. He hated her with a passion out of proportion to his memories. That was good. He relished the return of sensation, the awareness of time and acidic hatred.

Ten more steps, and he'd regained enough memories to know that he stood within the ruined city of Quellburn, on the continent of Quellbourne, in the world called Kulthea. That he'd betrayed Quellburn to its death, centuries ago; that the woman of the ruby ring had stood against him, had defeated him, had stripped him of his life and memory and left him an empty wandering wreck. Rage, again. It cleansed like cold water.

Two more steps. Memories that seared and terrified, and yet exhilarated — friends betrayed, enemies revenged upon, innocents slaughtered but unmourned. He'd wanted power. He'd gotten disaster at the hands of a woman wearing a ruby ring.

Yet that woman had died, and he had lived on, alone in this cursed place.

The last step, and he was out of the maze, blazing with restored memory and life and vitality. He sank to his knees, trembling, hands curled in his dark, silver-streaked hair, and began to laugh.

"You're gone, Alladyre. You're gone, and there's no one left to stand against me."
He opened his right hand to look at the ruby ring. The faceted edges had cut deep
grooves in his palm that flared bright red when released. He tossed it in the air and
caught it, smiling. "You've lost. I win. I — Zenon."

He put the ring down on the marble tile and brought his boot heel down on it until
it shattered into a thousand blood-red crystalline drops.

Thousands of miles away, curiously linked to the sorcerer, another dark-haired
man sat in the shadows and hugged his knees to his chest. He rocked back and forth
in a childlike gesture while his mind ranged out, crippled and distracted as it was.
There was something wrong, something direly wrong. It was his duty —

But it was too much to think of. Andraax let his head sink back down to rest on
his knees and deliberately let go of the strange warning.

It would take more than a warning to push him into conflict again.

› CHAPTER ONE ›

Iarsang sat with his back to the sheltering rock and stared dreamily into the storm. He was buffeted by wild shrieking gusts of wind, but none of his frightened charges dared to approach or disturb him even to ask after his health. There were no tales of a Navigator going mad, but — well —

A snap of lightning exploded just outside of the cave in an actinic fury; the inhabitants of the cave jerked back and cried out in panic. Nomaran Estvir, the senior of the two clerics, was praying in a frantic, hushed voice to his patron deity Phaon, but no one really expected a prompt answer to that. The senior gods of Kulthea, called the Lords of Orhan because popular theory put their home on that luminous moon, had a large but unfanatical following. The gods were casually considerate to the needs of their worshippers, but the deities (including Phaon) were far too busy to concern themselves with specifics — or individuals. Thus, the men of Kulthea had little confidence in divine intervention.

The second cleric, Benevolent Lady Astrid Haladan, sat in shaking silence as thunder poured over them like a flood; she clenched her fingers together until the pale skin whitened almost to bone. The handsome young man who gave his name as Civad the Jeweller (and was by all likelihood a thief) was in little better shape where he sat beside her. He'd originally been practicing magic tricks, but when his travelling companions remained unimpressed he'd taken to weaving a coin through his restless fingers. The gold shivered in the fitful lightning and seemed to move with a life of its own.

Only Iarsang seemed unaffected by the fury of the storm as he watched the Essence Flows dance in the tortured sky.

Iarsang was growing concerned, though it showed not a bit on his abstracted, handsome face. The Essence Flows were moving in strange, disturbing patterns as the storm energies pulled at them. Not a good night to be abroad, here in the shadow of Rihtoth Mountain and so far from the promised goal of Kelfour's Landing. Even had the storm been just a storm, which he could not say with any confidence, the winds were sweeping down the jagged sides of the Dragonsfang Mountains with enough force to take his little caravan without a trace.

Worse than that, his attempts to turn the storm or to reduce the winds met with no success at all. Here they were, and here they would have to stay until the storm lessened. At least his charges wouldn't argue.

They never did, really, once the gold was paid.

"Navigator?" The Benevolent Lady Astrid spoke over the crash of more thunder. Lightning streaked through the sky again, leaching color out of her skin and leaving her as pale as a corpse. Iarsang turned to look at her, polite but clearly distracted. She knotted her fingers even tighter. "Navigator, if I may ask, can we go forward?"

"It would not be wise," Iarsang answered her calmly as a shear of wind tore up a small tree by its roots on the mountain slope outside. His brown eyes were so completely blank that it gave her an unexpected chill. "Unless, of course, you would prefer to pay for a Jump past the range of this storm. I will cheerfully provide that service."

"How much?" Civad-who-was-probably-not-a-Jeweller asked quickly. The gold he'd been spinning on his fingertips mysteriously disappeared. The others looked less inclined to count coin, but Iarsang smiled.

"An additional fee of one hundred fifty gold pieces should be enough," Iarsang told him. And then, before they could all give a joint sigh of relief and dig for the gold, "Each."

"Each!" Nomaran Estvir squeaked, and was echoed by the others. "Master Navigator, the entire journey was only two hundred gold apiece! This is sheer thievery!"

Cleric Nomaran did not recognize the sharp upward tilt of Iarsang's eyebrow, but he registered it as a change of expression in the fine, handsome, Iylari-Elven face that thus far had shown only dreamy preoccupation. Iarsang's eyes suddenly looked uncommonly alert.

"The cleric meant no offense, Honored Navigator," Benevolent Lady Astrid ventured hastily, just in case that was the direction of Iarsang's thoughts. "It's only that — well — perhaps it might be better to wait out the storm. Surely Jumping past the storm would put us out of our way considerably."

"I would not think of causing inconvenience," Iarsang said. Whatever else he might have said was lost forever in the crash of an unearthly brilliant flash of lightning — and the thunder which followed almost immediately in deafening concussion. Even Iarsang found it prudent to move back a little from the cave entrance. As he was doing so, the glowing Compass on his arm pulsed and lit suddenly with a fury even brighter than the flashing storm. His clients crawled hastily backwards in the glare, but this was not some bizarre manifestation of a Navigator's pique; he wasn't even looking in their direction. He was looking out toward the mouth of the cave again, and past it, with strange, blank eyes and a face from which all expression, even bemusement, had disappeared.

"What is it?" Astrid cried as she shielded her eyes from the glow with shaking fingers. The light was so strong that she saw clearly the pale red rush of her blood shining under translucent skin, and the dark sticks of bone beneath. She shut her eyes as the flare grew brighter still. The cave filled with the burnt-copper smell of a close strike of lightning.

"Too late," Iarsang said clearly, very precisely. He was pale, whether bleached by shock or Compass-fury no one could say. "Flow Storm. This is just the edge of it, but I do not dare Navigate so much as an inch while it rages. I am afraid we now have no options at all."

Both of the clerics began praying again with desperate fervor, but no one really believed they would be heard. Surely even the Lords of Orhan feared to expose themselves to Flow Storm.

I am going to do this, Kella whispered to herself with cold determination. No more excuses, no more hesitation. I am going to kill him.

It was a terrible thing to be thinking as she stared at her husband, a thing that had been growing steadily and blackly in the shadows of her mind for months now. At first she had buried it in horror. Then, as time passed, as she grew more and more to hate the very sight of his mild stupid face, she had dragged that strange, violent desire out into the bright light and looked it over. Sometime in the last few weeks, it had ceased to horrify her at all.

There had been a stab of terror and guilt as she purchased the little vial of colorless liquid that rested in her skirt pocket, but even that had passed. Kella's right hand clenched over the smooth glass surface as she looked at Brion. She imagined him dead. The poison was quick and deadly (she was, after all, not cruel!). In only a moment, it would be over: a glass of cold wine, spiced with a few tasteless drops; a disbelieving gasp as the poison sank venomous roots deep in his body; the sound of his laboring heart slowing, faltering, and finally stopping. Kella felt dizzy and a little breathless. A muscle twitched in her cheek, as it always did when she was nervous. She rubbed it unconsciously.

"Quite a storm," Brion observed as he looked out of the window. No sound came through the weatherproofed glass or the sound-baffled walls. It was soothingly quiet. The room was the same as always, quietly beautiful, sprinkled faintly with the aroma of roses and Kella's perfume. It was familiar. Why did it feel so strange? Kella was looking at him again, that was part of it; he felt helplessly angry and grieved at the hate that shone so plainly in her eyes. He couldn't remember what had begun the dismemberment of their marriage, but plainly it had gone too far for anyone to put it back together.

"What?" Kella asked vaguely, as if she hadn't heard him at all. Brion sighed and looked back to the flashing bursts of lightning and rain.

"Nothing. If this keeps up we may have to activate the house shields. This lightning worries me."

"Is there anything that doesn't worry you?" Kella asked cuttingly. Why were her dark eyes so brilliant, so wide? Brion frowned unconsciously and looked around the quiet room. Lucky that Evan was safely asleep; he hated for the boy to hear these exchanges almost as much as he hated participating in them. He didn't despise Kella, truly, and he was tired. Too tired to summon energy to fight.

"Yes," Brion agreed quietly, and rubbed at the bridge of his nose to stop a budding headache. Kella turned quickly away and went into the kitchen. He was surprised and touched when, a few storm-wracked moments later, she returned with two glass goblets of ruby-red wine.

"For your headache," she told him, and handed him one. He gave her a smile of genuine thanks and saw her smile coolly back. Before he drank, he turned back to look out of the window. Lightning had exploded very close to the house. The smooth interior lights flickered and dimmed.

"What — " Kella began in alarm, and then the power failed altogether — lights, soundproofing, everything. Thunder crashed down. Brion could think of nothing, suddenly, except the sight of the lightning streaking parallel across the peaceful lawn straight for the window he faced. He spun, spilling the wine in a bloody stream across the immaculate white floor, and knocked Kella down under his sheltering body.

The window exploded in a frenzy of tiny shards. Brion was facing down and staring into Kella's terrified brown eyes; he saw the reflection in them of the forked blue-white death that crackled over their heads. It can't last, he thought frantically. It will fade in a moment.

When it did, it left a black rope of twisting darkness, sparked here and there with harsh moving colors. Brion rolled over on his back at Kella's horrified gasp and stared at it in disbelief; it wasn't anything he had ever seen or heard of. It was deep. It was like looking into —

Into a void. A rip in the world.

"Father?" Evan screamed from the doorway, and Brion twisted his head to look in horror at his son as the boy hurled himself toward his parents. Kella screamed, too, ordering the boy to go back, but Evan was deaf with alarm and wouldn't be stopped. Brion struggled up to his knees and reached for Evan's hands just as the void that rippled over all of their heads in the darkened room descended like a hungry cloud. Brion's hands brushed his son's, and then they were whirled apart by forces too great to battle. As fate's cruel whim would have it, it was Kella's trembling hands that grabbed her husband, and held fast as they fell, and fell, and fell —

Evan, alone and terrified, was falling too, in another direction.

"Master, is this wise?" Pelk spoke doubtfully as he and Vurkanan Tyes looked down the slopes of Mount Rihtoth at the storm raging unchecked below. "No offense, but it seems — well — dangerous."

"It is dangerous," Tyes agreed, gray eyes steady as he watched the clouds. "I've never lied about that, have I?"

"Not so that I noticed," Pelk grinned, and tossed his long blond hair back from his face. "Why? Are you planning to break new ground?"

"Perhaps." Tyes wasn't really answering that presumptuous question; he was still staring at the clouds below them, and Pelk had the strange prickling feeling that Tyes was using a spell of some silent working to look beneath that roiling fury of nature. "Something is happening that I don't understand. I have to see. It could be something the Loremasters need to know."

"How can we get down in that?" Pelk asked — not disbelieving, only a little concerned. He had been aide to Loremaster Vurkanan Tyes for almost ten years now, and there was little Tyes could do to really surprise him. Mostly.

Tyes wasn't listening again; his head jerked up, looking at the pale disc of the sun above and the deep blue sky, at the high white ridges of Mount Rihtoth and the more distant peaks of the other mountains that made up Dragonsfang. Pelk fell silent and waited while Tyes examined the signs. The lightning below that flicked and twisted among the black clouds was growing worse, a constant barrage of energy and destruction.

"That's a Flow Storm. It isn't centered here, but the edges are brushing the physical storm below."

"Shouldn't we get to safety?" Pelk asked in alarm. Tyes shook his head silently. "Master, it's a Flow Storm! Even the Lords of Orhan wouldn't stand here in the middle of a Flow Storm! Don't be a fool!"

"Quiet!" Tyes suddenly hissed, and his grey eyes burned in a face far too young for their power. "We're going down, Pelk. Now."

Pelk swallowed his protests and pulled his hood up over his pallid face. He had observed Flow Storms from a great distance, and the memory still froze him; great twisting voids opened and closed as Wild Portals were ripped between worlds, between times. Nightmarish creatures were thrown violently through only to be immediately thrust, screaming, into yet another opening Portal. It wasn't anything Pelk had a desire to see at close range ever again.

Vurkanan Tyes tapped an Essence Flow — one far enough away to be left unaffected by the storm — and poured it into the fragile structure of a Spell of Safe Transport. It was a foolproof sort of spell, for one of Tyes' great accomplishment. Pelk closed his eyes; the strange whispery touch of Essence wrapped around them, and there was a sickening jerk of disorientation as the Spell took effect. The nausea was gone before Pelk had a chance to really feel it.

When he opened his eyes, he was still blind — but only until a brilliant streak of lightning flashed across the sky. Then he was dazzled instead. A gust of wind caught his cloak and flared it out behind him like a banner; it looked impressive, he was almost sure, but in all practicality it almost choked him. Tyes, standing beside him, had no such problem. His cloak stayed firmly settled around his shoulders, flickering in its attempts to blend with the shifting, violent colors that ripped through the sky. He didn't seem bothered by the gusting wind or the choking clouds of dust forced on them.

"Master!" Pelk pointed. Tyes looked up through the pounding rain and saw the huge hole above them. Even as Pelk shouted, he saw the two pale bodies plunging down out of the sky towards the ground and certain death.

The risk was considerable, but Tyes had never been one to worry in the heat of action; he was one of the only Loremasters capable of reaching so far in such viciously treacherous conditions, but the Spell of Landing was the first any Loremaster learned, and he felt sure that it would respond to his call. It would lower the unfortunates gently to the ground — at least, he had faith that it would.

He was almost right. He called forth the Spell, fixed the targets, and began to guide them down — but then the Flow Storm maliciously twitched the Essence out of his grasp. The backlash flung Tyes back and to his knees, but he kept his grey eyes fixed determinedly on the two bodies falling, too quickly, toward him.

"Master, don't!" Pelk cried in alarm. Tyes grabbed at the Essence again. A failed spell made a Loremaster that much more vulnerable; in this storm, he was courting death, even for one of Tyes' immortal blood. Tyes shook his head and invoked the spell again. The Essence pulsed and shifted, trying to pull out of his control, but he held on with tenacity. The falling strangers slowed and drifted gently down to touch the rocky ground. Power flooded out of Tyes and merged again with the swirling maelstrom of energy above their heads. It left him faint and ill.

"I'm all right, Pelk; help them." Tyes ordered his young friend kneeling beside him. Pelk's intense blue eyes narrowed in obvious doubt, but he obeyed. Tyes bowed his head and tried to fight off a wave of dizziness. The rain was cold as it seeped into his straight black hair and ran down his neck, but the cold helped him to concentrate. No chance of using the Essence now. He at last recognized consciously what a risk he had taken, and shivered slightly from causes other than the cold.

"They're alive, at least," Pelk reported. Tyes climbed to his feet and joined them. The two strangers — one man and one woman — clung together shivering in the cold rain. They were not dressed for any sort of chill; their clothing was made of some thin material that soaked easily and clung to their skin, and neither of them wore any sort of cloak. Tyes glanced up at the sky and realized that the storm was lessening. The black rift in the sky above them swirled and turned in upon itself as it grew smaller. The Flow Storm, it seemed, was ending.

When it ended, the Portal that had delivered these strange wanderers would be gone forever.

"It can't be helped," Tyes told himself aloud, and looked back at the two. They looked something like the race known as High Men, he thought, with their dark hair and pale skin. Certainly they had little in common with his own Iylari folk — for one thing, their ears were plainly rounded, and that spoke of Mannish stock rather than Elvish. He tried the language of High Man, then a few other dialects. They both looked at him in blank incomprehension.

It would normally have taken only a second to work a Word Lore Mastery Spell to translate even into an unknown tongue, but Tyes reluctantly conceded defeat as the last of the Flow Storm faded away. His own powers had been severely stretched, and he dared not attempt a working as high as the translation spell. A lesser spell might be possible, in a few hours. Better to wait until then.

"We need to find shelter. Pelk, give them my cloak." Tyes stripped the changeling garment off; it went through an interesting chameleon flash as it tried to adapt to the colors of Pelk's garments and then stopped in confusion as he passed it carefully to the two shivering strangers. The man looked at them a moment and then cautiously took it. He watched the changing surface of the fabric in doubt and then swirled it around his damp body. The woman said something that Pelk instantly recognized as being a question, and the man replied. She turned away to look out over the rain-drenched slopes.

"She's looking for someone else," Tyes said quietly. "Pelk, see if you can spot anything. I'll try to make them understand me."

His aide quickly set off on the errand, but the woman seemed determined to follow in spite of her chill and shock. Tyes touched her on the arm to hold her back and was surprised when he saw her eyes. It wasn't only rain on her face.

The man said something to the woman and pulled her into the shelter of the cloak. He looked at Tyes and nodded a grim, exhausted thanks. Tyes nodded back.

Pelk came back in a few moments and reported that there was no one else to be found. In spite of the strangers' protests, Tyes and his aide managed to lead them up the mountain slope to the shelter of a cave. The rain might go on for a while, and neither of the strangers looked particularly hardy. Better to rest, and learn what they could later.

"Welcome," a light, smooth Iylari voice said as they stepped inside of the warmth of the shelter. Pelk threw back his hood and made sure that his dagger was ready for use, but an outstretched hand from Vurkanan Tyes calmed him.

"Navigator," Tyes acknowledged. His eyes adjusted to the dimness, and he made out the shadowy forms of the Navigator's clients. "The Flow Storm is over, I think."

"Vurkanan Tyes," Iarsang said respectfully. He stood to give him a properly executed bow. "Was it you using Essence in the eye of the Storm?"

"We all have our moments of foolishness." Tyes smiled slightly, and offered the Navigator his hand. "Iarsang, isn't it? It's been a long time. Four hundred years?"

"More or less," Iarsang acknowledged modestly. His Compass flashed briefly in the dimness of the cave, clearly illuminating the faces of his three charges; in typical Navigator fashion Iarsang paid it no attention. His face, never less than distracted, took on a complete dreamy abstraction that meant he was analyzing Essence Flows. "I could not manage to clear the storm earlier. The Flows were too erratic. Now that they have stabilized I think we can progress."

No question of that; they all looked toward the mouth of the cave and saw that the storm was shattering like a mirror under a hammer. Clouds scudded hastily overhead, taking the last vestiges of lightning with them. A pale, rapidly westering sun took the place of rain in less than a minute's time.

"Impressive," the Loremaster applauded. Iarsang gave him another slight bow. "How much?"

"Why, nothing, in your service. But what have you here?" Iarsang looked mildly enough at the two shivering strangers, and his eyebrow came up sharply. "Strange companions for a Loremaster."

"Strange companions for anyone, I would say," Tyes said. "A Portal threw them here. I believe there may be another nearby, but Pelk could find no trace of him."

The Benevolent Lady Astrid had come cautiously forward during their conversation, and now, to the surprise of both Iarsang and Vurkanan Tyes, she timidly stripped off her heavy fur-lined cloak and offered it to the two strangers. The woman looked visibly startled, but she took it. Astrid smiled encouragingly as the stranger draped it clumsily over her shoulders and hugged it close for warmth.

"They need dry clothes and warm food," Astrid said, and looked at Iarsang questioningly. He remained impassive. It was nothing to him if she chose to extend hospitality, but she knew well that he was not allowed or inclined to extend his own powers beyond the limits of his contract. When he made no move to stop her, she went back and began digging in her own stores to find something. The other cleric and the young man called Civad joined her somewhat less enthusiastically, being either less moved to charity or simply more inclined to eavesdrop on the conversation of their Navigator and one of the most famous of all Loremasters.

"I can look farther than you can, Loremaster, if you wish me to do so," Iarsang said calmly. Tyes put his head a little to the side and looked at the other Iylari with contemplative grey eyes. The two of them looked quite alike, except for Iarsang's greater height and stubbornly bemused expression. Iarsang raised an eyebrow. Vurkanan slowly copied him.

"At no charge?" Tyes smiled slowly. Iarsang nodded. "Then your generosity shall be kept absolutely secret, my friend. I know it isn't the kind of action the Navigators think of kindly. May I help you?"

"Thank you, no." Iarsang strolled outside, bending to fit his great slender height beneath the rock opening. The sun gilded his fine-boned face as he looked up. There was nothing to see but Iarsang standing silently for several moments, face blank and Compass pulsing in quiet, random colors on his wrist.

The strangers were still clinging together, but now the man began to speak in his strange tongue and make gestures. There was a clear air of urgency about him. Tyes tried to reach for Essence again, but so much in so short a span of time had left him unable to manage it. He looked at Pelk, but his aide spread his hands and shrugged.

"He says that his son is missing," Nomaran Estvir contributed haltingly. They all looked at him in frank amazement, this brown-mannered little cleric. He was so completely nondescript that no one had thought to ask him any questions. "Begging your pardon, Loremaster, but I have some skill in languages. His tongue has some similarities to that spoken in Murlis."

"How old is his son?" Tyes wanted to know. Estvir relayed the question. This evoked a torrent of speech from both the man and woman, with the cleric trying desperately to make sense of the jumble.

"Ten years old," Estvir finally answered. "At least it seems that is the answer. They are — deeply troubled."

"So would I be, were my son missing," Astrid murmured. She looked sympathetically at the pair. They took no notice of her, involved in their own quickly heating argument. The woman's voice grew shrill. Tyes threw a look at the cleric, who was sitting in quiet concentration.

"Personal matters," Estvir finally said unhappily. "She accuses her husband — his name is Brion — of not being concerned about the boy. Her name is Kella."

Tyes sighed and looked back out of the cave's mouth. Iarsang was coming back up toward them.

"Any luck?" he called to the Navigator. Iarsang nodded slowly.

"If you are looking for a boy, he came through a Portal near Smatoth."

"Is he still alive?" Tyes asked more quietly. Iarsang nodded again. "You seem disturbed."

"There was someone with him," the Navigator explained. "Can this be mere chance, Loremaster? That these people came here, that you were here to help them, that someone else was present to help the boy? It seems to stretch coincidence, does it not?"

"You have a point," Tyes agreed.

Iarsang's grey eyes met the Loremaster's, and Tyes felt a shiver of premonition. "The boy is in the company of a young man, black hair, silver-streaked at the left temple. The man's eyes are violet. He has six fingers on his hands."

"Andraax," Vurkanan Tyes whispered in dumb amazement and horror. "Andraax the Mad."

Iarsang nodded grimly.

"Father?" Evan whispered, and opened his eyes. It was very dark, and he was forced to sneeze at the musty damp smell. He reached out and touched a solid damp wall of rock. "Mother? Where are you?"

No one answered. Evan struggled to sit up; as he did, a light flashed behind him. It glowed with a steady blue fire. Evan twisted around to look.

At first he couldn't see anything at all, only a floating blue light and dark walls; then, suddenly, what he had taken for a pale formation of stone moved. It was a hand, and it reached up to push back the hood of a gray-colored cloak.

Are you well? the young man asked Evan. He should have looked scary, standing there in the glow of that strange blue light, but he didn't. Evan was fascinated by the hands that came out from under that gray cloak — they had six fingers — and it was a minute or so before he realized that he hadn't heard anything at all with his ears when the man spoke to him. Evan looked up with a jerk to find the young man staring at him with eyes that seemed to glow in the blue light.

"Where are my parents?" Evan asked instead of answering his question. The stranger looked at him in silence. "Who are you?"

"Who are you?" the stranger echoed in turn — this time aloud. The voice rang around the damp cave walls and seemed to wrap around the boy. It sounded like singing. "Evan. Your name is Evan."

"Yes. How did you know?"

"Do you always answer questions with questions?" the man asked calmly. Evan blinked.

"Sometimes. Don't you?"

That seemed to end the conversation. The man stared at him for another few minutes and then turned to go.

Evan jumped to his feet.

"Hey! You didn't tell me where my parents are!"

The gray cloak paused, and that strange blue light became a little stronger as the man turned to look at him. His eyes weren't really blue, Evan realized. They were a sort of pale purple. And even though he didn't look old, there was gray in his hair.

"I don't know where your family is, Evan," the man told him gravely.

"Well — can I follow you for a while? Until we get out of the cave?"

Evan didn't like caves much. This one was small and not very comfortable, and somehow he didn't feel like exploring. He was relieved when the young man shrugged and began walking on. It really wasn't very far to the exit, and there Evan hesitated and looked around. They were on the side of a hill. It didn't look anything like home, that much was sure. And there was no one around, no one at all.

"Hey, what's your name?" Evan called to the young man, who was continuing steadily down the hill. The boy jogged to keep up. In the light the man looked even younger, and his eyes were bright and strange.

Andraax he heard clearly in his head.

"Listen, Andraax, are you sure you don't know where my parents are? There was an accident — " Evan pleaded with just a touch of fear. Andraax looked down.

"Quite sure," he answered firmly. "It was no accident, Evan. There are no accidents here. You don't need a Loremaster to tell you that."

"Is that what you are, a Loremaster?"

Andraax seemed not to hear the question. He kept walking. For lack of any better ideas, Evan kept walking right along with him, shivering in the thin cold air. Andraax didn't seem to notice or to care.

But he did notice. After a while he took off the gray cloak and shook it three times. Before Evan could say a word the Loremaster swept it around the boy's shoulders and fastened it with a long silver pin. Evan thought it felt great, but then he realized that it was probably dragging the ground at least three ridiculous feet behind him. He looked back.

It hung perfectly at his ankles. He looked up at Andraax, who had to be at least as tall as his father and probably was taller, and remembered clearly that the cloak had been around his ankles. But that didn't seem to make any sense.

"Thanks," Evan managed to say. Andraax might not have even heard, since he was already walking again. His purple eyes were very strange and far away, and after only a few steps he turned slowly to stare at Evan. A cold stare, this time.

"Are you Thalan?" Andraax snapped abruptly. "Well? Are you? I've had about enough of interference from the Thalan. What do you want? I can't help you. I won't!"

Evan wasn't really qualified to answer this barrage of questions, so he just picked the first one.

"I'm not Th — Thalan," he finally stammered. Andraax hissed impatiently and suddenly began walking again. In a few more steps he stopped again and glared at the boy.

"Who are you? Why did you steal my cloak?" the Loremaster demanded. Evan stumbled backwards away from him; Andraax suddenly seemed taller and more menacing than before. "I warn you, I deal harshly with thieves of any age!"

There didn't seem any use in arguing. Evan reached up to unpin the cloak, but his finger caught on the long clasp. He gasped and pulled his hand back with a deep red slash in his palm. His eyes filled with tears as Andraax came toward him. The man suddenly lost his rage, and he looked at the boy with an almost frightening concern.

Careful, Andraax whispered gently into his mind, and took the boy's injured hand in six warm fingers. *Forgive me, Evan, I forget myself sometimes. There. Better?*

It ceased to hurt as Andraax spoke, and the Loremaster drew one long finger along the bloody cut. It closed as he touched it. Evan looked up, startled, and met Andraax's amethyst eyes; the young man knelt beside him to unfasten the cloak pin.

"I think perhaps I had better keep it," Andraax apologized with the faintest touch of regret. "I have been alone a long time. My mind isn't — what it was."

"I didn't mean to steal it," Evan said. To his own disgust he heard his voice tremble. He wanted to sit down, suddenly, and tears kept coming closer and closer even though he tried to fight them back. He kept remembering the terrible look on his father's face just as the cloud came down around them. Andraax was a stranger who seemed scary and kind by equal parts, no substitution for a missing father and mother. It was too much for a ten-year-old, even Evan.

"Yes, I know," Andraax told him aloud, and the warmth in that strange, beautiful voice broke down the last stubborn resistance. Evan flung himself heedlessly into the Loremaster's stiff, awkward arms and shook with tears. Andraax frowned slightly, and then sighed. His six-fingered hands slowly relaxed and began patting the boy's fair hair in long, soothing strokes.

"Please take me home," Evan finally whispered. The Loremaster's hands ceased their motion and pushed the boy away at arm's length.

"No one can take you home now," Andraax told him very seriously. "I will take you to your family, if you wish, but you must be do as I tell you and be very careful. It might be dangerous."

There wasn't a ten-year-old boy in any world who wouldn't have been intrigued by that, and Andraax felt a certain obscure satisfaction in seeing those dark eyes brighten a little beneath their film of tears.

"Is it dangerous here?" Evan asked him — and felt his spirit rising at the thought of adventure. Andraax's too-young face smiled slightly.

"I am dangerous, young one. Do not forget it."

Even though he smiled, his violet eyes were unwavering and distant. His thoughts were already far away, turned inward to a struggle that neither Evan nor anyone else could even guess at — a struggle to keep himself from utter, irretrievable madness.

"They aren't human," Brion said suddenly, and far too loudly. He stood, nudging Kella's head from his shoulder. "Kella, they aren't human."

"What?" she asked crossly. Brion, as usual, wasn't paying any attention to her. She stood up next to him and followed his gaze; he was staring at the two tall men standing outside of the cave's entrance. "Of course they are. Don't be stupid. Why are we waiting? We've got to find Evan!"

"We will," Brion assured her absently. "No, they aren't. Look at them. Look."

Kella looked. They were tall; the shorter one stood well above Brion's head, and he wasn't a short man. Granted, they were both amazingly attractive. Both young, younger than herself. They looked enough alike to be brothers, except that one was much taller than the other. Dark hair, both of them, and —

As Iarsang turned his head slightly, she saw his beautifully pointed ears parting his silky dark hair, and gasped aloud. Brion nodded.

"Not human," he said firmly.

"What about the others?" Kella asked in a suddenly hushed voice as she looked back at them; Pelk was looking at her with cool blue eyes, but the others were involved in their own heated conversation. Brion shot them a quick look.

"I don't know. Look, I don't think they mean us any harm — "

Kella, strung to the far edge of shock, wasn't in any mood for more of Brion's careful rationality. Her rage spilled over in a sudden, strangely cleansing wave.

"What about Evan! Anything could have happened to him! We've got to find him!"

"Kell, I don't think they — " Brion began. She pulled violently away from him and stalked over to Pelk, who was still watching her with interested amazement. He looked as if he was entirely at ease as he leaned back against the rock wall, but Brion wondered. None of these people was as simple as that.

"You!" Kella cried. "Where is my son?"

Pelk raised his eyebrows and looked toward the cleric who had done the translating earlier. There was no help forthcoming from that quarter; Nomaran Estvir was locked in a bitter, quiet argument with Civad and Astrid. Pelk spread his hands with a friendly smile and tried to convey polite ignorance.

"Kella, leave him alone. He has nothing to do with Evan," Brion said wearily. He was angry, but the anger was old and tired, and it had no real focus. "They're trying to help us, not hide him from us."

"And how do you know that?" she demanded acidly. Brion stayed silent, acceding that he didn't, really. It was only a feeling. Kella expressed her contempt for his feelings without saying a word and turned back toward Pelk.

What she said wasn't important, really, it was the fact that, once more, she had ignored him. It was contemptuous silence that ate at the fragile edge of his control and, finally, broke it. Brion reached out and grabbed his wife's arm before she could twist away, and when she tried to slap him he shook her. Hard. So hard her dark eyes filled up with glittering, hating tears and she went almost limp in his grasp.

Brion released her in a sudden painful spasm of self-loathing. She sagged against the rock wall and stared at him while her breath rasped in and out. She was frightened, he thought with stunned comprehension. All these years he had been nothing to her but an inconvenience, a necessary tool, and suddenly she was afraid of him. It should have made him feel better, he supposed. Instead, her fear made him feel worse.

Kella threw herself on him without the slightest warning, scratching, kicking, and screaming. Brion was caught entirely by surprise, but before she could do more than inflict a few minor wounds the young man Pelk had reached them. He pinned her and held her still until she sagged and began to weep as suddenly as she had burst into fury. Pelk looked at Brion.

Brion had expected the man to give him a look of cynical amusement; had he gotten it, there was no telling what Brion might have done. He was perched on that same hair-thin edge of rage from which Kella had so spectacularly fallen. Pelk, whether he sensed that or not, gave him a serious, grimly sympathetic nod. There was no condescension in it. Brion took in a deep, shaky breath and returned it.

The miniature battle had drawn an audience. The three in the corner had turned and were gaping unashamedly at them. Brion jumped slightly as he realized that Iarsang and Tyes had come in behind him — very quiet, they were. Very fast.

"We have reached an impasse," Vurkanan Tyes said as if nothing untoward had happened. His gaze was resting strangely on Kella and there was a faint frown between his grey eyes. "I find myself unable to help you in your search for your son. Navigator Iarsang is likewise constrained; he has accepted a contract to deliver his party safely to the city of Kelfour's Landing within twelve hours' time. However, we have arranged to provide you with another Navigator who will help you locate your child."

"For a price," Iarsang contributed softly. There was a brief pause while Brion looked uncertainly at the two tall Iylari and they looked back, and then Iarsang cut his eyes at Nomaran in unmistakable command. The cleric, out of utter fascination, had failed to translate. He hastily amended his lapse. Brion answered something soft and a little desperate. Nomaran sighed.

"He says that he has no money. For as long as I have travelled with Navigators, I have never known one to take a promise in place of gold."

"Nor will you," Iarsang shot back with a strange smile. "But that, too, has been arranged."

Vurkanan Tyes nodded to Pelk, who sighed in turn and jingled a pouch at his belt. "No great loss, I suppose," Pelk said. "Replenishing it will keep me in practice."

Civad, the dark-haired young "jeweller", looked up at that and made a quick, almost invisible motion with his hand. Pelk returned it with amazing speed and agility, and grinned. Civad raised his eyebrows in faint surprise and smiled back.

"One further problem," Iarsang continued. "My guild, the Navigators Guild, has no jurisdiction in this area. You must deal with the Order of Cypharia."

Pelk looked as if he had a joke riding on his tongue that would not be suitable for the company he found himself in. He looked at Iarsang and raised his eyebrows, plainly reviewing stories he'd heard about the beautiful women who made up the Order. The tall Navigator looked back at him with a dreamy lack of expression — but Pelk had heard stories, and some of them prominently featured Iarsang.

"I will return to Nexus and submit your request for hire. If a Cypharian appears before I return, don't allow her to convince you that I won't return. I will."

Watching a Navigator Jump was a strange business. Iarsang's compass flared briefly through a series of brilliant colors, then darkened almost to black. No one was exactly sure when Iarsang disappeared except Tyes, though they were watching. Brion and Kella watched with varying expressions of awe and distrust.

In the pocket of Kella's skirt was the smooth glass vial, still half-full of colorless death. Kella touched it like a holy talisman, a single anchor of reality in a world she couldn't comprehend and didn't want to know. She didn't see Vurkanan Tyes' frown grow alarmingly deep. There was a tiny disturbance at the edge of her mind as the Loremaster's slowly recovering powers sought entrance; Kella instinctively shut it out.

The time that passed was relatively short before opal light flashed again and disclosed the arrival of another Navigator. This one was a woman, not tall but exquisitely beautiful. She was obviously born of the same kin that had birthed Iarsang and Tyes, though her coloring was fairer and her eyes blue, she had the same upswept, aristocratic ears. Her clothing seemed ill-suited to the chilly mountain ranges, consisting mostly of diaphanous white robes, but she seemed immune to any discomfort. Her eyes flicked over the group, lingered on Loremaster Tyes, and blinked. That was the only expression of surprise she allowed herself.

"I am Varise of the Order of Cypharia," she announced herself gravely, and lifted her beautifully ornamented golden wand. "You wish to hire a Navigator?"

"These two are the clients, honored Navigator," Pelk said, stepping easily into the role of bargainer as if he had done it many times. In all likelihood, he had. "It is a slightly unusual contract. They don't wish to go to a specific place, they wish to find a specific person."

The Navigator Varise's pale brows rose slightly.

"Highly irregular," she protested. Pelk gave her a smile that might have melted enchanted steel.

"But hardly impossible, I'm sure. If you're worried about compromising the Guild's stand on military transportation, rest assured that none other than Vurkanan Tyes will vouch for their sincerity and innocence." Innocence, Pelk thought suddenly as he glanced at Kella, was perhaps not quite the right word. Well, too late now. "They are seeking their child."

"A missing child?" Varise didn't seem moved so much by sympathy as annoyance. It was likely she'd never priced such a thing before. Her blue eyes flashed with sudden suspicion. "A lost child, or an abducted child? There would be a difference."

"Oh, most certainly," Pelk agreed easily. "But the child has not been — "

"He is travelling in the company of Former Loremaster Andraax," Vurkanan Tyes said. This news brought the entire procedure to a squealing, snorting halt. Pelk's eyes went round. So did the Navigator's. "All Loremasters have been forbidden to interact directly with Andraax, even in a matter such as this. A Navigator is essential if the boy is ever to be found at all."

"Meddling in the affairs of a Loremaster?" Varise snapped sharply, and shook her head. "There is no price high enough to cover such a thing, Loremaster, as you very well know. Even you will not interfere with Andraax. We will not put one of our order in the middle of such a tangle."

"Afraid, Honored Navigator?" Pelk taunted with a grin. Her blue eyes levelled on him and narrowed dangerously.

"Afraid of Andraax? Anyone with a brain would be. That only proves you hopeless, alas." Varise looked back at Tyes. There was no warming of the chill in her manner. "The answer is no, Loremaster."

"Go back and ask Navigator Daphine if she will do it as a favor to me."

"I will not!" she flared. The Loremaster's eyes remained steady and insistent. Varise drew her shoulders back in a conscious attempt at dignity (it fell far short of Vurkanan Tyes' instinctively daunting bearing) and took a firmer grip on the golden wand in her hand. She deliberately turned a charming smile on the three huddled members of Iarsang's company. "Do the rest of you wish to continue your journey? I can bargain a rate with you for transport to Kelfour's Landing."

"We're already travelling in the company of Iarsang," Lady Astrid said firmly. Varise's mouth twitched slightly.

"And if I told you that Iarsang would not be returning?"

Lady Astrid opened her mouth to answer — from the look in her eyes, it wouldn't have been diplomatic — but she was cut off by a soft, amused voice from the cave's entrance.

"You'd be lying, Varise. But thank you for your concern." Iarsang's mild, distracted face smiled, but the brown eyes were strangely alert. "Go as the Loremaster instructs. Ask Daphine. She will agree."

"You're being ridiculous," Varise snapped, but she had lost her force. Iarsang cocked his head to the side and said nothing. She sighed impatiently and gestured with her golden wand. An opal flash, and she was gone.

"That was productive," Pelk grumbled. Iarsang nodded and came the rest of the way into the cave.

"Still, forms must be observed. Varise had to be dealt with first, but now — "

"Daphine will be reasonable," Vurkanan Tyes finished confidently. Iarsang's eyes gleamed with some private joke, but he said nothing. He urged the travellers to gather their gear, fast.

He could have, if he chose, told Tyes that in his experience the Daphine of the Order of Cypharia had been many things. Reasonable was not one of the adjectives that sprang immediately to mind.

But reckless — yes, that was apt.

Andraax didn't travel like anybody Evan had ever met. It was like something out of a dream, one of those dreams where you spread your arms and flew on the wind. It wasn't exactly like that, because Evan couldn't see anything but a strange, flickering mist all around, but there was that same sensation of drifting and soaring. They weren't walking, either. They were sitting down on what appeared to be a solid floor of mist.

Evan poked curiously at the fog with a finger. It gave a little, but not much. When he reached out to the side, though, the fog had no substance at all. He overbalanced with the effort he had put into his motion and almost tumbled over.

Andraax's six-fingered hand caught him and pulled him back. Evan began to stammer out a quick apology, but Andraax shook his head.

"Stay close. This isn't as solid as rock, and you can't see the edges."

"Can you?" Evan wanted to know. Andraax smiled faintly, and his lavender eyes warmed a little. He didn't look crazy. Most of the time.

"It wouldn't be much use if I couldn't, would it?" Andraax answered, and shrugged. "An acquired skill. You'll catch on."

"What's holding us up?"

"We're riding a Flow Stream, boy, an Essence Flow. You probably don't know about such things. They're unique to Kulthea."

"Kulthea?"

Andraax shrugged and made a globe-shaped motion with his hands.

"Oh. The planet." Evan sounded disappointed, as if he wanted to hear something more exotic. "I've never heard of Essence."

"It's a field generated by living things. It links Kulthea to other places, other times — and it is here to be used, by those with the ability. So we ride like this instead of walking."

"Oh," Evan said in the tone his father used when he really didn't understand but wanted to pretend that he did. "Kind of like the slidewalks."

"Yes, exactly," Andraax said, and smiled. "Slidewalks. You're thinking about little roads that move. You stand on them, and they take you where you want to go."

"Well, sort of. They can't go everywhere, but they can take you pretty close."

"Ah. It appears Essence Flows and slidewalks have that in common as well. We'll have to get off here and walk the rest of the way. The Flow turns out to sea at this point."

Andraax was in a talkative mood, and he gave Evan practically limitless descriptions of the entire land of Quellbourne that Evan found himself a sudden resident of, and the entire world of Kulthea. Evan hardly even noticed when Andraax grabbed his arm and stood up, but there was a sudden strange slippery sensation and then the mist road was gone. They were standing on the edge of a cliff. The sea was crashing in along a V-shaped shore far below. Evan gulped and stepped back, but Andraax seemed totally oblivious to the drop. He stood there with the tips of his toes hanging in the empty air and gestured wildly at the land to Evan's right.

"Kelfour's Landing. Lots to do there. Wineshops, bazaars, adventure around every corner. You'll like it." Andraax was almost dancing with excitement. Evan squinted down at the sprawling town and looked warily at his companion. Andraax was getting strange again. He was like a rubber ball, bouncing from extremes of suspicion and menace to the half-hysterical joy of a child much younger than Evan's own age. It didn't exactly inspire confidence.

"I thought you were taking me to my family," Evan said reasonably. Andraax's face froze into a sudden hard mask. His eyes looked black with pupil.

"You? Why should I? What makes you think I would do something like that for you?"

"Because you said you would," the boy insisted a little desperately. Andraax looked at him without comment. "Are they down there? In the city?"

"Kelfour's Landing could not possibly be called a city by the widest stretch of the imagination. However, it's the closest thing to civilization this backwater frontier has." Andraax shrugged and crossed his arms. "Do I look like a Navigator? Find them yourself. I have important tasks ahead of me."

"I'll wager," Evan scoffed, because he felt as if he were going to cry again. He turned angrily away and began walk along the cliff. There had to be some way down besides Andraax and his weird roads. People had to get there, didn't they?

He glanced back at Andraax, but the Loremaster was staring out into the sea. There was something strange in his face, as if he were listening to something far away. Evan shrugged, kept going. After a half mile or so (he turned around to look every so often, and Andraax was still standing there against the brilliant blue sky) he found a trail leading down one of the gentler slopes. It wasn't really a very good trail, but he was angry and determined to put as much distance between himself and Andraax as possible.

"I would not go that way," a mild voice said unexpectedly from just around the next bend. Evan, feet sliding unsteadily in the rocky shale, grabbed for support and stared uncertainly around the sharp corner. Andraax stood there with his arms negligently folded across his chest. He was still looking out at Kelfour's Landing with intent eyes.

He was standing on thin air. There was the slightest breeze that ruffled his dark hair and flared his cloak dramatically behind him, but he was hovering without apparent effort over a sheer killing drop.

Evan looked away and kept walking. Quicker, this time, even though it was really dangerous and frightening the way the gravel slid beneath his thin shoes. It hurt, too. He came down too hard on a sharp-edged rock, winced, and grabbed for the wall.

What he grabbed instead was a thin handful of spiderweb. His arm plunged into darkness, and his body followed it. He fell hard and began sliding down into the darkest cave he had ever seen.

"Andraax!" he screamed. He felt the rush of wind behind him, and something — it wasn't a hand, not even one with six fingers — grabbed his legs and pulled him back out with quick efficiency. Evan emerged back into the weak sunlight and laid very still with his face pressed into the gravel. His heart was pounding so hard it hurt.

"That's your first lesson, boy. Don't disregard my advice." Andraax's voice was still light and cool. He was hovering in the air a few feet away. "Now get up and keep going."

"Do I have to?" Evan whispered. A vast cold silence greeted him. He whispered something his parents probably wouldn't have approved of and pushed himself back to his feet. His legs were trembling. It seemed easier to rest a moment, so he did. "What's in the cave?"

"Nothing you would want to find," Andraax assured him briskly. "I'll see you at the bottom."

"Wait!" Evan yelled. Andraax grinned a maniacally happy grin and dropped like a stone. "Andraax, wait!"

The only answer was the occasional hissing slap of the wind as it pushed at him. Evan hesitated another moment, listening to the distant shrieks of birds, and began slowly picking his way down the path. Very slowly indeed.

By the time he got to the bottom, he was thoroughly exhausted, frightened, and grimy. It didn't help much to find his supposed savior on his hands and knees conversing with a rock.

"Why?" Andraax was asking. Evan came to a stop, supporting himself against the cliff face with one scraped hand, and watched him. The Loremaster's young face took on a fearsome frown as he stared at the rock, and without warning he suddenly sat up and pointed an accusing finger at it. "All right, I've asked you nicely. Now I'll ask you one more time: get out of my head!"

The rock didn't answer. Evan hadn't really expected it to, though he wouldn't have found it shocking either, given the kind of day it was turning out to be. Andraax didn't take the silence quite so well. He grabbed the rock in both hands and raised it high over his head, then tossed it far, far out into the crashing waves of the sea.

"There!" Andraax shouted exultantly after it. "Try following me out of that! Tell your fellows to stay out of my head or I'll fill up the sea with Thalan!"

"What exactly is a Thalan?" Evan asked him wearily. Andraax spun around and frowned at the boy as fiercely as he had at the rock; Evan, thinking about the strength that had propelled the stone, took a quick step back.

"A Thalan," Andraax said with careful, labored courtesy, "can be anything. They are creatures without form except the forms they steal from others. When they cannot find a body to appropriate they hide in inanimate rocks and trees. They are driving me mad."

"Why?" Evan asked innocently. Andraax sighed in exasperation and climbed to his feet. He dusted off his hands and frowned at Evan again.

"Now if I knew that, it wouldn't be driving me mad, would it? Who are you?"

"What?"

"It was," the Loremaster said patiently, "a perfectly simple question. Who are you and how do you know me?"

"You don't know who I am?" Evan asked slowly. Andraax's purple eyes went hard with irritation, and he raised his hands in a gesture that was as threatening as it was graceful.

"Now would I ask if I did?" he demanded. Evan stared at him and slumped dejectedly against the cliff face. "Great," he whispered, and limped over to the hissing white surf. He washed his cuts and scrapes in the salt water, wincing at the burn, and wondered what he was going to do. Obviously he couldn't stay with Andraax, could he? Maybe he could find help in Kelfour's Landing. Maybe his parents were already there.

He'd conveniently forgotten the endless hurting arguments between his parents, and the times he'd lain awake at night listening to his own miserable tears. It might have only been that fighting was more logical than staying with a man who talked to rocks.

He turned around to ask Andraax one more question and found himself alone on the beach except for the damp crater in the sand where the offending rock had been. Andraax, it seemed, was gone.

Evan walked toward Kelfour's Landing for nearly an hour before he decided to believe that Andraax finally had vanished for good. He kept glancing around at the cliffs vanishing behind him into the distance and around at the clean soft beach, but there was no sign of anyone or anything else but himself for as far as he could see. If Andraax was following him, he was doing it at a good distance.

Evan climbed up a gentle hill and took his bearings again. Kelfour's Landing was bigger than it had looked from the clifftops, and it was farther away. He was getting tired. He took another look down the beach and saw, just past another range of dunes, the top of what looked like a ship's mast sticking up. It rocked gently with the motion of waves. Evan ran down the hill, tripping in the loose sand, and cartwheeled to a halt at the base of the next.

Evan, don't, a voice whispered in his mind. Evan shut it fiercely out and flailed his way up the next sandy slope. If he had looked back, he might have seen, far away, the indistinct shape of a man hovering in mid-air. He didn't look. His attention was all focused on the breathless excitement of climbing this last, steepest hill. Sand slid in miniature avalanches from his flailing feet and hands, but he swarmed steadily upward until, finally, he was standing triumphantly at the top.

There was a ship, all right, a big, narrow-bodied ship with two huge masts. The sails were all down. There was a group of people walking along the beach toward a beached rowboat. Evan whooped and pelted down the dune toward them at breakneck speed. He lost his balance halfway down and rolled head over heels in a flurry of arms, legs, and dust.

When he slid to a stop, there was something looking at him that was stranger and much scarier than Andraax.

It stood about a foot taller than Evan (had he been standing up, and not lying flat on his back staring). Its skin was a thin grayish-blue covered with thick white hair, and even though it had sort of human features they were harsh and brutal. The eyes were small and set far back under a jutting ridge of forehead nearly buried under a wild mane of white hair.

It was wearing leather armor and carrying the wickedest weapon Evan had ever seen, two pointed blades joined together on one massive hilt. The weapon was pointed unwaveringly at Evan's unprotected throat.

"Up," the creature grunted, and stepped back. Evan scrambled hastily up. "Speak Seoltang?"

"I — guess so," Evan answered uncertainly. The words felt strange in his mouth; he guessed that Andraax had performed some kind of magic on him that had taught him this new language. Handy. Evan wished for a second that he'd had it in school.

The ape-like thing grunted again and grabbed the boy's arm in a crushing grip. Strong yellow nails probed at him arm as he yelled in surprise and pain. The creature's thick lips curled back from sharply chiseled teeth.

"Strong enough," his captor judged, pushing Evan down the beach toward the rest of the people.

Most of them weren't people, after all, most of them were the same blue-skinned apes that had captured him. There were about ten men, women, and children all huddled together in the center of the group — men and women that looked enough like Evan to be from his own world — and standing a little apart were three little gray-skinned creatures that clung together in a shaking clump. There was one other captive, heavily garlanded with iron chain around wrists and throat — tall, very tall, with elegantly beautiful features and long dark hair that fell far down his back. He didn't look very old at all, certainly younger than either of Evan's parents. From the way he grinned at his captors, he didn't act any older than Evan himself.

"Captives of Lord Warfarer Estenaak'n!" Evan's captor shoved the boy into the group of human prisoners. "Disobey my words and you die. These are your rules. Say nothing. Do nothing but what you are ordered to do. If you are slow to move, you will die. If you move too quickly, you will die. If any of you try to escape, you all die."

"Won't be very profitable if you kill your entire cargo," the young man in chains said in a light, careless voice. One of the women in the central group made an involuntary motion, either anger or distress, then controlled herself.

"Scum! You soon will feed the War God! Your blood will buy us luck." That was the pirate chief — at least, the creatures fit all of Evan's definitions of pirates — and he showed his huge fangs in an angry snarl. Evan gulped. The tall man lifted an iron-manacled hand to cover a yawn.

"How so, Kral?" the captive asked with an insulting smile and a careless wave at his chains. "It certainly hasn't done much for me."

The Kral chief shrieked in outrage and jerked wildly on his chains until the prisoner was on his knees in the sand. Evan bit his lip in nervous fear as the Kral danced and hooted their triumph. The man stopped fighting after a few seconds and sat passively with his eyes shut; the Kral soon tired of their sport and dragged him back to his feet. He was put in the boat and flanked by two heavily-armed Kral guards.

"In!" Evan's captor pushed the three little gray creatures toward the boat. They ran clumsily for it, still clinging together for comfort. The Kral's beady gaze fell on the humans. "You! In!"

No one seemed to want to move first, so Evan started walking. Slowly. He was looking at the dunes around them, hoping for a sight of a tall gray-cloaked man with a slash of silver in his dark hair.

There was only the wind hissing softly through the sand and, in the far distance, a shadow that might have been a bird circling lazily over the water.

"Ridiculous!" Navigator Daphine — newly arrived but never without an opinion — spoke briskly. She tapped her golden wand against the palm of one golden-ringed hand and glared at Iarsang through the gloom of the cave. "Was this your moss-brained idea? Trust you to suggest it and be conveniently too busy to carry it out. Iarsang, really!"

Iarsang raised both eyebrows without changing expression. His travellers were packed and ready to move on. The two Navigators looked at each other in unwavering silence for a moment, and then Daphine smiled slightly and turned to look in evident disfavor at the cave they stood in. She sniffed.

"What a charming and original location for shelter, Iarsang. It's obvious why you're so highly honored among your fellows for your ingenuity — if not for your taste. Lords Above, it smells like an ox died in here. I can't possibly continue to speak in this stench."

Iarsang smiled silently and made an open-handed movement toward her. A sudden fresh breeze blew into the musty cave, carrying the unexpected scent of lilac and sun-warmed grass. Daphine raised her eyebrows and bowed toward him, then turned to look at Tyes. The Loremaster was sitting comfortably against one wall, feet stretched out before him.

"Now, then, am I correct, Loremaster, in saying that your orders say that Former Loremaster Andraax is to be left strictly alone? That you are not in any way to approach him or interfere with him?"

"Correct," Tyes said quietly. He opened his eyes and studied his fingertips intently. "That's why I can't lead them to the boy. That, and other considerations. But I'm willing to pay you a more than fair rate."

"Fair!" Daphine exploded, and rolled her eyes. She tapped her wand against a shapely thigh. "Just like a Loremaster. Fair, as if there were any rate at all worth chasing after a man as half-mad and wholly dangerous as Andraax."

"Four times the regular rate," Tyes interrupted. A long, long silence fell. Pelk made a strangled noise in his throat and shut his eyes. "It would also be a considerable favor to the Loremasters. One that would be remembered."

"What is this boy to you?" Daphine asked in an entirely different tone. Vurkanan Tyes didn't look up.

"Almost nothing," he answered truthfully. "Andraax, however, is something else again. Four times the rate, Daphine. Something even your Order would hesitate to turn away."

Daphine glared at him for a moment, then looked at Brion. The stranger was standing alone in the shadows, just a pale ghost with dark hair and eyes. He looked exhausted. His wife had her back to him and was staring dry-eyed at the rough cave wall. It was difficult to tell whether that stubborn isolation came from shock or anger. Daphine felt a sudden tug of sympathy, and sighed.

"Four times the normal rate," she agreed in a doleful, soft voice. She had no doubt that she was going to regret this to her last breath. Money up front, of course; she held out her hand and let Tyes' human assistant Pelk drop the money bag into it. She weighed it professionally and nodded. "Of course, any extraordinary problems we might encounter will be extra."

"Naturally," Tyes nodded, and stood up. "So long as we are understood that a cloud crossing the sun does not constitute an extraordinary problem. Then we're agreed. You'll follow Andraax and the boy. Pelk, you'll go with them."

"Me?" Pelk echoed in astonishment. The tall Iylari adjusted the fit of his chameleon cloak and nodded.

"I'm going to see the First Speaker. I have to tell him that Andraax is here."

"Can't I come with you?" Pelk asked anxiously. Tyes rolled his eyes, not so much for his assistant's timidity as for his overwhelming caution.

"No. I promise to stay out of trouble, Pelk. Go with them. I'll be back as soon as I can."

"What do I do if we find Andraax?" Pelk demanded. Tyes gave him a rare wicked smile that was nevertheless full of warning.

"Be very, very polite," the Loremaster advised, and was suddenly — gone. Daphine's lips thinned in contempt.

"Flashy," she sniffed, and looked at Iarsang, who was motioning his travellers out of the cave. "Well? What favors do I collect from you for this incredible gift of goodwill?"

"I would not presume to bargain with a woman who just extracted four times a good price from a Loremaster," Iarsang told her coolly, and smiled. "Perhaps we will meet soon and discuss it. In Kelfour's Landing, perhaps."

"If you make it worth my while," Daphine said severely, and spoiled it with a smile as warm as summer's embrace. Iarsang bowed slightly to her and ducked out of the cave. Daphine turned back to look at her three charges.

It was a long regard, and not very forgiving. She finally sighed and shook her head. Without giving any warning at all, she took three swift steps across to Kella and put her hand flat against the woman's forehead. Kella tried to jerk away in surprise, but Daphine's left arm braced her in place. Kella's face went pale, then red.

"Stop it!" she cried. Daphine obligingly let her go. The dark-haired woman glared at her accusingly and scuttled backwards out of reach, though Daphine was standing with her hands resting easily at her sides. "What did you do to me? Stay away!"

"I have just wasted a Spell of Translation on you, one that isn't even included in the cost of your fee. I'm guiding you to find your son, mistress. That's what you want, isn't it?"

"Evan? You know where he is?" Kella demanded. "Where? Is he safe?"

"I can only lead you to him. We'll have to move quickly. I don't think we have time to waste."

Brion touched Daphine hesitantly on the arm and indicated his own forehead. She smiled slightly and invoked the spell again.

"You're taking us to Evan?" he asked. At her nod, his eyes lit up like rising suns. "Good. I don't know how to thank you."

"No thanks are necessary." Daphine's deep green eyes sparkled with sudden amusement. "Anything that puts Iarsang in the interesting position of owing me a favor, much less indebts the Loremasters, is certainly worth any risk. I might have done it for free."

"You charged me four times the going rate!" Pelk objected. Daphine spread her hands in a gesture of helpless resignation.

"And you paid it. Buyer beware, my friend. Now, let's be going."

"After what you charged, I hope you were including Jumps in that figure," Pelk grumbled as he picked up his pack and slung it under one arm. Daphine laughed outright and pointed her golden wand in his direction.

"You," she said in a tone of finality, "are going to be quite entertaining. As if I would give such things away. Really, Pelk. Do try to be reasonable."

"Reasonable," Pelk muttered and stalked out of the cave. "Navigators! The words don't even go together in the same breath!"

The weather outside, thanks to Iarsang's expert manipulation, was clear and mild. Daphine took a deep, sampling breath and looked down the mountainside, then up to where the other peaks of Dragonsfang loomed. A simple enough matter, this, sweeping out of her body and gliding far out toward Smatoth Mountain, to the place that Andraax had caught the boy as he fell blindly out of the gyrating madness of the Flow Storm. They hadn't walked from there. Daphine listened to the Essence of the path, listened to the tiny whispers that told the history to those who knew to hear, and found that the Loremaster and the boy had ridden the Flows away from Smatoth toward Kelfour's Landing.

"Hmm," she said aloud, and lifted her pale eyebrows in elegant surprise. "My. I hadn't really thought one such as Andraax the Mad would find your son such fine company. How very interesting. Has he any special talents, you child? Any magical gifts?"

It was such a relief to understand her question that Brion smiled again, quite unselfconsciously. He shook his head and stared at the distant, diamond-sharp silhouette of Rihtoth rising in the rapidly darkening twilight.

"Magic?" He shook his head again and laughed aloud. Daphine frowned a little as she recognized a touch of hysteria in it, but he quickly controlled himself and cleared his throat. "An hour ago, I would have sworn there was no such thing as magic. Not in any sane universe, anyway."

"Sanity is a relative term," Daphine noted, tossing long curling hair back over her bare pale shoulders. "As evidenced by mad Andraax. In any case, Andraax is most certainly intrigued by your son."

"Who is this Andraax?" Kella asked from a few steps away. She was staring at Rihtoth, the steep high peak covered in snow, with a look of stunned shock on her face that clearly revealed her disorientation and confusion.

"A long story, mistress, and one I'm sorry to say I do not fully know. He was once Loremaster Andraax, a very mighty and learned man. He was advisor to a great many distinguished rulers everywhere on Kulthea. Then he went mad, or so tales say. The Loremasters Guild no longer acknowledges him as one of their own, but who knows what Andraax thinks? He isn't often seen. He prefers to live in quiet solitude." Daphine sighed slightly. "He only occasionally indulges in outright madness."

"Is Evan in danger, then?" Kella prodded. Daphine's sea-green eyes, luminous and kind in the sunlight, studied her without comment for a long time.

"There are many worse things in this land of Quellbourne than Andraax the Mad, my friends. It may be that your son will encounter them unless we move quickly. However charitable Andraax is feeling, I would not trust him to hold to it for long." Daphine held them both, one after another, with her gaze until she was sure the danger had fully penetrated. Then she nodded. "Enough doomsaying, then. Give me a moment more to track them and we'll be on their trail."

"A little haste would be appreciated," Pelk said from behind her. He was staring upslope too, not toward Rihtoth's majestically whitened head but toward the closer cliffside. He was absolutely expressionless.

There was a sizeable war party of what seemed to be trolls edging out of the caves above them. Daphine pulled in a sharp breath and exchanged an unreadable glance with Tyes' assistant. He shrugged.

"Can you use that thing?" he asked, and flicked his fingers at the long Kynac at her belt. She smiled without answering. "Our guests have no weapons."

"That's not a problem," Daphine said with quiet confidence, and drew her long sword. "Just tell them to get behind me."

Pelk drew his sabre. He squinted at the horizon. The last feeble bit of sun was slipping behind the knife-edged bulk of Smatoth to his left. It wasn't an encouraging picture. He glanced again at Daphine, whose fine Iylari face looked completely composed as she held her weapon in one delicate hand.

"Six hundred gold pieces," Daphine said flatly without even looking directly at him. Pelk's mouth opened, but nothing much dared to come out. "You're about to ask me how much for a Jump to safety. I thought I'd save you the trouble."

"How do you know that was what I was going to ask?" Pelk demanded indignantly. A ghost of a smile played at her lips and spilled into her eyes.

"Why, Pelk," she said calmly, "everyone asks."

The trolls gave a howl of blood-chilling triumph as the last crescent sliver of sun disappeared. Before Pelk could so much as try to dig up the gold pieces (not that, in truth, he had them, but he certainly would have given a convincing imitation if given a chance) there were at least five full-sized trolls loping down the hill towards them.

"Behind me!" Daphine shouted to Brion and Kella, who stood frozen in amazement. When they didn't respond, she jumped quickly out in front and engaged the first two trolls to reach them. It looked utterly ridiculous. Daphine, while of average height for an Iylari woman, was completely dwarfed by the two hulking beasts that converged on her. Pelk instinctively started toward her, but her green eyes focused on his for a bare second of outright command. He stopped.

He had work of his own, anyway. There were three more still coming. Pelk worked his fingers nervously and wished, not for the first time, that he had a shield. He wished it even more devoutly as the first of his opponents skidded to a massive stop and swung a stone club the size of a tree trunk at his head.

Pelk ducked and slashed, catching the creature on one massive, hairy thigh. Blood spurted, but he had missed his much-hoped-for arterial stroke. The troll howled and brought the club down with amazing speed toward the young man's head.

Pelk dove forward just as the club smashed into the pebbled slope and ground several large rocks to dust. He lunged at full extension and caught the troll in the guts. The troll stumbled backwards, leaving Pelk at full extension and as defenseless as a baby.

There was, of course, another troll already looming over him. This one had a mace of obviously human manufacture — the property of someone not as lucky as the troll — and even though it looked tiny in his clawed hand, it wasn't. It was a good-sized war mace, bristling with ugly spikes.

It was sufficiently light that the troll would be able to swing it three times as fast as a stone club. Pelk recalled all of that in one blink of an eye, and began recovering his balance. It was far too late, of course, but he was not much interested in surrendering. The troll grinned a horribly toothy grin and drew the mace back for a splintering blow.

A wall of flame exploded searingly between Pelk and the trolls. The heat from it drove Pelk quickly backwards. He stared at it in outright amazement; it was a few seconds later that he remembered to look for Daphine and the others.

"Come on!" Daphine was shouting to him. He ran to her, leaping the still bodies of two trolls as he went. She had already sheathed her sword, but she had both hands outstretched toward the sizzling, crackling wall of flame that held the trolls back from them. "We must move quickly. Pelk, help Kella if she falls behind."

"What are you going to do?"

"Make us disappear." Daphine nodded toward the trolls. "Luckily, they aren't the hardest opponents in the world to fool. Go now. Run! Iarsang's probably halfway to Kelfour's Landing by now, but see if you can catch him."

"What about you?" Kella asked unexpectedly. Daphine spared her one startled glance and smiled.

"Oh, I'll be along. Don't worry. I have no intention of martyring myself for a troll family feast."

Pelk, the memory of the mace still hanging unpleasantly in his mind, grabbed Kella and Brion and shoved them bodily down the slope. He nodded to Daphine and plunged after.

"Wait!" Brion protested and tried to look back at the Navigator. "What's she going to do?"

"It's better not to ask!" Pelk nevertheless glanced back himself. He slowed, frightened despite good sense at the two remaining undamaged trolls looming angrily over the Iylari woman. The third was limping in to catch her from behind. Even as Pelk watched, Daphine seemed to suddenly tire and falter. Her hands dropped to her sides. The protective fires separating her from the howling trolls subsided to sullen ashes.

"No!" Pelk shouted in horror as the injured troll lunged for Daphine's back. He needn't have bothered. The troll's stone club passed through her thin body without encountering any resistance. The force of the troll's swing carried him forward and incidentally broke the arm of one of his brothers.

"What the hell — " Brion began dazedly. Pelk realized that they had all stopped running to gape. He cursed himself for a fool under his breath and shooed them on.

"Illusion. Just run. Don't talk." It was getting harder to see the footing, and even though there was a good coverage of grass, in places the rocks were loose and treacherous. Kella came down wrong and began to slide. She looked up desperately at Pelk, following right behind her, and threw out her hand. He grabbed it and pulled with all his strength. She was lighter than he had anticipated, and he overbalanced and fell flat on his back. Kella came down on top of him. She went rigid and stared into his blue eyes for a long, wild second before Brion pulled her off.

"Are you hurt?" Brion asked her anxiously. She shot him a furious glance and shook free of his hands. Pelk stood up and looked back upslope. The trolls were still up there, but they were occupied with a hysterically chaotic search for the vanished prey. There was no sign of the Navigator.

Pelk jumped as invisible fingers tapped him on the shoulder.

"Looking for me?" Daphine asked sweetly, and became visible in a sudden rush of color. Her face was flushed with excitement. "Hurry. They're stupid, not dead."

"Neither are we," Pelk finished softly. "Well done, honored Navigator."

She was ridiculously pleased, even though she made a good show of waving it off. Pelk smiled to himself and watched her as she picked their way down the mountainside. Ah, he loved Iylari women.

He had forgotten the strange sudden heat he had felt when Kella's wide and alien eyes had met his at such intimate range.

⟩ CHAPTER TWO ⟨

Evan had decided almost immediately that he wasn't going to enjoy this journey. Being captured by pirates was supposed to be adventurous and dangerous, but nobody had bothered to say anything about the way an overcrowded rowboat wallowed in the waves, or the smell of the filth and mold in the storage hold where prisoners were confined. It wasn't very big to be holding the fifteen of them and there was only a little light and air coming in from a tiny barred window above their heads.

Also, nobody had explained just how bad seasickness really was.

"Hey. Boy."

Evan was sitting with his forehead resting on his knees and trying — with little success — to keep his stomach under control. The room was spinning so much that he felt completely lost. He didn't dare look up.

"Boy. Drink this. It's warm, but it'll settle your stomach." A battered wooden cup appeared under Evan's nose. He felt his stomach come up again, but he grabbed blindly for the cup and drank in one quick gulp. It was only water, warm and strange-tasting. He held onto the cup for a moment and struggled to keep it down.

"Good," the soothing, lilting voice said. Someone pried the mug out of his clenched fingers. "Take deep breaths. What's your name?"

"Evan," he managed to choke out, swallowing hard. "Evan Kandris."

"Well, Evan Kandris, how came you to be dragged off all alone by the Kral, then? Have you no family to look after you?"

Evan looked up, half-expecting to find Andraax's bright, mocking eyes watching him, but it was the tall young man from the beach. He still wore his chains. They clanked dismally as he passed the water to the woman across from him. His eyes, though very bright, were also very blue.

"I'm looking for my parents," Evan confessed, and the stranger's brows drew down in concern. "Andraax said he'd find them for me, but — "

"Andraax?" The young man sat straight up as if slapped. The lilting drawl fell out of his voice. All around the narrow hold, people looked up and stared in amazement and some fear. "You saw Andraax the Mad? Where?"

"He was back there on the beach somewhere. I don't know where he is now." Evan looked up at the man — and up — and thought suddenly that no one, not even Andraax, was as tall as this. "How come you're in chains?"

The man laughed and swept long dark braids back over his shoulders in a gesture that should have been feminine but was not. His handsome face took on a conspiratorial expression.

"Because the Kral think I'm important," he told Evan in a confidential tone. The accent was back in force. Evan looked him over and thought that the man looked pretty important, even dressed in torn plain clothes and weighed down with chains.

"Are you?" Evan asked, interested. The man smiled, and his blue eyes were brilliant and wicked.

"Oh, aye, I suppose so. Since you've given me your name, it's only fair I give you mine — but don't spread it like manure, mind you. They don't know it. Not yet."

He stopped, clearly waiting for an answer. Evan nodded. The stranger's voice lowered further.

"My name is Tiernan O'Locklir. There. Now do you know me?"

Tiernan O'Locklir was still young enough to be a bit unhappy when Evan admitted his ignorance, but he just shrugged.

"That doesn't matter," Tiernan said philosophically, and stretched as much as his chains would allow. "Ah. Pardon me, my lady. No offense meant."

The young woman on the opposite side of the hold from him, rubbing her hip where Tiernan's long legs had hit her, glared at him. She was about as opposite to Tiernan as it was possible to get: tiny, barely taller than Evan; hair of a pure wispy gold that fell in wild curls around her sun-darkened face; huge eyes of deep, deep blue. Tiernan's eyes lingered on her, and he smiled.

"This is all your fault, prince," she whispered intensely. His smile faded.

"What? The Kral? Or your bruise?"

"Both!" she hissed back. "If you hadn't gone off on this harebrained expedition like a pouting child — "

"Did I ask you to follow me, Lady Magen?" Tiernan demanded coolly. She glared at him again.

"Don't be more of an ass than you have to be, my prince. If we get out of this alive, my father is going to skin you within an inch of your life, not to mention what your father is going to do!"

"We can discuss the delightful possibilities later. What have you got up your sleeve, most beautiful of magicians?"

"Absolutely nothing!" the lady returned sharply. "Tiernan, listen to me. This is serious! The Kral will choose a sacrifice to Kralta'ain. From the sound of it, you've already been voted most likely to lose your head! There's nothing I can do about it."

"Would you happen to have a simple lockpicking spell available?" Tiernan raised his chained wrists. The woman muttered something uncharitable under her breath and closed her eyes. The young man looked over at Evan and indulged in a solemn wink. "She loves me."

"I most certainly do not!" Lady Laurel Magen shot back, opening her eyes. Tiernan winced suddenly as the iron cuffs clicked open. He lost no time in dropping them noisily to the deck. "Really, Tiernan, would you mind not rousing the entire Kral race against us? I really don't feel up to it today."

"You did that deliberately," he accused her. She smiled with beatific innocence.

"Did what?"

"The damned things bit me, Laurel!" Tiernan sounded so wounded that Evan smiled, too. Lady Magen's lips twitched as she tried to hold back a laugh.

"Did they? Well, I shall have to work on that. Lockpicking is not an ability that comes in very handy in palace life, you know."

"I would have said just the opposite," Tiernan grumbled, rubbing his wrists. The sway of the ship made him ill in the pit of his stomach; he had no sea legs. The stink of the hold and the darkness served to frustrate and anger him; who dared treat him like a beast or a Kral? "What now? I'm free, but with no weapons we don't stand a chance against a ship full of armed Kral."

"That's what I've been trying to tell you!" The woman ran her fingers through her wild blonde hair. "You've still got a Navigator's Token, don't you?"

"For all the good it does us, yes. There isn't a Navigator in the world who'll take us anywhere on charity, you know. They're the most mercenary, cold-hearted — "

"Do you mind?" Lady Magen snapped irritably. "Meaning no disrespect, my prince, but we'd better think of a way to pay them, and quickly. Otherwise you'll be shorter by a head and I'll be fetching a fabulous price on the Trelkinaark'est slave block."

"I really don't see killing a Kral for spare change as an option." Tiernan eyed her doubtfully. "However, with the proceeds from your sale — "

"Beast," she said succinctly.

"If you do get out, will you take me with you?" Evan suddenly put in. They both looked at him, wide-eyed, as if the possibility hadn't occurred to them. He gulped down another wave of seasickness. "I was going to Kelfour's Landing. Can you take me that far?"

"Can we?" she asked the prince. He shrugged.

"I don't see why not, assuming we manage to pull this off at all. Certainly, boy. You look intelligent enough. Maybe we can take you all the way to court."

Lady Laurel Magen made a violent shushing motion as a shadow fell over the barred window above them. Tiernan looked up, and all of the warmth drained out of his face. He looked cold and dangerous as he stared at the foreshortened body of a truly huge, truly ugly Kral.

"That one," the Kral rumbled, and pointed to the prince. "The tall one. He is the most rebellious of the captives."

"Tier!" Lady Magen whispered faintly. "No!"

"Easy, Laurel," he whispered. "You always said I'd come to a bad end, didn't you? Well, you were wrong. This is worse than bad!" The barred opening slid noisily aside with a scraping of metal upon metal. Tiernan lowered his gaze to meet hers. He smiled slightly. "Tell your father I said he's a windbag."

"He won't appreciate it," she said, almost too softly to be heard.

"Always leave them laughing. My father the Bard-king's advice." Tiernan stood up as a Kral clambered down the rough ladder and pointed him toward the top. "Be careful, Laurel."

Laurel started to say something, but she lowered her chin and kept quiet. Tiernan looked at her for a few seconds and then smiled brilliantly, if a little falsely. He climbed the ladder as eagerly as if he were ascending into paradise.

"Up! You will witness the sacrifice to Kralta'ain!" the Kral shouted, and threw Evan bodily toward the ladder. Tiernan was already at the top and being pulled up. Evan looked down and saw Lady Magen being pushed up behind him. There didn't seem to be any choice but to follow orders.

The sun had gone down. There was only a dim glow of orange left on the horizon, and as far as Evan could see there was only water. He felt a surge of panic. Laurel Magen came up from the hold and was shoved into place beside him.

"I can't swim," he confessed to her in a tight, panicked voice. She nodded soothingly.

"That's all right. The Kral can't swim either." She wasn't really concerned just now with Evan's fears, since Tiernan was standing near the bow. The Kral, apparently baffled by his escape from the irons, were binding his wrists behind his back. Laurel's breath caught painfully.

"What are they going to do?" Evan asked her. She reached out without any conscious thought and put her arm around him, more for her own comfort than for his. Tiernan was deliberately avoiding looking at her, and the expression he had on his face was the same bored, dreamy one he wore to annoy his father at court. It almost always worked. She wanted to scream, but somehow she managed to hold it in; the Kral pushed him forward to the edge of the deck.

The other prisoners slowly clambered up out of the hold, even the three little grey creatures. They looked even more frightened than before, if it were possible. The Kral sneered and pushed the captives forward, then saluted as another Kral, a female dressed in a long (obviously captured) purple cloak, came forward with a huge sword in her hand. She had the commanding attitude of someone who expected obedience.

"Kralta'ain, the Great God of War, has smiled! We have taken many captives and much wealth! I, Lord Warfarer Estrenaak'n, give honor to Kralta'ain by the blood and head of this captive!" She thumped the sword's point into the deck for emphasis. Evan winced and felt Laurel's arm tighten around him.

The Kral crewmen roared and stomped their feet. Tiernan yawned pointedly and tried to conceal the fact that he was, in spite of all his bravado, trembling and wishing devoutly that he had never put himself — and, yes, Laurel — in this predicament.

If only his hands were free, he might have at least taken a few Kral with him. As it was, he could only stand very straight while the Kral female brought the sword up and prepared to relieve him of his head.

Laurel Magen bit her lip, hard, and tried not to scream. Her eyes filmed over with tears, making the glitter of the sword cruelly brighter as it caught the dying sunset on the way toward Tiernan's neck.

She did scream, despite her best efforts at bravery, but it wasn't really because of Tiernan's imminent death. There was something far more unexpected and shocking that appeared in a looming wave over the railing just beyond him, something that caused the Kral Lord Warfarer to drop her sword and stumble backward, mouth open and eyes agape.

It was a Sea Drake, the most deadly and dreaded creature in all of the oceans. The drake's head was almost as broad as the body of the ship it faced, and the cruelly sharp beak gleamed along the edges like the Lord Warfarer's abandoned sword. It was a brilliant blue in color, except for the eyes — and those eyes Evan knew. Lavender eyes, with round, human pupils. Even though they were five hundred times larger than they had been in a human face, they were unmistakably the eyes of Andraax the Mad.

No one else could possibly have known that. Giddy from an unexpected reprieve, Tiernan twisted to look over his shoulder and gasped at the sight of the dragon. The huge beak opened. It was deep enough for a tall man, even one of Tiernan's immense height, to stand comfortably — but he didn't aspire to try, not now. Tiernan dove hastily out of the way and banged against the Kral's Lord Warfarer. She was struggling to get to her knees, but it seemed her legs would not support her.

"Menachrahan!" one of the other Kral shouted from behind the prisoners. "Menachrahan demands a sacrifice first!"

"Who?" Evan asked in incomprehension. Laurel was staring in tranced horror at the sea drake.

"The Kral's sea god," she answered vaguely. "It's a drake! Even the Kral fear them."

Evidently. The Kral had all begun screaming "Menachrahan!" They threw treasure by the double handfuls over the side at the dragon, which seemed indifferent to the process. Its huge purple eyes swept over the assembled prisoners, searching — and Evan knew what it was searching for. He sidled back behind Laurel. He didn't want anything to do with Andraax, particularly not when Andraax was a dragon. He was crazy enough as a human being.

"Tiernan! Look out!" Lady Magen screamed. The prince turned, too late, as one of the berserk Kral crewmen picked him bodily up and carried him to the railing of the ship. Laurel ran toward him, but another Kral pushed her violently back. Tiernan was hefted up over the Kral's head and thrown into the open maw of the sea drake.

Laurel Magen screamed as the dragon's mouth closed. The drake slid silently back beneath the waves.

The Kral, berserk with terror, poured a mountain of gold and jewels over the side. The Lord Warfarer had regained her wits, and she screamed a torrent of abuse at the crewman who had tossed her sacrifice over the side.

Evidently, his answer did not please her. The Lord Warfarer picked up her sword and, in one angry swing, sent his head rolling bloodily across the deck. It rolled and thumped against the far rail amidst a drift of broken pearls and discarded golden coins. The Lord Warfarer glared at the suddenly quiet crew, daring someone to challenge her. No one did. She rested the bloody sword point down on the decking.

"He profaned the chosen sacrifice by offering it to Menachrahan. His head, therefore, has been chosen to honor Kralta'ain." A few muttered after that, and she raised the sword again. Blood ran wetly down the blade and dripped to the deck. "I await volunteers to join him."

Not even Krals were as stupid as all that.

The sea drake suddenly surfaced again, in exactly the same spot. Evan, caught in the open, could only stare at those great lavender eyes as they looked at him, and he could have sworn one eye winked. Then the huge mouth opened again, and a jet of water erupted out of it. The wave washed two or three Kral overboard, but it deposited Tiernan O'Locklir in a damp tangle on the deck, still alive and coughing.

Then the dragon sank again without as much as a backward glance.

The Kral looked at Tiernan with hysterical, superstitious dread. He tossed long black hair back from his face and laughed. If it was slightly uneven, no one except Laurel knew him well enough to notice.

"It seems neither of your gods has any taste for me," he said. There was a long silence. No one, particularly not the Kral, thought the jest was funny.

With guttural threats and spears, the Kral threw them all back in the hold again.

Iarsang was leading his party at night to make up for lost time. It was a matter of pride, of course, because he had simply never missed a promised delivery date, and not even a Flow Storm was going to smudge his perfect record! Besides, he might have someone waiting in Kelfour's Landing, if all went well. It had been some time since he and Daphine had dallied together, and in spite of himself he smiled. There was something to be said for the Order of Cypharia, most notably that they attracted the most beautiful and most passionate women in all the world. And Daphine, of course, was a different order of magnitude altogether.

Pleasant memories were distracting him from his work. Iarsang put Daphine and all of her admittedly enchanting arts firmly out of his mind and cast forward along the Path again. Nothing except small nocturnal creatures and, at Path's end, the bustle of Kelfour's Landing. It was still four or more hours away, but that would put them in well under Iarsang's contracted schedule. He smiled in satisfaction.

Now, that was odd. Iarsang's smile vanished and his face became totally abstracted. Random flashes of color from his Compass increased in intensity. Pathsight seemed clear, and yet there was something — unclear. Iarsang cast a Hazard Sense True and received a dead quiet silence. Nothing. But it was a nothing he didn't much like.

"Wait!" He brought them all to a halt.

"What is it?" Civad asked. Iarsang stood for another moment in silence and then shrugged.

"I do not know. Perhaps nothing. But — "

Civad looked around at the others and drew his sword. It was a wise gesture. The male cleric quickly unlimbered a long wooden cudgel, and Astrid produced a long-bladed dagger that looked formidable and well-used. Only Iarsang did not arm, preferring to use his concentration on the strange clouding of his vision.

"Navigator!" Civad pointed at a stand of trees nearby. "What is that?"

It was an aura, like the one that faintly limned Iarsang himself — except that where Iarsang's was a glimmer like starlight, this one was visible by its very darkness. It seemed so dark that it made the very night pale by comparison. Iarsang felt a shiver of true fear shake him.

"Unlife," he whispered. "And powerful. Back. Go back!"

Estvir, recognizing the truth of what he said, immediately turned to go. He was the first to die as a silent, deadly missile struck him in the heart. While his body crumpled, Iarsang reacted without thought, pushing the others down and reaching for a Jump. Their only chance was to reach neutral territory. He was pouring Essence into the spell as the first arrow hit him, and then the second. The third disrupted his control to the point of no recovery, and the Jump was lost. Iarsang sank to his knees as he fought to stay alive. None of the arrows had hit in immediately fatal places, but shock was making it more and more difficult to breathe.

There was still the option of returning to Nexus, the Navigator's island, and saving his own life. Almost any Navigator would have done so, knowing that to stay was death, knowing too that his party was as good as dead already. Iarsang looked at his two surviving charges and rejected the idea; whatever he could do, even if it cost him his life, he would do.

Still, this was going to ruin his record.

Astrid cried out as she saw the arrows that had pierced the Navigator, and again when the shadows began coming out from the trees and advancing on them. She composed herself with difficulty and stood up to face them, dagger in hand. The first of them, a wild-looking man wearing uncured animal skins, jumped at her with a spear. She held the dagger out in a straight line toward him and directed all of the force of her mind in one single, dreadful blow. It streaked through the knife like lightning and struck with awesome force. Astrid's attacker exploded into white flame and fell, twitching and screaming, to the ground.

A knife hissed past her ear to bury itself in the throat of the second of the enemies. She glanced back, startled, to see Civad readying another dagger. He had a brace of them in the lining of his cloak. There was an arrow in his shoulder, but it wasn't affecting the accuracy of his casts. She traded a look of sheer terror with him, and then raised her dagger in trembling hands to meet the next enemy.

Her powers as a Mentalist were severely limited, almost of necessity; the mere fact of her religious calling interfered with mastering true control of her own Essence. She was a formidable opponent, but only in carefully measured strikes. The first use had clearly, in this battle, been her last. Now she would have to rely on strength and skill — and luck.

Luck deserted her as surely as it had Iarsang and the others. Civad's skill accounted for three more of their enemies, and Astrid's dagger killed another and wounded two more, but in the end they were disarmed and pinned helpless on the ground. Only then did the last attacker approach, a short man dressed in a black robe trimmed with silver. He was cadaverously thin and as pale as a thing walled up too long in darkness. Only his eyes gave an impression of vitality, and they were glittering with excitement. He rubbed his skeletal hands together in satisfaction.

"Fine, very fine. They will do excellently." His voice was a bloodless whine. "Bring them along."

"Who are you?" Astrid shouted. The savages pulled her to her feet and lashed her arms tightly behind her. A barely checked moan from behind her indicated they were treating Civad with no more care. The black-robed man came a step forward and touched her face with bony, greedy fingers.

"Merely a servant of Hraask," he said casually, and smiled at the fear that exploded in her eyes. "Quickly, now. Take them to the temple."

Both Astrid and Civad struggled until their captors knocked them unconscious. The black-robed priest moved over to look at Iarsang, who was lying quite still next to the dead cleric. The Navigator wasn't dead; his grey eyes were open and focused.

"And you, Navigator. A little venom for you? No, perhaps not. That wasn't the agreement."

"No, it was not," another, colder voice agreed. Iarsang's eyes shifted to look beyond the priest to the one whose aura had first alerted them to danger. Not Iylari, this one, nor any other good kind of Elven blood. And that left only the disheartening choice of Dyari, the dark Elves. The Elf came closer, and closer still, until he was kneeling beside Iarsang and looking deeply into his eyes. "The agreement was that I should have this one before he died. You would be wise to keep to it."

"Here he is, alive," the priest answered a little sharply. He didn't seem to care much for the Dyar, even though he was obviously afraid of him. Iarsang closed his eyes, cutting off that searching gaze, and felt the Dyar's cold fingers slide down his arm to touch his Compass.

Iarsang's back arched in sudden, breathtaking agony at the dissonance that flared through his Compass. His heartbeat slowed and faltered. The Dyar laughed.

"Not yet, Navigator. Not quite yet. I understand that your Compass ceases to function at your death. What a pity! I must adapt it to my own ends. Therefore you must, regrettably, live a while longer." Even as he spoke, Iarsang's heart steadied. The Dyar's fingers touched the platinum bracelet around his wrist and found it seamless. "However, I fail to see a way to remove this from you."

"Take his hand off," the black-clad priest suggested. The Dyar cocked his head and regarded Iarsang with mild interest.

"Should I?" he asked. Iarsang opened his eyes and made his face as expressionless as he could.

"If you wish," he answered indifferently. The Dyar smiled.

"Ah, no, that would be — wasteful. No, there is a way, I think. And I think you know of it." The dark Elf bent forward until his face was only inches away from Iarsang's. "Tell me how to remove it and I spare you your hand."

"No," Iarsang whispered. There seemed to be no sound anywhere in the world except for the beat of his heart, the drip of his blood falling slowly to the ground. The Dyar kept smiling.

"Your self-sacrifice is repulsive. Do you think it makes any difference? I will take it, then. And remember, it's by your own choice."

The Dyar didn't, in the end, actually remove his hand. The metal of the bracelet yielded first. However, the raw ruin that was left was more horrifying, in its way, than a simple amputation would have been. The Dyar and the Hraaskain withdrew with their prizes and left only the dead and dying.

"How long will this take?" Brion asked their Navigator as they walked on through the darkness. The mountain was receding behind them. Pelk was following last, on Daphine's instructions, and that left Kella alone and isolated between a man she didn't know and one she didn't want to know. If the idea bothered her, it didn't show. Her expression was conspicuous by its absence of emotion.

"That all depends," Daphine said pleasantly. "I can find your son, of course. There is no difficulty in that. However, there are a number of ways you might go to reach him — for instance, we might walk the entire way, a journey that promises to take several days; we might ride the Essence Flows, as Andraax and your son did, to take us to their destination; we might even Jump to that point. Each takes progressively less time."

"There must be a reason why we're not doing the one that takes the least time," Brion said. She smiled slightly.

"Indeed there is. Neither Pelk, his master, nor you has enough gold to pay for such an exorbitant piece of extravagance. Such a Jump would beggar a king. No, I am afraid we must settle on the compromise — riding the Essence Flows to the point Andraax and your son chose as their destination."

"How long will that take?" Brion pressed. Daphine looked at her slender golden baton a moment and shrugged.

"Not long, once we reach a Flow. Of course, we must walk to get to it, and that will take a little time. Andraax was fortunate in that he was able to catch one almost at the very spot he started. We must go out of our way a bit." Daphine looked back at him and thought briefly about how it must be, to have a child missing in such frightening circumstances. Her face softened a little, and lost some of its professional poise. "Not long now. Another few miles and we will be able to enter the Flow. From there it will go very quickly. We can cover great distances in moments."

"You've been very kind to us," the man began haltingly. She cut him off with a wave of her elegant hand.

"No, I haven't. Please don't forget, Brion, that I am a hired guide, nothing more. I haven't been kind. I have been businesslike. You'll ruin my perfectly good reputation if you say otherwise, particularly around Iarsang." Daphine smiled again, for no particular reason, and thought about Kelfour's Landing. A dreary little backwater of a town, really. But it did have beds, and with Iarsang for company she wouldn't lack for entertainment. "He's a great one for repeating things at the least opportune times."

"He didn't seem all that talkative," Brion commented a little gloomily. Daphine smiled again, realized that it was inappropriate, and controlled it almost as quickly.

"That all depends upon the circumstances. I'm not all that friendly with most of my clients, as a rule."

Pelk, from the back, laughed at that. Daphine turned her head to look at him, and he quickly shut up. She shook her head.

"Pelk, of course, being the exception," she acknowledged. "Pelk is notorious for bringing out the worst in everyone, including his master. You know, Vurkanan Tyes used to be the very symbol of good sense before he took up with that rogue back there. Now he throws himself headlong into every problem that comes his way."

"It is the virtue of a Loremaster to be curious," Pelk said piously. It sounded like an axiom. Daphine laughed again.

"Did he tell you that? It's the chief virtue of a Loremaster to keep himself out of trouble. Your master and that professional troublemaker Randae Terisonen certainly keep the Order of the Loremasters jumping, and I've heard neither of them are in very good favor with the Council at this moment. True?"

Trapped by his own loud mouth, Pelk contented himself with a superior air and a disdainful face, as if he whiffed a Troll nearby. Daphine cocked an eyebrow at Brion as if to say she had been proved right, and not for the first time. He smiled at her, and she was surprised to realize that he really was quite attractive, in his dark, strange kind of way. She'd not noticed the gentle weariness in his eyes before, or the patches of gray beginning to creep through his smooth dark hair. He was older than she'd originally thought — or perhaps he only acted older.

"What happens after we find my son?" Kella suddenly spoke up from behind Brion. She hadn't been as oblivious as she had seemed, after all. "How do we get him back?"

"Ideally, we won't have to," the Navigator said carefully. "I can't imagine Andraax having any use for your son beyond sheer curiosity, and Andraax's attention span is extremely short. He'll forget about your son and find something else to interest him, if he hasn't already. We have only to wait."

"What if he's — what if Evan's hurt? What if this Andraax doesn't want to give him up? What do we do then?" Kella asked. They were uncomfortable questions, but clearly required answer. Daphine retreated further into her professional shell.

"I am not responsible for anything but getting you to your destination. What actions you choose to take when you reach there is not my concern." Daphine hesitated a moment, then glanced at Brion. "But in all honesty I can't think of a way you could force someone like Andraax to do anything he didn't want to do."

"I intend to have my son back if I have to kill this Andraax to do it," Kella declared quietly. Pelk took a long step forward and fell in next to her with a concerned frown. He lowered his voice a little when he spoke, not from any desire to hide his words but to make her listen more closely.

"Mistress Kella, Andraax is so old that he may as well be a god. He's destroyed evils that would have made a second's work of you or me. Without power, you have no hope of threatening a Loremaster at all, and particularly not Andraax."

"Then how do I get power?" she demanded a little desperately. Pelk shook his head.

"There isn't an easy way, mistress. It takes years of training and complete dedication."

"I haven't got years. How do I get it now?" she shot back. He spread his hands helplessly. "I see. Your world isn't any different from mine, then. The powerful can take everything from you and you have no way to fight back."

"That isn't so!" Pelk protested, stung. "If no one cared, why would my master have risked his life to help you? Why would the Navigator have accepted such an outrageous assignment at any price? Why would I be risking my life? You have many more friends than you like to think."

"What are you going to do to help me get Evan back?" she shouted, covering her mouth with trembling hands. Brion sighed and turned toward her, arms outstretched. She struck his support away with an angry moan.

"Stay away from me!" Her face was as pale as a corpse's, except for the vivid spots of rage that colored her cheeks. "Damn you! I don't need your help!"

"You need someone's help," Pelk murmured softly. She took a deep breath and didn't look at him. "Kella. I want to help you."

"No," she said, a lost, arid voice. Her face was empty and distant. "No, you're just the same. You can't understand how it feels. What's he to you? Just a boy you've never met. You don't know — "

"We're wasting time," Daphine interrupted. Kella said nothing, only stared straight ahead with dry, feverish eyes. Pelk frowned at her a moment and then shrugged. "Pelk. Watch the rear."

And don't involve yourself, she finished silently, but knew there was no use dispensing such gratuitous advice. Pelk had been a Loremaster's companion long enough to know his limits — and yet —

There wasn't nearly enough detachment in his face when he looked at Kella's bent back.

Iarsang, she thought enviously, would never have had these problems.

They trudged along in silence for a while, as the moons rose brilliant and strange over the horizon and bathed them all in soft whispery light. Kella averted her eyes from them, sanity shaken again by the evidence of her own eyes. It was one thing to know you had been flung across worlds into utter strangeness; it was another to see it, to have your comfortable assumptions blasted open by the smooth fall of too much moonlight and strangely placed stars.

"Here," Daphine finally said decisively, and turned to her little party. "Brion, take my hand. Pelk, hold onto Kella. Stay close, all of you."

"It looks just like every other bend in the road we've passed," Brion said doubtfully, but held his large square hand out. Her cool fingers closed over it. "What makes it different?"

"Essence," she said with a quick smile. "Think of it as a current, if you like, except that it moves through space instead of water. Be careful. Like a current, it's unforgiving of error. Pelk — "

"I've ridden Essence before," he shot back, a little annoyed. She nodded.

Despite her firm grip on Brion's hand, the disorientation and sheer strangeness of what happened next made him waver and nearly fall. Daphine proved unexpectedly strong. She steadied him and turned immediately to peer through the gray nothingness for Pelk and Kella. They were immediately behind. Pelk was wearing an expression of bored patience, but the glitter of his eyes gave him away. No one tired of the unusual — not even Navigators or Loremasters.

"Where are we?" Brion finally choked out as his queasiness finally calmed to a rolling boil.

"Nowhere, at the moment," Daphine told him. "Or, to be more exact, we're part of the Essence. The markers would mean nothing to you, even if you could see them."

"We're heading toward Kelfour's Landing," Pelk put in quietly. Daphine shot him a wryly amused glance.

"Full points for your master's tutelage," she murmured. "Quite right, though the Flow will not quite get us there. We'll only go as far as the shore, and then we'll move upcoast toward the town."

"Do you think he's going to this town?" Kella asked. Daphine raised her eyebrows and shot an unreadable glance aside at Pelk. "Well?"

"Anything is possible with Andraax," the Navigator said noncommittally. Pelk nodded. "We will have to be very careful. And Kella — make no mistake. Andraax is dangerous if annoyed. Don't confront him, not even if we find him. Leave that to me."

"You?" Pelk echoed, startled. Daphine smiled thinly.

"Even mad Loremasters understand the sanctity of a Navigator, I should think. You, on the other hand — well. You look like a thief, Pelk."

"I do not!" he protested. He looked at Kella with a comically earnest expression. "I have an honest face, don't I? Well?"

Kella was quiet a long time, but she kept looking at him. Really seeing him. Pelk found that encouraging.

"Maybe honest in your world means something different than honest in mine," Kella finally answered, and got a laugh even out of Brion. Pelk squeezed her hand and smiled. She smiled hesitantly back, and some of the tragedy in her beautiful dark eyes lightened.

Then, with no warning at all, the world went mad.

It was only Daphine's strength that managed to hold Brion close to her, and only blind luck that Pelk lurched forward and into her other grasping hand. There was suddenly no down, no up. They were not weightless; rather, it was as if gravity was pulling in all directions with shifting, capricious force, tossing them this way and that, up and down, without any logic at all. Kella screamed, but her voice was muffled against Pelk's chest as he held her desperately close.

The wind — if it was wind — whipped her borrowed clothes into suffocating waves around them. Pelk's fingers were locked around Daphine, his one last lifeline — but the spinning insanity was slowly but surely stripping his white-nailed fingers away. Daphine was trying to say something, but the wind drove the words back in her throat.

"What is it?" Pelk called over the roar. Daphine's skin was bleached white with shock and effort, her wide eyes dotted with pupils so small they were almost nonexistent. Still, she heard him.

"Someone is pulling us!" she shouted back. "Disrupting the Flow! I don't know — maybe a Compass — "

Pelk tried to ask why a Navigator would do such a thing, but he couldn't manage the effort. His fingers, slick with sweat, were losing their last desperate grip. He felt Daphine's skin sliding out of his grasp — and then her own hand turned and locked around his wrist. The world seemed to spin again, and yet again, on some crazily moving axis like a wobbling child's toy. Somehow, Daphine hung on.

"Don't let go!" She devoted all of her power and concentration to breaking the hold that their enemy — whoever it was — had over the Flow. It was like embracing acid. Daphine flinched and forced herself to sink deeper, no matter how it seared her soul. Unlife. There was no mistaking that terrible mark.

In spite of the pain, she wondered how such an obvious master of Unlife could wield and shape the Essence, the very antithesis of evil. It seemed impossible. And yet, clearly, it was possible. The black cancer of Unlife ached in her Compass and beat through her Essence-linked senses like the living heart of a vast invisible beast.

She no longer had a choice — to delay was to die. They were hurtling without clear direction through the Flow. She had to gain control before their dark captor finished whatever evil he intended.

No one would ever know, not even Daphine herself, how much the effort cost her. In her last fleeting moments of consciousness, she looked off into the shifting gray of the Flow with a face bleached so white it looked corpselike, and recognized the faintest taste of presence. It terrified her far beyond anything that had come before.

The power was — or had been — Iarsang's.

"Oof!"

Pelk sprawled ungracefully on the ground and collected a mouthful of grass and dirt as a body fell atop him. He laid there for a moment, grateful for unmoving ground, and then twisted around with a groan and flipped over on his back. The protest of his unhappy muscles made him sick.

Daphine was lying crosswise on him. She looked surprisingly frail in the halflight; Pelk thought in alarm that she wasn't breathing, but then he saw her chest move in a barely perceptible gasp. Still, she didn't open her eyes. Pelk struggled up to a sitting position and eased her off of his legs.

Brion and Kella were lying twisted together not far away. Brion appeared to be unconscious, but Kella was stirring. Pelk could see the exact moment when she realized where she was, because she stiffened in Brion's embrace, even though it was entirely accidental. She shoved her husband away, heedless of his condition, and scrambled to her feet. Pelk caught her as her head reeled and betrayed her balance. He was afraid she would resent his touch, too, but she didn't pull away.

"Where are we?" she asked weakly.

Pelk glanced around. The moons were high, but revealed little enough. They had come far from the Dragonsfang peaks, at least; the white jagged blade of Rihtoth glimmered dimly in the wash of starlight, but it was distant. Pelk tried to determine how close they were to the sea, and failed utterly. His own head was not much steadier than Kella's.

"I'm sure we're safe," he assured her, releasing her to offer Brion a hand up. The other man braced himself against a dimly-seen tree and rubbed at his temples with shaking hands. Pelk sympathized, but he was more concerned by Daphine's white, motionless trance.

"Is she all right?" Brion asked.

Pelk got down on his knees next to the Navigator. Pelk turned her face gently from one side to the other, then felt carefully around her neck. Brion waited in silence.

"Brion, what do you do?" Pelk asked suddenly. Brion blinked and came a step closer.

"Do?"

"Where you come from. Are you a healer?"

Brion smiled and looked at Kella, who was ignoring him. His smile looked a little sad and a little strained.

"I build things," he answered quietly. "Towers. Buildings."

He was trying to find a word that didn't yet exist in the language of Kulthea, but Pelk understood him well enough. The thief continued his gentle examination of Daphine without pause.

"Pity. I was hoping you had healer training of some sort. Well, that can't be helped." Pelk sat back on his heels and frowned at the unmoving Iylari woman. "Nothing broken that I can tell. She's just not waking up."

Something moved at the edge of Pelk's eye, a shadow among shadows. A thief's instincts made him spin to his feet and draw his sword in one fluid motion. He looked menacing enough, except for the trembling of his hands as his head betrayed him again. Brion stumbled backward in surprise at the sudden move.

"What is it?" Brion yelped. Pelk stayed perfectly quiet and still, waiting. Apparently, for nothing. It was some long minutes later that he lowered his blade. He didn't sheathe it.

"Nerves," he finally said, but didn't at all believe it. The night was silent and breathless around them, and the moons shone in serene indifference.

Half a mile away, Iarsang crawled another hundred feet and lapsed again into unconsciousness.

"What are we going to do?" Kella asked as Pelk sat down again beside Daphine and settled himself comfortably keeping his sword in easy reach. Pelk looked up at her and couldn't read anything in her face; the moonlight disguised it, but he suspected that even in full daylight it would have been the same. She was practiced at hiding things, he thought. Her small hands were fisted at her sides, almost hidden in the oversized gray robe that she wore. If her nails were longer she would have had blood running from her palms by now.

"We wait," he said succinctly. It wasn't what she wanted to hear, but there wasn't any way to garland the ugly truth. "We wait until Daphine gets better."

"But she said time was running out!" Kella protested. Pelk sighed and looked down at the Navigator, begging her without a word to open her eyes and save him from this acutely uncomfortable conversation. "We can't wait. Evan can't wait. You're talking about the life of my son, Pelk, don't you understand?"

"Yes, I understand," he snapped back. "And you're not going to help him blundering around in the dark with no good idea of where we are or where we're going. I told you before, Kella. You need the Navigator."

"We have her wand." Kella bent to take the golden etched scepter from Daphine's limp fingers. Pelk snapped a hand out and shook his head, blue eyes suddenly harsh and unmoving. "Why not?"

"Just don't try. I'll stop you," he said, and she had not the slightest doubt that he meant it. Kella pulled her own hand back as carefully as if she were drawing it out of a lion's mouth. His eyes, still wary, watched her with the intensity of a predator's. "Sit down, Kella. Try to relax."

She didn't bother to debate the impossibility of that; instead, she turned her back on him and stared at Brion, waiting for him to speak. He was listening, but he sat silently. Helplessly. Pelk, still watching her, saw a brief flash of emotion chase across her still face and vanish again. It spoke louder than words. Pelk thought that were he Brion, he'd be watching for sharp objects at his back.

Pelk wished Tyes hadn't gone; whether it showed on his face or not, he felt completely out of his depth. Four of them, only two who had the faintest idea of how to fight, and the only magic user fallen and useless. It was enough to make his teeth ache.

They were taking no chances with Tiernan this time; he was double-shackled to the slavehold wall, and the chains were so tight that he hung with his toes barely reaching the deck below. Uncomfortable. Tiernan drew in a slow breath and tried to ignore the pain, but it grew like sly wildfire along the base of his ribs and up into the strained muscles of his arms. He tried to form a smile, conscious of Laurel's wide stricken eyes on him from across the way. That hurt too.

"You know, this is kind of relaxing," he said lightly. "You should try it, Lady Magen. I'm sure it does wonders for the circulation."

"Tiernan — " she began, and shut her mouth without finishing. His smile drained away, leaving only the warm steady light in his eyes as he watched her. It had to hurt, she thought a little hysterically. How could he look that calm?

"Hush," he whispered, barely audible over the creaking of the ship and the sounds of the other captives coughing, talking, and moving uneasily like caged animals. For all that, she had no trouble hearing him, or understanding the look in his eyes. "Why did you follow me, Laurel?"

"I want my dowry back," she said calmly enough. Her heart was beating faster and her skin tingled with suddenly alert nerves. I will not blush, she told herself sternly. I'll keep that much dignity, at least. "I told you that in Jaiman. I want my dowry back."

"No," Tiernan answered simply, and implacably. His eyes were very bright and wicked. "Your parents and mine made an agreement, Lady Magen, and your whims don't have any bearing on it. Your father turned over the gold. My father accepted it and gave it to me. Business, Laurel. Just business. Because you decided to break that agreement is no reason to expect your goods back."

Laurel had quite forgotten her sympathy for him. She was chained, too, though not nearly as tightly, and now she sat straight up with as much dignity as she could salvage from a ragged dress and rumpled hair, and a face too smudged and tear-stained to be called beautiful.

But, Tiernan thought, she was beautiful anyway.

"I demand that you return my dowry, Lord High Prince Tiernan."

"When you agree to marry me," he answered easily. She blinked and tried to think through the fine illogic of that, then decided that it was just another of Tiernan's pointless games.

"That's stupid," she shot back. He raised his elegant dark eyebrows.

"Why? You're eminently marriageable. The daughter of one of the most powerful of Loremasters — and you'd make a valuable addition to any household." Tiernan's eyes raked her deliberately from stem to stern, insultingly direct. "As you obviously seem attached to me — "

"You arrogant — overbred — petty — manipulative — "

"You forgot annoying," he supplied helpfully. Laurel glared at him. He cocked his head to one side, heedless of the painful stretch of muscle, and admired the way anger lit up her face. Very fine.

"All right, annoying!" she spat, and got her temper in hand with difficulty. "I mean what I told you in Jaiman, my lord. I'm not going home until I recover the dowry you cheated out of me."

"I hope you packed for all seasons," he smiled back, and then suddenly gasped as his muscles spasmed. His head slammed back against the hard wooden wall, and for a brief moment his vision swirled and eddied like smoke. Only Laurel's face stayed in focus, and all of the anger in her drained out like water from a shattered jar. She strained against her chains in instinctive protest, and muttered an irritated word under her breath. Her chains clanked open.

"Tiernan?" she asked. She was so much shorter than he that even standing on her toes her head barely reached his chin. She swore softly and worked her magic on his locks as well. Tiernan fell forward into her arms, still gasping for breath, and even through his excruciating discomfort he still appreciated the way her body fit against his, the way the smooth skin of her neck felt against his lips.

"Here, sit down," Laurel murmured, and dumped him back on the rolling deck. Tiernan coughed and drew in blessedly unimpeded gulps of air. "Did you say something?"

"You taste good," Tiernan said very clearly, and grinned at the blush that rose to her cheeks. "Thanks, Lady Magen. As always, I am in your debt."

"Then pay it. Promise me the dowry."

"Promise me your hand."

"I'll give you the back of my hand if you don't drop it!" she snapped, and sat back against the wall facing him. "Why are you insisting on this insanity?"

"Why not?" he replied just as archly. She made a frustrated noise in her throat and shook her head. "Really, Laurel. Why not?"

"Because we aren't suited! Just look at us! You're of royal blood, and I don't have half the pedigree, much less the wealth and the position. You should marry a princess, not the daughter of a wandering sorcerer."

"Oh, you object on the grounds of station," Tiernan said, and rubbed his chafed wrists. "Hardly a valid point. My father may be well-born, he got his position by hard work and a large dose of ruthlessness. Besides, we both know that your father is much more than a wandering sorcerer. Loremasters are a step above royalty — just ask anyone. Except royalty!"

"We haven't a thing in common," Laurel continued ruthlessly. He smiled grimly.

"Naturally we do. I think you're beautiful. You think I'm an obnoxious fool. We have both agreed to disagree. What better basis could we have for marriage?"

"Love," she said instantly, and regretted it as his remarkable eyes fixed on her. There was no laughter in them, though his face retained a blandly polite expression.

"Love." Tiernan's voice was low and drawled. "Ah. Well. That's different, I suppose."

Whatever she expected, it wasn't that simple, dry reply. She felt a chill run up her spine, and opened her mouth to reply. Nothing came to mind under the piercing intensity of his gaze. Laurel turned her face away and busied herself with surveying the rest of the slaves chained in the hold.

Evan was beside her, curled up in a protective ball. He was sleeping normally, the sleep of the young and untroubled. Laurel brushed his fine dark hair back from his face and sighed at the pallor of his skin.

"He's so young," she murmured, half to herself. Tiernan's warmth appeared at her shoulder.

"How is he?"

"Tired. He was scared up top, you know. I think he likes you, Tier." Her voice turned just the slightest bit acidic, but it was still teasing. "Perhaps it's because you act about the same age."

"Vicious," he observed languidly, and bent to put his lips beside her ear. They just brushed the skin, making her shiver. "Do you love me, Laurel Magen?"

Her laughter, to her surprise and pleasure, sounded entirely natural. She turned slightly and looked at him, blue eyes steady and amused.

"Don't be foolish! My father sold me to you, like some expensive cut of meat. How could I possibly love you? Does the cow love the farmer?"

She had finally succeeded in hurting him. It was only the briefest flash of pain in those pale, beautiful eyes, and then the long lashes lowered and disguised it. His mouth tightened in a mocking smile.

"I warn you, I could marry you against your will. The bargain was sealed and accepted — "

"Not by me!"

"The gifts have been exchanged! The only thing that remains is the ceremony." Tiernan was suddenly conscious of a shameful desire to frighten her, to see the same pain he felt mirrored in her face. He covered with a humorless grin. "Or we could skip the ceremony. If you want to compare me to a farmer, then I suppose we could just begin the spring plowing and be done with it."

He had the muted satisfaction of seeing her blush from her brow to the hollows of her collarbone. Laurel jerked away from him and backed as far as the tiny confines of the hold would allow. One of the other prisoners gave a sleepy protest, but one icy glare from her silenced him. Tiernan stood there without moving, smiling that strange, heady smile and looking down his arrogant, aristocratic, flawless nose at her. There was challenge in it, and the barest hint of need.

Lady Laurel Magen pulled in a deep, steadying breath and held to one of Tier's empty manacles as the ship rolled on another swell.

"If this is how you woo the ladies, I'm surprised you aren't still virgin, prince. Enough of this silliness. We must find a way out of here."

"That would be nice," Tiernan agreed more seriously. "But I don't see how. Unless you have more up your sleeve than your alabaster arm?"

For answer, Laurel smiled slightly and flipped her sleeve back. His brows rose again, but his eyes remained shadowed and hidden.

"Attractive, but hardly effective."

"Now you see it," she said. Her eyes shimmered — then her head — her body — and finally Tiernan was staring at a blank space. She had succeeded in startling him. She succeeded again as her voice whispered warmly against his ear, sending him spinning to look. "And now you don't. But I don't see how it could help us get off of this ship, and once we're in Trelkinaark'est there's no chance to get away. You're the strategist. What do you think?"

I think I love you, Tiernan wanted to say, but didn't dare. He couldn't see her. She might hurt him.

"Useful," he said instead, and tried to sound more like a responsible fighter than a hopeless lover. "Don't waste it, mistress. As you said, we have no chance so long as the ship's at sea. In view of that, why don't you rest. I'll think about it."

Laurel became visible and curled herself up beside Evan; it wasn't long before exhaustion pulled her lids down even against her desire to keep them open. Tiernan sat there opposite her and watched her with wide blue eyes as sharp as new steel and as soft as dawn's fog. He was supposed to be thinking of escape, of course.

He wasn't.

، CHAPTER THREE ،

Vurkanan Tyes arrived on the quay of the Loremasters' island of Karilôn without ceremony or warning. No one took much notice. He had to move hastily out of the way of a young man in student robes; the earnest young scholar was carrying an armload of scrolls, and wouldn't have seen a drayhorse standing in his way, much less a Loremaster. Two more followed him, each as heavily burdened, and the rear was held down by a hugely muscled older man with neat white hair and a smooth face that belied his years. His sharp eyes didn't miss the dark-dressed newcomer, and he advanced on Tyes with a wide grin.

"Vurkanan! Nice to see you. You're back early, aren't you? I thought you just visited six months back. Heard you were in Jaiman." It was Ghislain Ryancourt. Everyone on Karilôn agreed that Ghislain's passion for gossip was faintly embarrassing — and never more so when it was your latest escapade on his lips — but he was such a true charmer that even his prying seemed forgivable. Tyes, despite his long familiarity with the older Loremaster, was no more proof against Ghislain's blandishments than anyone else.

"Or some such," he agreed pleasantly. Ghislain's expression sharpened, a hound sniffing meat. Vurkanan moved hastily to distract him. "Anyone interesting here?"

"Oh, the usual. They called Terisonen back in, you know, some more trouble in Kelestia. Sooner or later, Kirin Tethan's going to pull that boy's feathers, don't you agree? Anyway, Terisonen's here. Oh, and Yael Ziriv-Kari, and Tethan, and T'vaar Dekdarion. The other council members are all off attending to business, I think. Malim Pelax just sailed off on that damned flying yacht of his, so you needn't worry about running into him, but I heard that — "

"Randae's in trouble again?" Tyes finally asked, to derail Ghislain from a long and probably embarrassing account of Malim Pelax's latest outrage. Ghislain nodded so violently that his white hair fluttered. There was something strangely childlike about the old Loremaster; looking at his wide and earnest brown eyes, no one would ever believe that the man had stood down a Dragonlord with nothing more than a wooden staff and a mountain of courage. Tyes believed it. He remembered it vividly — even when Ghislain was trying hard, as now, to make him forget.

"Got into a direct confrontation with some minor lordling down there; had to do some fancy work to stop an evil cleric. Most unpleasant, I understand." Ghislain's brows drew together. "I've never seen anybody with the penchant for falling into trouble like that young man. It's most — mystifying."

"Not even me?" Tyes grinned. He fell into step as Ghislain started up the path toward the Tower. Ghislain snorted and rubbed at his forehead.

"Vurkanan, you've had your days. No, I'll go further; you've had your years. When I was on the Council I was ready to dive from the Tower at some of your more — interesting — antics. But in your worst, most mischievous, most reckless moments, you've never done the things that Terisonen has done — and you know it very well."

Ghislain was quiet a moment, looking ahead at the laboring backs of his students. "He's lucky this time. He should be dead. He must have a patron deity among the Lords who had an idle day, or he would be."

"Is he badly hurt?" Tyes asked in sudden concern. Ghislain shrugged.

"Minor repairs. Nothing too devastating, it appears. Maybe if he lost a major body part in one of these little scuffles he'd be more cautious." Ghislain smiled, for no discernible reason, and shot Tyes a measuring look. "Not that it did much for your discretion, though."

"I didn't lose a body part," Tyes protested. The older Loremaster shook his head sadly and lifted his face to catch a cooling sea breeze. "Well, I didn't. Not quite."

"You can thank Terisonen for that, I suppose, because if he hadn't shown when he did — "

"I'd be missing my life instead of a few inches of skin and a few broken bones. Oh, yes, I haven't forgotten. Randae's good to have at your back."

"Randae," Ghislain said dryly, "isn't good to have anywhere close. That boy attracts disaster the way a Gark attracts stink. Enough of Terisonen! Why not tell me what's doing to pull you in from Jaiman on this short notice?"

The last thing Tyes needed was to let Ghislain get wind of Andraax's reappearance; Ghislain had deep and abiding feelings about the mad Loremaster, and Tyes certainly couldn't afford any opposition. While he was searching for a good response, Ghislain's head came up and he put a sudden hand out to touch Vurkanan's arm. They both came to a dead halt. Ghislain tugged the younger Loremaster into a convenient alcove near a breadseller and shushed his objections impatiently.

"I don't have time for seek-and-find, Ghislain, this is — "

"Important, yes, I have no doubt of that. But look. Look."

Because he knew very well Ghislain wouldn't let him go until he did, Tyes looked. Then he pulled in a deep breath and kept looking, even after Ghislain shook his arm for emphasis. He went hot and cold in one vivid, convulsive flash, and even when the other Loremaster spoke again it didn't seem to make sense. Tyes forced himself to shut his eyes and listen.

"You see? I thought it might be best to keep the two of you apart." Ghislain's voice was patient and slightly disapproving.

"Why didn't you tell me she was here?" Tyes asked, too sharply. Ghislain sighed.

"And have you tear about the island looking for her? I was hoping, since you seemed to be in such a possessed hurry, that you'd be gone before the issue came up. But as usual, my only luck is bad luck." Ghislain slowly relaxed his hold on Tyes arm and watched him guardedly. "You aren't going to follow her, are you?"

"No," Tyes said calmly enough, but he was trembling all over. The older man craned his neck around the corner to watch the woman across the way from them. She wasn't shocking to look at, just an elegant, aging woman dressed in the outlandishly patchwork leathers of Thuul under a brown cape trimmed with white feathers. She had cut her hair again, this time in a smooth silver cap around her ivory-pale face. She was haggling with a grocer for a piece of fruit, and as she pointed at one Tyes saw the flash of silver on her right wrist.

"She's still wearing my marriage gift," Tyes said, aggrieved. "She must be here for a reason. Give, my friend. There isn't a leaf that falls on this island that you don't know what knocked it down. What brought Isseline here?"

"She doesn't talk to me," Ghislain confessed a little petulantly. "But according to Yael she's here complaining about the behavior of the Loremaster who mediated the recent dispute over Thuul's ports — "

"What? I mediated the treaty!" Tyes blurted, astonished and furious. Ghislain raised his eyebrows, unsurprised.

"I am at a loss to understand your former wife, my friend. The two of you fight like cat and dog, and for no better reason." Ghislain leaned on his staff and grinned mischievously. "But you didn't really call her a stone-hearted bitch to her face, did you?"

Tyes glared at him.

"I haven't time for this," Vurkanan muttered, and swore under his breath. "Not now. Not now. Can we get by her, do you think?"

"Isseline?" Ghislain's disbelief was comical. "Your wife — "

"Former wife."

" — has been known to track a wounded deer the length of the island in a pouring rain and never lose the trail. I hardly think she's going to overlook prey of your size." Ghislain's lips pursed briefly in annoyance. "Or of mine, come to that."

Across the way, Isseline del Banov shook her head and said something to the merchant. She was leaving. Tyes breathed a cautious sigh of relief.

Too soon, Isseline stopped and turned to look straight at him. She was a strangely compelling figure, dressed in her barbaric leathers and with her hair chopped as short as a warrior's; the way she stood, head elegantly high and her silver eyes catching the sun, made Tyes remember happier encounters.

Then she smiled, a professional smile with little warmth in it, and he remembered the rest.

"Come out, Vurkanan, or are you so terrified? Oh, and Ghislain. Greetings to you both." Isseline's voice was low and lilting, the Thuul inflection still strong in spite of long years absent from her homeland. "I've been waiting to find you, Vurkanan. I thought I'd be waiting the season away."

"You might have left word. I'd have gotten back to you — eventually." Tyes returned her stare flatly as he stepped forward. "Please be brief, Isseline. You had a complaint about my performance?"

"Not since the last time we shared a bed," she countered coolly, a hit Vurkanan took with no visible reaction. "It was the only way I could get onto the island without too many questions being asked. I came for a serious reason. It cannot be true, what I heard."

"What?" Tyes snapped. Ghislain had retreated a prudent (if cowardly) distance, so the look that Isseline levelled on her former spouse only did minor frost damage, and no innocent bystanders were struck dead. "I'm not playing games, Isseline. I haven't time. If you have something to say, say it!"

"You promised my daughter in marriage to that arrogant young idiot prince in Jaiman, didn't you? Without so much as consulting me?" Isseline's voice, warm and musical as it was, could be as much of a weapon as her eyes, and Vurkanan this time betrayed a slight twinge.

"Yes."

"Without even consulting the girl?"

Tyes shrugged wearily.

"It was perfectly obvious that she was in love with him — "

"Obvious to everyone except Laurel, it seems, since she stood right up and refused the entire arrangement — and in front of the court!" Isseline's cold beauty thawed a little as she smiled. "She showed uncommon good sense, considering how little I had to do with raising her."

"Good sense?" Tyes hissed. His gray eyes grew hot enough to spit sparks. "She might have made her point in a less devastating way. In her excess and her temper she is certainly your child. Prince Tiernan was gracious about the entire scene, but I was not, and when I get back to Jaiman I intend to have quite a long talk with your daughter!"

"She isn't there," Isseline said flatly. Tyes just stared. "Prince Tiernan packed his sword and mail shirt and left without so much as a word. I dropped in to congratulate Laurel on her good sense and she was gone — following the fool, I suppose. I don't have to tell you the kind of trouble he's likely to lead her into."

Tyes spat at the ground.

"Fools! Both of them! Are you going to search for them?"

"Oh, certainly, and it might be nice for you to contribute a little time as well. Where do you suggest I start?"

"Go to Jaiman. As soon as I finish my business I'll join you." As she turned away, Tyes reached out and caught her elbow. "I — I'm glad you waited to tell me. I would have thought you'd enjoy leaving me in ignorance."

"Wrong," she said unnecessarily, and stepped away. She looked at him a moment more, gray hair whipping around her face in the fresh sea air, and then vanished as if she had dissolved on the breeze. Tyes let his breath out in a rush.

"Tell me something, Vurkanan," Ghislain said contemplatively. Tyes looked up to see those clear blue eyes surveying him far too shrewdly. "Did you ever love her, do you think?"

"I can't remember," Tyes snapped, and turned back up the street. Ghislain had to hurry to keep up with his long, angry strides. "Any particular reason you forgot to tell me about my daughter?"

"None of my business," Ghislain responded serenely, never mind the truth. Tyes swore under his breath and tried to bring his mind back on his problems: on Andraax, principally, and on the rather precarious promise he had extended to Navigator Daphine. He was trying to think of a way to explain that when they rounded the corner and came within immediate sight of the Keep. The Tower of Winds lifted into the air like a blinding staff of light; far above, the pennons of the current Council members fluttered in riotous, colorful confusion. There were four gates leading into the courtyard, each guarded by powerful spells; Ghislain walked with Tyes to the easternmost.

"This is where I leave you," Ghislain said, and offered his hand. Tyes took it with a belated smile and word of thanks. "No need of that, I've not done you much good yet. I've got duties to perform in the Library; while I'm there I'll see what more I can learn about your daughter — and her mother, while I'm at it."

"There's little to know about Isseline," Tyes said hollowly. Ghislain smiled slightly.

"You say that now, my friend, but I remember a time not so very long ago when you would have said differently. She is vulnerable, you know. You did hurt her."

"I know," Tyes sighed, and shook his head. "It's habit. My thanks again, Ghislain, but if you find nothing — my thanks anyway. I may have to reconcile myself to spending time with Isseline, whether I wish to or not."

"Good luck."

Tyes shook his head and turned into the gates. Ghislain watched him as he strode quickly across the white marble courtyard, returning greetings to other Loremasters as they paused in their own business. It was really none of Ghislain's affair, of course, except insofar as he had appointed himself chief gossip of Karilôn, but sometimes Vurkanan Tyes could be a total fool where women were concerned.

Ghislain sighed philosophically, remembering his own wayward and wandering youth, and started up the path toward the Library.

The sun was a dim threat in the east, coloring the horizon but not doing much toward lighting the landscape. Pelk rubbed his eyes and brought himself back to alertness again — it was an effort — then reached across to touch Daphine's wrist. Her pulse still beat slowly beneath the pale skin. She hadn't moved since Pelk had shifted her off of his legs, and his efforts to revive her — some of them extreme — had been ineffective.

"Anything?" Brion asked from a few feet away. Pelk sat back and braced his aching back against a tree trunk.

"She's still the same. Go to sleep, Brion. I'll wake you if there's any change." Brion grunted an assent. Leaves rustled as he shifted into a more comfortable position. Pelk listened to the sounds of the forest at night, and then frowned slightly. "Kella? Where are you?"

There was no answer. Brion sat up again. Pelk reached over and quieted him.

"Kella?" he called again, louder. There was no answer. "Damn. Where has she gone?"

"I'll go look for her," Brion volunteered. He climbed to his feet.

Pelk held on to his shoulder and kept him firmly seated "No, you won't. Stay here — and don't move! I'll be back."

Pelk scrambled up to his feet, wincing at the needle-stabs of returning circulation, and drew his dagger. No use having a sword at the ready if he was stumbling around in the dark; he'd be as likely to split himself open as he would anything to kill anything hostile — but, in this place, with his nerves stretched as taut as bowstring, Pelk didn't feel comfortable without some length of steel in his hand. He took a deep breath and listened to the forest. There seemed to be a strange silence toward the north. Perhaps that way —

Kella clung to a tree and tried not to breathe as Pelk passed within feet of her. He was barely visible in the dimness; she was sure that if she stayed still and silent, he would pass her by. Her patience was rewarded. Vurkanan Tyes' assistant moved past her and deeper into the woods.

"Kella?" Brion's voice came faintly. Her fingernails dug painfully into the bark of the tree, but she said nothing. She hadn't been able to sleep; her mind had kept replaying lurid pictures of Evan in danger, injured, dying, dead, and matching that against Brion's cool fatalism. Damn him. He was no father to his son. It was up to her to save her child, and not even Pelk could be trusted to help.

After she was sure Pelk was out of immediate range, Kella began picking her hesitant way through the trees. It wasn't easy. Many times she stepped down awkwardly and made more noise than she wished, but it seemed Pelk was searching a different area and didn't hear her. She ran into a web stretched between the boles that clung to her face like a damp, sticky hand, and it was all she could do to hold back a scream of utter terror. The unseen insect that had spun it squirmed in her hair; she clawed at it frantically until she was certain it was gone, and then slumped against a rough-barked tree and tried to regain her courage. Her heart was racing painfully against her ribs, and she was breathing in shallow, panicked gasps. She couldn't go on, she couldn't — she fought back a sudden surge of nausea and sank to her knees. The leaves were cool and damp against her skin, steadying her and giving her a chance to recover. She shivered in reaction and felt her heart slow a little.

Pelk's voice called, too near. Kella gasped and bolted to her feet again, spinning off into the darkness with no clear purpose except escape. Things were too mixed in her head for her to understand why she fled, or where she was planning to go; all that she had left to cling to, in this strange world, was hate for her husband and love for her child. Good or bad, she was choosing love over hate.

She had no way of gauging how far she had come from the clearing, but the sun was beginning to show its light. She caught glimpses of the dawn through the branches overhead, but it seemed it would take hours for daylight to fully penetrate this place; it was still as dark as midnight beneath the branches. Kella pushed on. Once she heard Pelk's voice quite near, and froze into instant immobility, but he moved to the east and lost her. She wanted badly to call out to him for help, but she didn't dare. Going back meant defeat. Kella's sanity — never very strong — couldn't take another defeat, no matter how well-intentioned.

The total strain of the journey hadn't left her as much strength as she'd hoped; as the sky turned a bright morning blue above the trees, and light began to distantly filter down to touch the forest floor, Kella sat down to rest. She fell instantly into exhausted sleep.

Her dreams were strange and disturbing. She rarely dreamed of Brion, but this time he wasn't the contemptible man she hated. He was — frightening. A strong man, a man who held power she could never understand and never match. She whimpered a little in her sleep as her fingers brushed the glass bottle hidden in her pocket, but she didn't waken.

She didn't even stir when the black vines she had used at a makeshift cushion began cautiously moving around her limbs. She shivered as the plant began sinking fine, almost invisible spines into her exposed skin, but the pain was distant and unreal. She had lost the will to move, even if she had known her danger.

A cold shock of water on her face opened her eyes in spite of the lethargy, and she blinked back confusion and water droplets to focus on the most beautiful man she had ever seen. He was frowning in concentration, and before she could so much as ask him his name he had grabbed at her hands and pulled. Kella fairly flew out of the deadly plant's embrace and into his arms. He covered her mouth with one hand as the pain hit her in a shrieking wave; blood droplets began to appear all along her skin where the spines had been jerked away. She rolled her eyes in panic as the drops began sliding damply down her body, but the man shook her roughly out of her hysteria.

"No sound," he warned her, and his voice was as beautiful as his face — cool, rich, and dark, alien with accent like nothing she'd ever heard. His black eyes looked at her without compassion. "You won't die. The dreamvines didn't drink long enough."

He removed his hand from her mouth, but held it ready to clap it back if she showed an inclination to scream. Kella didn't scream. She stared.

He was beautiful. His dark hair fell to his shoulders, and his face was as pale and perfect as a stone god's. There was an air of menace about him — of power. About his left wrist he wore a glittering jewel that reminded her of the bracelet the first Navigator had worn — Iarsang — except that where the Navigator's stone had shimmered with color, this bracelet's stone was rippling with shades of darkness.

"Who are you?" she whispered. He smiled slightly.

"Jadel. And you — " His long, pale fingers touched her face lightly. A droplet of blood was licking its way along the line of her jaw; he touched it and smeared it into a thin red film over her translucent skin. "You are Kella."

"How do you know me?" she asked. He shrugged, the question unimportant. "My son. Do you know where my son is?"

"Evan? Yes, I know. And I know where your husband is as well. I have been waiting for you, Kella." She tensed a little, reacting to the dark laughter in his eyes, but he held her shoulders and wouldn't let her draw away. He was stronger than any man she'd ever touched. "I want to offer you help. Not like these others; they've done nothing for you but waste precious time and lie to you. I offer you the chance to find your son, and take him from the madman who holds him captive."

"But Pelk said — "

"The slave of a Loremaster!" Jadel sneered. "I say it can be done. I say if any of them cared for your son, they would have showed you the road to power long ago. It's easy, Kella. And it's fast."

Kella opened her mouth to answer, but she was hit by a sudden rush of desire so intense it made her voice lock in her throat, made her tremble all over. Her gaze locked with the tall man's, and for the first time she noticed that his ears, like Vurkanan Tyes', like Iarsang's, like Daphine's, were sharply and elegantly pointed. Not a man, then. And yet —

And yet, it made no difference to the intolerable, inexplicable agony of lust that went through her flesh like acid.

"I have other things to offer you than power, Kella," Jadel murmured, and she felt herself pressing against him until she could feel every line of his body through the thin fabric of their two sets of clothes. His eyes were a black well of promises. She felt dizzy and a little afraid, but the desire hit her again with horrifying, exhilarating force and drew a low moan out of her. Jadel smiled slowly. "I can make you the woman your husband never could. I can give you pleasure so great it will be pain. I can give you pain so perfect you will weep when it is gone. And when I am done, Kella, when I am done, you will be my equal — in power, in pleasure, in all things. Doesn't that please you?"

"I — " Kella's eyes spilled over with tears. She couldn't articulate — didn't even guess — how deeply she had wanted all of those things, and how much she would give for them. "Yes. Yes. My son — "

"Your son will be saved," Jadel promised offhandedly, and slid his hands around her back to hold her hard against him. "And so will you. But only if you ask it."

Kella shook her head a little frantically, dazed by the speed of her attraction and not realizing in the least that it was mostly fueled by Jadel's black, potent will. He didn't let her go. He bent his head down and touched her lips with his. She gasped in recognition of feelings and needs she'd never imagined, needs that welled up from the invasion with awkward, anxious hunger. He pushed her away and held her there in spite of her struggles.

"Not yet," he told her. She stopped struggling to listen to the hot beauty of his voice. Her eyes were like the eyes of one drugged, or dead. "There remain some tasks. First, your husband. Have you forgotten? He threatens us — and he threatens your son. You know he has to die."

"Die?" she repeated numbly.

Jadel nodded. "You have the means." He reached deftly into her pocket and removed the glass vial. He dangled it in front of her face in the dim morning light, and the light it reflected was lost in the velvet darkness of his eyes. "Don't hesitate now, Kella. You can't. What does his life matter against your son's? Against your own? All those years wanting freedom, and now you can have it as easy as this. Do it. You must."

For a long, frozen moment her eyes looked back at him, bruised and shocked and hopeless. He twirled the bottle so that it caught the light and threw prismed patterns across her face. When there was no reaction, he shrugged and turned away. He hadn't taken three steps before she was blundering after him, hands outstretched.

"Wait!" she cried desperately. He whipped around quicker than a striking snake and grabbed her wrists in one long-fingered hand. As pale as her skin was, his was nearly corpse-white next to it. He shoved the poison vial between her hands and pressed them painfully together.

He grinned, a dead man's grin full of empty humor.

"I will wait," he assured her. "Go, Kella. Go."

She stumbled when he released her, but she stood there staring at him. Jadel cursed under his breath in impatience and pulled her into a brutally tight embrace, levering her unresisting lips apart and wrenching open the door of her soul in the same cold motion. She clung to him like moss as he dragged the plain soft fabric of her robe down over her shoulders. His fingers left bruises on her where they paused. His kiss burned and chilled and clawed savagely at all of the sanity she still possessed. It was only a moment, but that fleeting moment suffocated something still feebly burning inside of her—and lit another, darker flame that found rich fuel in her despair. It hurt, and yet she welcomed the pain as a long-lost friend. Jadel played with her a moment longer, then pushed her away. Kella stumbled as her ripped clothing slipped down, and she sat there in the welter of damp leaves staring at him with misted dark eyes. His face was bland and calm.

"Go," he told her again, as if nothing had happened. His expression hardened and took on a cold, cutting edge. As she watched in drugged disbelief an inky translucent light began to crawl from his bracelet up the white-roped muscle of his arm, and then it slid smoothly around like a second skin to cloak all of him except his face in whirling darkness. Kella forgot to breathe as her heart lurched with desire and terror.

"Don't disappoint me, Kella," Jadel said, too softly. And laughed. It scraped at her mind like a raw scream. Kella screamed herself, a breathless, aching sound, and clawed her way back to her feet. She had disappeared into the sheltering forest before he had stopped finding her amusing, which was lucky for her. His laughter stopped as if sliced with a sharp knife, leaving only the silent, timid sounds of morning, and the progressively more distant thrashing as Kella fought to run away from her fears, or toward them.

Benevolent Lady Astrid had never been overly coordinated, so it didn't injure her pride much when she overbalanced and fell headlong into her cell at a shove from her captors. They didn't laugh, although she was fairly sure it was a ridiculous sight; it wasn't often one got to see a senior cleric of Eissa's order floundering about with her skirts up to her knees. But then, she was also fairly sure that the Servants of Hraask had no sense of humor. Worship of Hraask, that unclean mockery of a goddess, tended to destroy that virtue first.

Something wet and slimy skittered over her bare leg, drawing a shriek from her as she thrashed backwards. No one among her captors paid any attention as they turned the well-oiled lock on the door. Astrid escaped from the unseen creature, only to wriggle back against a soft, yielding bulk that gave a very human wince as her weight came down on it.

"Uh — Benevolent Lady —" Civad, the thief from Iarsang's party, choked. She twisted off of him (it was a difficult task with her hands tied so tightly behind her) and set her back against a damp but blessedly still wall. "Thank you."

"How are you?" she asked him. Her voice was steady, which was an unexpected blessing. He grunted softly in the darkness and did a bit of thrashing of his own, apparently squirming into a sitting position beside her. Except for a tiny, depressingly grilled square of light in the door, the cell was as black as a Dragon Lord's heart.

"I think I'll live," Civad sighed. He didn't seem overly excited with the prospect. Astrid couldn't honestly blame him; her mind sheared away from the horrible prospects facing them, and insisted on focusing on immediate discomforts.

"Your shoulder?" she prompted, remembering his injury. He said nothing. "Is it still bleeding?"

"No. It's stopped. I'm just a little weak, that's all."

She wasn't convinced by his tone. He sounded more than just a little weak. Astrid concentrated a moment on the thick knots around her wrists, but no matter how she contorted her fingers she couldn't seem to get a close enough grip on the rough hemp. She gave up and let her abraded hands rest.

"I hope you're praying, Lady Cleric," Civad said quietly. Again, she didn't like his tone, colorless and limp. "We could use some divine intervention right now."

"I wouldn't plan on that, my friend; the Lords of Orhan are hardly known for personally intervening in the affairs of lesser mortals, and I can't Channel any power without being blocked off by the clerics of Hraask. Rather than look to the skies I suggest we look to ourselves. Can you reach these knots?"

"What a novel point of view for a cleric," Civad marvelled only a little sarcastically. "Here, turn a bit — forgive my hands — "

"Can you untie them?" she asked anxiously as his fingers skimmed competently over the rope. He snorted.

"If I can't, I should find a new profession. Hold still. This will take a little time."

He exaggerated; it seemed less than a minute before Astrid felt the ropes slide loose. She sat up and rubbed her aching wrists in relief, then turned and tried to peer through the darkness at her fellow captive. He was just a dim shadow on the floor.

"Thank you," she smiled. He didn't move. "Civad?"

"My pleasure." He sounded much weaker. "Forgive my discourtesy. I think I'll lie here a while, if you don't mind."

"Your shoulder?" she asked as she settled in beside him. He said nothing, but when she touched his arm he shuddered, and a little hiss escaped him. Astrid attacked the knots of his bonds. Her clumsiness demonstrated itself again; she was glad that the darkness hid the inevitable flush that worked its way up from her collarbone to her hairline.

"Sorry," she apologized as the ropes finally came free. He cautiously moved his arms, caught a moan between his teeth, and cradled his injured arm close against his side as he sat upright again.

"Sorry for what? Untying knots in the dark isn't a required skill for clerics, as I understand it. You did better than I did when I was an apprentice thief." Civad sighed and probed gingerly at his shoulder. "My master said I'd never make much of a thief. He told me to stick to making pots."

"Why didn't you?" Astrid moved his hand aside and began examining his wound with practiced gentle fingers. Healing was the only task at which she was not clumsy. He sat back with a sigh of relief.

"Stick to pots? Too noisy. All that banging. I have sensitive ears."

"Well, I suppose thieving's a quiet business," Astrid observed. Her tone grew serious. "Civad, the arrow's broken off here. I'll have to take it out."

"Wonderful," he said sourly. "Can't you wait?"

"I can, but I doubt you'd be grateful later."

"I suppose this is going to hurt."

Astrid smiled, even though he couldn't see it in the darkness, and touched the back of her hand gently against his cheek. It was rough with a day's growth of beard and slick with sweat. His body radiated a feverish smell of pain and fear.

"Very probably," she agreed, as gently as she could, and set one hand on either side of the wound, front and back. "Do you think you can hold still?"

She felt his nod as a tensing of the muscles under her hands. Astrid bent her head until her forehead was almost touching the blood-marked fabric of his shirt and began to slowly invoke her deity's power. It came sluggishly, in halting gradual steps — balked, she assumed, by the power of Hraask, the Spider-Goddess, and her detestable clerics. Astrid hoarded what little she received and began easing the arrow fragments out of the wound with as much care as she could. Civad went rigid with pain.

"Not long now," she assured him a little breathlessly. A piece of wood worked its way free under her fingers, and then the sharp bulk of the point slid out. A fresh gout of blood came with it. Astrid hastily put her fingers into the wound and clamped off the spurting vessel. Civad cursed in a low, miserable voice, but she ignored him until she was sure her power had sealed the damage.

"There," she said with a sigh, and absently wiped her bloody hands on her robe. "So long as you don't strain it, you should live."

"But will I enjoy it?" he groaned weakly, and began slipping sideways along the wall. Astrid caught him and held him upright. "I'm all right, Benevolent Lady, don't fuss."

"I'm not fussing," she assured him, and cast an apprehensive glance around their inky prison. "At least, not about you. What do you know about the worshippers of Hraask?"

"What any boy growing up in Quellbourne knows," Civad shrugged — or tried to. He settled for a grimace that went unseen in the darkness. "A thirsty goddess, their spider-lady. Likes blood and torture. They appease her with all kinds of abominations — and they keep Great Spiders for pets. Sometimes they feed them with captives."

"Oh, come now," Astrid scoffed in nervous disbelief. "Surely such things are said about half of the cults on Kulthea. Eating babies, drinking blood — foolish talk — "

"Then why is your voice shaking?" Civad asked without humor. She bit her lip. "I grew up in Kelfour's Landing, Benevolent Lady, and you can believe this: no one travelled close to the lair of Hraask. Those who did never returned."

"Why did the Navigator take us into such deadly territory?" she demanded. Civad sighed.

"He didn't. We weren't near the Temple when we were ambushed — or at least we weren't any nearer than anybody else. They came deliberately looking, I think. Did you see the Dyar? The one hovering over Iarsang?"

"Yes," Astrid relied faintly. The memory made her shake. It wasn't his appearance; like all of the Elven race, the Dyari were beautiful. It had been the oily black evil that had hung around him like a cloud, and the flat menace in his eyes. "Do you think he led them?"

"I don't know." Civad shifted uncomfortably. "I wish I did. Do you think Iarsang's dead?"

"Yes," Astrid answered, sick at heart. "Yes, I have no doubt. It would be madness to leave him alive. Of course, it was madness to attack in the first place; don't they know the navigators will strike back? I hope that we'll be missed. Maybe someone can rescue us."

Civad didn't bother to point out what both of them already knew: that chances of rescue were slimmer than the personal manifestation of Astrid's patron goddess wielding bolts of fire. He let the throbbing agony of his shoulder lull him into a dull stupor. Astrid sank back against the wall beside him, a comforting, warmly human presence. She slid slowly into sleep and let her head drop onto his shoulder — his whole one, thankfully. Civad found he didn't much mind. It was faintly surprising, really. He wasn't much for clerics.

A chain clanked faintly on the far wall, hidden by darkness. Civad tensed so suddenly that he bounced Astrid's head from its pillow. He'd been intending to jump to his feet in the fury of his panic, but the strident voice of his pain reasserted itself before he was more than crouching. He braced himself against the wall and slid up to a tottering standing position, left arm held tightly against his side.

"What is it?" the cleric asked anxiously as she dragged herself up beside him. He put out a hand to touch her arm and still her.

"Who's there?" he asked. The chain clinked again, a purposeful sound, not accident. Astrid reached out and cupped one hand in front of her. Another expenditure of precious, finite power, and a dim blue light began to glow in her fingers.

"Merciful gods!"

Afterward, Civad couldn't swear who uttered the half-prayer, he or the cleric. Suffice to say it was uttered, and hung in the air like the unearthly light of the Benevolent Lady's spell.

Against the far wall, dimly limned with blue, hung three men in chains. They all bore the marks of torture and bad use, and the rags they were still barely wearing were so ripped and bloodied it was hard to identify them. Still, Civad had a feeling — and, as he locked gazes with the cleric beside him, he knew he was right.

"Sir?" Astrid said timidly, and advanced to within a few feet of the smallest man, a wizened old human who had his eyes open and watching. He hardly seemed to notice her. The pupils of his faded blue eyes constricted in response to the light, but that was all. She waved it back and front before his face and sighed.

"Drugged?" Civad asked.

"I don't know. Can you get him out of these chains?"

"I doubt it. They took all of my tools, even down to the wire strips in my cuffs. And I had a hard enough time with rope." Civad looked at the little man thoughtfully. "He's wearing the robe of a Scribe of Nomikos."

"What there is left of it. And these two — " Astrid indicated the other two men, apparently hanging limp in their chains and in deep sleep. "These two are Changramai warriors, sent to guard him. Scribes never travel without them."

"Doesn't appear to have done him much good," the thief observed. He was watching the Changramai. Neither moved. "But then I heard that the Changramai weren't so much action as talk. Good for guarding a library, but in a fight — "

One of the heads lifted to reveal a stony dark face and eyes that glittered wild blue in the witchlight. That was all the Changramai did, but it was eerie enough. Civad forced a smile.

"Well, hello. I thought you might be awake. There's nothing like insulting a warrior's honor to get his attention, I always say."

"Thief," the Changramai whispered contemptuously, and closed his eyes again — to all appearances, unconscious and dead to the world.

"I'll bet he thought he insulted me," Civad remarked, and stepped closer to look at the old scribe. He had heard chains clank, but he couldn't imagine the Changramai wasting motion, and the old man seemed lost in deep trance.

"Civad!" Astrid cried, and dragged him back without deferring to his wounded arm. It was as well she did. The old man's eyes came brightly alive with menace, and a thin ropy arm swung a length of chain with lethal force. It grazed Civad's cheek in passing, leaving a pink scrape but nothing more permanent.

Both the Changramai were watching now, as tense as hunting cats. Their stares were unsettling. The menace from them was so palpable that Astrid and Civad, without a word spoken or a look exchanged, took two voluntary steps back and stood with their shoulders touching. It didn't much matter that the two Changramai were chained more effectively than guard mastiffs; the impression that they gave off was one of unstoppable, uncontrollable ferocity. Civad let out a slow, shaky breath as adrenaline subsided and allowed a fresh wave of pain to wash over him.

"Are you all right?" Astrid asked quietly.

"Better than I deserve," the thief answered, and studied the old scribe with intent eyes. "Why did he strike at me?"

"Look at him. I think he'd strike at anything within range: man, woman, or beast." It seemed true enough. The old man's watery eyes were still fixed on Civad with malignant intent, but his face was slack and stupid. Civad shivered and resisted the urge to take another step away.

"Mad," he judged grimly. "Poor bastard. I suppose we're lucky our jailors had the good sense to restrain him — and the Changramai, because the Changramai would kill anyone who laid a hand on him."

"I'm amazed they have Changramai alive at all," Astrid commented. The two warriors shifted their eyes as one to stare at her, apparently alert and intelligent. "I thought they would die before being captured."

"Many did," the left-hand Changramai replied very quietly. "We were ten warriors and three Scribes. What you see before you is all that survived."

"Gods," Civad murmured, a little awestricken at the ferocity implicit in that bald statement. "I meant no harm, you know — I only meant — "

"You made your comments to see if we were conscious. Yes, we understand that. But as you love your life, do not approach the Scribe."

The Changramai wasn't altogether referring to the old man's madness. Civad nodded a quick affirmative.

"Warrior, I am a lay healer. May I see to your wounds?" Astrid asked slowly. The Changramai's eyes slid over her, dissecting and judging, and he nodded once. She exchanged a cautioning look with her companion and came forward — carefully staying out of the Scribe's range — to probe gently at the first warrior's wounds.

"You two are not mortally hurt," she finally judged, and stepped back. "I haven't enough power to do more than accelerate your healing, so your wounds will still trouble you — "

"They do not trouble us," the second Changramai said stonily. She looked at him, then nodded.

"Of course. If there were some way I could approach the Scribe — "

"It is no use," the first warrior said with just a whisper of regret coloring his even voice. "His reason has been gone for days now. He will not eat or sleep, only does injury to anything he can reach. Do not approach him."

"As you say. Do you know why they've taken us?"

"Where were you taken?" the Changramai asked her. Astrid looked aside at the thief, who was rubbing absently at his wounded shoulder.

"On the Rihtoth road to Kelfour's Landing." Civad raised his eyebrows. "We were in the company of a Navigator."

"The dogs of Hraask attacked a Navigator?" It seemed to come as much of a surprise to the Changramai as it had to Astrid and Civad. "Then they were desperate indeed. We knew they were, to have fought us at such losses — or to have fought us at all. They are cowards, mostly, preying on lone travellers and the weak and old. Yet they were brave enough to take two desperate risks that will eventually destroy them and this foul nest."

"Do you think so?" Astrid asked. She settled down cross-legged on the damp floor of the cell and set the witchlight to hovering over her head like a crown. Civad remained standing. "Oh, granted, the Navigators would raze this temple to the very stone if they thought the worshippers of Hraask had killed one of their own — and I'm certain the Changramai have their own ways of dealing with those who fail to respect the neutrality of Scribes. But do you think anyone will know who took us? Surely they are not that foolish."

The Changramai remained silent. Civad shook his head.

"Unless one of us can get word out or free himself, no one will ever know. As for razing this place to the stone, don't you think it's been tried, warrior? Every few years a group of fools bands together and decides to challenge the might of the Hraaskain; if they're ever seen again it's because their nerve broke before their heads did. It's more than mere ferocity. The Hraaskain have magic. And — " Civad cast a significant look at the door. "And they have the Giant Spiders."

Outside of the door there was something moving. It had too many legs to be anything near human, and the soft breathy noise it made had an insectile keening edge to it.

It effectively killed any conversation anyone might have managed.

There were good days and bad days, even in the august chambers of the Loremasters Council. There were days when the beautiful room, with its polished warm wood and elegant velvet, was a restful haven full of friends and good conversation.

There were also days when the fine rose-petal incense smelled overpowering, and the wine tasted too new, and no one agreed on the color of the sky above the crystal dome. This, the head of the Loremasters Council reflected, was one of those days.

Kirin Tethan rubbed at the bridge of his fine-boned nose and pushed back another wave of exhaustion. Across the table from him, Yael Ziriv-Kari turned her jeweled bracelet idly over in her fingers and watched the resulting rainbows with every appearance of mindless interest. T'vaar Dekdarion was pacing from one end of the Council Chambers to the other in brisk, no-nonsense strides that proclaimed him for a warrior louder than the close-fitting black leathers he wore.

Basically, it was another example of how little the three of them agreed today.

"I still think you're too hard on the boy," Yael said suddenly. Her slanted violet eyes moved up to meet Kirin Tethan's with no trace of deference. "Terisonen is headstrong, but we haven't enough of that to go around. The entire order has gotten so cautious we won't take a brisk walk around the island in case we might be rained on. He has a good heart, and no matter what you may think of his methods — "

"His methods?" Tethan interrupted cuttingly. "The puppy has no methods. He charges right into any kind of trouble he can smell. You heard him! He stood right there and told us he got dragged into this entire debacle over a woman! A woman!"

"And have you never made a fool out of yourself over a woman, Kirin?" Yael asked archly. He glared at her, hazel eyes snapping. She smiled. "No, probably not. What about you, T'vaar? Have you?"

"Made a fool of myself over a woman?" the tall man asked without pausing in his restless circuit of the room. "Only over you, Yael. But then I'm hardly alone in that."

"Careful," she warned him — but her smile was forgiving. "You might spoil your reputation as a cold-blooded Changramai."

"Former Changramai, if you please!" He sat down unexpectedly in one of the tall upholstered chairs scattered aimlessly around the huge domed room. Brilliant lights flickered across the glass canopy above them, random flashes along the lines of the Tower's defensive spells. T'vaar ignored them. He propped his pointed chin on one fist and looked at his two fellow Council members. It was difficult to tell what he was thinking; his face had the typical Changramai stillness, and those deep blue eyes the aloofness of the ocean. The only concessions he made to personal expression were his unrelieved black attire and the startling violet streaks in his short blond hair — both remnants of his upbringing on the country of Tanara. He was the least obviously Elven of any of them, with his muscular frame and human-proportioned features; except for the sharp points of his ears, he might have passed for a prince of any human land.

"Well?" Tethan demanded sharply. "Aren't you going to join her in defending him?"

"Why?" T'vaar wanted to know. "Yael rarely needs help in expressing her opinion, right or wrong. And as it happens, I'm not on her side today. Terisonen needs more self-control. I'm not particularly grieved that he managed to rid Kulthea of another minion of the Unlife, but I am certainly not pleased that he did it for the wrong reasons. I am even less pleased that he put the entire district at risk in doing so."

Yael Ziriv-Kari dropped her bracelet on the table and glared at him. She pouted most prettily, whether she intended it or not. T'vaar shrugged silently and got up out of the chair again to resume his pacing.

"Then you're agreed he needs correction?" Kirin Tethan rapped. T'vaar made a lazy gesture of acquiescence. Yael, still pouting, gave an angry shrug. "Well, that's progress. I've a mind to pair him with Kedrik Bularis for a time. If Kedrik can't teach him the value of caution, no one can."

"Are you certain Kedrik's not too cautious?" T'vaar asked. He paused to examine an enchanted axe that hung on the wall with apparent fascination, though he had looked at it every day for more than four hundred years. As he cocked his head, an amethyst earring caught the light and sparked answering fire from Yael's discarded bracelet. "I wonder sometimes if he didn't get too much of a scare on his first Jump. He's always struck me as exactly the type Yael described: too ready to run from a fight."

"Send him out with Tyes again," Yael suggested puckishly. T'vaar threw her an ironic look.

"I seem to recall that we already tried that. We nearly had two dead Loremasters to show for it."

"But what we ended up with were two live Loremasters and two Fifth Pale demons banished from Kulthea. Results," Yael pointed out triumphantly. Tethan snorted.

"Considering how long it took Tyes to recover from those results, I wonder. T'vaar, who do you recommend we pair Terisonen with?"

"Malim Pelax," the black-dressed young man said. He was prepared for the outburst that followed, and he wasn't disappointed.

"Are you mad? Malim Pelax — "

"Is a perfectly respectable Loremaster, if not quite to your taste, Yael. An acceptable arrangement, T'vaar. I will give the orders." Kirin Tethan speared his most outspoken adversary with a challenging glance. "Unless our colleague has an objection other than her obvious personal feelings."

Put that way, of course she didn't. Yael shut her mouth and gave him a frosty nod. Tethan smiled slightly.

"T'vaar, will you see to it? Fine. Now to the next matter: Vurkanan Tyes has requested an emergency meeting."

"Is he here now?" Yael asked. Tethan nodded. "Fine. Vurkanan isn't known for wasting our time, most certainly. Shall we see him now?"

"He's on his way." Tethan stood to do a bit of pacing of his own — if only as far as the wine cabinet. He held up a bottle of red and raised inquisitive eyebrows at his two fellow council members. T'vaar Dekdarion shook his head, as he always did. Yael accepted. Kirin Tethan carried two full cups back to the table, then a third that he placed in front of the traditional visitor's chair.

He knew Tyes well enough to know the man wouldn't turn down a cup of red wine.

When Vurkanan Tyes pushed through the doors and bowed to them, Yael and Kirin Tethan exchanged startled glances, and T'vaar's blue eyes narrowed in thought.

Tyes had always seemed — invincible. Today there was exhaustion in every line of his body, shadows ringing the vibrant gray eyes, and a barely perceptible tremor in his hands. He gulped down his wine with a bare word of thanks.

"Forgive my appearance, my friends. I have not had time to change my apparel."

"It appears the wear goes deeper than just clothing, Vurkanan," Kirin Tethan said. T'vaar was a quiet, steady shadow in the corner. Yael's eyes were compassionate and concerned. "How can the Council help you, Loremaster?"

"I came to ask you to lift the restriction against opposing Andraax the Mad." There, it was said, bald and grim. Tyes got reactions from two of them; predictably, the former Changramai warrior stayed expressionless and still. "He may have stolen a child. We all know that his logic is — uncertain. I deeply feel that we need to intervene in this matter."

The silence stretched until every beat of his heart was audible in the stillness. Kirin Tethan's knuckles were white around the base of his goblet. T'vaar Dekdarion, apparently disinterested in the entire matter, removed the enchanted axe from its place on the Tower wall and began inspecting the edge. Like the amethyst in his ear, it caught the spell-lights from the dome overhead and cast them back in rainbow sparkles.

"From the beginning, Loremaster," Kirin Tethan finally said. Vurkanan Tyes took in a deep breath and obeyed. The telling occupied some few moments, but no one interrupted with comments. Yael Ziriv-Kari's violet stare was on Kirin Tethan rather than the speaker, and she was not much pleased with the white lines around his mouth. He hardly seemed to be listening, and there was a barely perceptible flinch every time Andraax's name was uttered.

"What business is it of ours?" Yael asked when Vurkanan was finished, her voice light and dry. Kirin Tethan flashed her an unreadable look.

"Andraax, mad or no, is a Loremaster. His actions reflect on the entire order. We can't let him bring harm to these strangers or their child." Vurkanan was braced for a blow. He wasn't disappointed.

"You," Tethan said in careful, precise tones, "have overstepped yourself, Tyes. You should never have put yourself at risk in a Flow Storm. You should certainly have never interceded for these strangers, nor concerned yourself with their problems. That is the kind of mistake that Terisonen would make, not you. And this — promise — to the Order of Cypharia — "

"Too vague to be called a promise, surely," T'vaar put in. He tossed the axe idly in the air and caught it with blurring speed. "And if anyone overstepped, it was Andraax. What man, Loremaster, madman, or both, has the right to take a child from its parents unless there is true danger? Surely Tyes' actions were in perfect accordance with his position. I see no difficulty."

"I suppose you see no difficulty in letting him chase after Andraax!" Tethan snapped. Dekdarion shrugged. He picked another axe from the wall and began juggling them. Behind the flash of steel, his eyes were steady.

"No," he agreed evenly. "I do not, Kirin. Do you?"

"You hardly knew Andraax!" Tethan burst out. "I tell you that he is dangerous and unpredictable. I will not risk any of our order around him; there is no saying who he will see as friend and who as enemy. He has the strength to crush you like an insect, Tyes. There is no one — not even me, who is his closest contemporary — who could stand against him in open conflict."

"I think," Yael said from behind her wineglass, "that perhaps you are more frightened for Andraax than you are for Vurkanan. Am I right?"

"Ridiculous!"

"Is it?" she pressed. "I think your restrictions were not meant so much to keep Loremasters safe as they were to make sure Andraax was left free. Ever since his madness struck, you have built up this image for us of unrelenting savagery and danger. Yet, I wonder. We have always obeyed your restriction, Kirin, but I wonder."

"You wonder what, Yael?" Tethan asked in sudden weariness. Yael's eyes were drawn to T'vaar, who caught the hafts of both axes in one facile hand and stood very still as he watched them. Across the table, Vurkanan Tyes was just as quiet. All friends, here, all Loremasters, and yet she was teetering on the brink of unforgiveable offense. Not a healthy situation.

T'vaar's stolid expression begged her to reconsider.

"I wonder if perhaps your love for him hasn't blinded you to the realities of his position — and ours. I know how close you were to him, Kirin, and I am sorry to break open old wounds, but something must be done! We can't simply let him roam over the whole planet doing just as his mood strikes him. He isn't answerable to anyone, he isn't afraid of anything — he really could be dangerous, you know. It would disastrous to discover such a grim fact while bent over a child's bleeding body." Yael was as delicate in her tone as she could manage, but she still felt the walls come up around Kirin, and the pain. "You know Tyes is right, Kirin. Let him go. He won't hurt Andraax unless he has to."

"Hurt him?" Vurkanan Tyes wondered aloud. "More likely you'd be a year gathering up all of my body parts. I beg to remind that I didn't volunteer for this. I'd be just as happy to hand it to a Council member, believe me. I've no desire to be a hero — or a martyr."

"There's a job for Terisonen," T'vaar observed lightly from across the room. Tethan covered his face with unsteady hands.

"No. No. I am not lying to you, my friends, and I am not letting love blind me to fact. Do not interfere with Andraax. Do not approach him, do not track him, do not so much as breathe the same air with him. Am I being clear to you, Loremaster Tyes?" Tethan's voice was soft, but it was unmistakably menacing. "If you do, you will be in violation of Council edict that was set down almost five hundred years ago. And we are not repealing that edict today!"

"Why not?" T'vaar asked quietly. He put the axes back on the wall with a grate of metal on stone and crossed to the table. Even now, he didn't sit; he leaned on stiffened arms over his chair and looked at each of the others in turn. "If a majority of us want to reopen the edict, we certainly can. And that is the law, Kirin."

"I know the law!" Tethan snapped, and his hands came down to rest palm down on the table. He looked calm, but there was an underlying tension to him that was coiled like thin biting wire. "I helped write the law, and so did Andraax! Do not presume to lecture me on the law, T'vaar."

T'vaar was probably the only Council member, past, present, or future, who could stand eye-to-eye in opposition with the First Speaker of the Loremaster Council and not blink. Tyes, for his part, was looking meekly down at his wine and trying to appear insignificant — which he was, for this confrontation.

"I question the wisdom of allowing Andraax free rein on Kulthea, First Speaker. And I wish to put the matter to discussion." T'vaar's voice was icily controlled. He and Tethan were having a positive war of stares. "It's a formal request by a full member of the Council. Are you going to refuse it?"

Yael's lips parted, maybe to urge T'vaar to greater caution, but she didn't have to speak. After a cold, cold moment, Kirin Tethan smiled.

"Of course I'm not going to refuse it," Tethan assured him with false geniality. "I'm going to subject it to full Council review — which of course will mean waiting until our absent members are back in the Tower. Perhaps three or four months. And then we'll have a full discussion session — not to exceed one year — and a formal vote. That, my friend T'vaar, is the law of repealing an edict."

"Then recall the members. I do intend to pursue this. Yael will support me." T'vaar shot a look at her, more to stiffen her resolve than verify her intentions. She nodded glumly. "In the meantime, Vurkanan — "

"As First Speaker, since you invoked my rank," Tethan said evenly, "I have the right to summarily assign Loremasters to new fields when the circumstances warrant. I will have orders drawn up to remove Tyes from this area of — temptation."

Tyes shook his head in instinctive argument, but Yael Ziriv-Kari put one slender hand on his arm and squeezed in warning. He looked down at his glass again. T'vaar said nothing. The silence was sharp-edged as Tethan rose from his chair and began pacing.

"Perhaps we are all speaking in haste," Yael ventured finally. She was patently uncomfortable in the role of peacemaker, being more accustomed to stirring up trouble than smoothing it over, but she rose from her place and glided over gracefully to put her hands on Tethan's arm. She was a tiny woman. Many times the touch had worked to her advantage when she opposed men the height and strength of the First Speaker. His eyes softened despite themselves as he looked down at her beautiful, fragile face.

"Perhaps," he admitted, and sighed. "Andraax is a sore subject, you know that. The Lords above know there should be a resolution, but I am not certain there is any correct one. Let us postpone this to full Council, as T'vaar suggests."

That was more like the Kirin Tethan they all knew. T'vaar drew in a deep breath, the first indication from him that he had been affected by tension at all, and Tyes tossed back the rest of his wine. Yael continued staring at the First Speaker. He hadn't finished, she sensed.

"But I have not changed my mind, Vurkanan. You are far too involved with these — strangers. It is not the place of a Loremaster to play nursemaid. Let the others deal with this. You will be reassigned."

"I'm sure Vurkanan has no objection," Yael answered quickly, and turned Tethan a little farther to the side. "But tell me, Kirin, can we not at least observe the situation from a distance? Surely we cannot afford to be caught by surprise if Andraax has some purpose in all this."

Her right hand, shielded behind the folds of her flowing purple robes, gestured impatiently in Tyes' direction. He cast a look across the table at T'vaar, but the other man was looking with deliberate interest at the dome above their heads. Tyes slid carefully out of his chair and moved to the door; not hurrying, but not dawdling either. T'vaar's eyes flicked toward him, then back up to the ceiling. Yael continued to talk in a low, calmly hypnotic voice, and Kirin Tethan — for all of his age and wisdom — was not proof against the wiles of an Iylari woman as accomplished as the diminutive Loremaster. Tyes slipped out of the door without attracting any attention.

He had to stop at his rooms and get a change of clothes, and then he intended to be gone before Kirin Tethan could find time to issue firm orders for his reassignment.

"Wait! Vurkanan, wait!"

Tyes kept walking, afraid that it was some last-minute summons from the Council (he wasn't convinced that even Yael Ziriv-Kari could keep an old fox like Kirin Tethan bemused for long, and was even less certain that T'vaar would cover for him when all was said and done); he glanced back over his shoulder as he rounded the first set of spiral stairs down from the tower and came to a sudden teetering halt as he recognized the tall gangling form that trailed him. Even as he did, Randae Terisonen missed a step and had to grab for the railing to save himself from a fall. Tyes swore under his breath and lunged back up the steps to steady him, and received a brilliant smile in return.

"Randae," he sighed, and shook his head. "Come on. I'm in a hurry."

"Yes, I figured that. Did you get your hindquarters roasted, or do they only reserve that privilege for me?" Terisonen sounded gloomy. Tyes concentrated on negotiating the next in a seemingly endless wind of stairs, and shook his head.

"I assure you, when Kirin finds out I'm gone I'll be lucky to come away with only my skin seared. What's this I hear about you being in trouble again?"

"They're pulling me off circuit again. Oh, they haven't said so yet, but they will — or worse, they'll stick me on circuit with a dead fish like Kedrik or Malim Pelax." Randae shivered in emphasis, almost missing another step. "What did you do?"

"Me? Nothing. Overstepped myself, apparently."

"Oh. I haven't done that one since — yesterday, I think. You'll have to think of something better, Tyes, I'm way ahead of you in this game."

"And what did you do?" Tyes asked, resigned. Randae dug in his pockets for answer, turning up all kinds of odds and ends, and as they reached the main floor of the keep and turned into the part of it holding the Loremasters' personal quarters he pulled out a tiny silver locket and pried it open. He passed it to Vurkanan, who took a long, critical look at the picture inside.

"Pretty," he admired. He wasn't being polite. The girl — human, by the shape of her face and the dark shade of her hair — was beautiful. Randae looked at the picture himself as if in disbelief, fingers skimming over the painted surface with longing.

"Yes," he agreed softly. "That's what got me in trouble, you see. I shouldn't have cared when her parents promised her to Corith Danen, but I did — and I followed him. I just wanted to be sure, you know — that he was good enough for her. He wasn't. He was a servant of the Unlife, a dark mage, and he was going to kill her in one of his unclean rites. What else could I have done, Vurkanan? What would you have done?"

"I take it the Council wasn't overly sympathetic to noble purposes and lost loves." Tyes nodded to another passing Loremaster and deactivated the wards around his rooms with a wave of his hand. He pushed the door open and crossed briskly to his clothes press.

"Not particularly, no. What would you say to the possibility of me marrying her?" It seemed to be a casual question, but it wasn't, no matter how offhanded Terisonen was trying to be. Tyes paused in the act of pulling out a new black tunic and turned to look at him with raised, incredulous eyebrows. Randae's hazel eyes were wide and innocently hopeful.

"I think that the matter deserves more thought," Tyes finally said diplomatically. Randae's expression fell like a half-baked cake.

"You don't think it can work," he accused. Tyes sighed and pulled out a pair of black breeches with a thin white stripe down the right leg. Unmindful of his friend's presence he began stripping off his travel-stained clothing and yanking on new pieces.

"No, I don't. And neither do you, really, or you wouldn't be asking me. I tried it, if you'll remember; Isseline is a lovely woman, and I loved her, but the life of a Loremaster isn't something that permits partners. You know that — or you should."

"At least you've got a child to show for it." Randae looked down at the picture in his huge fingers with a lost-little-boy expression. "Even if you don't know where she is."

"Lords and Powers, does everyone know about my daughter's escapades except me?" Tyes laced his breeches. His boots were still serviceable, so he jammed his aching feet back into them. As his head emerged from his tunic, he saw that Randae was looking at him again — and he looked guilty.

"Well, I was talking to Isseline — "

Tyes swore and dropped his dirty tunic on the bed and walked bare-chested across the room to stare at close range at his friend. Randae blanched further and tried to step back, but his back was at the door. Tyes crossed his arms and waited.

"Ah — she left. Prince Tiernan was upset about the broken engagement."

"Not any more upset than I was," Tyes said grimly. Randae nodded nervously. "Go on. What did Tiernan do?"

"He took his arms and horse and disappeared. The court was in an uproar for days, but no one went after him — no one except Laurel. She took a horse from the stable — "

"Stole a horse, you mean," Tyes frowned. Randae said nothing. "Isn't anybody in Jaiman looking for them?"

"Nobody in Jaiman seems inclined to care; there's trouble enough to go around, what with the Dragon Lord agitating and politics flying. His father's too busy to worry."

"And my daughter?"

"Laurel's got her own mind." Randae looked down at his picture again. "Surely she's all right."

Tyes swore again under his breath and crossed back to the bed. He dragged his new tunic on and belted on his swordbelt over it; inspecting the cloak, he found it undamaged.

"Thanks for the news, Randae; I'm sorry I can't help you with your troubles." Tyes looked at his friend and managed a smile. "You don't want a child. Trust me. She'll cut your life expectancy in half."

"Are you going already?"

"Yes. I'm sorry, I must. If you see Ghislain, will you tell him I'll come back soon? I have urgent business — "

He was standing by the door now, with one hand on the latch. It began turning before he could exert any pressure. It seemed a day for swearing, so Tyes did it again and backed up next to Terisonen. He knew it was one of the Council members.

He wasn't disappointed. There were two of them: little Yael Ziriv-Kari let herself in without fanfare and nodded briskly to both of those in the room. T'vaar Dekdarion was a black-clad shadow at her back. He shut the door behind him and set his back to it, a formidable human lock.

"You're wasting time," Yael said flatly. "Why are you still here?"

"I can only move so quickly. I'll have to leave the keep in order to Jump back to Quellbourne. I presume that's where you want me to go?"

Yael smiled slowly and glanced aside at T'vaar, who wore his customary blank expression.

"I came prepared to offer you an additional incentive, my friend. I have news of your daughter, Laurel Magen. She was seen following Prince Tiernan of Jaiman by ship to Quellbourne."

"What a coincidence." Tyes' voice flatly said he doubted it. Yael lost her smile.

"No plan of mine. Your daughter's will has led her into danger, Loremaster. I think there may be more awaiting your attention in Quellbourne than just a mad Loremaster and his new apprentice. I would recommend that you go at once. Tethan is in a frothing rage, and he's determined to cut you off."

"I can't leave from here. I must make it to the walls. Can you arrange that?" Tyes asked tensely. She glanced back at T'vaar, who shrugged.

"I think I will take the spells down — just for a moment," T'vaar said contemplatively. "To check them, of course."

"Handy, having the master of the island's defenses around," Randae noted, and fell immediately silent as T'vaar's chilly eyes swung toward him. He shuffled his feet uncomfortably. Tyes took one last look around the room and nodded.

"I'm ready, then."

Yael reached out and pulled his face down to her level to deliver a gentle, comradely kiss on his cheek. He returned it with real gratitude.

"Be careful, Vurkanan. Come back to us — and we will settle things for you here."

"If anyone can, it's you two," Vurkanan smiled, and felt the spells that blocked exit from the keep dissolve around him. He reached for a Jump, saluting T'vaar with a nod as he did so. T'vaar's lip curled into a barely identifiable smile.

"I don't suppose you could make exceptions for me," Randae said wistfully. The form of his friend collapsed into rainbow afterimages and was gone. Spells prickled at the edges of his consciousness as T'vaar reactivated them. Yael patted Terisonen familiarly on the arm.

"No," she simply said.

Pelk stumbled wearily back to the clearing, no wiser and certainly less well-tempered than when he had left. All he had collected for his hours tramping the wood were a fine assortment of scrapes and insect bites. He resisted the overwhelming urge to scratch them and sank down wearily next to Daphine. She hadn't so much as blinked an eye, it appeared. He stretched his overheated legs gratefully out on the morning-sprinkled grass and relaxed — and then tensed.

"Don't tell me," he said grimly, and sat upright with a snap. He was staring at Brion, across from him — and, farther away, with her back turned stubbornly to everyone else, Kella. "I've offended a minor god. I must have. There's no other explanation."

"She came back about an hour ago," Brion apologized. "I didn't know how to get word to you."

"Next time, just scream it out loud and maybe I'll be able to avoid such exertion." Pelk sank back prone on the soft grass and spread his arms wide. "I'm not made for this kind of work. I'm a thief, not a scout. Next time you should plan these emergencies better. Damn it, where did she go?"

"I don't know," Brion answered. He looked almost as tired as Pelk, and about as disheartened. Pelk saw a flash of pain in his dark eyes. "She won't say anything. She — she won't let me touch her. Her dress is torn."

Pelk sat up again.

"Probably on loose branches," he said without conviction. "It was rough going."

"Yes." Brion leaned his forehead against clenched fists. "Yes, probably so."

Pelk sat there another moment while his scratches and scrapes argued with him, and then levered himself painfully back to his feet. He walked over to where Kella sat huddled and paused a foot or two away.

"Kella, are you all right?" he asked her more gently. She didn't answer. "Where did you go? Did you — meet anyone?"

He edged around her a bit, wary of startling her, and saw that her gown had been torn from neck to waist. In the gaps he glimpsed the purplish beginnings of fresh bruises. It was a bit of a surprise, the sad anger that went through him, and the equally sad knowledge.

"No one," Kella answered faintly. "I'm sorry, Pelk. I'm sorry."

"Don't be sorry," he said. He got cautiously down on one knee next to her and leaned forward. She didn't flinch away. "Will you tell me what happened?"

"I got lost. I went to sleep and — there were some vines — I woke up and they were all over me. They were stinging me." Kella held her arm out, like a child presenting a hurt for inspection; Pelk examined the punctures. They were tiny bites, but they looked red and angry. "That's all. I ran back here."

"Your dress is torn, Kella," Pelk said. Her eyes flared in panic, and she began to draw back. His very stillness kept her from it. "Please tell me if you saw someone. I need to know to keep us safe, do you understand? Tell me."

The panic faded to sad embers in her beautiful dark eyes, and then went curiously blank. She folded her arms across her chest and shivered, but she shook her head.

"You can tell me, Kella."

"I didn't see anyone. No one at all." It wasn't Kella's voice, really; the voice was stripped of all emotion and character, just a meaningless collection of words. Pelk carefully reached out and touched her face with warm, gentle fingers.

"As you wish," he sighed. "Don't go far, all right? Stay close to me. Tyes will be back soon."

Tyes, he thought, sick at heart, had better be. Kella didn't even glance at him, only stared out into the still morning air. Pelk watched her another moment and then got up to return to where Brion sat.

"Is she all right?" Brion pushed his sweat-streaked dark hair back from his eyes. He looked as unhappy as Pelk felt. Pelk sank down next to him and pulled up a handful of long green grass. His restless fingers began to braid the blades into a tiny wreath.

"No," he answered honestly. "I think she's met with trouble, Brion. Someone has hurt her."

"I'd say I was angry," Brion replied distantly, not looking at him, "but I can't lie. I'm just tired, dear God, I'm so tired, and I can't feel anything anymore. Is that terrible? Damn it, I should care, she's my wife — "

"Gently," Pelk said soothingly. "I know that there's trouble between you. I don't blame you — but she needs someone. It's as if she's drifting farther and farther away, and she needs someone to grab hold of."

"Not me," Brion whispered, and quite suddenly his dark eyes spilled over with tears. He blinked them back and shook his head. "You try, Pelk. I can't do it anymore. There's just nothing left between us, nothing at all."

"Nothing?" Pelk snapped back in sudden anger. He reached out and shook the other man lightly. "She's your wife, man. Perhaps that means less on your world than mine, but she deserves your effort, at least! If nothing else, she's the mother of your child. Don't you owe her honor?"

"She does not honor me," Brion said. Even to his own ears, it sounded petty. He rubbed his face with aching, trembling hands. "All right. I'll try, if you think it will do any good. You're right, I've been — afraid. Afraid to try."

"Maybe it's time you started." Pelk's voice was cool and quiet, but his eyes said something else, hot with sad anger and impatience. Brion took a deep breath and got clumsily to his feet. After a second or two to gather strength, he started over to where Kella sat in a huddled heap; it was like watching a man approaching his own hanging. Pelk shook his head and walked the opposite direction, toward where Daphine still lay in pale, tranced slumber. Her skin felt cool and waxy under his fingers, and when he carefully lifted each eyelid her pupils were fixed and huge. Except for the stir of her breath and the slow beat of her pulse in the white column of her throat, she looked dead.

Wake up, he begged her silently, wishing again with futile desperation that he'd been able to learn Tyes' lessons more effectively. He didn't know what to do, and sooner or later someone was going to figure that out — or maybe his nerve would break and he would confess.

Daphine's eyelids fluttered, revealing glazed green eyes. She moved one hand slightly, clenching white-knuckled fingers around her Navigator's rod. Pelk whooped in excitement and waited for her to fully wake.

She didn't. Except for the one brief second of movement, she was as still as she had been all night and day. Pelk watched in a growing black despair, hardly aware of the voices murmuring across the clearing, hardly aware of the growing hot ache of his weary, strained muscles. The warming air was heavy with moisture, adding to his discomfort, and he shifted to a more comfortable leaning position. He kept his eyes on the silent Iylari woman and waited for anything — anything at all.

"Get away from me!" Kella screamed in a raw, horribly desperate voice. Pelk looked up with a snap in time to see Brion stumble back out of range of a wildly flung slap. Kella's husband was white-faced with anger and hurt as he stalked away; behind his back, Kella crouched as if to spring. Pelk stared in frank astonishment at the expression on her face. It wasn't the blank distance she'd shown him when he'd tried to help, and it wasn't her normal expression of annoyance.

It was an expression of cold, murderous, desperate intent.

Silently, Kella rose to her feet. Brion trudged away with his shoulders slumped in defeat. She had one hand in her pocket. As Pelk began moving as well, alarmed by the look of fury on her face, she suddenly sank to a kneeling position on the soft grass. Before he could do more than stand up, she was stretched out full length in the shade with her eyes shut.

"I told you," Brion said bitterly, and walked right past him. Pelk paid no attention. He was still watching Kella, aware of his pulse moving too quickly under his skin. He realized that he was holding a knife in his right hand under the concealing shadow of his cloak. He sheathed it with fingers that trembled with suppressed tension, and felt the hair on the back of his neck standing up.

"Tyes, I swear to Orhan —" he began in a shaky whisper. There was a flash of light behind him that didn't improve his jangled nerves; he came down flat-footed with the knife held again at ready. He needn't have bothered. Vurkanan Tyes pushed his hood back and cast an ironic, startled glance at the bare steel in his assistant's hand.

"You called?" he asked mildly. Pelk juggled his dagger in exaggerated indifference.

"Cursed is more like it. Kind of you to show up, master. I was beginning to wonder if you'd met a woman."

Tyes would have smiled, but the image of Isseline del Banov took all of the humor out of it. He glanced around the clearing, reading the tension with startled eyes: Daphine lying stricken and silent; Brion standing with angry defiance and only just now turning to gape at Tyes' sudden reappearance; Kella appearing as dead and senseless as the Navigator. He didn't miss the strain on Pelk's face, either — it was far too unusual.

"I see you've been busy," he noted mildly. Pelk's mouth tightened. "Tell me."

Pelk did, in as few words as he could manage. The amusement faded from Tyes' face — and there had not been an abundance to begin with. Pelk, by contrast, began feeling better almost as soon as the words left his mouth.

"There's something wrong here," Tyes observed grimly. Pelk raised one eyebrow in perfect imitation of his master's usual gesture, patently and elaborately amazed. "It's like a shadow covering this place. It's even affecting you, Pelk. Can't you feel it?"

In truth, he couldn't. Pelk shook his head and swiped irritably at the sweat beading his forehead. Tyes stared at him until he began to feel unnerved. The Loremaster turned away and walked to Daphine's side. He took her hand and held it for a moment, then stood up and turned with distant eyes to face the south. Pelk started to speak, but something in his mentor's expression stopped him.

"Iarsang," Vurkanan Tyes finally whispered, stricken, and snapped back into vital focus to turn back on his apprentice. "Pelk, stay here. I'll be back."

"Not again!" Pelk protested. Tyes's gray eyes flared impatiently, and he raised one warning finger. Pelk sighed. "Yes, master. As you say."

Tyes didn't waste any time; he was already Jumping before the words were complete. Pelk kicked irritably at an innocent clump of grass and began to look around for Brion. There was little he could do, but at least he could keep the pot from boiling over any worse than it already had.

Daphine, unnoticed, opened her eyes and tried to speak. By the time Pelk glanced her way again, she had been swallowed up again by the dark shell of her struggle. There was no sign that she had ever moved.

Tyes blinked to banish a sense of disorientation — two Jumps following each other so quickly tended to have that effect — and looked quickly around the small shaded pathway. A body lay just off of the trail; he turned it over and recognized the death-distorted features of the male cleric in Iarsang's party. He had died quickly, from all appearances, which was probably a mercy. Tyes searched the area in methodical steps and noted the signs of struggle and blood drops that spotted the green leaves and thirsty ground. A desperate battle, by all evidence. He felt a surge of uneasiness.

There was a long, bloody swath that led away through the tall grass. Tyes followed it and felt the pull in his mind grow stronger with each step. The blood was fresher the further he went, and there, ahead — a tall, gray-clad figure crumpled on the grass at the edge of a patch of sunshine. Iarsang's hair gleamed with macabre cheerful glory where the light struck it. Tyes fell to his knees beside him and gently turned him over so that his head rested on Vurkanan's bent arm.

Iarsang's eyes were open and gentle in spite of the terrible pain that washed over them like acid. He smiled slightly with lips far too pale even for Elvenkind, and whispered something Tyes failed to hear. In bending closer to catch the repetition Tyes saw the red bleeding ruin of Iarsang's left hand, and froze in horror.

"You come in good time, Loremaster," Iarsang croaked. Tyes tore his appalled gaze away from the Navigator's injuries and groped for his water flask. He held it carefully to Iarsang's lips and let the man drink.

"I obviously come a good bit too late," Tyes said grimly. "Who did this thing?"

"Dyar," Iarsang said faintly. "And Hraaskain. In my case only the Dyar; I'm not certain whether I was not to the Hraaskain's taste, or whether the Dyar enjoyed himself too much to share. It hardly matters. He's using my Compass, Loremaster. He must be stopped. I felt him — pervert it. He is using it to attack Daphine, I think; I have only the faintest connection to it — "

"Save your strength," Tyes begged. The Navigator's voice was growing fainter with each breath. A new fresh stain was breaking open on Iarsang's chest around a shattered arrow. "Iarsang, please. Be still."

"Can't," Iarsang whispered. His good right hand closed with painful strength on Tyes' shoulder, and those distant, distracted brown eyes sharpened to cutting intensity. "Help me. Swear. Help me get the Compass."

"I'll do what I can," Tyes sighed. "Now, quiet. These wounds need healing."

"This one—" Iarsang moved his bleeding hand painfully. The fingers were frozen into mangled claws. "This one stays. To remind me, until we get the Compass. It can't be healed. The Dyar made sure of that."

Tyes ignored him and delved into the delicate, painful work of knitting torn and abraded tissues. The lost blood he could do nothing for. When he moved to bring his powers to bear on Iarsang's hand, he realized that the man was right; there was Unlife sunk into every twisted cell of the wound, every drop of blood. It was poisoned as surely as if it had been doctored with venom — and although Tyes' powers over Essence kept the Unlife from creeping further, it could not banish the corruption. He pulled away from contact, his gray eyes brimming with rage, and took out a clean roll of bandage from his pouch. He wrapped the hand as tightly as he dared and avoided Iarsang's steady gaze.

"I must send word to your guild," Tyes finally said.

Iarsang shook his head. "This is Navigator's business. The loss of a Compass is a serious problem, and one they'll want to settle themselves."

"No," Iarsang said again. His face was lit with nearly maniacal determination. "It's mine, Vurkanan. I'm going to get it back if I have to follow it across Kulthea. It's my responsibility."

"You can't do it alone," Tyes said simply. Iarsang struggled up to a sitting position. "Look at you. It's a miracle you aren't as dead as your friend over there; I can't imagine how you survived. You couldn't wrestle a girl of five, much less defeat a Dyar with all of the power of a master of Unlife."

"You could," Iarsang insisted harshly. It was Tyes' turn to shake his head — vehemently.

"No. I have other business, my friend." He stood up and hauled Iarsang to his feet. "Back to work for me, I'm afraid; once I can revive Daphine, you'll return with her to tell the Navigators of the theft. Agreed?"

"No."

Tyes didn't have strength or time to argue. He put one arm around the wavering Navigator and Jumped the two of them back into the clearing where Daphine's shattered little party waited.

Pelk was showing steel again when Tyes reappeared. His assistant, Tyes reflected, was jumpier than a skinned cat. The woman, Kella, was still lying in a fetal ball across the clearing, and her husband stood at Pelk's shoulder. Pelk mouthed something that probably wasn't a blessing and sheathed his knife again with an exhausted grimace.

"Come here! Help me," Tyes ordered. Pelk and Brion both came forward to help as he eased Iarsang's nearly limp weight from his shoulders. "Careful! Watch his arm."

"I've got him," Pelk murmured. "We don't seem to be having much luck with Navigators, do we?"

"Navigators don't seem to be having much luck with us. How is Daphine?"

"Quiet. She looks dead, except that she's still breathing." Pelk looked up to meet his master's steady gray eyes. "You were right. There's something strange about this. We've all been at each others' throats since we got here."

"Unlife," Tyes said quietly. "It's hanging over this place like a cloud. For my sanity's sake, Pelk, keep your hands away from your knives. There's too much malice in the air. I don't want any mistakes."

Pelk's expression tightened in anger, but he choked it down and recognized the truth of the Loremaster's words. He'd felt it himself, a killing fury that seemed to hang in the humid breeze and attach itself like a leech to the unsuspecting. He'd seen it in Kella's eyes, and briefly in Brion's. Most uncomfortably of all, he'd recognized it in himself.

"It's the Dyar," Iarsang whispered. He was looking even paler than before, but his brown eyes were unnaturally bright. "Can't you feel him?"

"All I feel when I feel anything at all is tired," Pelk returned unhappily. "Master, what about Daphine? What can we do?"

"Iarsang, keep an eye on my friend, will you?" Tyes asked with a fleeting smile. Iarsang nodded gravely. Tyes turned away before Pelk could get out an indignant protest and went to look down at Daphine.

She lay utterly still. The Loremaster put one hand gently on her hand where her fingers wrapped around her Compass.

"Careful," Iarsang whispered from across the clearing. Tyes nodded absently. There was a black evil clawing at the protective shell of Daphine's defenses, an evil that tried to tear control of her Compass away from her. Tyes took a deep breath and plunged himself headlong into the maelstrom of Essence and Unlife that surrounded Daphine in unseen waves.

It was like bathing in freezing salt water. He gasped and hung tenaciously on, tracing the Unlife's reach back through maimed Essence flows. In some incomprehensible way it was easy, easier than tracing Essence itself. The Unlife left a huge terrible trail of desolation behind it; Tyes could clearly see the black slash across Essence flows that had derailed Daphine so disastrously and brought her to this place.

It was a trap, a web of darkness binding the entire area like a sticky dangerous net. Tyes had no more power against the void of Unlife than anyone else, but he could reach through to Daphine and give her the strength she so desperately needed. He felt the contact like a physical jolt and hung on grimly while the dark power turned on him and battered at his control of Essence. Under the gentle touch of his fingers, Daphine's hand moved to grasp his like a drowning woman reaching for a drifting lifeline. The physical contact steadied them both. The invisible black maelstrom around them slowed, faded, and stopped.

Daphine's green eyes slowly opened, revealing no confusion, only a vast painful exhaustion. She spared a weak smile for Tyes and struggled up to a sitting position. The smile quickly disappeared, and she squeezed his hand in sudden agonizing memory.

"Iarsang!" she whispered. "Loremaster, Iarsang — "

"Better than could be reasonably expected," Iarsang's light voice answered — not so light anymore, nor nearly so melodious as she remembered. Daphine twisted to look over her shoulder and saw him sitting up with most of his weight resting against Pelk's hands. Her face lit up with a flash of utter joy. "Are you all right, Daphine?"

"Apart from some pains and bruises, yes." Daphine, recalling the presence of spectators, made a valiant effort to tone down the depth of her relief. It didn't fool anyone. Iarsang wasn't as easy to read at first glance, but his face was a little less abstracted, a little softer than was his custom. Daphine realized that she was staring — and Iarsang was staring back — like a moon-eyed lover, and busied herself suddenly with brushing off her clothes.

"I don't mean to interrupt," Pelk said dryly, "but can someone tell me where we are?"

"Kelfour's Landing," Iarsang answered, "is a few hours that direction. The Temple of Hraask is two hours that way."

Pelk followed his pointing finger and looked off into the impenetrable mass of forest. He couldn't quite suppress a groan.

"Why would we be going to the Temple of Hraask?" he asked. "Or will I be sorry I asked?"

"Because that's where the Dyar is," Iarsang said simply. "The Dyar, and my Compass, and my two missing travellers. So that is where I go. The rest of you can do as you like."

"Iarsang — " Daphine began. He raised his bandaged hand so that she could see it, and watched her face blanch almost as pale as her diaphanous robes. The bandages were already soaking through. "I know how you feel, but you can't — the guilds will take — "

"I don't want the guilds to take care of me," Iarsang cut in with vicious precision. He lowered his injured hand and stared at her with suddenly intent eyes. "My inattention cost the life of one of my charges. It cost me my Compass. Two more of my people are captive to the Hraaskain, and a dark Elf holds the keys to Essence. Do you think I can forget that? Don't you know the damage he might do with a Compass?"

Daphine whitened further. She had never seen Iarsang in such a mood; not many people, alive or dead, had. The tall Iylari stood up, no longer bothering with Pelk's help, and came to her side. He stood there like a force of Essence himself, brown eyes burning in a face pared to pale bones and certain purpose. He leaned forward to look her directly in the eyes.

"Will you help me?" he demanded softly.

"I — but — "

"Will you help me?"

There seemed to be no other answer than 'yes'. Daphine made it and felt a great weight of tension dissolve out of her; Iarsang seemed to run suddenly out of passion and strength, and wavered uncertainly again. Tyes caught him and eased him down next to Daphine. The Loremaster put his hands on his hips and looked at the two Navigators with a stern, unforgiving expression.

"You two are determined to make my life miserable, aren't you?" he said. Iarsang's familiar dreamy smile touched his lips.

"That was hardly my intention."

"Daphine, do you intend to go with him to the Temple?" Tyes demanded. She nodded. Iarsang's right hand touched hers in silent thanks. "Then I suppose I have no choice but to go with you."

"What about us?" Brion asked. He'd been so quiet that his voice startled all of them. "What about Evan? We've got to find our son, Loremaster. You promised us that."

"So I did," Tyes said unhappily. Daphine avoided his eyes. "It appears that priorities have changed. I haven't forgotten, I assure you, but I can't stop Iarsang, and I can't let them go alone in this condition. What if I can assure you that I will take a personal interest in your son's rescue as soon as this is done?"

"Why not now?" the man demanded.

Tyes looked at the two Navigators and smiled. "Because at the moment not one of us is up to the task. We all need rest. Even you, Brion — and especially you, Pelk. A few hours sleep is no longer a luxury. If you want any of us to function effectively, it's necessary." Tyes stood up and stripped off his cloak. He folded it into a neat, practiced bundle and handed it to Iarsang, who put it under his head and rested his head against the softness with a grateful sigh. The cloak look on a strange mixture of colors — green for the grass it touched, and glossy black to match Iarsang's hair. It appeared that his head was floating four inches from the ground. Daphine sank back herself against his shoulder and felt the slow beat of his pulse against her face. It frightened her that she had come so close to losing him, and herself. As if in response, Iarsang's right hand moved up and touched her hair, feather-light. Daphine closed her eyes and let the slow sensuous caress take her into an exhausted, dreamless, healing sleep.

Iarsang fell asleep seconds later with his fingers still covered in a blanket of her silken hair.

Pelk grabbed up a discarded blanket and took it to Kella; she was lying asleep in the cool shade. He touched her arm lightly, but she didn't wake. Her skin felt too cold. Pelk spread the gray wool over her and watched her for another few seconds, remembering the time she had laughed at his joke, and remembering too the look of implacable fury she had directed like a weapon at her husband. She looked so lost now, so weary. Pelk contented himself with easing a strand of dark hair away from her face and pushed himself back to his feet. Brion had already lost his edge of antagonism and was lying down on the other side of the clearing. Pelk shook his head and rolled up in his own cloak a few feet away from Kella, telling himself that it was only because the spot was so cool and so pleasant. He didn't really fool himself.

Tyes used the last of his stored strength to set wards around the makeshift camp, and fell into an exhausted sleep himself.

"Kella," the wind whispered. Kella's eyes flew open. The sun had moved several degrees, but no one showed any signs of waking. Pelk was lying not far from her, but as she watched him his chest rose and fell in the measured slow rhythm of sleep. She waited and felt a shiver travel through her flesh despite the warmth of the blanket that covered her. The wind spoke again. "Kella, now. Do it now."

She knew that voice. It rooted itself deep inside of her, as black as the anger that she had buried for so long, and touched parts of her that had never been exposed before. She hated the voice, and yet she needed it more than she'd ever needed anything in her life.

Even her son.

"Now," the wind told her again. Across the clearing, Vurkanan Tyes twitched uneasily in his sleep, and the wind quickly became just an innocent breeze. It didn't matter. The wind was in Kella's head, now, where only she could hear it, and it whispered thoughts of blood and pain and pleasure that made her tremors grow more violent and constant. Kella's hand slipped into her pocket and took out the vial of poison.

The wind told her that poison would be too difficult with so many witnesses. A knife, it whispered icily in her mind. Pelk's knife, there on his belt. He was lying on his side, and it would only take a little care not to wake him —

Kella crawled out of the hot embrace of the blanket and crouched there on the grass on hands and knees. Her eyes were wild with anguish and need. She was sweating, even though her skin still felt cold to the touch, and she had to wipe her forehead with a trembling hand. She crawled slowly toward Pelk, stopping in terror every time he breathed. The afternoon was deathly still, and every rustling move she made sounded like the roar of thunder. Pelk slept on, oblivious.

Kella's sweat-slick fingers touched the hilt of his knife. His breathing continued regular and even, even as she slowly pulled the blade up and out of its sheath; the point came free with a little *chinging* sound, and Pelk's eyelids fluttered. Kella froze and sat there in utter stillness with her heart pounding painfully against her ribs, but he only shifted a little and went on sleeping. She reversed her crawl and climbed to her feet.

Brion was sleeping on the other side of the clearing. As Kella crossed into the sunlight he turned over without waking. His face was still tensed even in sleep, and there were tired lines around his eyes and mouth that she couldn't remember seeing before. Kella stood there breathing in great gulps of air and took the last step into the shadows where he lay. Strangely enough, she felt no hatred now, only a vast need to end this, to empty her heart and feel some variety of peace, however brief. Kella lifted the knife and tested it against her finger. It was so sharp that the cut it made was painless. She smiled a mad, cruel little smile and got down on her knees beside her husband. She looked for a second as if she was weeping, or praying, but her shoulders were trembling with wild horrified laughter as she raised the knife in both hands and prepared to bring it down.

Pelk's hands caught hers at the high point of the arc and jerked her backwards. Kella twisted, snarling, and struck out at him; the razor edge of the knife caught him in the arm. His own unnaturally fast reaction kept the blade from severing muscle and veins, but the cut was long and bled badly. Pelk still held her left hand and jerked her close, twisting the knife out of her hand. She looked up into his face with tears in her dark eyes, and he felt another astonishing burst of pity. The knife fell in a glittering arc to land on the grass beside Brion and sprayed a little spatter of Pelk's blood as it hit.

Something shattered the wards around the camp as if they were made of glass. Pelk's hands tightened instinctively on Kella's wrists as the sun turned to swirling darkness, and she screamed a name he didn't know. The others were moving. Tyes was on his feet and summoning up defenses, but Pelk and Kella seemed all alone in the center of a black hungry void. Kella's wrists were wrenched out of his grip, whether by her own will or another's Pelk couldn't be sure. He reached instinctively out for her, and saw the tall Dyar step out of the swirling darkness behind her. Their eyes met; Pelk's were burning with sudden fury and Jadel's were mocking and cold. Jadel took hold of Kella's left hand and raised it to his lips. She was still looking at Pelk, and so he could see the horrifying ecstasy that swept over her, and the fear. Pelk reached out again, and his fingers closed over hers. Hers felt small and cold, as if Jadel's chill presence had somehow frozen her soul.

"Kella, no," he whispered. Her dark eyes were wide and blank. Pelk's blood ran down his wrist to cover both of their hands. "Please, Kella. Let me help you."

"I can't," she replied, and it was just words again, nothing of Kella behind them. Jadel pulled on her left hand, and despite Pelk's strength the woman slid out of his blood-slick grip. She was still looking at him, that anguish and fear in her eyes, as Jadel dragged her back against his black-robed body. The dark Elf lifted Kella's bloody right hand to his lips with evident hunger, but his gaze was still on Pelk.

"Mine," Jadel mouthed silently. Pelk felt a flash of pure hot rage burn through him; he caught up his knife off of the grass and flung himself at the Dyar. He dimly heard Kella scream, and heard Tyes shouting something, but he was too busy to heed it. The Dyar flung Kella out of the way and grabbed Pelk's wrist in one unnaturally strong pale hand. This close, Jadel's beautiful face had the look of a porcelain mask, and the dark eyes the malevolence of a well of writhing serpents. All of Pelk's quickness and strength couldn't budge the grip the Dyar had on him. For the second time, and from the second hand, his knife spun to the grass trailing blood.

Pelk couldn't stop a scream as he felt Unlife seep through his skin like corruption.

From nowhere, another hand was tugging at Jadel's rock-hard grip; for a dazed moment Pelk thought it was Kella's, but then he realized that Brion had managed to get to his feet and was grappling with the Dyar. That was unusual enough, but it was positively astonishing, the look that went over Jadel's face as Brion touched him. Pure and total revulsion. Jadel flinched away from the contact as if it burned him, and Pelk fell to his knees. The bones in his wrist felt as if they had been ground to black splintery powder.

Jadel cast another malevolent look at Brion and stepped back. Kella was still held captive by the Dyar's other hand; Pelk reached futilely out again, and she tried to meet him. Their fingers grazed each other and slid away. Behind Jadel's back, a black Portal had opened, and the Dyar stepped backwards into the void. Kella went with him, hand still outstretched. Just before the Portal closed, Pelk saw her whisper his name.

The wind, the black vortex, the aura of Unlife—all had vanished. The clearing was littered with broken leaves and twigs and dots of Pelk's blood, but there was no sign of Jadel or Kella. Pelk's reaching hand wavered and fell, and then his whole body followed. He was unconscious before Brion caught him and eased him down to the ground.

Civad woke with a start and managed to push Astrid's head from his shoulder yet again. She began an irritated protest, but then she heard it: a key scrabbling in the lock of the cell door. She pulled Civad up to his feet and shivered once as the hinges of the door shrieked in protest, then shivered again at the sullen blaze of torchlight and the faces it revealed.

One of them was the Hraaskain priest who'd overseen their capture in the forest. There were four others with him, and despite the differences in their physical appearance they might have been cast from the same mold. Their expressions held no hint of mercy.

"You see?" said the shortest man, evidently carrying on a previous argument. "Five sacrifices. I was right."

"One of them is mad," came another voice — Astrid thought it was the youngest cleric, a smooth-faced boy with the eyes of a demon. "Useless for the ceremony. Use that one."

"I don't want that one!" the short cleric shouted angrily. "I want the woman! Do you know how long it's been since they had a woman? The Goddess' pets deserve a special treat, don't they?"

"Faeldin, if you're trying to imply that I'm not faithful to the Goddess — "

"Shut up, both of you," snarled a third. "Karamon, you'd best remember that it's because of your incompetence that the Night of the Troll is in jeopardy. The Goddess may not be pleased, even if you've provided the right number of victims."

"But the quality of the victims — " Karamon, the young one, began nervously. The third speaker waved an impatient, menacing hand and cut him off. He didn't appear to have taken any notice of the prisoners, but now he walked past the Changramai and the Scribe manacled on the wall. He looked back at Karamon.

"Why are the victims chained? They should not be harmed."

"The Scribe — the Scribe's mind turned and he became too dangerous to leave free. The other two are Changramai warriors." Karamon gave the older man an ingratiating, faltering smile. "The first time we've ever captured Changramai alive. I ordered them restrained because they will never be controlled by either threats or drugs."

The older man looked at them a moment. The Changramai returned his stare with flat intensity. He shrugged and turned to give Astrid and Civad a cursory glance.

"There's something wrong with the man as well," he noted indifferently. Karamon sent a resentful glance toward the man who had overseen Astrid and Civad's capture.

"You might ask the Fang of Hraask about that, not me," he grumbled. "I did not order him injured."

"Trandel?" the third speaker asked. Trandel cleared his throat. "My troops are not weavers and bards, Honored High Priest. It isn't a mortal wound." Trandel cast an assessing look at Astrid, and his lips curled into a menacing, distracted smile. "Besides, the woman is a healer. She should be able to mend such small breakage."

"Which brings us back to my original suggestion," Faeldin jumped in eagerly. "Let me have the woman. She's of the least use here, certainly."

"The Goddess will find the sacrifice of a cleric particularly powerful," Karamon argued hotly. "I tell you — "

"I tell both of you, shut up or you'll both be food for the Goddess!" the High Priest shouted. The other two priests fell fearfully silent. The High Priest's cool, distant eyes flicked over Civad, lingered on Astrid, and then he nodded.

"Yes, she would be a nice morsel for the spiders." The short cleric, Faeldin, beamed in fierce vindication. "But I think she would be more pleasing as a direct offering to Hraask. Take the Scribe, Faeldin. He's of no use to the Goddess."

"It only leaves us with four sacrifices," Karamon reminded the High Priest a little unhappily. The older man's eyebrows rose.

"Your concern, Karamon. Since you failed in your duty to secure a Troll for tonight's ceremony, law requires you to provide four live victims in its place — or die yourself." The High Priest smiled a black, amused smile. "Perhaps you should pray that none of them takes injury before tonight, eh?"

Karamon glared, but didn't dare argue. He shouted out into the hall, and two huge shaggy men dressed in torn animal hides entered the cell.

Karamon handed over the keys and stepped back. The servants unlocked the Scribe's manacles, ignoring his curses and the vicious blows he rained on them, and dragged him out of the room. Faeldin scuttled after, for all the world like a fat spider himself. Astrid flinched as the High Priest's impersonal, grimly hungry eyes raked her again, and then he turned and left. They all left, except for Karamon, who came up and looked her over at closer range.

"You might be useful," he said, as if Civad were not even present. Astrid took an involuntary step back and felt Civad's hand steady her. "Perhaps you'd like to buy your freedom, yes?"

"With what?" she scoffed. He reached out and cupped her chin in one hand. His skin was soft and pale, and she shivered at the touch of it. He was young and passably handsome, but no one would have felt anything but disgust for the red malice in his eyes. "Don't touch me."

"We run short of women here," he told her, and his hand slid insinuatingly down the column of her neck. She struck it angrily away. "A pity."

"I told you not to touch me," she hissed. He smiled tolerantly and reached out to slide his hands around her waist. She slapped him, hard. Karamon stumbled backwards in utter shock, hand raised to retaliate and fury burning like the red mark on his beardless face. She didn't flinch.

"Go ahead," she taunted softly. "I have ears, scum of Hraask. I heard him tell you to pray for our health. Would you really dare to damage me when your own life might pay for the pleasure?"

For a moment she thought she might have misjudged him, but he pulled his temper back under trembling control and turned to go. As he did, a shriek of inhuman agony echoed through the hall. Karamon turned back and grabbed her arm in a brutally hard embrace; before she could fight him and before Civad could intervene, the evil cleric dragged her to the cell door and held her there in spite of her struggles.

At the far end of the hall, three Giant Spiders were feeding. The screams were coming from the Scribe, who had rediscovered sanity at an unfortunate moment; as she watched in frozen horror, the third spider bit down on his stomach. The Scribe convulsed, but his struggles were hampered by the two huge spiders already weighing him down.

"They're injecting him with reduction poison," Karamon said next to her ear. His hands held her shoulders so tightly she felt bones creak. Astrid felt his body trembling behind her — not with fear, as her own body was trembling, but with awful pleasure. "What you're watching is the reaction as he feels his organs and muscles dissolve into a liquid mush. It's very painful."

As if in agreement, the Scribe screamed again. Astrid felt a light-headed nausea take hold and fought to keep from disgracing herself. Karamon's mouth moved closer, lips just brushing her ear. His hands were moving insinuatingly down the curve of her shoulders.

"Now the Goddess' pets are feasting. A magnificent sight, isn't it? They suck all of the juices out of his body until there is only a dry sack of bones left. That's what I've saved you from, mistress. That's why you owe me."

Before Astrid could stop herself — or want to — she drove her elbow back hard into his stomach. He was unprepared for the blow, and staggered back with a *whoosh* of expelled air. She pushed past him and went back to Civad, who had watched with tense interest.

"Bitch," the priest of Hraask coughed, trying to drag air into his frozen lungs. She watched him and wished in a most unclericlike fury that he had been a foot taller so that her elbow could have done permanent damage. "I'll see to it that your death is as painful as possible, do you hear? You will regret this!"

He retreated, still holding his stomach protectively with one hand. Civad watched him until the priest had turned the key in the lock again, and then looked at Astrid. Her mask of bravery was cracking a little with Karamon's withdrawal, and her hands were trembling uncontrollably. She managed a smile at his look of inquiry.

"You must have an interesting love life," he said dryly. "You seem to attract the most interesting types. Anything broken?"

"My bones, or his?" she smiled. "I'm all right, Civad. But the Scribe — "

"Yes, I know," he whispered. She began shaking all over, and clenching her hands didn't seem to help. Worse yet, her eyes filled up with blinding tears. "Easy, Benevolent Lady. You're safe."

"It isn't that," she gasped, and the tears spilled over in a silver stream over her cheeks. "He — he — poor man. Oh, the poor man. I should have done something more."

"There was nothing you could have done."

"I know." Astrid covered her face with her hands and wiped irritably at the tears. "I know. But I could have tried. I shall never forget — "

Civad patted her awkwardly on the shoulder. He was distracted by a gurgling sound from one of the Changramai on the wall; he looked over and saw in dumb amazement that one of the warriors had gotten a bleeding wrist free of the manacle.

He was using that freed hand to choke his still chained companion. The second Changramai's face had gone a dark red — but he wasn't struggling.

"Hey!" Civad yelled, and sprinted over to try to pry the madman's fingers away from his fellow warrior's throat. "Hey, are you crazy? What are you doing?"

"Leave it," the Changramai told him grimly. The other warrior was just hanging there quietly, dying. Civad swore and punched the madman in the stomach with as much force as his wounded body could muster. It popped the Changramai's fingers loose from his companion's throat — and wrapped them around Civad's. Astrid managed to drag him free.

"Don't interfere," the Changramai said in a voice as harsh as broken glass. "We failed to protect the Scribe. This is Changramai custom. Stay out of it."

"You can't do this!" Astrid shouted frantically. The Changramai ignored her and took another hold of his friend's neck. "What can possibly be gained by his death?"

"When he is dead, I will follow," the Changramai said woodenly. It was as if he were discussing the sunrise or a meal, not murdering a friend. "And if the Hraaskain do not have four victims to offer up, their sacrifice will be invalid."

"Granted, that would cause Karamon considerable pain — the little weasel — but I don't think it's worth it." Civad eyed the second Changramai nervously. He was unquestionably dying. "Damn it, no! No!"

"Without a Scribe to protect, our lives are over," the Changramai said very softly, and for the first time there was emotion in his smooth mask of a face. "We failed in our duty. For that we must die."

"Wait!" Astrid said frantically, and managed to pry the Changramai's fingers away again. The second man gasped for breath through a terribly bruised throat. "Wait. What if you had another Scribe to protect?"

"There is no other Scribe. All of them are dead."

"I was on my way to Nomikos to become a Scribe," Astrid said in a rush. Civad looked at her in frank astonishment. "Will you allow me to fulfill the Scribe's mission?"

"You are not a Scribe."

"I will be! I will be if you keep me alive. But I'll need both of you, do you understand? You must swear to protect me." Astrid had their attention, at least; both of the warriors were looking at her doubtfully, but they weren't committing suicide or murder. She found that unreasonably heartening. "What was your mission?"

"Do you swear on your oath as a cleric that you will go to Nomikos and become a Scribe even if we do not survive?" the first Changramai asked. She winced slightly.

"Yes. I swear it in the name of my patron deity Eissa. I will go to Nomikos and become a Scribe."

The Changramai looked at one another and communicated in some silent, strange warrior's language. They both nodded in concert.

"Very well," the first man answered for both of them. "The Scribe was to investigate a ruined city that lies far inland. Quellburn. We will take you there."

It seemed to be as simple as that. Astrid watched them for a few moments, but they said nothing, they did nothing. Civad let out a sigh of relief and sat back against the far wall of the cell. After another hesitation, Astrid sat down next to him.

"See?" he asked her softly. "Now you've saved a life. Things do balance, Benevolent Lady."

"Do they?" she asked him grimly, and rubbed her hands together in convulsive distaste. "All I've done is postpone their deaths and maybe make them less pleasant. Are you sure that was praiseworthy?"

"Aren't you?" he asked. "Are you really going to Nomikos? I mean — "

"Yes," she answered distantly. "Yes, I really was, and I really am. You know the funny thing, Civad? I'd decided to give up my calling as cleric because I was tired of life-and-death decisions. It seems I've only traded one burden for another, doesn't it?"

Civad couldn't think of any answer for her, so he closed his eyes again and tried to sleep. Even though the old Scribe wasn't screaming anymore. Civad's dreams echoed with the sound of the spiders feeding.

The moons were rising over the trees, suspended on the eerie waves of chanting that rose up from the valley. There was a large cleared space that still looked raw, in spite of its obvious age, and in the center rose the dimly gleaming black Temple of Hraask.

It had been built to strike fear into the hearts of anyone who stood in its shadow, whether faithful servant or hapless victim. The Temple loomed six times the height of a tall man at the center of the dome; the only door in or out of the grim brooding colossus lay at the mouth of the spider, a huge portal that lay in the knife-sharp shadow of basalt fangs. Above the entrance shone eight moonstones that seemed to suck up the cold moonlight and hold it in an internal, obsessive embrace.

It was the most frightening thing Kella had ever seen. When her eyes cleared, and her mind began to accept the sudden change of scene, she lifted her hands to her mouth in involuntary denial. Her fingers were wet; she realized they were black in the moonlight with smears of Pelk's blood and wiped them convulsively on her gown. The sight before her was so still, so eerie, that Kella nearly screamed as Jadel's white, cool hand slid around her shoulder.

"The Temple of Hraask," he told her with a certain distaste. "Elaborate, isn't it? I'm told they dipped each piece of stone in blood to christen it."

Kella's body spasmed under his hand in unmistakable horror. Jadel's smile was lost in darkness; he patted her shoulder in false fatherly concern.

"No need to worry, my dear, it won't bite." He found that amusing, and his laughter echoed distantly back from the black shell of the spider. "Or at least it won't bite you. Come on."

"In there?" she whispered, and resisted his pull on her arm. His dark eyes caught hers, glowing like the moonstone eyes below.

"I won't repeat myself, Kella." His words were calmly dispensed, but his fingers were so tight they were forcing the blood from her arm. She stumbled along with him more from fear than from desire, but it really didn't matter. Either served his purpose.

There were several rudely-constructed huts clustered in front of the spider. As Jadel and Kella stepped into the clearing people emerged from them with weapons drawn. Jadel held up one hand, and all movement stopped. Men and women stood aside like an eerie avenue of statues and watched the Dyar and his captive walk toward the Temple. Only their eyes moved, glittering with fear and hunger.

Kella was almost relieved to be in the shadow of the Spider — until the fangs curved around, cutting off the world from view, and that almost-relief vanished into terror. The moonstone eyes, set far above the level of her head, glared down with barely contained fury. When Kella tried to turn back in panic, Jadel shoved her forward against the unforgiving stone and held her. The huge iron doors swung silently inward.

"Jadel, no," she whimpered. His cruel grip dragged her inexorably into the darkness, blocking out the half-hearted light from the rising moons. The chanting grew louder. Someone was standing at the far end of the darkened room. As Kella's eyes adjusted to the dim corpse-pale torchlight she realized that it was a short old man. He looked at her and dismissed her all in an instant, but he was elaborate in his obeisance to Jadel. The Dyar took it as his due.

"The ceremony has begun," Jadel observed. He seemed bored by the prospect. "I suppose we shall have to observe."

"High Priest Valtar asked me to extend his personal invitation, Lord Jadel. He would be pleased if you would add your voice to ours in our worship of Hraask."

"Frankly, the prospect bores me, but it seems you have little else to offer in the way of entertainment." Jadel studied the short priest with luminous, predatory eyes. The other man drew himself up to his full height — it wasn't impressive even to Kella, who was dwarfed by Jadel. She wasn't inclined to laugh, though, not in the face of the rage that spread like oil over the shining surface of the priest's eyes.

"Don't mock the Goddess," he warned softly. "Not even you can mock Her."

"I would not dream of it," Jadel recited in a tired monotone. "Shall we go in?"

"Go," the priest snapped. He jerked his head toward the iron door behind him. Jadel waited. The priest finally pushed it open for him. As Kella was dragged along in the Dyar's wake, she felt the little man's eyes boring into her back and edged closer to Jadel's chill-burning presence.

In contrast to the dimly lit anteroom, the central chamber was so brilliantly lit that the shadows cast by the chanting priests and servants looked sharp enough to cut. Kella was immediately stricken with claustrophobia; even though the ceiling stretched many times her height above her, it was of dead black stone shot through with delicate red tracery that reminded her alternately of spiderwebs and veins. Her mind reached two frantic, equally inhospitable conclusions: she was either in the lair of a huge and poisonous beast, or in its stomach.

The worshippers were scattered around the walls. The dominant feature of the temple was the altar that lay in the center. Made of the same black stone as the ceiling and floor, it stood almost Kella's height. There were four manacles — red — set in the four corners of the altar. They were, for the moment, empty.

"Ah, we're in time for the opening," Jadel noted with mild approval. He pulled her to an empty spot near one of the eight entrances to the room. He held her tightly.

"Jadel?" she summoned the courage to ask. He glanced at her. "Why are we waiting here? Why can't we find my son? Please?"

"I'm waiting for something," he told her in a tone that warned her against further questions. She felt his grip tighten on her wrist again, and winced. "We'll have our time soon enough, Kella. Perhaps they have guest quarters here. Would you prefer to stay?"

"No," she whispered. His smile was quiet and menacing, and filled her with fear.

"Then we will go on as soon as I have what I need."

There was activity at one of the doorways; several shaggy-looking servants emerged leading four chained captives. The first two captives weren't familiar, but they looked dangerously quick and alert. The other two stumbled as they were pulled ruthlessly along, and as the brilliant white light caught their faces Kella drew her breath in sharply. She touched the borrowed, ripped fabric of her clothes.

"Do you know them, Kella?" Jadel asked her. She nodded. "How unfortunate. Well, these things do happen, don't you agree? The hazards of travel."

"They were kind to us," Kella whispered almost silently. Jadel shrugged and didn't seem to need to answer. Kella bit her lip and hid her face in the smooth cool fabric of his robe. He stared down at her head for a moment, frowning in perplexity, and then put his hand on her smooth dark hair. His fingers twined in it, prepared to pull in casual malice, but then slowly relaxed. He looked back at the bedraggled procession without expression.

They weren't taking any chances with the prisoners. The priests locked the first Changramai down on the altar before they loosened the chains that bound him to the others. There was a stirring in the darkness behind the prisoners, and the servants pulled them aside. The chanting grew louder. Two priests hovering near the altar backed quickly away.

The Great Spiders picked their way out of the tunnel with almost graceful caution. Jadel looked them over with clinical interest, noting the stench of Unlife that surrounded them. The smallest of them stood the height of the altar — at least four feet — and the largest nearly at a level with Jadel's head. They ignored the chanting worshippers, but they seemed to sniff the air in Jadel's direction with suspicious eagerness.

"The chants protect us," a priest whispered by Jadel's ear. "Raise your voice to Hraask if you would survive."

"I could smash these bugs before they presented a threat to me," Jadel shot back irritably. The priest laughed.

"So you could, great Master. But could you smash their Great Mistress, She Who Waits? Do you dare to stand against a Goddess in Her Temple?"

They were good questions, regardless of how much Jadel resented them. He forced a smile onto his lips and picked up the chant in a ringing, mellifluous voice. The Spiders lost interest and circled toward the altar where the first Changramai waited in stoic calm.

They all stopped several feet away and froze. Except for the restless movement of their fangs, the spiders might have been a macabre and lifelike addition to the Temple's statuary. The chanting faded away into echoing silence. A tall older man stepped forward from the worshippers to stand at the chained captive's head.

He held a golden helmet in the shape of a spider between his hands, and slid it over the Changramai's head before pushing it firmly into place. The Changramai stiffened and trembled all over, but his struggles ceased after a moment. There was nothing to be seen of his face except his wild, glittering eyes, bound on either side by the golden fangs of the spider.

The priest lifted his face toward the highest point of the dome and let out a shrieking, keening call that echoed eerily from the smooth ceiling. Kella shivered again; she looked up as Jadel did and cried out.

Part of the dome was moving. It fell with slow, graceful precision, and as the light identified it Kella had to stifle her screams with all of her strength. The dome's red-veined stone had been perfect camouflage, because like the stone it was shiny black and delicately painted with crimson web-patterned marks. The spider's shell looked as thick and glossy as armor; eight eyes glowed like the moonstones set in the temple doorway outside. It dwarfed the Great Spiders that backed away and crouched as low as their bulk would allow. The priests prostrated themselves on the cold stone and echoed the terrible shrieking cry of the high priest. The monstrous thing touched down with a metallic click of its armored legs and pivoted to survey its domain.

It faced Jadel and Kella, who were still standing, and went as still and quiet as its children. Its fangs clicked together in a deliberate, menacing gesture. Jadel smiled.

"I would not," he said softly. "I would be a difficult meal to swallow, Mother of Fear, and you know it."

The spider looked at him for a time-stopping moment, and then turned to look at the Changramai on the altar. He seemed unable to even strain against his manacles, but his eyes were open and aware. Kella felt a rush of some dark, overwhelming power, and grabbed at Jadel's hand for support. He caught her without effort.

The Mother of Spiders leaped on her prey and sank her black fangs into his exposed chest. The Changramai's body jerked and twisted in reaction as she pulled her knifelike pincers down through his abdomen. Skin parted like rotten silk, bathing Changramai and spider alike in blood.

It was plainly evident even from the far wall where Kella and Jadel stood that the reduction poison was melting the Changramai's organs into a viscous red mush. As the monstrous, obscenely beautiful creature began to noisily feed, Kella fainted in Jadel's arms.

He dropped her limply to the stone and watched in detached fascination as the carnage continued.

"Eissa, Lady of Mercy, look down on us and have pity," Astrid Haladan was whispering. She was bone-pale but standing. Civad, chained next in line to her, said nothing, but he was trembling.

"Louder," he advised shakily when she was finished. "Do the gods take bribes? Not that I have anything to bribe a god with — "

"This place — it's like being buried alive," Astrid whispered. Tears spilled out of her eyes and coursed down her dirt-smudged cheeks. "Not even the gods can hear us in this place. We're alone."

"Except for her," Civad said, and nodded toward where Kella had slid limply to the floor. The tall, too-pretty man next to her was watching the spider accept her sacrifice with dreamy eyes. "I knew she was trouble from the beginning. That bastard's Dyari if I haven't gone blind as well as mad."

"You have not," Astrid said mournfully. "Gods, what's happening? Is the whole world mad?"

The second Changramai, the one who'd been ready to die in the cell at the command of his fellow warrior, moved closer with a clank of chain. If he was disturbed by the horrible death of his friend, he hid his fear well. His face was a dark mask.

"Stand ready," he whispered. As softly as he spoke it was an unmistakable command. Astrid and the thief exchanged wide-eyed glances; she nodded. The Changramai lapsed back into stony silence as the young priest Karamon came to their side and smiled at them.

"A volunteer? Who's next?" he asked cheerfully. No one spoke. He touched Astrid's arm in casual covetous appreciation, then nodded to the massive servants who guarded the prisoners. "The woman, I think. Yes, definitely."

"No!" Civad shouted. Karamon beamed at him.

"You want to go in her place, little man?" he asked sarcastically. Civad opened his mouth, then shut it. He looked down. Karamon nodded and took hold of Astrid's arm.

She would not scream, not out of any last vestige of pride but out of the knowledge that once she screamed she would not be able to stop. Servants were clearing the limp sack of skin that had once been a living man away from the bloodstained altar, and the bloated gleaming shape of the spider waiting, motionless. Karamon took hold of her arm again, and suddenly the touch of human skin felt very comforting — even the skin of a priest of Hraask.

"I will walk," she said with trembling dignity. He bowed mockingly to her, eyes brilliant with malice and satisfaction. The servants unlocked her from Civad — she only had time for one quick, desperate clasp of hands — and pushed her toward the altar. It seemed a thousand miles away, and yet all too close.

No one made a sound as she crossed the distance. Karamon beckoned to two servants and they pulled her unresisting onto the surface of the stone. Astrid couldn't stop a cry as the red manacles snapped closed around her wrists and ankles, but she pulled in deep, steady breaths and vowed to die as a cleric should — as a martyr dies. It was a great deal more difficult than she would have imagined.

"Here," the Changramai warrior muttered in Civad's ear, pressing a tiny length of iron into his hand. Civad's nimble fingers turned it over curiously. His eyebrows rose. "Hurry."

Civad did. He freed the Changramai in less than ten seconds, as the manacles snapped shut around Lady Astrid's limbs. He was hampered at working his own escape by the injury to his shoulder, but he managed in spite of a black sheet of pain that spread through his body. Well before he was free, the Changramai had exploded into lethal, unexpected movement.

The Servants of Hraask, strong and intimidating as they were, were no match for a surprise assault from a trained, angered Changramai warrior. The freed captive hit the nearest man and broke his neck in one swift, enraged twist; before the servant was more than an inch or two into his fall to the floor, the Changramai had wrenched the battered sword from his dying fingers. It was more graceful than a dance, the spin that took the warrior from a dead opponent to face a live one. There was a certain deadly elegance in the way he caught the servant's half-raised axe with the upswing of his blade. The axe spun glittering in the harsh white light and landed in the body of a cowering priest behind them, but neither the Changramai nor the Servant he faced noticed. The Servant stared at the warrior, stricken with mortal terror, and opened his mouth to scream. The Changramai reversed the direction of his swing with effortless ease and took his head with one careless blow. The impetus carried him into combat with a third man, this one standing at shaky guard with a knife and sword.

Civad wormed his way out of his bonds with a whispered gasp and scrambled across the dead servants to reach the fallen axe. It was stuck in the priest's spine. He felt a black wind at his back, swore, and yanked the blade loose in a convulsive twist. He swung wildly without bothering to look, and his steel clanged against an upraised spiked mace, throwing him off balance across the body of the priest.

It was fortunate that his balance failed, because the downswing of the mace missed him by inches. Civad rolled away and swung, catching his opponent across the thighs. The servant staggered backwards. Civad sprang back upright with an urchin's delighted grin on his face — but it quickly disappeared. The man had looked huge when Civad was looking from a prone position. He topped the thief by more than two feet.

Civad, bowing to fate, went in under the man's next ponderous swing and buried the axe in his unprotected side. Blood jetted out to splash the wall of the temple, mingling with the red web patterns and disappearing except where it slowly trickled down. The servant toppled to his knees with a surprised oath. Civad kicked the mace out of his hand, and buried the axe in his neck. It went only halfway through, but that hardly mattered; it most certainly killed him. Civad yanked the steel free and turned to look at the scene behind him.

The Changramai was hard-battled, four Servants of Hraask ringing him in a deadly circle of steel. He was bleeding from a few wounds, mostly minor. As Civad watched, one of the servants feinted and drove in to strike him, but the warrior twisted impossibly fast and grabbed his enemy's extended wrist. The Changramai pulled the servant out of position and threw him into the oncoming swords of two of his fellows. Civad darted in behind them and hamstrung one before anyone was aware of his sudden presence. The other man was still struggling to free his sword of his dead comrade's body, but he caught Civad with a kick square in his wounded shoulder. The thief went spinning and collapsed against the spattered stone of the altar.

A massive, black-armored, chitinous leg was only a foot from his face.

The only sane thing to do was roll away and pray for divine aid, but Civad was laying no claim to it, not now. He scrambled up to hand and knees, then to knees, and without looking at the bulk of the killer spider in front of him, swung his axe at the joint of the leg closest to him.

To his undivided surprise, it went through the spider's limb with difficulty. The huge monster flexed back on its undamaged legs and made a sound that eclipsed all other terrible cries in the room, a wail that made Civad drop his axe and cover his ears with shaking fingers. The shadow of the spider fell over him like a black sheet.

The Changramai exploded out of the melee behind him and cleared Civad in one leap. Before he had landed, he was rolling under the belly of the creature. Civad watched in disbelief as the warrior swept his sword through three of the supporting legs of the spider and rolled out of danger as the huge bulk crashed down on the severed legs. The Changramai came up to his feet with grace

"Get up!" he yelled at Civad, who realized that the spider was trying to drag itself toward him — or toward the altar. Worse yet, the four smaller spiders were scuttling out into the killing ground, and not all of them were heading for the Changramai. Civad grabbed his fallen axe and got to his feet just in time to meet the rush of the largest of the Great Spiders. He was slammed back against the chest-high stone of the altar and cried out as the oversized fangs snapped at his throat. The spider's bloated belly jerked and sprayed him with a sheet of clinging, slimy netting that fouled his axe hand. Civad, finding more strength than he thought he could possibly possess, ripped at the silk with his free hand and swung the axe to meet the lunge of the spider's head. The bright steel buried itself to the hilt, shattering black chitin and sending a foul-stenched wave of reddish blood over Civad and the altar. The fangs lunged for him again in dying reflex, but he was able to twist aside. The spider collapsed at his feet in a strange and macabre show of homage. The breathless thief stared at it for a few seconds in frozen astonishment before he realized someone was calling his name.

It was Astrid, whom he had almost forgotten. She was trying hard to keep her voice calm, but when he finally looked her way she couldn't keep a tinge of desperation out of her expression.

"Are you all right?" Civad asked her, shaking off his shock. She gave a convulsive nod.

"Please get me free. Please!" She jerked at the manacles for emphasis. Civad searched in his pocket for the tiny sliver of metal that the Changramai had discovered, and set to work freeing her bonds. Astrid watched with tense impatience, hair plastered to her face by a combination of sweat and spider-blood. She jerked her right wrist free with a gasp of relief as he smiled in triumph and moved away. She brushed her hair frantically out of her eyes and looked around.

The Changramai — her Changramai — was down, but he was still fighting. Even as she watched, one of the spiders charged in to nip at his hamstring, but he leaped away and steel whirled to drive the monster back. Strange, she thought, that only now the priests were beginning to react; they were babbling and milling like a lot of geese, but a few of them were mustering around Karamon and the high priest, Valtar. Karamon had drawn a long dagger with a transparent blade; within the blade, she could see a vein of virulent yellow. Karamon was watching the Changramai with astonishment and rage, but now his head turned and his eyes focused on her, and on Civad's unprotected back. He raised the dagger and came for them in a shrieking rush.

"Civad!" Astrid cried, and pointed with her free hand. He spun around and caught Karamon's hand as it brought the dagger down. Fluid dripped from the tip to splash on the stone altar by Astrid's head. Where it landed, stone melted with a smoky hiss. "Civad, careful!"

Karamon's greater weight bent him backwards above her. The dagger got dangerously close to Astrid's face. She was able to flinch just far enough to allow the next drop of poison to miss, but it was a near thing. Civad abandoned caution — and honor — and jerked his knee up hard. Karamon gagged and fell limply on him. Civad dumped him over on the floor and shoved him with all his strength; Karamon slid across the slick stone toward the crippled monster spider. She was maddened and beyond discrimination; Karamon had time for one panicked, despairing scream before the fangs crunched together and sank into the skin of his neck just above his collarbone. His lifeblood jetted out and bathed her in new red patterns.

Civad grabbed the priest's abandoned dagger and held it in one shaking hand. He was facing the remainder of the Priests of Hraask, and the High Priest, who had both hands outstretched in front of him. As Civad lifted the transparent blade, Valtar grinned and spread those hands wide. A red rippling fog began spraying out of his fingers, reaching for Civad. The thief shrank back against the altar, but there wasn't anywhere to run; the altar at his back, and more Hraaskain closing in from behind, the crippled, maddened spider still dragging itself inch by torturous inch toward him, pushing the ripped corpse of Karamon before it.

"Civad?" Astrid whispered. His free hand reached around and found her freed one, and squeezed. She closed her eyes.

The outer door to the hall flew open under a tremendous blow. Hraaskain scattered like frightened ground birds at the wind that shrieked through. In the center of that wind, apparently untouched by it, ran a mixed and welcome group: the Navigator Iarsang, left hand hidden in a rough sling but holding a huge golden broadsword in his right; the Navigator Daphine, moving at his side and readying a long Kynac as she did; Vurkanan Tyes, who had no weapon ready but who was already moving his hands in a spell to counter the Hraaskain priest's conjuring; Pelk, standing at his master's side and ready to defend him from less magical assaults.

To Tyes' other side was Brion: the man looked terrified and out of place, though he was holding a dagger in a grip that looked death-tight. Civad gave a shout as they flung themselves as a unit toward the altar. Iarsang smiled and lifted his broadsword as the surviving Giant Spider scuttled across his path; white flames licked along the sword's edges: though he only had one hand to wield it, the steel slid effortlessly through the tough arachnoid shell and scorched the life out of it. He kicked it aside and pushed his way through the Hraaskain to Civad's side. Civad gave him a look of relief and confusion, then bent to work on Astrid's manacles again. Tyes was standing not far away with his hands outstretched in nearly the same position as the Hraaskain's, but what formed at the tips of his fingers threw even the bright cold lights of the temple into pale shadow. It shot toward Valtar and was barely deflected by the red fog swirling around the older priest. As Tyes readied another bolt, Valtar turned and ran for an exit. Pelk started to follow, but Tyes pulled him back with a negative gesture. Pelk went to help the Changramai warrior, busy with two axe-wielding Servants of Hraask.

"We must go!" Tyes shouted over the din. "The temple defends itself here. Move!"

Iarsang pulled Astrid from the altar as Civad unlocked the last manacle. She staggered. The Navigator's attention was elsewhere — on the corner where a dark-clad, eerily handsome Elf stood with his arms crossed across his chest. On the Dyar's left wrist was a Compass, and it glared with all of the colors of darkness.

Iarsang walked toward him as if they were alone in the temple and stopped ten feet away. He could get no farther against the Dyar's defenses. Jadel smiled slightly and bowed his head in mocking respect.

"You have formidable strength, Navigator. But it won't help you now. The Compass draws its strength from your body, and the more it is mine, the weaker you will grow. It is the nature of things. Give up."

"I will have it back, Dyar. Now."

"Take it," Jadel taunted. His evil glee was palpable now, illuminating the dead-dark eyes and revealing things that made even the priests of Hraask give way and flee after their leader. The fighting died as the servants withdrew after their masters into the bowels of the temple. The silence that fell was broken only by the gasps of the wounded and the slow tortured scratch of the huge spider dragging itself towards it prey. Iarsang forced himself a step nearer. Jadel didn't move.

"Iarsang, get back," Tyes said quietly. Jadel's gaze flicked to him. Tyes stood there just as easily as Jadel, and his eyes were fierce and implacable. Iarsang nodded and stepped back. Tyes raised his hands, and Jadel laughed.

"Oh, Great Loremaster, I shake in my bowels. But I have something of value to you, I think."

"What?" Tyes snarled. Pelk was the first to guess, even before Jadel reached down to grab Kella's limp arm and turn her so that her face was revealed. Only Tyes' outstretched warning hand stopped him from charging forward to certain defeat. "No, I don't think so. She left of her own will."

"That doesn't change your strange fascination with good and evil, Tyes. And if I say that her life stands at risk — "

The Dyar moved his hand, and a blade appeared in it, a curved, wickedly sharp instrument that fit around Kella's throat as if it had been forged for the task. Perhaps it had. No one said anything, not even Pelk. Tyes watched him for a bare second, and then nodded.

"It won't stop us for long, I warn you. You will be punished for what you've done, that is certain. If not here — then somewhere. Rely upon that."

"I look forward to another meeting," Jadel said, and smiled. His teeth were sharp and menacing, and gave his face an inhuman cruelty that made them all flinch. Jadel put the blade away with exaggerated calm, hoisted Kella in his hands, and looked at Iarsang again. The Compass on the Dyar's wrist flared; Pelk could see a thin black thread leap from its swirling surface to touch Iarsang's chest. The Iylari jerked as if struck by lightening, and only Daphine's instant support kept him from going to his knees. By the time he could stand on his own again, Jadel and Kella were gone.

"Out!" Tyes shouted, breaking the paralysis. Tiny apertures were opening all around the dome, and out of them came small red spiders, no bigger than a thumbnail. It might have been laughable, except that there were thousands spilling out from every direction. They swarmed toward the people standing in the center of the temple. "Out, quickly! Brion, help the cleric. Hurry!"

Beginning at the far end of the dome, iron gates slammed down over all tunnel entrances. Pelk sprang toward the entrance and reached it just as the iron grille began its descent; he dropped his sword and caught it. He couldn't support its weight for more than a few seconds, but that was all that was needed; Tyes was there in another heartbeat, taking part of the load, and together they held it up as the others ducked under and into the outer hall. Tyes and Pelk looked at each other as Brion and Astrid cleared the threshold, and Tyes' eyebrows rose. Apart from the sheen of sweat on his skin and his damp hair, he looked as cool and composed as ever.

"We go together," Tyes said calmly. "On three. One, two — "

At three, they threw themselves aside, and the grille slammed down with stunning force. That didn't stop the spiders, of course; the little red bodies tumbled through the gaps in the iron in a growing tide.

The outer door was shut. Tyes touched it and jerked back burned fingers. He shook his head. Pelk, without a word said, pushed his way past and set to work on the lock.

"Careful, " Tyes cautioned. "There will be traps."

"Careful, and hurry, yes, I know," Pelk waved it aside. He slid the point of a borrowed dagger into the lock and began delicately fiddling. Tyes watched him a few seconds, then looked where Iarsang was pointing.

"Trouble," Iarsang said succinctly. The tidal wave of spiders was fanning out into the outer hall: it was only a few steps away. Tyes reached through the thick interference of Hraask's influence and found an Essence Flow. Fire blazed up in a line between the party and the spiders.

"That should hold them," Tyes said. Pelk, oblivious to other problems, swore and jumped backwards as a knife-blade shot out of the wood beside the lock. Its tip dripped poison. He rolled his eyes and set back to work.

"It isn't holding them," Iarsang observed with careful restraint. The spiders were spilling right through the fire, untouched. Tyes nodded.

"You have boots, don't you? Step on them," the rescued Changramai panted. Civad gave him an incredulous look.

"You step on them, friend. I'll back you up."

"Shut up and let me think," Tyes snapped. He stretched out for Essence again, found it, and this time the barrier that formed was steaming ice. The spiders scrabbled for purchase against it, apparently unaffected by the numbing cold but unable to climb it. Iarsang smiled.

"I had no doubt," he assured Tyes.

Tyes shrugged. "Pelk?" he asked. Pelk grunted and didn't answer. He heard something crack under the pressure of his dagger and leaped back from the lock. A thin yellow vapor began seeping from the lock.

"Back!" Daphine shouted, and Tyes called the wind again to sweep the poisonous gas out through the cracks in the door. Pelk shook his head and bent to work again. Civad came to crouch beside him.

"Need help?" the younger thief offered. Pelk shook his head and wiped sweat from his forehead. "Try down and side. It worked on the manacles."

"Down and side?" Pelk repeated, and did it. The lock gave a quiet click. He grinned and nodded. "Down and side it is. Everybody out! Move!"

He swung the door wide. Civad darted out ahead and disappeared. Tyes gestured everyone else out, then looked back at the ice barrier. It was melting with unnatural quickness.

He swung the door shut as the first of the red spiders wriggled over the top.

"Are we all present?" Daphine asked lightly, and scanned the group as they gathered in the little cleared space between the closed temple door and the narrow opening of the fangs. She frowned slightly and looked again. Lady Astrid Haladan was doing the same, and it was she who spoke first.

"Where's Civad?"

"Up here!" the thief called down. He was standing on the left hand fang. By stretching recklessly out over the slick black surface, he could reach the first of the eight great moonstones that made up Hraask's Eyes. He grinned, hidden in the darkness, and worried the point of his dagger under the edge of the stone. He felt it give a little at the pressure.

"What are you doing?" Tyes called angrily. "Get down here. Do you wish to die?"

"I want to have something to show for my trouble," Civad panted, and pushed a little harder. The moonstone made a grating, encouraging sound. Civad's palm slipped a little on the temple's surface, and he hugged the wall closer. "A little more —"

"I'd better help him," Pelk said quietly to his master. "He's in no condition for this kind of play."

"Go," Tyes said without taking his eyes from dim specter of the thief hanging above him. "Hurry."

"Almost got it," Civad called triumphantly, and gave his wrist a practiced flip. The huge jewel jumped free of its housing — and stopped after moving two inches. He frowned, reaching behind it, and felt a trigger moving. In spite of his reflexes, in spite of his sudden knowledge, he had nowhere to go.

A blade, filled with the same yellow acidic poison that had come so close before, sprang out from the stone at the level of his stomach, sinking deep within his bowels. Civad screamed and fell into Pelk's arms as the other thief sprang up on the wall beside him; the two of them tumbled into the dust of the forecourt between the fangs.

"Master!" Pelk cried. Civad convulsed. Tyes and Lady Astrid Haladan both reached the fallen man at the same moment, touched him, and drew back. Civad's body gave one final, tormented spasm and stilled. His eyes had turned dead white, like moonstones. The blood that ran from his wounds was silvery in the moonlight.

Lady Astrid screamed and began to sob, but there was nothing any of them could do for him. There was no time for anything but a hasty blessing from her shaking hands. Tyes called down fire on the body. They watched him burn for a few moments, solemn and silent. Daphine turned to Iarsang with a question in her green eyes. His own face was tired and dispirited.

"The Dyar's gone to Kelfour's Landing," the Navigator said heavily. Daphine took his hand, held her other out to Brion, and the others linked hands for the Jump.

When dawn broke, there was only a smoldering pile of ashes to mark Civad's death, and a moonstone hanging out of place against the stone of the Temple of Hraask.

˒ CHAPTER FOUR ˒

He came upon a woman crying hopelessly in one of the curtained alcoves off the Great Hall. In his present grim mood, Tiernan had a mind to walk past her just as any of his royal brood of brothers would have, but the sorrow in the sound woke some answering chord in him. He stopped next to the heavy velvet drapery that concealed the little room. She wept. Tiernan stood there in awkward indecision; she was probably a kitchen maid, crying over a harsh reprimand, or one of the young girls new to court and overwhelmed with strange rules and stranger games. She wouldn't thank him for seeing her in such a state, he knew, whoever she might be.

And yet, the agony in that sound —

"Are you all right, my lady?" Tiernan asked very softly, softly enough that she could choose not to hear him. The weeping vanished into hiccuping gasps, and then silence. Tiernan touched the velvet curtains, then lowered his hand again. "Can I get you something? Someone?"

The curtain shot aside in a scream of bronze rings, startling him back a step, and he looked down in the tear-streaked, outraged face of Lady Laurel Magen.

Oh, gods.

"The only thing you can get for me," she said with dangerous, careful precision, "is a box to bury you in when I'm done with you. You! You — I don't know what!"

"Would you like to explain why you're so intent upon violence as a solution to this ordeal?" he asked with what he thought was remarkable calm. She glared at him and wiped a shaking hand across her face. It didn't improve her looks, but Tiernan had enough of an instinct for self-preservation to refrain from saying so.

"I have nothing to say to you," Laurel declared shakily, and tried to sweep by him. Tiernan blocked her way with an outstretched arm.

"You owe me an explanation, Lady."

"Do I?" she demanded.

"Yes. You've humiliated me in front of the entire court, you've embarrassed your own father, you've made us the laughing stock of Jaiman and for all I know the known world. I think you owe me an explanation, woman!" Tiernan hadn't even been aware of his anger before it came spilling out. Laurel stepped back from him, but he knew her better than to believe it was out of fear. If Laurel backed up, it was to get a better view of her target.

"I need not explain anything to you. How dare you make this kind of assumption? How dare you go behind my back and bargain for me like some particularly interesting piece of horseflesh? As for making you a laughing stock, Prince Tiernan, you'll survive. Your friends will probably chuckle about it for a few days, and then you'll find some new expensive toy and forget all about this one. I don't intend to be your latest castoff."

"Gods preserve me," Tiernan said grimly, and bent closer to look at her. She held her ground. "Lady Magen, I don't understand you. Do you think I meant this as some kind of game?"

"Game?" Laurel laughed, a harsh sound that hurt her as much as it did him. "Oh, I don't doubt you were serious, my prince, and that you would have stayed serious for at least half a day after the marriage. But I know you, Tiernan. Half a day is your limit. After that I'd be another expensive, discarded hobby, on the same shelf with your hawking gloves and your broken lutes and your dying plants."

"How can you say that?" he whispered. She bit her lips, blue eyes wide and eerily brilliant with tears.

"Because it's true, Tiernan. You go through women like a scythe through ripe wheat. I'm not going to be another acquisition."

"Another — " Tiernan began to repeat it, and stopped. He dropped his arm and simply looked at her for a long moment, feeling the same sick weightless sensation he'd felt since Laurel had stood up and quite calmly repudiated his formal proposal of marriage. "Is that what you think of me? Do you really think I'm no better than that? That I would treat you so badly?"

She didn't answer, but the tears that overflowed from her eyes were answer enough. She had reason, he thought distantly in some part of his brain that wasn't being shaken with rage and pain. He'd played the fool enough, for want of anything better to do; as the youngest prince of a long-lived line, he had little position and less responsibility, and he'd attacked life with reckless abandon. He'd wenched his way through the court with glee, he'd careened from one interest to another as his quicksilver moods took him, he'd ignored his father's efforts to restrain him and resented his brothers' disapproval. And always there had been the elusive elfin beauty of Lady Laurel Magen watching, and judging —

"I meant what I said," Tiernan said slowly. "I want your hand in marriage. For more than a day."

Laurel gave something between a gasp and a sob and tried to push past him. He grabbed her shoulders, surprised as always by the delicate feel of her, and held her still. She writhed away and put all of her strength into a slap. It rocked his head back; the sound echoed like a shout in the great empty room.

He slapped her in return, all of his rage and pain behind it, and she fell backwards and struck the stones with a sound that terrified him. Tiernan dropped to his knees beside her, babbling incoherent apologies, and pulled her into his arms. Her head hung oddly, like a straw doll's hugged too enthusiastically by a child. It was only as he saw the blood pouring from the back of her head that he knew what he'd done.

Tiernan put his head back to call for help, but what came out of his throat was a raw, inhuman cry of agony that echoed and echoed in the deserted Great Hall, and in his head, like a death bell.

"Tiernan! Tiernan, wake up!" It was Laurel's voice, bless the powers and gods and lords above; Tiernan reached for it like a dying man and found his hands holding her face between them. Laurel's blue eyes were huge and alarmed, waking an echo of that horrible vision again, and he felt an absurd need to weep. He pulled his hands away and clenched them instead into hard fists. "Tier, what's wrong?"

"Nothing," he managed to stammer.

She frowned. "Nothing? You scream like seven kinds of damned and it's nothing? Tiernan, I've never so much as heard you whimper!"

He didn't say anything, only took in a deep breath and looked around the dark slave hold. It hadn't changed, unfortunately, still a tiny, dank, overcrowded cell reeking of sweat and fear. Evan was sitting across from him with his dark eyes wide and frightened, and Tiernan made an effort to straighten his back and smile. It may not have been very convincing, but it soothed the boy. Evan smiled back.

Laurel was still watching him, unsmiling and tense. He glanced at her, then quickly away.

"You had a nightmare," Evan said. Tiernan nodded. "Was I in it?"

"Um, no, sorry." With a huge effort, Tiernan thrust the dream aside. The prince cocked his head, listening to the lap of water on the other side of the hull. "We're in shallow water. We must be about to dock."

"Wonderful," Laurel sighed. "Do we have a plan yet, or are we following your usual strategy of a suicidal frontal assault?"

"Of course I have a plan, my beauty. How could you doubt me?" Tiernan stood. He had to stretch, but the tiny confines of the hold made that a complicated operation. Laurel watched him steadily, blue eyes far too aware and suspicious. He gallantly offered her a hand up, which she took, and held it when she tried to pull it away.

"Tell me, do you remember the day I found you crying in the Great Hall?" he asked her very softly. She blinked, startled, and then nodded.

"Oh, yes. You made me furious, you know. Did I ever apologize for hitting you? I am sorry for that. At the time, though, it only made me angrier that you walked away."

"Be glad I did," Tiernan whispered, and his eyes were luminous and strange. "But do you remember how I left Jaiman?"

"I — " Her mouth closed with a snap as she realized what he meant, and she shook her head. "Oh, no, you madman. Not me, and not this poor boy — or had you forgotten him? I'm not risking his life in a leaky little rowboat for three days, not at this time of year."

"We may not have any choice. Look, if you can throw your invisibility around the three of us, we can cut a small boat loose and not be noticed."

"And what about provisions? Tiernan, you have a rock where your brain should be. Why don't we just buy our way out?"

"With what?" he wanted to know.

She smiled brilliantly. "Why, that's up to you, my prince. Liberate some funds."

"I suppose that Loremasters' daughters don't steal."

"Not very well," she confessed. "I'll keep you unseen. How difficult can it be to cut a few purses when you're invisible?"

Tiernan looked at her doubtfully, then smiled himself, as brilliant and as false a smile as she had levelled on him. Despite herself, Laurel Magen warmed to the scheme and tried to pull her hand free. He lifted her fingers to his lips despite her struggle and kissed them.

"You must be demon's get, my beauty, because you always seem to be leading me into crime and mischief." His eyes danced. "And sin."

"And I always thought that you had a perfect sense of direction," she shot back, and twisted her fingers loose. "What about these others, Tier?"

"I think that at this point we'd better worry about our own necks, don't you?" When she would have protested, the prince touched her lips with an outstretched finger. "We can't save the world, Laurel. At this particular moment, we may not be able to save ourselves."

Evan watched her as she picked her way cautiously back to an empty space on the floor. She sank down wearily and rubbed at her forehead with dirty fingers, leaving long streaks across her fair skin. Evan looked up as Tiernan sank down on his haunches next to him, and the prince smiled.

"How do you feel?" he wanted to know. Evan shrugged.

"I'm not seasick anymore. Tiernan?"

"Mmm?"

"Are — are we going to die?"

Evan's voice trembled on the last word, but it didn't break. Tiernan looked down at the top of the boy's dark head and felt a sudden surge of fear. It was the dream that had unsettled him, he decided, and ruffled the boy's hair lightly.

"No, we're not going to die," he said softly. "I won't allow that."

"Is anybody going to ask your opinion?" Evan asked sourly, and sounded in that moment so much like Laurel that Tiernan laughed, a pure silver that drew Laurel's hungry eyes and trapped her heart.

"What's the good of being a prince if you can't guarantee a little thing like that? Here, boy, think about it as an adventure. Didn't you ever wish for adventure?"

"I've gotten over the wish," Evan growled, but he smiled anyway. Tiernan slapped him lightly on the back and stood up. The top of his head bumped against the weathered wood of the deck above.

"Listen," Laurel breathed. Everyone froze. A metallic rushing sound came echoing through the hull, and one of the other prisoners gasped and began sobbing. The silence was oppressive.

"They're dropping anchor," Tiernan said quietly. "We have no more time. Laurel!"

"Coming!" She picked her way to his side. They sat in tense silence as the creaking and groaning of the ship died into faint moans, and the footsteps of the crew on the deck above became agitated. There was a rasp of rusty metal, and the hatch to the hold was thrown open. Sunlight speared down, agonizingly bright to the dark-accustomed eyes of the captives.

"Now," Tiernan breathed. Laurel put her entire concentration into the spell. It worked much more quickly than before, mostly because she was rested but also because she was painfully aware of how much depended on her skill. There was a peculiar brushing sensation over her entire body, raising the fine hairs on her arms. Tiernan stiffened next to her and disappeared with a startled look on his face. Evan was just opening his mouth when it — and he — disappeared.

"Wow," Evan breathed, subdued. Laurel reached out for Tiernan.

"Laurel, either you have awful aim or wonderful taste, but this is my hand." Laurel, suddenly glad for the invisibility that hid her blush, jerked her hand back and found his sliding down her unseen arm. "I've got Evan. What now, oh wizardess?"

"Quiet," she hissed. The other prisoners, too occupied with their own troubles to worry about the three so suddenly missing, were crowding back from the ladder as a Kral crewman descended. He wasn't searching for anyone in particular, luckily; he just grabbed the nearest to hand and began shoving bodies up toward the upper deck. Wails and screams rose as the prisoners were driven out into the open air. Laurel took the chance to lean close to where she guessed Tiernan's head to be.

"Wait until they're all out. They'll probably leave the hatch open, and we can get out after that."

"You hope," Tiernan whispered back, lips brushing her cheek. She drew in a deep, quick breath that was almost a gasp.

"Yes," she murmured. "I hope."

Quite suddenly, before she could do anything at all about it — or even decide if she wanted to — Prince Tiernan's unseen lips moved to touch hers, a hesitant kiss unlike his usual arrogant pose. Soft and as warm as summer wind.

Laurel didn't move.

"Forgive me," he said, with his lips still touching hers. The words were almost lost in the uproar around them. "Some things just have to be tried. You can slap me now."

He felt her arm tense, but he didn't move, providing her an easy target. She didn't hit him. Instead, she leaned forward, her own mouth searching for his. Tiernan made a lost sound deep in his throat as heat rolled over him and her lips pressed and opened on his. His hand slid up her arm again to trace the unseen line of her cheek as his mouth matched hers in abandoned need. It seemed impossible, for her to be so undeniably real to all of his senses except vision — so he shut his eyes and enjoyed himself without distraction.

Evan was tugging on his hand. Tiernan gave Laurel another light parting kiss just under the line of her jaw and felt her shiver, then drew regretfully back and looked around. The last of the slaves was being prodded up the ladder. Tiernan froze as the Kral crewman looked around with a ferocious frown; beady deep-set eyes swept over them. Then the Kral snorted and clumped back up the ladder toward the sunlight. Laurel gave a tremulous sigh of relief, barely audible. It was cut abruptly short as the crewman cleared the hatch and slammed the lid down, leaving them once again trapped in darkness.

"Great," Tiernan said in an even tone. He looked toward Laurel but could not see her in the pitch-black hold. "What now?"

"I don't know. I don't specialize in miraculous escapes, you know; you must have me confused with my father." Laurel's voice sounded light and whimsical, but there was a very real current of tension underneath. Tiernan squeezed her hand reassuringly and was annoyed as a distractingly tactile memory of the cinnamon taste of her skin intruded.

"They'll miss us soon. We haven't much time."

"No kidding, Tiernan, I never would have guessed that." Laurel was getting irritated. Tiernan opened his mouth to reply, but Evan tugged impatiently on his other hand.

"They didn't lock it — the door. It's open."

Tiernan cursed himself silently and counted to ten.

"I don't know," Laurel said doubtfully. "Someone might see the hatch lift — "

"There's no other way," Evan said simply. Tiernan sighed.

"You're right. I'm going up, Laurel. Evan, you stay right behind me — and Laurel, you hold onto his ankle. The last thing we need is to lose each other. Be ready to move fast."

"I'm ready to outrun your father's entire mounted army," Laurel assured him. Tiernan took her hand and passed it to Evan's, then slid out from between them. "And you, prince — be careful, you fool!"

"Nag, nag, nag," his voice floated back, eerie in the stillness. Laurel urged Evan toward the ladder. He climbed until his reaching hand came into contact with an unseen leather boot.

"Tiernan?" Evan whispered. A disembodied chuckle drifted down like smoke.

"Who were you expecting? Be ready, now — it sounds quiet above. Go!"

Tiernan lifted the heavy hatch and eased it over, mindful of the squeaking hinges. No one was looking toward them, though there were several Kral working nearby. Tiernan swarmed up the remaining distance and put the hatch all the way back against the deck. With luck, the crew might assume someone else had left it open. As he straightened (and oh, it felt good to finally do that!) a hesitantly reaching hand struck his leg. Evan. Tiernan lifted him the last few feet and set the boy noiselessly on the deck next to him. Laurel came up next, moving just as carefully.

There wasn't enough activity to cover conversation, so the prince led his two charges over to the side. There was a rough wooden gangplank fastened at the forward end of the ship, but there were too many Kral around it; invisibility or not, Tiernan didn't trust his luck that far.

The dock was built high, so it was only about a ten foot drop from the ship onto the gray wood of the quay, but Tiernan wasn't pleased with the possibilities. A turned ankle just now for any of them would be disaster. All in all, the gangplank was a better bet — though it gave him a crawling nervous feeling in the pit of his stomach.

He had Evan by one hand and Laurel by the other. Tiernan took a deep breath and began marching them toward the knot of Kral clustered at the exit.

"What are you doing?" Laurel hissed, so softly that if it hadn't been for the urgency pushing the words they wouldn't have even reached their target. Tiernan squeezed her hand, a silent "trust me" that got only doubtful silence. They stopped a foot or so away from the Kral that blocked their way. Though she had better sense than to say it, Tiernan knew the woman was thinking he was a fool. He was beginning to agree with her.

Evan's hand slipped out of his.

Tiernan, panicked, grabbed for the boy but missed. He didn't dare say anything, only waited in breathless fear for discovery. Gods, he prayed silently, this is ridiculous, a little punishment for rashness is all well and good but this —

One of the Kral blocking the way bellowed and grabbed at his buttocks with both massive hands. He whirled around to glare at the other Kral next to him, taller and slighter. The second Kral blinked at the enraged one, clearly wondering what was going on. The first Kral snarled and launched his hugely muscled body into attack. The two rolled roaring away past Tiernan and farther to the center of the deck. The other Kral, making a peculiar hooting sound that he guessed was laughter, abandoned the gangplank for the much more amusing spectacle of their fellows ripping each other to shreds.

Tiernan just restrained a whoop and dragged Laurel down the sloping wooden ramp to freedom.

Well, relative freedom. What lay at the bottom of the ramp was a milling confusion of slaves, heavily armed Kral, and the occasional evil-countenanced traveller. As Tiernan looked the mob over doubtfully, a body slammed full-tilt into him from behind, sending him sprawling. He twisted around to look, but there was no one to be seen — and then someone as invisible as he tripped over his chest and went tumbling. It wasn't Laurel, because she was still holding Tiernan's right hand.

"Evan?" he said quietly.

"Here! I'm here!" The boy flung his arms out and grabbed Tiernan's chest as if he were not ever planning on letting go. Tiernan winced and sat up, finding new bruises as he did so.

"Good job, boy! What did you do?"

"I poked him in the butt. What else could I have done?"

Tiernan shook with sudden half-hysterical laughter, but he hugged the boy anyway and got to his feet. This time his grip on Evan's hand was firm.

"Look! Isn't that the captain?" Evan pointed with Tiernan's hand. Tiernan looked in the indicated direction and saw the purple-caped Lord Warfarer of the Kral ship talking with a plain-looking young man dressed in a brown, vaguely clerical robe. The two were standing next to a dejected, chained group of captives — the others from the ship — and the man indicated them with a frustrated, angry gesture. The Kral roared something in response and headed for the gangplank. The cleric, if he was a cleric, followed. Tiernan herded his two followers back in time to let the Kral pass without incident, but as the man swept by he paused and turned. He couldn't possibly see us, Tiernan's mind argued, but those cold brown eyes focused and stared. All three of them instinctively froze. A smile flitted across the man's face, and then he turned and followed the Lord Warfarer up the ramp to the ship. Tiernan breathed a sigh of relief.

"No time," Laurel said sharply, and tugged on his hand. "Come on, let's go. Do you think you can do this, or do you want the boy to steal for you?"

Tiernan looked around at the fat swinging purses of the passersby and felt himself intrigued. It held all of the forbidden lure he'd always found fascinating — but it held an equal mixture of shame. He shrugged aside the doubts.

"I think I'm going to enjoy it," he confessed, and lifted Laurel's fingers to his mouth. "Stay here, my lady. I may need to find you in a hurry."

Two drunken Kral sailors weaved by, and Tiernan fell into step behind them. He made three tries before he eased the dagger out of the sheath, but it finally slipped free without incident. As he pulled it toward him, it entered the realm of the unseen, along with the rest of him. Tiernan grinned like an urchin and began looking for plump targets.

He had collected three fat purses before he felt luck turning, and he had the good sense to stop after the third attempt at the same belt bag failed. Tiernan patted the three golden lumps inside his shirt and turned back to survey the ramp.

The Lord Warfarer and the brown-robed man were coming back down the ramp, still arguing. The Lord Warfarer said something harsh and final and stalked away, leaving the man at the foot of the ramp — not two feet from where Tiernan had told Laurel to stay. He had a sudden dizzying presentiment of danger and began dancing his way through the crowd toward them, but now luck was throwing obstacles in his way. He ducked when he should have dodged and hit hard against the burly body of a Kral soldier — unfortunately sober. The Kral frowned and swiped at the apparently empty air. Tiernan ducked again, just missing the swinging arm, and snuck a quick look at the ramp.

The brown-robed man was turning to look at the spot where Laurel and Evan probably stood. There was absolutely nothing to hold his interest about the area unless he could see through Laurel's illusion. Tiernan whispered a frantic curse and shoved a frightened slave out of his way as the brown-robed man lifted a casual, graceful hand.

Laurel screamed. The sound went through Tiernan like a burning knife, and he surged forward, not caring about revealing himself now, only caring that too much distance lay between him and her. He was taller than almost anyone else in the entire throng, and so he saw he cleric's hand come forward and touch — nothing. From that touch color spread like thrown paint: stained gray gown, pale golden skin, wide blue eyes, a fall of corn-yellow hair. Laurel pulled back from the contact with a gasp and fell to her knees with bruising force. Evan was becoming visible too. He pulled frantically at Laurel's limp hand, but she couldn't move. Tiernan burst out of the crowd, still invisible, just as the man in dirt-brown robes moved his hand again and Laurel toppled limply forward on the paving.

Tiernan's body collided with the other man's with force enough to send them both over the edge of the dock and into freezing water. He didn't care. He was frantic with rage and worry; the water registered only as a convenient means to drown his new enemy. Tiernan came up and gasped air, then fastened his quick, clever hands around the other man's throat and began to squeeze.

Two things happened at once, neither of them pleasant: Tiernan became visible, and stunning power raced through him and knocked him almost into unconsciousness. Choking his opponent became a wishful memory. Tiernan fought instead to keep his own head above water; his opponent calmly pulled himself out of the water and watched his struggle with little evidence of concern. Tiernan breathed water and gagged. Somehow he was looking through several inches of liquid. How had that happened? He tried to draw breath, and inhaled water again. There was no way his leadened muscles could propel him back to the surface again. Blood spun in fiery wheels across the surface of his eyes, and he remembered clearly the vision of Laurel lying dead in his arms, dead by his own hand —

A massive hand closed painfully on his neck and yanked him out of the water without ceremony. He was dumped in a dripping, gagging heap on the stones of the quay, and even if he had been in fighting shape the sight of his savior would have beaten any ambitions out of him. This Kral was twice his breadth and almost his height, and the ugliest specimen his race had probably ever produced. Tiernan coughed up more salt water and shut his eyes.

"Prince Tiernan O'Locklir," the man in robes said, drying himself with a piece of sacking. There was a strange sense of familiarity about the sound of his voice; Tiernan, as he coughed up burning salt water, realized that the accent was the sound of home, a plain provincial dialect he'd heard all his life. An accent of the farmlands of Rhakhaan, in Jaiman. It went oddly with the formality of the words. "I've been expecting you. Oh, don't strain yourself. Your Elven sorceress is alive, as is the boy. It's up to you whether or not they stay in that enviable condition."

"Who are you?" Tiernan gasped out of a throat raw with salt. The man smiled and wiped water from his face.

"Your deadliest enemy, sir."

That didn't sound particularly encouraging, all things considered. Tiernan put his head down and heaved up more water. His Kral captor dragged him up to his feet and locked something heavy in place around his neck. As Tiernan lifted his hands to touch it, the Kral yanked on the chain attached to the iron collar and dragged him a few feet until the prince decided it was better to cooperate. The Kral led him to a draggled line of prisoners and chained him to the lot. Tiernan looked around him as he coughed out the last of his collection of ocean water and saw Evan watching him, wide-eyed. At the boy's feet lay Laurel, still limp but wearing now an iron collar that was a mate of the one around Tiernan's neck. Evan wore one, too, a child-sized version that made Tiernan's brows come together in brief, distracting anger, but he pushed it aside and dropped on the cold stone next to Laurel.

"I think she's all right," Evan told him shakily. "She seems to be sleeping."

When Tiernan tapped her gently on the cheek, her blue eyes shot wide open. She looked around and shook her head in fierce anger. No disorientation there, Tiernan thought with amusement.

"I'm sorry, Tiernan. I should have guessed — I should have been able to do something. Are you all right?"

"Apart from inhaling half of the sea, yes." Tiernan gave a pitiful cough for effect. She snorted. "We're not in a good position, Laurel."

"So I see. Well, I've run out of ideas. There isn't much good illusion will do for us with these chains on except make us more obvious — " Laurel's voice trailed off as she stared into the distance. "That man saw through my illusions. And he cut through my defenses as if they weren't there."

"Magic," Tiernan nodded grimly. She snapped back into focus.

"Naturally," she said dryly. "And he's drained me so badly that I can't even open these simple locks. I need time and a lot of distance from him."

"I wish I could provide that." Tiernan was dead serious, and she gave him a weak smile.

"Don't worry, prince. We aren't dead yet."

"No?" he asked and looked around. There was a darkness in his eyes she couldn't remember seeing before. "Then the Lords of Orhan must truly favor fools. Think of something, Laurel. Please."

He wasn't teasing, she realized with an unpleasant shock. He didn't even look at her directly. Sweet Lords, all this time she'd been praying for him to grow up and recognize the unpleasant realities of life — but just now she would have sold her soul for a brash impulsive hero.

"Me?" she asked with a bright, insincere smile. "Why, Prince Tiernan, rescues are clearly within your demesne. I wouldn't dream of trespassing."

"No jokes, Laurel. No more jokes." Tiernan remembered the way she had fallen limply at the brown-robed man's feet, and his stomach turned. "This is different."

A unit of leather-harnessed Kral marched toward them, prodding slaves to their feet as they came. Evan jumped up and tugged on Tiernan's arm until the prince stood. Laurel gratefully accepted Tiernan's help as the chains connecting them clanked and swung about; his fingers held hers tightly. Even though he didn't say anything, she understood.

It was an inconvenient time to be in love.

The slave-line moved in through a low jagged gate in the walls of Trelkinaark'est. Despite his sudden attack of worry, Tiernan couldn't help but wonder at the brooding size of the massive stone bulwarks; they stood many times his height, and he was easily the tallest being within sight. The stone was the same boiling, troubled gray as the sea beyond, pitted here and there with reminders of long-lost attacks and the biting action of sea and wind. On the dimly-seen tops of the walls were black iron spikes, curving out like greedy talons.

He remembered Laurel's father once remarking that the Kral fortress had never fallen in all of its recorded history. That wasn't for lack of angry foes, either; the frontier town of Kelfour's Landing had seen the launching of many brave fleets, but those ships and the warriors they carried were all decaying at the bottom of the seas. Not even the Navigators went to Trelkinaark'est — not without a great deal more money than Tiernan could reasonably imagine.

He still had the gold in his shirt, but he knew better than the believe it would buy their passage off the island, even if he could get the others free. As he brooded over the problem, a shadow passed over him; then he stood inside the walls of the Kral fortress. The uncheering thought intruded that many others had seen it before him, and they were almost all still here — dead or alive.

"Hey! Can you see where we're going?" Evan was craning his neck in an attempt to see over the crowd as the slaves were driven forward, but he was even shorter than Laurel. Tiernan glanced over the other bobbing heads with ease.

"It seems we're in luck," he said without much humor. "We're just in time for the daily slave auction."

"Is that the good news?"

"It is."

Evan didn't bother to ask for the bad news, and Tiernan didn't volunteer it — but there was a separate compound on the other side of the slave market, and as he watched a fat old man was dragged to the door and thrown inside. Tiernan knew instinctively that to go inside that compound was to die. The man's terror told him that.

"How much gold did you get?" Laurel asked him softly. He looked down at her.

"Not enough."

"Ah. Perhaps enough to bribe our owner — "

"Or owners," Tiernan finished unhappily. She nodded. A Kral overseer snarled in their direction, and they fell silent as the snaky little slave caravan wound through the crowd and up toward the raised stone platform that constituted the Slave's Market.

"Tiernan, have you thought of a plan yet?" Evan asked nervously. They were standing at the foot of the narrow stone steps, perhaps sixth in line.

"No," Tiernan snapped shortly. Laurel sighed.

"Maybe Andraax is nearby." Evan tried to look around, but the press of bodies was overwhelming. He ended up huddled against Tiernan. The prince's arm came around his shoulders, steadying him, and Tiernan's blue eyes raked the crowd with restless impatience. No familiar faces —

Yes. One. The brown-robed cleric was standing motionless at the foot of the platform. There was a crush of excited buyers in that area, massively muscled Kral jostling each other for position and calling out bids at the top of their voices. Yet a two-foot empty space extended all the way around the pale-skinned young man. Tiernan shook his head and kept looking.

"You! Next!" Tiernan came back to the present with a shock to find a Kral overseer prodding Laurel impatiently with the tip of a blunted lance. "Go! Go!"

Another Kral turned a key, and her chain detached from Tiernan's and fell to the ground. The overseer grabbed it up and bounded up the stairs. She was forced to follow quickly or be dragged. Tiernan didn't move. He didn't dare, knowing that the remaining Kral was standing a foot behind him and ready to beat him senseless at the least sign of trouble.

Besides, he couldn't do anything. Not yet.

Laurel had barely stumbled to a halt before the crowd in front of her shrieked out unintelligible bids. The uniformed auctioneer seated in a crude wooden chair was writing something down in a ledger on the stand in front of him. So fast. She was taken by one arm and yanked toward the steps on the far side of the platform. She had time for one last desperate look over her shoulder and saw Tiernan striding up to stand in her vacated place. He wasn't looking at the crowd. He was looking at her, eyes gone black and furious in a face too young to frame them.

"Stay!" the Kral overseer barked. He locked her chain to an iron ring at the foot of the stairs. There were a few others chained near her, some she recognized from the ship, but no one looked minded to share conversation. She didn't much blame them. The platform was too tall to see over, but Tiernan was up there, and soon he would be through it and down here next to her —

It seemed to be taking an unmercifully long time, or was that just her own anxiety? The roar rose to deafening proportions. She flinched and rested her burning cheek against the cool rusting metal of the chain. The sharp scent of iron cut through even the accumulated stench of the slave ship and the odorous crowd around the platform. Laurel found herself suddenly, passionately wishing for the sybaritic luxuries of court life: clean clothes, hot baths, Tiernan's easy, pleasant good humor —

Someone was chained in place next to her. She turned to face him with a glad smile.

"Tiernan — "

Evan's white face looked back at her in terror. Laurel jerked around to stare past him, but there was no one else new. The older captives stared apathetically back. "Where did they take him?" she demanded of Evan, who was clinging to his chain as if it were a baby's blanket. "Evan, please tell me. Where is he?"

"I don't know. I thought he was with you." Evan's eyes suddenly filled with tears. "Is he okay?"

Laurel couldn't answer. She reached out for him, but their chains were tethered frustratingly short, and the most she could manage was an awkward half-embrace. A sudden crash of thunder sounded overhead — the weather of Trelkinaark'est was notoriously changeable — and then the first warm drops of rain began to fall. The crowd scattered except for a few hardy souls who had more money than sense; in a few more seconds the rain came down in a pounding curtain that drenched slave and master alike to shivering skin. The drops were driven with such force they were actually painful. Laurel turned Evan toward the wall and tried to shelter him as best she could, but there was no keeping him dry; in a few heartbeats water was running from her like a stream from a sluice, and soon enough he looked as drowned and miserable as she did.

"Here," someone said, throwing a rough wool blanket around her shoulders. Laurel pulled it up over her head as her chains loosened. She pulled Evan in under the makeshift umbrella and turned her face her benefactor. Thanks died on her lips at the cynical smile he displayed.

"Where is my friend?" she demanded. The man in the brown robe — magically still perfectly dry — shrugged slightly.

"You don't need to be evasive, Lady Laurel Magen. Prince Tiernan is quite well, if too aggressive for his own good. He is resting."

"What did you do to him?"

"Made him sleep, much as I made you sleep earlier. I haven't harmed him." The man's smile widened. "It isn't the time or place for that. Come along with me. Oh, and I should warn you that you are now legally my property. If you attempt to escape or to harm me, all I have to do is raise my hand and you find yourselves in the deepest dungeons of this barbaric place. Believe me, you'd wish for death."

"I understand."

"And you, boy?" the man wanted to know. Evan looked up. His dark eyes were unreadable.

"I understand."

"Good. Come, then. We have a long and trying journey ahead of us."

"Journey?" Laurel prodded, following him from the shadow of the slave market into the rapidly clearing streets of the Kral city. The rain continued unabated. There wasn't any sign of Tiernan, despite the man's words.

"Our ship leaves on the morning tide." The man turned to look back over his shoulder at her. For the first time she realized that the rain was actually vanishing into this wisps of steam around him, and she was glad she hadn't tried to touch him. "For Jaiman, my lady. For home."

Somehow, there wasn't a lot of comfort in that short, sweet word. Home.

Tiernan hit the door and bounced back three painful feet. The wood didn't even rattle on the hinges. He sank down on the rickety narrow bed and tried not to wonder what he'd done to his throbbing shoulder. The even deeper ache came from not knowing, being helpless —

He rubbed at his abused arm and tried not to think about Laurel and Evan, alone in this stone mountain. He hadn't had one chance in a thousand against the cold-eyed cleric who'd bought him — and if the cleric had bought Laurel, where was she? Tiernan was afraid to even speculate on how the man knew him. It didn't bode well for future escape attempts.

The door rattled. For a second Tiernan's only thought was that he'd gone insane — who'd ever heard of a door rattling a minute after being hit? — and his second brought him bolt upright, throbbing shoulder and all. Someone was removing the bolt from the outside.

Evan edged in around the opening door. He stood there looking at the prince for a few seconds, dark eyes shining, and he smiled.

"Hi," he said awkwardly. Tiernan smiled in return.

"Greetings, Master Evan. Where's Laurel?"

"Here," she said, and the door swung open wider. She crossed the threshold and stopped. The door swung silently shut behind her, fitting into place with an audible click. The bolt shot home with a thud. "How are you?"

"Dry," Tiernan answered, eyeing their dripping clothes, and stood up to strip the thin blankets off of the bed. He tossed one to Laurel and began toweling Evan dry. "Was it your turn to fall in the ocean?"

"No, the sky fell on me." Laurel wrapped the blanket tightly around her body and shivered. She stifled an explosive sneeze. "And I'm getting a cold."

"I don't wonder, Lady Ice Maiden."

"No comments from you, you — fool of all fools!" Laurel scrubbed at her dripping hair with the rough fabric of the blanket, never taking her gaze from his face. "I was worried about you."

"Why?" Tiernan asked lightly. "I'm too stupid to die, you know that. And too stubborn."

She didn't answer him, just kept rubbing her hair dry. After another few seconds, she smiled and looked down.

"We're going to Jaiman," Evan suddenly put in. Laurel and Tiernan both looked at him. "That's what he said, didn't he? That we were going to Jaiman? Isn't that where you're from?"

"Why would he take us back to Jaiman?" Tiernan wondered aloud. "Maybe he's a friend in disguise."

"It's a great disguise," Evan said stiffly. Laurel covered a laugh and sat down next to him on the bed. "I can't go to Jaiman, Tiernan. I've got to find my parents. Can't you do something?"

"Not a lot," the prince admitted, folding himself down into a comfortable cross-legged position on the floor. His shirt clinked. He pulled out three full bags of coin and dumped the contents out on the floor; the gold and silver clattered cheerfully on the bare boards. Evan grabbed a handful and examined the crests with a half-frown.

"Different from your home?" Tiernan guessed, and held a rough-edged silverish coin up to examine it. The symbols were unfamiliar, but the metal was undeniably good. Evan imitated him with a heavy gold piece that looked to have origins in southern Jaiman, in the unsettled kingdoms.

"We don't have money — not money like this."

"Do you have one?" Tiernan asked, interested. Laurel rolled her eyes. "Really, Laurel, I wasn't going to rob him. I was only curious."

"I don't have one," Evan admitted, and looked down at his clothes. "These are my sleep clothes. See, there was this storm — and this lightning — "

"Those are sleep clothes?" Tiernan broke in with raised eyebrows. "How odd. What do you normally wear?"

"All kinds of stuff. Breeches, like yours, and shirts, and boots — I guess it isn't too much different from yours, except that yours is a lot better."

"Not everybody gets to dress as well as Prince Tiernan," Laurel put in tartly. "Do either of you have a constructive suggestion, or are we going to discuss fashion until morning?"

"My, she has quite a temper when she gets wet." Tiernan dodged out of the way of Laurel's blow. "I have a suggestion. It may not be very useful, but it's all I can think of."

"Well, then, spit it out! This may be fine adventure for the two of you — men — but I'm cold, and tired, and hungry, and I want a hot bath and clean clothes and peace!"

Tiernan sat there a moment more, passing coins back and forth to Evan for inspection. Then he reached up into his hair and began untying one of his long braids. A black disc about the size of a coin dropped down in his palm. Tiernan held it up between his thumb and forefinger.

"I wish to summon a Navigator," he said. There was a short, breathless silence before Laurel laughed aloud.

"What? You think a Navigator's going to come for this paltry little amount? On Trelkinaark'est? I think you were underwater too long, my friend. No Navigator on Kulthea is going to show up for that — "

Tiernan's expression stopped her dead in her verbal tracks. He looked — stupefied. And delighted. Laurel turned to look behind her, following the line of his gaze.

"Your pardon, gentlefolk. You wished to summon a Navigator?"

There was a slender, white-haired young man standing behind her. Laurel took a few seconds to digest his appearance, but she felt a wild leap of excitement. A Navigator, unquestionably, dressed in the uniform of a Guide of Vurn-Kye. He wore their formal black well in spite of being almost as short as Laurel herself. There was an indefinable air of elegance about him; perhaps it was the incredible beauty of his face, or the vivid purple of his eyes, but she didn't think so. He reminded her of the oldest of her father's friends — ageless.

"Yes," Tiernan finally said. "Ah — how much to reach Kelfour's Landing?"

"Kelfour's Landing — " The Navigator stood there a few seconds deep in thought, and then spread his hands. "For you, gentle people, no charge."

Laurel and Tiernan looked at each other. The prince slowly raised his eyebrows.

"No charge?" Laurel echoed softly. "You are a Navigator?"

"I will take you to your destination," the youth nodded. Which didn't exactly answer her question, she noticed. As she was thinking that, she noticed another thing: the young man, even though he wore the uniform of Vurn-Kye, complete to gold braid around his tunic, ornate jeweled emblem on the shoulder, and the famous black gloves — the young man wasn't holding a Compass.

"Maybe we'd better wait," Evan said uneasily. The man's purple eyes flashed to him and stared. Evan looked down. "How do we know he'll take us where he says?"

"If you wait for morning, you will be on a ship bound for Jaiman in the company of a renegade cleric named Walerin. You, boy, will never reach the coast. You will cease to be of interest to him and be cast over the side, where you will drown." The young Navigator looked at Laurel. His eyes were as cold as chips of ice. "You will killed by the Kral sailors to propitiate their gods. You, Prince Tiernan, will reach the shores of Jaiman alive — but there you will die and be the cause of endless death and suffering to your people. All of your royal family will owe their murders to you — and so will your companions. You will be cursed for generations!"

The silence was deep. Prince Tiernan had whitened during the merciless recital, and now he slowly stood up. He towered over the Navigator. For the first time Laurel saw an echo of his father in him, in the steady, searching look and the commanding presence.

"You are no Navigator," Tiernan said softly. He smiled slightly, but his eyes remained still and intent. "Or if you are, your guild has an interesting new sales approach. Tell me, do you enjoy frightening women and children?"

"I say what I must," the young man returned, unmoved. "And if I am no Navigator, I can still take you where you wish to go. Are you in a position to be judgemental, Prince?"

"I suppose not. One thing, maybe-Navigator. Do you farsee, or is this just supposition?"

"The things I have told you will come about, if you wait and board that ship. I can tell you no plainer than that." The Navigator looked past him to Laurel — and to Evan, who sat in the circle of her arm. There was no recognition in the boy's eyes, not yet. "Think of the boy, then. Think of his need, and come with me."

Tiernan tossed his long hair back over his shoulders with an arrogant gesture — looking very much the Tiernan of Laurel's memory from the royal court — and nodded.

"Yes." The prince turned to look at Laurel, who gave him a look of silent inquiry. "Well, if nothing else, we'll survive to tell how we bargained a Navigator into the lowest prince in history."

"He's no Navigator," Laurel said with dead certainty. Tiernan shrugged.

"He's the only alternative we seem to have. Evan, get the money, we may still need it. Unless you'd like to reconsider, Master Navigator?"

146

Stormriders

The so-called Navigator stepped forward to look at the glittering pile of coins. He shot a quick look at Evan, then bent and pulled something from the pile. He held it up to the light.

"This is sufficient," he said.

"A tenth-piece?" Tiernan inquired. The Navigator put it in a pouch at his belt.

"You seem to have overvalued yourself, Prince Tiernan. Come. Gather your coin and we will be gone from here."

By stuffing one of the stolen moneybags almost to bursting, they were able to get all of the coins into one bag, which Tiernan put back in his shirt. Evan and Laurel rose and stood next to him, facing the Navigator — and the Navigator, for the first time, smiled.

"Excellent," he said, and raised one empty hand.

The door flew open under a tremendous blow and banged back against the stone wall; splinters flew everywhere. Armed Kral poured into the room. Behind them, came the brown-robed cleric that the Navigator had named Walerin.

"Quickly!" the Navigator shouted, and his hand shot out to grab hold of Evan's and Laurel's — and Tiernan grabbed for them to complete the circle. The cleric was shouting something too, but the words were lost in a growing rush of wind. The Kral weren't coming closer — but the cleric was pushing through at a run.

The four of them wavered and were gone like a mirage in the desert. Walerin, just reaching them, went with them.

The Kral, ever practical, began searching the room for something to scavenge. He found a fingernail and sniffed at it.

"This is it?" Brion asked in disbelief, and pressed himself against a rough wooden wall as a passing horseman shouted for right-of-way. Mud splashed up to cover him as the rider thundered past. Pelk rolled his eyes and pulled the man over closer to the ramshackle walkways that lifted the town of Kelfour's Landing above the perennial mud.

"What were you expecting, Eidolon?" Pelk wanted to know. Brion gestured helplessly around at the unpainted wooden buildings, the sea of mud that passed for a thoroughfare, the thick log palisade that they had just passed through. The narrow walks were jammed with ruffians and toughs of every description and race, and the smell — Brion had never faced such a stench in his life. It was ripe with decaying offal and new wood, exotic spices and old sweat. Pelk felt right at home.

"I don't know. Something more — permanent."

"Permanent it is. Elegant it is not." Pelk looked around and took a deep breath. Brion watched him doubtfully; he was trying to keep his breaths as shallow as possible. "I love the city."

"This isn't a city," Brion grumbled. "This is a cesspool."

The word obviously translated, because Pelk gave him an amused look and shrugged. He caught the arm of Vurkanan Tyes, who walked a little ahead of them. "What now, master?" he asked. Tyes looked around and took his bearings.

"Iarsang, how are you?" he asked. The Navigator straightened and made an eloquent dismissing notion — but Daphine's lips were pressed tightly together. She traded a look with Tyes that clearly disputed Iarsang's assessment of his condition. "I don't suppose I could ask you to rest?"

"No," Iarsang simply said. Tyes nodded.

"Then this is what we'll do: Pelk, you take Lady Astrid and Brion to get us some better weapons." Tyes frowned distractedly at the dark presence of the Changramai who hovered like a shadow at Astrid's back. "Better take the Changramai too — it'll save a useless argument. Daphine and Iarsang and I will try to pin down Jadel's location."

"Wait," Iarsang said, and turned to look at Lady Astrid. "Benevolent Lady, my contract with you was to take you to Kelfour's Landing. You are here. If you wish to stay here, no one will think ill of you. This chase has personal meaning for the rest of us, but you — you go into danger for no reason. I urge you to stay here."

"Civad was my friend," she said very quietly. "And the woman, Kella — she needs our help. I would be no kind of cleric to turn my back on that. No. I'll come with you."

"You said you would go to Quellburn," the Changramai said harshly at her back. They all looked at him, a little dumbfounded, because he'd been so silent for so long that they'd forgotten he even had the power of speech. "You lied to us."

"No! No, I didn't lie," Astrid said hastily, and caught his hands in hers. "I'll go to as soon as this is finished. Don't you want to avenge your Scribe? Your companions?"

"You are my Scribe now," he told her stiffly. "I must protect you. This journey will be dangerous."

"Scribes must go many dangerous places, to discover knowledge — isn't that correct? If I ran from danger, I would make a very poor Scribe." Astrid smiled slightly and sadly. "And no kind of cleric at all."

"As you wish," the Changramai said, bowing. She looked back at Iarsang. He was watching her with an all-inquiring look.

"I — we — will continue with you," she said, and raised her chin, daring him to contradict her. He gave her a little bow of amused agreement and spread his hands helplessly.

"Pelk, have them back to the Raging Threk in two hours. No arguments — we're going to have a peaceful night's sleep in good beds tonight." Tyes actually looked as if he thought someone might challenge that, but they all seemed to take the blow cheerfully. "Be careful. I don't want to have to bail you out of trouble."

"Me?" Pelk asked innocently, and spread his hand over his heart. "When have I ever gotten into trouble? It's always trying to clean up after you — "

"Come on, before you say something you shouldn't," Brion muttered, and dragged the young thief around. Tyes smiled and looked at the Navigators as the others walked away.

"Any ideas?" he asked. Iarsang's brown eyes grew dreamy and distant.

"It's here." His expression cooled. "And so is he. He'll know we're coming for him."

"I'm certain of that." Tyes narrowed his eyes against the noon glare and looked up and down the street. "This way."

"Why?" Daphine asked. He shrugged and cast a wry look at Iarsang.

"Why not? Kelfour's Landing isn't that big. How hidden can he be?"

"Not hidden enough," Iarsang said grimly. It had the ring of a promise.

"Hey! Out of the way!" a voice roared from behind Tyes. He turned to look and found himself face to face with a man who had to be at least half Troll — or worse. The ruffian leered at him from a knife-scarred mouth and leaned forward. "You're taking up the walkway, little man. Talk in the mud!"

"I would not do provoke him, friend," Iarsang advised quietly. The tough looked him up and down.

"No, I wouldn't guess so," he sneered. "That supposed to scare me?"

"Only fools attack Navigators," Daphine warned, and lifted her Compass. He raised his hands and stepped back.

"I wasn't talking to you, Navigator," he said hastily, and eyed Tyes again. "But you're no Navigator, fancy-man. Out of the way!"

He swiped one huge arm and caught Tyes in the ribs, catapulting him off of the narrow wooden walk and into the ankle-deep mud. Unfortunately, Tyes didn't land on his feet. He sat with mud dripping from his hair and glared up at the tough and his friends, who laughed and cheered.

"Don't do anything stupid, Tyes," Daphine called, jabbing her Compass into the stomach of the ruffian. He let out his breath in a surprised *chuff.* "My friend is a sorcerer. You don't really want to live your life even uglier than you are, do you? Get down in the mud and help him up."

"What? Are you mad, woman?" he barked. She narrowed her eyes and stared at him — and Daphine had a truly impressive stare. The laughter died into an uneasy, tense silence. "I'm not getting in the mud."

"Yes, you are, unless you want a free trip to someplace very unpleasant — the peak of Rihtoth, say? The winds there will scour the flesh off of you in ten minutes, they tell me. What do you say?"

"Easy, easy, I'm going — " The tall man jumped off of the walk and landed with a splash in the reddish muck. He extended a hand mutinously to Tyes, who took it and stood up. Without taking his eyes away from his tormenter, Tyes levitated himself back up to the walkway and removed the clinging mud with a whispered spell. He stood there in the center of a respectful silence, and then reached down to offer the ruffian a hand up.

The man declined hastily and trudged off through the mud. His friends hastily disappeared. Tyes lowered his hand and looked at Daphine.

"Was it something I said?" he asked innocently. She looked back at him critically.

"No, I don't think so. You're not bad at illusion. I rather like the glowing red eyes."

"Overdone," Iarsang said critically, and staggered. Tyes quickly grabbed for his arm and saw that the rough bandages around his hand were soaked through again. "It's nothing, a little dizziness."

"We must get you to the inn and change those bandages — and then you're going to rest, do you hear?" Daphine took hold of Iarsang's other arm. Iarsang shook himself loose of both of them.

"I'm not going to feel better," he said bluntly. "I will only be worse and worse, and then I will die. If you would help me, then help me get to him."

Tyes agreed. For the just a moment the illusion that had so frightened the ruffian flickered again, lighting his eyes with ruddy fires. "I promise you that, my friend. Tell me which direction, and I will get you there."

As the three of them set off to the north along the walkway, the knife-scarred tough grabbed one of his friends and drew him into the shadow of a doorway.

"Follow them. See where they go."

"Where're you going?" his friend growled. Knife-scar slammed him painfully back into the wood.

"None of your business. Keep your mouth shut, and I'll cut you in, eh? Now move! Don't lose them or I'll lose you."

"I'm going, I'm going — " The little man disappeared into the crowd after Tyes and the Navigators. Knife-scar grinned tightly and rounded the corner, heading home.

Kella was asleep, curled into a protective ball under the disarranged sheets. Jadel sat cross-legged on the floor on his discarded clothes, naked except for the black sparkling circle of the Compass around his wrist. He reached for Unlife; unlike the Essence flows that Loremasters and other adepts tapped, the Unlife knew no currents, no cohesion. It trickled in from a thousand disparate directions, a thousand little destructive acts and actions that fueled only chaos and death. When he had drawn enough, he began forcing it through the matrix of Iarsang's stolen Compass — Iarsang's no longer. It still fought his control, but its struggles grew weaker as its former master did. By the time he had drawn all of its fangs, he thought appreciatively, Iarsang would be dead and the Compass would be changed quite beyond recognition.

Enough, for now, that it could be turned to the use of reaching his apprentices.

"Master," came a tinny voice, faint and far away. A shape shimmered vaguely in the air above the Compass, painted in shadow. Jadel concentrated, and it solidified into rough focus. "Master, I have them! Just as you said — the woman was not easy to control, but the Prince is headstrong and foolish — "

"Do not underestimate him, Walerin. We've made the mistake of underestimating the monarchs of Jaiman for far too long. Whatever his reputation, he comes from a long line of clever and resourceful rulers, and he might prove troublesome. Anything else?"

"We're leaving for Jaiman on the morning tide. Oh, and there's a boy with them — a strange-looking child. Shall I get rid of him?"

"Show him to me," Jadel ordered, and the shadowy figure gestured. A second picture appeared in the air — a boy of about twelve, small for his age, with black hair and wide dark eyes. Jadel smiled a faint, pleased appreciation for the workings of fortune. "I know the boy. Save him. He will be useful to me as a second control to the mother."

"Of what use is his mother?" Walerin asked, and laughed. He didn't need to ask. Jadel made a rude but imaginative gesture, and his apprentice laughed again in delight. "The boy looks rather interesting, in a strange way. Shall I instruct him?"

"On no account." Jadel thought of the unsettling touch of the boy's father, and damned again Kella's failure to be rid of the man. "The boy could be dangerous in himself. Be careful. Losing him would be unhealthy."

"I am always careful of my health, master," Walerin grinned. The grin faded. He looked around in sudden agitation. "Master, something's happening. I must go."

"Remember what I said," Jadel warned, and put his right hand over the Compass. The picture and sound cut off instantly. Jadel rubbed his thumb absently over the crystalline surface, dark eyes far away. "Don't fail me, Walerin. Don't dare to fail."

Warned by a sudden intuition, he turned his head. Kella's eyes were just opening, fuddled with sleep and something more. Jadel rose from his place on the floor and stretched himself out on the bed next to her, pale strong fingers running from her shoulder up to her neck.

"I heard from my assistant," Jadel told her without preamble. "Your son is safe."

Kella gasped and tried to sit up, but his grip held her still as he rose on one elbow to look down at her. There was unspeakable strength in his hand. It slid down the column of her throat to pull away the sheet that covered her body. She felt she should protest, but she no longer knew how — and she no longer wanted to. There was a delicious, almost painful hunger waking in her that she'd never known before.

"Is Evan all right?" she whispered. Jadel lifted his dark eyes to meet hers. They held no particular expression.

"Evan is under my protection. Once we solve the problem of your husband and his friends, we need never fear for his safety again."

"Brion wouldn't — hurt — " She lost her voice in a sudden gasp. Jadel smiled slightly and kissed the white skin of her collarbone, thinking again how fragile that skin was, and the bone beneath. The thought added a certain — zest — that was otherwise lacking.

"He could — and would — take your son away from you. You'd never see him again, Kella. Is that what you want?"

"No! No, I want him, I want him back — "

"Then we have only one option." Jadel's lips touched hers, a light but intimate caress that left her breathless. "As long as he lives, Brion is a deadly danger to us, Kella. Remember that. I promised to show you the road to power, did I not?"

"Yes," she whispered fiercely. He pressed her tightly against his body, pinning her so that she couldn't have resisted even if the thought had occurred to her.

"Then learn," he whispered in return, and poured the Unlife into her. She screamed, but they were used to that in Cheldar's Bathhouse. No one came to see.

It was almost an hour later that the ruffian knocked respectfully on the door. Jadel gestured it open and finished pulling on his black tunic. The man shuffled his feet and looked frightened.

"You have something for me?" Jadel asked impatiently. The man's eyes cut away from him and lingered on the sight of Kella's half-covered body still lying on the bed.

"You wanted to hear of any strangers. There's a big group just come in — I went to see them close, and got a good look at three of them. One of them was a Navigator, a woman. The other one was an Elf, had his hand bandaged. The third was a sorcerer."

"Tall, dressed in black and white, Iylari?" Jadel fastened his black cloak around his shoulders. The ruffian nodded.

"That's him. There were four others, but they went in another direction. One of my men is following the first three."

"You've done well," Jadel said. It was an unmistakable dismissal, but the man's scarred face clouded over with anger. He advanced one step and drew the full force of Jadel's stare. He stopped.

"I thought there'd be some money in it," the tough said mutinously. Jadel's smile had all the charm of a drawn dagger.

"Then you thought wrong, my stupid friend. Get out. And tell your friend not to follow them. I know where they're going. Now get out before I grow displeased with you."

The man didn't immediately move, so Jadel lifted one hand. Black fire began licking around his fingertips. The ruffian, having seen his fill of magic for the day, fled without further incident. Jadel looked at the black flames dancing on his hand and gently blew on them. They went out.

"Kella, get dressed. We're going to have a bit of fun."

She stood up and reached for her clothes. He barely even glanced at her, not even remotely interested in either her flesh or the anguish and dead agony in her eyes. She held up her trembling hand and concentrated.

Black fire danced on her fingertips.

Pelk signalled a halt. His little parade—and they were a motley crew, no doubting that, from the ragged Changramai to the bloodstained priestess to Brion, who didn't fit into any good category — straggled to a stop and stared mutely at him.

"Tyron's Arms," Pelk mused, and looked doubtfully at the rusting sign that flapped outside of the building. "Well, it's worth a try. Brion, what weapon do you prefer?"

"I've never used one," Brion confessed. Pelk turned to stare at him in open-mouthed amazement.

"What? Never?"

"Not everyone lives as militant a life as you," Lady Astrid said with a laugh. "I myself can defend myself with a dagger, but I haven't any strength for swords."

"A bow, then?" Pelk asked. She shook her head.

"I fear not. I have terrible aim. At the shrine they say that it's good I became a cleric; I haven't the temperament to be a wife or the skill to be a fighter."

"Scribes do not fight," the Changramai pronounced. It was obviously law. Astrid caught Pelk's eye and winked.

"That's one problem solved. What can I get for you, then — " Pelk looked at the Changramai with a chagrined look on his face. "I've never heard your name."

"Ziv," the Changramai said shortly. "Any weapon. I am trained in all."

"You can't carry all," Pelk pointed out. "Pick a few of your favorites, why don't you?"

He swung open the door and went inside.

"My," Lady Astrid breathed, and turned to look around the room. "How unexpected."

"An understatement," Pelk said softly. Brion leaned forward.

"Why are we whispering?" he wanted to know. Pelk gestured vaguely around him and the carefully ranked weapons — all of beauty and quality, from the tiniest ladies' knife to swords that looked too big for Trolls to lift.

"We stand in the presence of greatness."

"Welcome, my friends, what can I interest you in?" a voice asked, deep and rough. Pelk looked around as if waking from a dream, but he didn't see anyone. There was a long counter at the end of the store, but —

The man who came out from behind the counter, wiping his massive hands on his shirt, would have been remarkable by any standards — but to find him in Quellbourne was a rarity beyond words. Pelk bowed slightly and looked down — and down — into the little man's eyes.

"I didn't know there were any dwarves living in this part of the world," he said. Tyron shrugged, revealing rippling muscles all over his compact body. He came barely above Lady Astrid's waist, and she wasn't a tall woman.

"That's Kelfour's Landing for you; a pleasant surprise around every corner."

Tyron eyed them with an assessing glance. "You people look like you could use a change of clothes more than weapons. What are you, bards one and all? As I'm not a clothier, what can I sell you?"

"The question is, what can't you sell us?" Pelk meant it for a rhetorical question, but Tyron raised his chin. They all followed his gesture, and this time even Brion was stricken. He looked down at the swarthy little man with shining eyes.

"You made that?" he asked.

Tyron shrugged. "Commissioned by Gerdar the Duelist — heard of him? He's a professional, takes on duels for those who don't have the guts or training to do it themselves. He paid me, then told me to leave it hanging up there. If you want it, all you have to do is defeat him in a little harmless combat."

"That's all?" Pelk grinned without taking his eyes off of the shining thing above their heads. "And no one's done it? When did you hang it up there, yesterday?"

"She's been waiting for nearly a year, boy, and that's not for lack of suitors." Tyron crossed his arms. "She's my best work. The blade's so fine it looks like white water. Genuine Threk hide on the hilt, there, and the pommel's of genuine ivory. A king's sword."

"Well, since we aren't kings, perhaps we'd better look at common weapons," Astrid said firmly. Tyron's leathery face wrinkled in a grin.

"You don't want any of this light stuff, my friends; most of it's bronze. If you're meaning to go into a real fight, you need good quality steel. Here, let me show you — "

The rest of them followed as the little man stumped up toward the front of the shop, but Pelk stayed where he was and watched the dusty sunlight touch the white sword. A strange feeling came over him as he stood there, a feeling almost of lust.

"Is that a fair price?" Brion inquired of Astrid as he examined at a wickedly sharp iron dagger. She shrugged and made a so-so motion with her hand. Tyron looked affronted.

"I do beg your pardon, Benevolent Lady, but my goods are of the finest quality, dwarf-forged. In any other land you'd pay twice the price and be grateful for a bargain!"

"Careful, Tyron. Stretching the truth to a cleric is always risky," she smiled. "I have little skill with weapons, I admit, but your price strikes me as a little high for Quellbourne — "

Pelk's eyes snapped down from contemplation of the sword. He walked toward the others, cutting off conversation as he did. Tyron raised his eyebrows in inquiry.

"The sword," Pelk said flatly. "I want it."

"You're not alone," Tyron rumbled in amusement. Pelk stared at him.

"How do I challenge this Gerdar?"

"Bah!" Tyron said sourly, and took a close look at him. "Listen to me, young man; Gerdar's not someone to play with. He's fast and tough. He's beaten twelve men in the last few months, and they were every one bigger and faster than you. Don't be a fool. Buy your weapons and get out of here with a head that works, that's my advice."

"Gerdar," Pelk repeated. Tyron rolled his eyes and looked beseechingly at the others, but they weren't inclined to step into the fray. The dwarven smith shrugged massive shoulders.

"Wait here," he barked. He was obviously unimpressed by Pelk's chances, but he had a fatalistic attitude about fools. It was clear where Pelk stood in his estimation. The dwarf stomped out of the room.

"Are you certain of this?" Astrid said. Pelk nodded. "You remember what the Loremaster said: no trouble. Pelk — "

"There won't be any trouble."

The Changramai ignored the exchange. He was searching through a display of swords with single-minded thoroughness, testing each blade with breathtakingly graceful moves. He paused in his evaluations as a gong sounded to the rear of the shop.

Tyron came back in and began adding up Astrid's, Brion's, and Ziv's purchases without further comment. Pelk chose nothing for himself, though he did get remember to add a beautifully fashioned longbow to the pile — not for himself, because he was an indifferent bowman, but for Daphine. He had a sense that the little Navigator would be frighteningly precise with it.

"You're not going to reconsider?" Tyron asked as the gold was exchanged. Pelk shook his head. "Right. Take your fight outside, then. No brawling in my store."

"Where's Gerdar?"

"In the street, waiting." Tyron reached beneath the counter. "Here."

Pelk reflexively caught the battered wooden sword the dwarf tossed him. Tyron's mouth quirked in a quick, morose smile.

"Well, you're quick, I'll give you that. Good luck, man."

"Luck," the Changramai said softly, contemptuously. "A warrior doesn't need luck."

"A warrior never kicks good wishes in the teeth, either," Tyron shot back. He flapped his hands dismissively at them and ushered them quickly out of the store and into the hot sunlight.

A man stood lounging against the wooden wall of Tyron's store. He didn't look particularly tough, but the Changramai went silent and still at the sight of him, and touched Pelk on the arm.

"That's him," Ziv said shortly. Pelk studied the tall man as he straightened and began walking toward them. He didn't look fearsome.

"How do you know?" Brion asked curiously. Ziv flicked his fingers in some mysterious Changramai gesture and shrugged.

"He moves well," Pelk said under his breath. He fell silent as the man approached to within a few feet and stopped. He had a long, graceful reach, and within that pleasant, unremarkable face dark brown eyes missed nothing. He looked at each of them in swift, dismissive stages, lingering on Ziv, and ended with Pelk.

"You must be the one," Gerdar said. Pelk raised his eyebrows. Gerdar grinned. "You've got the shine in your eyes, man; I can always tell. You understand the rules? We use only the practice swords until one or the other yields or is unable to continue. Your friends don't interfere — and neither do mine."

"Fine," Pelk said shortly, hoping that the tension in him wouldn't show in the one word. Gerdar smiled again, dashing his hopes. "Where?"

"Here." The duelist made an expressive gesture at the muddied street. When Pelk hesitated, he chuckled. "Afraid of a little mud? Or simply afraid?"

"Me? You're the one who specified practice swords. Afraid of seeing a little of your own blood on your fine shirt?" Pelk hefted his practice sword and jumped down into the mud with a deliberate splash. Gerdar looked down at him with expressionless eyes, then joined him in the muck.

"The reason I specified practice swords is because I can always use the exercise, and I don't have to go to the tiresome expense of paying for a fool's funeral or the exertion of slaying his foolish friends and relatives. I'd kill you. It's what I do, and I'm good at it." It was a flat recital, with no modesty and less arrogance, but it hurt all the same. Pelk took a ready stance. Gerdar hadn't even lifted his own weapon.

"Confident bastard, aren't you?" Pelk said through gritted teeth.

Gerdar shrugged. "I've fought over a hundred men in my life. A third of them fought for possession of the sword. It still hangs in Tyron's store." Gerdar's lips thinned slightly, the only hint of his emotion. "The other two thirds fought for my life. I still stand here, and they do not."

"Is he kidding?" Brion asked Ziv, who stood motionless at his side. The Changramai slowly shook his head.

"To be a duelist takes more than skill. It takes genius." The warrior's quiet blue eyes studied the two opponents with impartial calm. "Pelk cannot best him."

"He could get lucky," Astrid whispered back fiercely. Ziv took another look and shook his head again.

"No," he simply said.

Gerdar was moving. It was like trying to watch a striking snake. Gerdar's blade snapped up, a perfect extension of his arm, and without any pause cut at Pelk's head. Considering that the practice sword was blunted, the blow could have at the least knocked the victim unconscious; it was remarkable that Pelk was able to jerk his own sword up in time to counter it, but even Astrid's untrained eye could recognize the difference in speeds. Pelk was fast, as a thief had to be — but Gerdar was something else. Wood cracked on wood, knocking Pelk's weapon out of line, and Gerdar reversed the line of his attack with smooth, effortless precision. Pelk managed somehow to parry again, but the blow tossed him two steps back. He looked stunned. Gerdar had hardly moved any part of his body but his arm, and the amount of control he exerted over the heavy wand was truly intimidating.

"Yield," Gerdar said softly. Pelk shook his head mutely and lunged. His attack was swept aside like an annoyance. Gerdar regarded him with implacable arrogance. "I give you no more chances. Yield now, or eat mud."

Pelk snarled something he couldn't even identify and put every iota of strength into a crossbody cut that even Ziv found acceptably impressive. Surprised, Gerdar parried and launched an attack of his own that slapped Pelk's defense down like scythed wheat. Pelk wasn't able to parry the next blow, and it caught him full on the arm with bruising force. It might have been a crippling blow, except that Pelk's native agility had allowed him to roll with the force of the hit enough to cushion it — but even so, his left arm hung limp and useless, and pain shot over him like in a hot net. Gerdar waited. Pelk shakily brought his own wand back up into guard position.

"Pelk, retire!" Astrid called, alarmed, because she could see the pain in his eyes, and the anger. Pelk didn't even hear her. "Ziv, stop this. He's going to be hurt!"

"It is his right."

"His right!" Astrid swung around on the Changramai with blazing eyes. "Men! Do you consider it an honor to be maimed and crippled? He could die, Ziv, and for what? A fancy sword?"

"He does not fight for the sword," Ziv explained patiently, as if to a child. "He fights for honor."

"Honor!" Astrid sighed. She was startled into silence as her eyes caught what was happening in the muddy street. Pelk had staggered forward, playing on his injury, before lashing. For the first time, he beat Gerdar's speed and hit the fighter solidly in the side. Gerdar staggered back, stunned. Pelk braced himself for the return and wasn't disappointed; Gerdar lunged. Even though Pelk was expecting it, he couldn't counter the blow. The heavy wooden sword caught him in the chest, partly deflected by his last-second attempt at parry. He lost the air in his lungs and could not breathe.

Pelk's vision grayed, but he somehow stayed on his feet in the treacherous muck. Gerdar moved in like a hunting cat, sword raised for a last — and possibly fatal — blow. There was a cool anger in his eyes that alarmed those who watched. Pelk tried to raise his hands in surrender. He couldn't quite manage. Gerdar was aiming for a blow to the head or neck, knowing that a full strength blow could break Pelk's neck like a chicken's.

"No!" Astrid cried. Ziv stiffened. Brion lunged from the walkway and bowled Gerdar over from behind. The two of them went flying into the mud past Pelk, who fell forward into unconsciousness. Astrid hurried out to his side and rolled him face upwards, relieved to see he had begun to breathe again. Only then did she think to look for Brion.

The two men got to their feet. Gerdar held his practice sword and wiped mud from his eyes with the back of his arm. He levelled the blunt point at Brion.

"You," he hissed angrily. "You interfered. Pick up his sword."

Brion said nothing, did nothing. Ziv climbed down into the mud next to Astrid and fished the wooden sword out of the muck.

"I accept the challenge," Ziv said calmly.

Gerdar shook his head. "No. He interfered, and he will finish it. Take the weapon, man, or I'll beat you as you stand."

"I don't know how to use a sword," Brion answered slowly.

Gerdar grinned; for the first time they saw the wolfish cruelty that lurked beneath his smooth surface, the intensity that had taken so many lives.

Gerdar attacked.

Pelk's challenge had drawn a noisy crowd from a few neighboring establishments; betting had been furious. Now the onlookers fell silent and shuffled their feet uneasily. It was one thing to cheer a match between two armed men, but this was cold-blooded murder.

"Ziv!" Astrid cried. She grabbed his arm.

Gerdar moved with all of his speed, a deadly blur that brought the hard wooden wand down with bone-crushing velocity. Ziv tensed himself in readiness to act, but Brion stepped into the attack, grabbed Gerdar's arm, and threw the duelist smoothly over his back into the muck. Gerdar hit with a stunning splash.

Brion backed away, flushed with fear and triumph. Gerdar struggled to his feet. His eyes burned with purpose; he could not afford to lose this fight, if Ziv read the facts right. Gerdar's reputation was at stake; he would show no quarter, not even to an unarmed man.

Gerdar advanced upon Brion, cautiously this time. Brion waited. Gerdar held his sword horizontally across his body, apparently guarding, but as Ziv hissed a word of warning, the duelist swung the sword up above his head, landing a hard blow on Brion's ribs. The man staggered backwards, almost losing his footing, and turned to protect his injured side. Gerdar displayed no triumph and came in again at full strength, landing another blow hard along Brion's thigh. Brion gasped and almost fell.

The crowd jeered Gerdar. Whether or not their disapproval penetrated his consciousness, he overreached himself in looking for his next strike. Brion balanced on his good leg and kicked his opponent's legs out from under him. Gerdar collapsed into the muck. Brion fell on top of him and fastened his hands around the duelist's throat.

"Yield," Brion gasped out harshly. Gerdar said nothing, struggling to throw him off. Brion increased the pressure on his grip until Gerdar's struggles weakened and he fell unconscious.

Astrid caught Brion as his bruised leg folded, and Ziv helped her conduct him back to where Pelk waited. The thief was still trying to pull air into his bruised lungs, but he held his hand out to Brion, and the other man took it with relief.

"I thought you couldn't fight," Pelk croaked. Brion sighed and braced himself against the wooden side of Tyron's Arms, rubbing his bruised thigh.

"Not with your weapons. Unarmed fighting is a kind of sport among my people. I'm not very good at it."

Ziv gave a snort of disbelief. Brion wiped mud from his face and looked at him questioningly.

"The Changramai know fighters when we see them," Ziv said. "You fought well."

"Pelk wore him down," Brion smiled, and coughed painfully.

Pelk sucked in a deep breath and winced. "Next time, you go first."

Gerdar slowly pushed himself out of the mud in the street, shaking his head to clear it. No one helped him. The crowd had dispersed, turning its back on him in eloquent scorn: whether for attacking an unarmed man, or for losing, it was impossible to tell. He cast one black, unfathomable look at the four travellers and limped down the street, a scarecrow figure that Astrid felt a surge of pity for —despite her own better judgement.

"What will happen to him?" she asked in a low voice.

Ziv shrugged fatalistically. "He has lost a fight. There will be a great many who will come for him now, and soon he will lose again, maybe his life."

"That's terrible," she whispered. Ziv's calm blue eyes blinked in mild surprise.

Pelk stretched out his aching limbs and coughed again. "It would have been much more of a tragedy if he'd won," he noted, standing. "Now, if we can collect our winnings — "

Tyron was standing in the doorway to his shop, a wrapped bundle in his arms. He looked at each of them in turn, then unfolded the cloth to reveal the ivory pommel of the white sword. As Pelk caught his breath and stretched out his hand, Tyron took a step back from him.

"The sword goes to the winner," he said stubbornly. Pelk stared at him a few seconds, then looked at Brion, who held out his hand and took the sword. It slid out of Tyron's hands almost unwillingly, and the smith took a step backwards. The cloth fell away, revealing a scabbard of rich Threk hide. Brion slid out the blade: the white metal warped the sunlight and threw it back like a faceted jewel. Pelk's eyes teared at the glare, or from his passionate disappointment, but he said nothing. Brion put the blade back into the scabbard with a clash of steel and held it mutely out to Pelk.

"Why?" Pelk asked without taking it.

"What would I do with it?" Brion asked. "Take it."

They stood there looking at each other before Pelk slowly put his hand on the pommel. He pulled the blade part way from the scabbard and slid his palm along the razor edge, then held up his hand to show Brion the bleeding cut.

"By my blood," he said slowly, "I will help you get your son back or fall in the attempt. The Lords of Orhan and these people gathered before us are witness to my oath."

"I so witness," Ziv said. Astrid echoed him. Pelk held out the bloody hand to Brion, but before he took it Brion cut his hand on the white sword. They clasped hands over the pommel, then Pelk let go and took the scabbard in his undamaged hand.

"Let me see your hands," Astrid insisted, grabbing for Brion's. "A foolish thing to do — "

She turned it over, but under the blood there was no sign of a cut. Pelk held up his hand wordlessly and displayed a palm innocent of wounds. They looked at each other for a moment before Tyron cleared his throat. They'd almost forgotten the little man, but now he drew all eyes.

"It seems the Lords of Orhan witnessed, all right," Tyron remarked blandly. "Better hope it wasn't an empty promise, friends. Use the Lady in good health."

"My thanks, Tyron," Pelk said, and held up the sword.

Tyron glared and went back in his shop. "Fools," he grumbled, and slammed the door.

The wind was bitterly cold and bit at Evan's exposed skin like a wolf.

That was the first thing that Evan noticed, in the disorientation of travel; he instinctively huddled closer to Tiernan's warm body and opened his eyes to see a forbidding, rough-edged landscape that looked even colder than the cutting wind felt.

The Navigator — if that was what he was — released Evan's hand, then Laurel's. A gust of wind threw a curtain of cold sand over them, causing them to cough and close their eyes against the blown grit; Laurel shaded her eyes and peered into the growing sandstorm. The sun was going down behind a ragged hill in a blood-red blaze, but there was no sign of anyone else.

"Navigator!" she yelled, receiving no reply. "Where have you taken us?"

A frightening blanket of darkness fell over them; Laurel felt Evan's hand slipping out of hers. She grabbed for him, felt Tiernan do the same; her fingers met the prince's, but the boy was gone. She cried his name, but it was impossible to see in the fury of the storm and the unnaturally swift fall of night. Tiernan grabbed her and held her trembling body close, trying to force warmth back into her chilled flesh.

Evan opened his eyes to see Andraax sitting cross-legged facing him on the sand. He could distantly hear the shriek of the cold wind, but he and Andraax sat in a protected little bubble of warm, still air as blown sand scoured the outer flesh of the bubble in rushing waves.

Andraax was floating a few inches above the ground, apparently unaware that he was doing so. Evan watched him for a second, then stood up to look outside of the bubble.

"Careful, it's fragile," Andraax cautioned him.

Evan turned back to stare at him. "You brought us here," he accused. "You pretended to be somebody they could trust, and you brought us here."

"Not exactly. I would have taken you to Kelfour's Landing, boy, but there was a complication in my plans. No matter. You are safe here."

Evan crossed to stand only a foot away from the placidly floating magician, and in that moment he looked a great deal like his mother. His eyes snapped with anger, and his face was a stiff, unforgiving mask. Andraax looked at him uncertainly.

"What about my friends?" he demanded. Andraax said nothing. "You're going to leave them out there? They don't even know where they are! You can't do this!"

"I can," Andraax corrected him calmly. "I will not oppose this minion of the Unlife directly, and for your friends, it is too late for intervention. You will come with me."

"Not without Laurel and Tiernan," Evan shot back stubbornly. He crossed his arms and glared at the smooth, expressionless face of the former Loremaster. Andraax felt a tired surge of exasperation.

"I have given my answer, Evan. Come." Andraax held out his hand. Evan backed away quickly — and Andraax floated forward. "Evan! Stop this. Any farther and you will — "

There was an audible popping sound, and the bubble collapsed; Evan passed through it. The storm shrieked, smothering Andraax's warning as the magician shot to his feet — but Evan was already running blindly away. Andraax started to follow, then stopped. The sand swallowed him up like a phantom.

"It's all right, hush, it's all right," Tiernan whispered against Laurel's hair as she clung to him. "He'll be fine. We must find shelter. Come."

"He's lost, Tier, he's alone in this — we have to try — " Laurel gasped for breath, resisting an overwhelming impulse to weep, and buried her face against his chest as his hands pulled the damp blanket she held around her shoulders closer. "Yes. Shelter. I'm sorry."

Tiernan said nothing, only took her hands and began towing her through the smothering windstorm. The darkness left as suddenly as it had fallen, leaving them bathed in lessening wind and waning sunlight. There was a sharp-edged outcropping of rock rising not too far away; he led her to the leeward side. In a sheltered little space too small to be called a cave, he settled her before climbing to the top of the rocks to survey the surroundings.

"Can you see him?" she asked. Tiernan braced himself against another chilling blast of wind.

"No, nothing. Damn it, where could he have gone? I can understand why my tutors were exhausted most of the time." Tiernan jumped down from the stone perch, landing in a crouch. "Laurel?"

Only the wind answered. He straightened slowly, feeling tension knotting up in his muscles and fear in his stomach, and walked back to where he'd left her.

"Nice of you to return so promptly, Prince Tiernan," Walerin said. He held Laurel Magen by the throat with his left hand. His right hand was twined in her golden hair. Tiernan took an instinctive step forward, and the hand on her neck suddenly sprouted long black claws. Those evil claws trembled on her pale skin, leaving little red marks where they touched. Laurel made no sound, but she closed her eyes.

"Leave her, you bastard," Tiernan whispered. Walerin didn't move from where he sat.

"You are in no position to demand anything, my friend. The woman is not important to me, except as she is important to you. I don't know how you managed to get this far from me, but from now on I want your position in this affair made abundantly clear. Any resistance from you, man, and she forfeits what's left of her life. I don't even need to be near her." Walerin retracted the black claws and drew his fingers in a suggestive, chilling line around her throat. Where they passed, a black collar came into being — real and solid, but so thin it was almost weightless. Laurel reached up to touch it, then jerked her fingers away in loathing.

"What is it?" Tiernan asked harshly. Walerin held up his left hand and began to slowly curve his fingers inward. The collar contracted, cutting into Laurel's throat. She gasped and then gagged for breath. "Stop! I understand. What do you want?"

"Oh, many things, prince, but few that you can grant." Walerin smiled slightly and gestured at a space opposite him. "Sit down."

Tiernan sat, unwilling to get so close and terrified lest Walerin should move his left hand any more. Walerin, as if reading his thoughts, smiled and relaxed. The collar abruptly released; Laurel breathed in unrestricted gasps.

"Not much of an inventor, are you?" she asked Walerin when her voice was steady enough. "My father could have thought of something much more original."

"Your father will have much more troubling things to think about," Walerin said absently. "Now, Prince Tiernan, now we have a bargaining position. Your cooperation for her life."

"You're taking us to home," Tiernan said. "Why?"

"What difference to you?" The cleric's hand moved suddenly, half-closing. Laurel convulsed and grabbed helplessly at her throat. "If I shut my fist, it will cut her head from her shoulders, as neat as that. I don't think you want that to happen, do you?"

Tiernan shut his eyes, briefly, forcing his terror into the back of his mind. Once again the terrible dream-specter of Laurel dying in his arms ran across his thoughts.

"I will cooperate with you," the prince whispered softly. He didn't open his eyes, but he felt a sudden dizzying surge of relief as he heard Laurel able to draw breath again. She was weeping. "Damn you! Have you no heart?"

"No," Walerin said almost cheerfully. "Which is why I shall outlive you. Sit still, Prince of Rhakhaan. If you move — "

"I know the consequences," Tiernan said woodenly. He opened his eyes to watch Walerin slide out from behind Laurel to approach him. Laurel, her wide blue eyes blazing with burning hatred, looked as though she would attack the cleric barehanded, but Tiernan's urgent expression begged her not to risk her life. Walerin disappeared behind him, out of his field of vision. Then the evil cleric's fingers traced a cold line around his throat. Tiernan felt instinctively for the cause and touched a slick, oddly unsettling ring that was not metal or any other substance he could identify. Like Laurel, he jerked away from its unhealthy touch.

"There," Walerin said in some satisfaction. "Now I can trust you to think of each other's continued health, and I need not worry that you might attempt anything — unwise. To your feet! We have a long way to go."

Laurel was shivering violently, despite her blanket, and she needed Tiernan's help to rise. The prince looked at Walerin, who watched without expression.

"She's weak," Tiernan said flatly. "She needs rest. Can we not travel later?"

"Always the gallant, aren't you?" marvelled the cleric. His sarcasm was all the more effective for being delivered with a ridiculously provincial accent. "No. If she cannot travel, she will account for one less mouth to feed. You choose, woman. Walk or die."

"I'll walk," Laurel whispered. Tiernan took her hand, his eyes bitter and full of rage.

"Save your threats, Tiernan," Walerin said before the prince could find words to fit his anger. "If you want to keep her with you a little longer, devote your energy to cooperation. I have a very short temper — and if there's one thing I despise, it's royalty."

"What did you do with the boy?" Tiernan asked softly. Walerin glanced around.

"Oh, the boy. He's been watching us for some time now. Boy!" Walerin's voice echoed on the rock. "Time to join our little band. I have been more than patient with you."

Silence. Sand hissed from impact with rock, and the sun completed its slide into night. The temperature was already beginning to plummet. Tiernan pulled Laurel closer as he felt her begin to shiver violently. Don't do it, the prince begged in his mind. Run, Evan, two of us is more than enough —

Evan slid down a sandy slope less than twenty feet away and ran to stand with his friends.

"A wise decision, young master," the cleric told him softly, and lowered his hands.

Evan raised his chin defiantly. "I didn't have much choice."

"But that is why you are wise! You know when you have no choices. Your turn for a pretty necklace, boy — stand still — "

Evan didn't move, although he flinched as Walerin came close. Walerin touched the boy's throat —

And screamed. He jerked back from the boy with an expression of ludicrous betrayal. His fingertips were burned a painful red.

"Deceitful little swine!" he screamed, raising a hand to strike him. Tiernan's hand shot out and forced Walerin's arm back; the cleric, taken by surprise, fell off-balance onto his back and laid there staring at Tiernan's cold grimace.

"If you want to fight, worm, fight me," the prince hissed.

Walerin squirmed backward through the cold sand until he was out of the man's reach. Only then, when he was safe from a sudden attack, did he extend his hand toward Tiernan and clench it.

"I don't have to fight," Walerin said. The black collar shrank inward to cut off Tiernan's breath. "Who's the worm now? You probably don't remember me, Prince Tiernan of Rhakhaan. I wasn't worth your notice, but I remember you. Arrogant, worthless, thoughtless — worm."

Tiernan pitched from his knees over to his side, mouth open and straining desperately for air. Laurel clawed desperately at the constricting collar, but her fingers slid off as if trying to hold something alive. Evan skidded to a stop next to her and tried to help, but for all of his seeming invulnerability to Walerin's spells he couldn't save the prince from them. The boy looked up with wide, desperate, anguished eyes.

"Stop it!" he commanded. Walerin bared his teeth in a menacing grin. "Please stop it. He never hurt you. Why do you want to hurt him?"

Walerin watched the prince writhe in the sand a few seconds more, then relaxed his hand. Tiernan pulled in a deep, sobbing breath, and opened his eyes, eyes which regarded the darkening sky blankly. Laurel touched his face with trembling fingers.

"For my sake, hold your temper," she whispered in his ear, easing his long dark hair away from his sweaty face.

"For your sake?" he gasped just as quietly. His perfect eyes turned to look at her. His pupils were too large, too slow to react.

She winced. "All right, for your sake. But you take — all the fun — out of life."

He wasn't too badly damaged — or if he was, he was too proud to show it. Laurel resisted a sudden urge to drop his head back into the sand and looked up at Evan, who still stood staring at the motionless cleric. Walerin stared in return. Evan finally looked away and sat next to Tiernan and Laurel.

"We're in trouble, aren't we?" he asked softly.

Tiernan raised one hand — it was an effort, but he managed — and smoothed the boy's dark hair. He smiled. "I'm always in trouble," he assured him.

Laurel rolled her eyes. "Do what he says, Evan. Don't make things worse."

Evan looked down. "I'm sorry you got hurt."

Tiernan raised his shoulders up from the ground and sat up. Walerin brought his hands up in instinctive defense, but Tiernan only tossed his long hair back over his shoulders and laughed. If it was a hollower laugh than usual, and his face was four shades paler, only Laurel recognized it.

"Easy, cleric. You have the advantage."

Tiernan gave him a mocking bow. "You have my undivided attention."

"On your feet," Walerin said savagely, getting to his. Tiernan rose as smoothly as before, but it cost him; he blinked hard against a surge of dizziness and felt his limbs give slightly in a hot rush of weakness. Stupid, he raged at himself silently, a stupid display and you're only weakening yourself —

Then again, Tiernan thought as doubt moved in Walerin's eyes, then again —

Evan lagged behind as they began walking, looking over his shoulder for some sign of Andraax. There was no one following except for a swirling storm of sand at the top of the far hill. Evan stared hard at it, wishing, but it died and left nothing behind.

It was getting colder by the step.

"You what?" Jadel snapped. There was a short, breathless silence. The shadow-figure that balanced atop his dark Compass bowed in abject apology. "You allowed a Navigator to interfere? Why did you not destroy him?"

"I'm sorry, master, but it was so sudden — all I could do, I did. I turned the Navigator from his planned course, but we were thrown into the sands near the Seolburn."

"You recaptured them all?" Jadel demanded. Walerin's dimly seen figure stayed in a submissive posture.

"I did, master." He hesitated briefly. "Except for the Navigator — "

"Navigators chatter like birds." Jadel's languid beauty sharpened, became cruel. "A change in plans, then. The subjugation of Rhakhaan must wait. You are close to Quellburn. Meet me there with your captives."

"The boy, too?" Walerin asked. He seemed nervous.

"Of course the boy! Is there something you haven't told me, Walerin?"

"He — he resists my power, master. There's something odd about him. I fear he may be difficult to control."

Jadel thought for a few seconds of the boy, of the father — and of the mother, who sat limply across the room and heard nothing of what he said until he intended her to. An interesting heritage for any child — and this one seemed to be a lodestone for trouble.

"Use whatever methods you must," he finally said. "Only keep him alive. I may need him in Quellburn."

"May I ask why we go to Quellburn, master?" Walerin asked; it was a stupidly impetuous question, but the ruination of the kingdom of Rhakhaan in Jaiman had been his pet project for years, and he was petulant at the prospect of delay.

Jadel, far from taking offense, smiled. "You may not ask, Walerin, but I will tell you: my spies within the walls of the palace in Rhakhaan report that I will need something much more than the spells I possess to enter. Something like what the traitorous sorcerer Zenon used to break the defenses of the city of Quellburn." Jadel trailed his long fingers slowly over the dark slick surface of his Compass. Interference flickered through Walerin's image. "No one has dared to enter the city since its destruction. But we will: to recover Zenon's dark knowledge."

"Why do you need the boy?" Walerin wanted to know.

Jadel's dark eyes shifted slightly to look at Kella, who sat with her eyes shut. "I may need some expendable coin to buy my way into the city. There are forces there unfriendly to us. The boy should do nicely." Jadel's voice chilled even further, if that was possible. "If not, there is always the mother, though she is progressing well. It would be a pity to waste her — but more of a pity to waste this opportunity. Enough explanation, Walerin. If your Prince of Rhakhaan should prove difficult, kill him; the more gruesome his body by the time it is found, the better for us. I need him alive far less than I need him dead."

"The woman?" Walerin asked.

Jadel shrugged. "Yes, master. I set out for Quellburn immediately."

"No more Jumps. If the Navigators are alerted, they will prove troublesome."

"Master," said Walerin's image before winking out like a doused flame. Jadel stood and stretched. He snapped his fingers absently in Kella's direction, and she opened her eyes.

"Brion's here," she said coldly. "I feel him. He's with those others."

"They seek your son." Jadel was gratified to see her dark eyes catch fire. "When they find him, they'll take him where neither you nor I could rescue him again. We must act to stop them now."

"Show me how," Kella whispered. Jadel crossed the room and took her wrists in his hands, pale strong fingers circling the warm flesh and feeling the pulse beneath. "Show me, Jadel."

"So fierce," he wondered aloud, and touched his lips to hers. She shivered and tried to draw her hands away, but he held them fast. "Don't fight me, Kella. You can't."

"I wasn't trying to," she whispered, her lips moving tantalizingly on his. "Let me go."

Jadel's hands released her. Kella reached up and wound her fingers in his long satin-soft hair, touching the strange, sharp angles of his face and the curve of his ears, and then slid down his neck to ease the dark fabric of his robe off his pale shoulders. He stood very still, watching her with black eyes that were no longer cold. Her eyes were as hot as burning tar. Kella's mouth touched him delicately at the base of his throat, teeth grazing the skin in instinctive hunger, and then travelled down the smooth hairless line of his chest. Jadel lifted his hands to unfasten his robe at the waist, and stepped out of it when it slid to his feet. Kella stood to meet him.

Their bodies melded together like water, and Jadel took her back onto the bed. He paused there, bracing himself on raised elbows, and stared down into her dark hungry eyes.

"Don't worry about our enemies," he whispered to her then. "I have arranged a suitable welcome for them. You and I have other concerns."

"Now, Jadel," she begged breathlessly. Her fingers tightened on his back. Her fingernails left red marks, and Jadel smiled in quiet pleasure. He held still, feeling the heat exploding in her body, feeling it scorch his own in delicious sympathy. "Don't make me wait. Now!"

"Patience," he whispered, and kissed her again. She moaned and tensed against him, but he was too strong, too commanding. "This is the second lesson, my lady. With power must come patience."

But, he had to admit, it was a half-hearted lesson, and it did not last very long.

"This," Iarsang said softly, "is ridiculous. I am fine. Daphine, if you do not stop fussing at me — "

"You aren't fine," she shot back, peeling away the last layers of bandage to reveal his hand. She froze, staring at the ravaged flesh and shattered bone. When she managed to speak again her voice was colorless and too thin. "You need a healer."

"Tyes has tried." The other Navigator wrapped his undamaged hand around hers. "Daphine."

She didn't look up at him, but only turned to the bowl of clean water at her elbow and began viciously wringing out wet cloths. He watched her with a faint, distant expression, but she was too busy wrestling with her own anger and pain to notice his. She took his mutilated left hand gently in hers.

"This is going to hurt." She felt rather than saw his nod of agreement. He didn't stiffen or make a sound when she washed the wounds, even though it must have been terribly painful; Daphine blinked back useless tears and began wrapping it again. Despite the passage of time, the wounds hadn't even begun to heal, and they still wept blood as she covered them. She wrapped it as tightly and as completely as she dared, stricken by the speed with which blood spread over the frail cotton bandages, and as she was tying the ends she happened to touch the patch of white skin on Iarsang's left wrist where he'd once worn a Compass. It was flushed with sunburn.

"If I'm not careful I will end up finding that more painful than my hand," he joked faintly. She looked up at him, more astonished at his humor than his bravery, and saw the weariness in his brown eyes. "Once I have my Compass back, our lives will be better, I promise you."

She didn't answer but only watched him. After a long silence Iarsang leaned forward and touched her on the face, a slow caress that had less of urgency in it than gentle appreciation. She turned her head and kissed his fingers. Unable to say anything of what she felt, Daphine gathered up her bandages and cloths and retreated to the far corner of the room.

Iarsang wondered just how things had changed so drastically, from a pleasant but unimportant little assignation to this strange painful need. He wondered too if their lives were better, or worse.

"Daphine," he said, surprising himself and her. She jumped a little and turned to look. "How long have I known you?"

"What?" She frowned at him. "I don't know — a hundred years? On and off?"

"On and off," he echoed. "Why have I never noticed how kind you are?"

She almost dropped the water basin. "I'm not kind," she said finally, when she had basin and hands and voice under control. "Navigators are not kind, as a matter of principle. We are businesslike."

"Not you," he said, stretching out on the long bed with a sigh. Kelfour's Landing had enough of a cosmopolitan community to have beds long enough to fit Elven height, a blessing he'd not dared to hope for. "Do you know, until yesterday I never doubted myself, never doubted my ability as a Navigator or a man — and in one short moment everything has changed."

"No it hasn't," she argued, and came back to perch on the edge of the bed, looking down at him. His eyes, no longer vague, had a wounded look that went beyond physical pain.

"Yes," he corrected softly. "I lost the lives of my charges. I failed in my duty. I permitted a Compass to fall into evil hands."

"You survived!"

"Is that praiseworthy?" he asked her in a voice so completely stripped of emotion that she almost missed the terrible doubt underneath. "I failed, Daphine. I have never failed before."

"You won't fail now," she told him, and felt his right hand touch her cheek. She shivered. "I won't let you fail, Iarsang."

"You see?" he whispered. "So kind."

Her lips parted to protest, but his long fingers moved to touch them, and she was silent. Neither one of them moved, lost in the moment, lost in a strange new world of emotion that was as alien to Navigators as charity.

For just a moment, as he leaned forward to touch her lips with his, Iarsang forgot all of his grief and anger, forgot even the aching fury of his wound. Daphine responded to his kiss with a strangely awkward eagerness. She slid her arms around him and sank back with him to the smooth, blessedly soft sheets. After a long, hazy moment, she opened her eyes and found him looking at her. It was unsettling, that look. And strangely moving.

"All this time wasted," Iarsang whispered. She shook her head as her hands slipped down his chest, carefully unknotting his laces and baring skin that still held marks of arrow hits. His body was feverishly warm to the touch.

"Not wasted," she told him. "No moment I spent in your company was ever wasted, Iarsang. I intend to keep you alive from entirely selfish reasons, you know; you shall stay with me for a long, long time."

"Agreeable," Iarsang murmured. Her long hair drifted down over his chest, pleasure driving away fading pain. "You drive a hard bargain, Navigator."

"You," Daphine smiled, "haven't seen anything yet, Navigator. Wait until you recover. I intend to get my full value out of you."

"It sounds like pleasant duty," Iarsang said solemnly, and she covered his lips with hers. Conversation came to a halt.

They were understandably startled and irritated when the door slammed back on its hinges and Vurkanan Tyes hurried in. He looked from one of them to the other with raised eyebrows.

"Am I interrupting?" he asked politely, but brushed it aside. "The Dyar and Kella — they're in the bathhouse. I've tracked them as far as that. I'll need the two of you. Daphine, can you and Iarsang together put us in the right room?"

"I expect so," Daphine said, recovering her composure. She slid off of the bed with a last glance at Iarsang, who was sitting up with a certain regret of his own. "You're certain they're in the bathhouse?"

"Positive."

"We should wait for the others," she said doubtfully. Tyes shook his head.

"Jadel is too dangerous. The fewer ungifted I expose to his influence the better; I'm not even certain I'd risk Pelk to him at close range. You and Iarsang are well-protected"

"What about Kella?" Daphine asked quietly. Tyes met her eyes squarely.

"If we can get her away, we will. But I don't think she wants to be helped, Daphine. I sensed it in her from the beginning — a kind of despair, a darkness — and whatever it is that this Dyar offers it goes far past what we can. But yes, I will try."

"One more thing," Iarsang said, coming to his feet. He hid his mangled hand in the folds of his cloak, and he looked almost his old self, except for the purpose and sharp awareness in his eyes. "Don't let him take you alive. Either of you. I shall not."

"It will not come to that," Tyes answered. Iarsang looked at him without expression.

"It may," he insisted, and linked hands with Daphine. Tyes came forward and completed the link. Power swirled and swept around them, and then they were gone.

Gone, yet not arrived —

"He's warped the flow again!" Daphine screamed.

They plummeted in some strange direction again, out of control and blind. This trip was short. They landed hard in a nondescript little room roughly furnished with a rumpled bed and little else. Tyes rolled to his feet and threw one comprehensive look around as he offered an arm to Iarsang. Daphine was already rising.

"Where are we?" he snapped. Daphine frowned.

"In the bathhouse. This is the room where he was — "

"Yes," Iarsang affirmed. "I can feel him. He's near."

"Lead," Tyes ordered curtly. Iarsang yanked the door open, almost wrenching it from the rickety leather hinges in his haste, and strode into the narrow wooden hall. The bright fire of his stolen Compass burned in his mind, all but blinding him to the mundane sights around him. He shouted something wordless and broke into a run as he saw the doorway at the end of the hall.

"Wait!" Daphine did her best to follow. Even so, he had a lead of a few feet on both her and the Loremaster when he reached the door and slammed it.

Jadel and Kella stood at the far end of the room, wearing identical smiles of contempt and triumph. Iarsang took two steps forward.

"You came," Jadel said, as gratified as the host of a failing party whose best guests just arrived. "Be welcome, Navigator. Ah — and you too, mistress — and the Loremaster. Vurkanan Tyes. I have something for you, Tyes."

"Kella, come here," Tyes called. She kept smiling, her dark eyes brilliant with malice, and pulled aside the curtained alcove next to her.

Behind the curtain lay a young half-Iylari woman, tiny for her blood, cloaked in a cloud of golden hair. Tyes caught his breath, gray eyes going wide and fixed, and he took one step further. Jadel laughed.

"I am merciful, Tyes. If you want our child, come and get her. I'll not stop you." He laughed again and took Kella's outstretched hand. "I won't have to."

The door slammed shut behind Tyes' back, and he felt strong wards shimmer into existence around them. Trapped — but he wasn't too worried. It would only take a few untroubled minutes to dissolve them. Then, what?

Jadel, seeing his confusion, pointed to the floor between them.

It was dissolving into a black starless void.

"I must go now, Loremaster," he said. "But I'd hate to leave you lonely. I hope you like my friends."

Kella put her arm around the Dyar priest as he held his stolen Compass out in front of them. Iarsang gave a wordless cry of anguish and reached out, but they were gone.

The Compass wrenched most of what strength he had left away from him in its passing.

"Back!" Tyes shouted, and dragged Iarsang back as he saw that the tall Navigator was unable to move. "Back! Don't interfere! Daphine, get him out of here!"

"What about you?" she asked anxiously. The hole in the floor was forcing them back, but that wasn't what had Tyes' face bleached so white, or what raised the hackles on the back of Daphine's neck. "What's happening?"

"The fool," Tyes whispered in disbelief. "Against the wall! Go! He's torn a hole into the Pales. I have to shut it!"

As he spoke, the first of the demons had hooked a clawed hand over the edge of the hole and was coming up. Tyes swore under his breath and abandoned finesse. The first demon jumped up to face him, almost eye level to the tall Iylari Loremaster, and swung a massive club. Tyes flung himself backward and tossed an attack of his own — a fireball of frightening proportion. The demon erupted into unnatural green flame. A sorcerous blast of wind pushed it back over the edge of the hole, and Tyes took a step forward. Already more demons appeared, more than he could fight with ease.

Jadel had seen to it that Tyes couldn't abandon the fight, not merely because of the presence of his daughter on the other side of the room but because he'd raised the demons in such a dangerously populated area. To abandon the fight was to let the demons rage unchecked throughout Kelfour's Landing. Yet to fight so many was to die —

He'd said at the outset what had to be done. Now, with all of the years of experience and power in his possession, Vurkanan Tyes bent to the task of sealing a hole into hell.

Essence exploded into visible life around him as he drew on every source available, from the powerful currents above the island to the wandering, unpredictable washes that floated near the city and in the mountains. It was too bright to look on, but Tyes didn't need eyes; he shaped it into a huge circle and began forcing the flows over the rift between worlds, making the demons give ground. Some of them lost their grip and fell screaming; others encountered the burning raw touch of Essence and exploded into nothing, utterly unmade.

It was more Essence than any one Loremaster could safely handle, and it was taking a terrible toll on Tyes. He held it, somehow, though the power surging through his body set every nerve to burning, every muscle into raging convulsion. He fell to his knees, then to his hands. Sweat dripped from his brow onto clenched fists and reflected the rainbow storm of Essence that glittered before him. Not enough, he thought distantly. He would have to force it still farther, whatever the cost —

The whirling storm of Essence circled tighter, then tighter still, driving the rift inward until there was only a tiny circle of darkness remaining confined by the light. Tyes' burning forehead rested on his sweat-streaked hands, and he forced himself to one last, ultimate effort that ripped through his body like the thrust of a sword. A rib shattered under the force that rushed through him, then another. He cried out, and the darkness disappeared under a solid sheet of Essence.

The light winked out, leaving them with dazzled eyes. The floor was whole but scorched, and as Daphine hesitantly stepped forward she hissed in surprise at the heat still simmering in the wood.

"Loremaster?" she asked, profoundly awed and not a little concerned. Tyes stayed in his prone position for another few torturous seconds, then slowly rolled over onto his back and gasped for breath. His face was drained utterly of color, a shockingly pale mask that was made even paler by the blood that ran from his mouth and nose. His gray eyes were huge and pupil-less with shock.

He whispered something she didn't catch, even as she knelt at his side and began dabbing at the blood on his face. She bent closer.

"Top that," he croaked in weak but unmistakable triumph. "Top that, you Dyari bastard."

It seemed the Loremaster, too, had learned to take things personally.

"We have to stop," Tiernan said in a voice long gone hoarse from abuse and weariness. The cleric kept walking, and he showed no signs of slowing. Laurel staggered again; she wouldn't protest, but she was gasping for breath and shivering desperately. Evan was a dead weight in the prince's arms. He'd long ago been too exhausted to continue. No shame in that; even Tiernan's legs were turning to mush in the constant exertion of pushing aside cold sand.

"Walk or be left to die," Walerin said without turning. Tiernan cursed wearily and tried to support Laurel as much as he could, which wasn't much. He felt a surge of desperate anger. He couldn't carry them both —

And he couldn't choose to leave one, either.

"Laurel," he whispered to her. She kept walking, eyes glazed with effort. "Laurel. You must keep up. Understand? You must! I can't carry you."

She didn't seem to hear him for a moment, then shook her head slightly to clear it. Awareness came back to her face, along with a deadly weariness.

"I'm tired," she told him in a lost, tiny voice that made him want to weep or scream. "I have to stop. Make him stop, Tier."

It was the first time in a very long time she'd asked anything at all of him. Tiernan felt a hot flash of pain around his chest and tightened his grip around her arm. Even in the darkness, she was too pale. She looked like walking dead.

"Walerin," Tiernan called. The cleric ignored him. Laurel stumbled again, dragging at the prince's arm, and he halted. She stayed on her feet, but it was a struggle. "Walerin, wait. What do you want out of me?"

The cleric halted and turned, and in the dim moonlight his expression was thoroughly unpleasant with triumph. He said nothing. Tiernan stared at him, feeling the trembling of Laurel's whole body next to him, feeling the dead weight of the sleeping boy in his arms, and slowly bent and put Evan on the ground.

"Do you want me to beg?" he asked even more softly. Walerin still said nothing. "Please. Please let us stop. You'll kill us."

Walerin turned and began walking again. Tiernan slowly got down on his knees. Cold arid wind shook his hair back from his face, revealing the despairing intensity therein.

"Walerin," he said again. When the cleric looked back, Tiernan slowly performed a full obeisance in the style of the Rhakhaan court, the kind used by convicted felons and traitors. He stretched his body full length in the cold shifting sand and rested his forehead on clenched fists.

"I beg you, let us stop," he whispered. Because he couldn't stand to look up he failed to see the hot flash of gratification on the cleric's face.

"By all means." Walerin seated himself on the sand. "Rest. You see, Prince Tiernan? Humility is such an excellent tool."

Tiernan slowly crawled up to a sitting position. Laurel had collapsed next to him with none of her normal grace; he pulled her into the warm circle of his arms and pillowed her head on his chest. She needed a bath, he thought with a flash of grim humor. They all did.

"I know you, Walerin," he said mildly, drawing the cleric's eyes again. "I remember you now. You were a stableboy on the palace grounds."

Walerin dug out a full waterskin from his pack and drank deeply, ignoring the thirst of his captives. He smiled a little.

"Yes, I remember too. Interesting, what coincidence can do." His dark eyes glittered in the moonlight, as harsh as the rest of him was bland. "But I'm honored that you remember me after all this time, Prince Tiernan. After all, I was a mere stableboy —"

"You fired the stables," Tiernan said with bitter force. "I saw you. Do you have any idea how many horses died in that fire? How many had to be destroyed because of injuries?"

"Doubtless enough that you would have hung me if you'd caught me," Walerin guessed, and shrugged. "I had nothing against the beasts. I did, on the other hand, have something against you."

"Me?" Tiernan echoed, puzzled. Walerin unwrapped a bit of cheese and bit into it, still grinning.

"Oh yes. You. The perfect little royal brat. Your horse was never properly groomed, your tack never shiny enough, your stall never clean enough — and every word you said against me was taken out of my hide by the Master of Horse, or didn't you know that? I only did what you would have done, in my place: I took my revenge."

"You burned twenty horses to death," Tiernan said colorlessly. "Animals who never did you any harm. If you think I would have done that — "

"Oh, no, the great prince wouldn't have done any such thing, I'm sure," the cleric retorted with a sneer. "You would have challenged your enemy to a fight to the death, and then spared his life. You would have won, of course, because you've never lost."

"I'm sitting here, aren't I?" Tiernan pointed out. "You whine about your problems, cleric, but it doesn't explain what you did, or excuse it. If you had a complaint of me, you should have faced me. What you did was the act of a madman."

"But you would have seen me hang anyway."

"Yes," Tiernan whispered, and his face convulsed in memory. "I'd see you hang now, you bastard, and not just for the horses."

"Your doxy lives, Prince. For now." Walerin's laughter was a faint, joyless sound that cut like the cold wind. "Lucky for her I have other tastes. Iylari women turn my stomach."

Tiernan felt Laurel shiver again in his embrace, but it wasn't because she had heard their captor's words; she was asleep, but her skin was bitterly cold. Tiernan pulled her closer.

"We need a fire if you expect us to live through the night," Tiernan said. Walerin looked at him a minute.

"Surely there are better ways to warm a woman," he said in mocking surprise. "Surely you know them, Tiernan. I might enjoy that spectacle very much."

"Your enjoyment will have to wait," Tiernan growled, just barely holding to his temper. Laurel's life was so desperately precarious; he couldn't afford to antagonize this madman any more. "Please, Walerin, a fire. I can't keep them both warm."

Walerin thought a moment, then nodded. He gestured at the sand between them, and a green-tinged flame sprang up out of the bare dirt to flicker thinly in the cold wind. It was unnatural, but it warmed. Tiernan put Laurel as close to it as he dared, then wrapped Evan carefully in his blanket and put the boy on the other side of the fire. Walerin watched him silently.

"No blanket for you, princeling?" he asked. Tiernan lay behind Laurel and wrapped his arms around her body, struggling to retain his own warmth and force some into her chilled body. "Ah. So much more interesting than a blanket. Enjoy her while you can."

Tiernan couldn't bring himself to close his eyes, not while Walerin was watching with that terrible intent gaze, so he hugged Laurel's sleeping body closer and stared back. Walerin seemed amused, but he didn't look away.

"Don't you sleep?" Tiernan finally asked. Walerin inclined his head affirmatively, but he didn't move. "Well, if you're just sitting there you might as well tell me why you're taking me — us — back to Jaiman."

"I'm not, not directly." Walerin's expression was briefly unhappy. "But perhaps you'd benefit from the plan. It really is perfect. It gives you a whole new usefulness, Prince Tiernan. Youngest of a pack of sons — that must have been a trial. Too young to inherit, too young even to marry profitably — and very little wealth of your own. A landless prince. You really are useless, aren't you?"

Whether he intended it or not — and Tiernan was deadly certain that he did — Walerin had struck.. Tiernan trusted it didn't show in his expression, but in his heart the old bitter helplessness welled up. Walerin smiled slightly, or perhaps that was a trick of the greenish light.

"More useful than a failed stableboy, certainly," Tiernan murmured. Walerin's smile vanished, replaced by nothing in particular. Tiernan felt the merest pulse of pressure along his neck. Just a warning. He smiled in turn. "Go on. It's fascinating."

"Yes, isn't it? You see, Tiernan, the paradox is that your brothers are all older than you, better placed than you, better trained and stationed and influenced — and yet it's you who holds your father's heart, you whom the people of Rhakhaan adore. I've always found that a charming bit of irony. I'd been contemplating how to reach you for years before you presented me with this amazing opportunity."

"If you only wanted to apologize, you could have done it by letter. I'm not fussy."

Walerin stood and walked around the fire, squatting just in front of Tiernan, just in front of Laurel's sleeping body. He was so close that the prince could smell the acrid stench of his sweat and the strange metallic odor of Unlife that seemed to enfold him. So close that his brown eyes looked like dried blood in the moonlight.

"You're such a fool." The contempt in the cleric's voice struck Tiernan like acid. "Don't you see what you've done? She did. That's why she came after you. That's why she's thrown her life away so uselessly. She came to defend you.

"Hadn't you even contemplated the fact that you're a perfect hostage — or a victim?"

Taken off-balance, the prince could only stare. Then he laughed. The laughter faded uncomfortably away under the dry, avid heat of Walerin's eyes.

"I'll perform a miracle for you, Prince of Rhakhaan," Walerin continued. "I'll foretell the future. You see, some day very soon your body will be discovered just at the coast of Jaiman, and the things that will have been done to you — well, it defies the imagination of a mortal. Your lovely sorceress will be likewise pitifully murdered. An outcry will go up. Who's done this thing? Bandits? Pirates? Servants of Unlife?

"Sadly," Walerin grinned suddenly, "no. It will be discovered that the murder was done by factions within your father's own court. Factions with substantial followings. Those lords — who will be well aware of their own innocence, but unable to prove any such thing — will have no choice but to flee for their lives. And they will raise up forces to protect themselves.

"A hypothetical question, then: what will your father and brothers do? What will your people do? What will be the result of that, soon-to-be-ex-Prince of Rhakhaan?"

Tiernan stared back at him from a face gone pale and expressionless. He didn't speak for a long moment, just watched the hot hunger in his enemy's eyes. It was suddenly hard to draw breath through the knot of anguish in his chest.

"War," he whispered faintly. "You are going to start a war."

"A civil war," Walerin corrected him precisely. "And every man, woman or child who carries the blood of O'Locklir will die. Every one. Is that clear enough for you, you pitiful idiot? In the midst of this carnage and confusion, we will appear, and where there is still order we will ensure chaos. When the dust settles, our puppet will be on the throne, and I will have the best revenge of all for my years of servitude: I will crush your people. I will eradicate your family. I will destroy every thing you have ever held dear to your heart."

Walerin's voice had picked up a strange intensity, though it didn't get any louder. He reached over and extended one hand to touch Laurel's cheek. Tiernan's hand shot out to intercept him. Their eyes met again, both cold as death.

"But first," Walerin whispered very softly, "first I will have the two of you, and that will be enough for now. Enjoy her tonight, Prince Tiernan, while you still can. Tomorrow I may decide to watch her die."

Tiernan bared his teeth in an uncontrollable snarl, but he didn't move. The fury was there, locked in every muscle, crushing in the force of his grip on Walerin's hand, but he didn't dare vent it. Walerin pulled out of his grasp and smiled again.

"Now I can rest," he commented in deep satisfaction to the night sky. Walerin walked back to the other side of the fire. He stretched out on the cool sand, apparently at his ease. "Pleasant dreams, princeling."

Tiernan closed his eyes and felt the tears he had denied earlier rising in the hot emptiness of his heart. He forced them back again. There was no time for despair, no time for rage; he had to think, and think quickly.

But he could not think.

Laurel shifted in his arms as if moving restlessly in her sleep, and she turned until she faced the prince. She was still utterly relaxed, but her eyes were wide open.

Tiernan, she mouthed silently. He stared at her in blank confusion. She rolled her eyes in frustration. Down. Lie down.

Tiernan threw a mistrustful glance across the fire at Walerin, but the cleric's eyes were closed. The young prince lowered himself until his cheek was resting on his crooked arm, and he was eye level with Laurel Magen. Incidentally enough, he realized, his face was blocked from Walerin's direct view.

"Good," she breathed, barely perceptible even this close. She shivered again, and he pulled her tighter against him. "Lords, it's cold."

"Did you hear?" Tiernan whispered. She studied his face for a moment, then nodded. "It's a perfect plan. Perfect."

"Of course it's perfect. Anyone who knows you stormed out of Rhakhaan alone and unprotected might have come up with it. You're not so foolish as that, Prince Tiernan. You must have known the risk you were taking."

It was Tiernan's shame and shock that he had not. He wasn't about to admit it to Laurel's bright, knowing eyes, though, and so he smiled his most brilliant smile. He had the sinking feeling that she wasn't really deceived.

"In any event, we have no choice," Laurel continued softly. "We must distract him and reach him."

"And once we reach him?" Tiernan asked with an innocent face.

She frowned at him. "I leave that to you. But we must take him by surprise, and we musn't fail. There won't be a second chance — not for any of us." For just an instant, her shell of control cracked, and she reached out to hold Tiernan's hand in both of hers. "I'm afraid for the boy."

"I'm afraid for you," Tiernan whispered, and in spite of the danger that loomed all around them he couldn't help leaning forward to touch her lips. They were cold, but they warmed quickly under his. "Can you provide the diversion?"

"Am I diverting you?" she asked. Their lips were still touching. Tiernan kissed her again and wished most passionately that Walerin and all of his evil were a thousand miles and a Pale away. He also wished, uncharitably but just as understandably, that Evan were the same distance — in the opposite direction, of course.

"Me? Oh, no. That's because I'm a man of enormous — "

"What?" she asked, all wide-eyed innocence. He felt a wild breathless urge to laugh.

"Concentration," he finished. "If you don't have anything constructive to offer, shut up and kiss me again."

"Oh, but I do," she told him, and all of the humor was suddenly gone. "You're not going to like it."

She was right, as always.

"Is he all right?" Brion asked Pelk in an undertone. They were all afraid to speak above a muted whisper. Pelk pulled his long hair back from his face in a distracted, uncharacteristically awkward motion and shrugged. He seemed to want to say something. His eyes lingered on the figure of his master and friend Vurkanan Tyes bending anxiously over the prone form of a young, blank-eyed woman.

"Who is she?" Brion pressed. He felt events speeding by, and it was a feeling he didn't much like. Pelk's lips thinned further.

"She looks like Laurel Magen," he said shortly, and in a tone that defied identification. As softly as he spoke, he still drew a stiffened stare from his master across the clearing.

"Do you doubt it?" Tyes asked him bluntly. The Loremaster's face was still marked with faint traces of strain and blood, but his gray eyes were as sharp and demanding as ever. Pelk looked down.

"She has her features," Pelk agreed very quietly. It wasn't a true answer, but Tyes forgot it for the moment and looked down again. His long fingers eased a blowing strand of curled blonde hair back from ivory skin. Except for the steady, faint rise and fall of her chest, the girl might have been dead.

"Who's Laurel Magen?" Brion asked. His frustration gave more volume to the question than he wanted, but when Tyes looked up it was with a sad, distracted smile.

"This is my daughter, Brion. Forgive me. It's only that — "

Brion looked at him for a few seconds in silence. There was some shared sense of grief and anguish that echoed in the air between them. Brion nodded.

"I know," he told the Loremaster, and he did. He took a deep breath against the sudden painful memory of his son's frightened face and turned to Pelk, who was the only one of the party who seemed to have any energy and direction at all. "What can I do?"

"We'll stay the night," Daphine said unexpectedly. She rose from where she had been kneeling near Laurel's still body and crossed to Iarsang. He raised his head at the touch of her hand on his shoulder, but his brown eyes were vague and dim with exhaustion. Daphine's gaze hesitated for a frozen moment on the bandages wrapping his left hand, and lingered at the sight of the blood that soaked it yet again. She tore herself free with an effort. "We all need rest. Even if we lose time."

"We know where he's going," Iarsang said faintly. That drew everyone's eyes, even the silent and watchful Changramai. "He's going to the ruined city of Quellburn."

"You can feel that?" Tyes asked. It was not quite doubt. Iarsang smiled faintly, but it never reached beyond his pale-rimmed lips.

"There is little else I can feel just now. He grows stronger." Iarsang raised his uninjured right hand and regarded the violent weakened trembling of his fingers with dispassionate calm. "And I grow weaker."

No one spoke. No one wanted to agree, but it was self-evident. Brion looked away at the others. Benevolent Lady Astrid was huddled against the bole of a huge ash tree not far away; she looked asleep, except for the constant trembling of her body and the ashen gray of her face. Her Changramai warrior stood over her like a guardian tree; only the slight rise and fall of his chest and the occasional blink of his eyes demonstrated he was alive. Daphine hovered over Iarsang like a mother cat over an injured cub, and Tyes was consumed with the plight of his daughter.

No one seemed in the least concerned with his son.

"Which way?" Brion asked, startling them and himself with the firm authority of his voice. Pelk looked sideways at him and raised his eyebrows in silent inquiry. "If you'll tell me which way to go, I'll start walking."

"Brion — " Pelk began reasonably. Brion closed his eyes and felt a sudden weird pressure building up behind his eyes, a pressure that frightened and confused him. He opened his eyes, but that didn't help; the sky was too pale, the sun too bright, the trees just slightly wrong. He put his hands to his face and blotted out the sight. "Brion, you need rest. We all do."

Pelk reached out to touch his shoulder. Before he even knew he was moving, Brion's hand slashed out and knocked him back. Pelk gave ground in astonishment. Brion slowly lowered his hands from his face and stared at him with burning dark eyes.

"Don't touch me. I want to find my son. You promised me, Pelk, you all promised — and I'm not waiting any longer. Either you help me or get the hell out of my way!"

Pelk made a cautious calming gesture, but Brion took another step toward him. Pelk cast a glance over his shoulder, but Tyes was simply sitting and watching. Not that his master could offer much in the way of support — he was exhausted, much more worn than Pelk could remember seeing him. Iarsang could barely lift his head. Daphine —

Daphine was moving very slowly in behind Brion, whose attention was focused on Pelk. To keep it, Pelk spread his hands wide.

"Brion, I haven't the faintest idea of what to tell you. We can't go on. Look at us. Iarsang can barely walk. My master needs rest if he's to take us anywhere at all. The girl — " Pelk's eyes shifted again to where Laurel Magen's body lay, oblivious to everything, "the girl needs help. Do any of us look in shape for a fight?"

Brion shouted something in a language that Pelk didn't even recognize. Pelk backed up again and shot a look at Ziv, but the Changramai folded his arms and looked blankly back. So much for help from that quarter. Ziv wasn't going to leave Astrid's side for an instant.

Which left Pelk in the most uncomfortable position of fighting someone he considered a friend.

Before he could think himself out of it, he sighed and charged forward. He slammed into Brion with stunning force (which didn't do his ribs any good) and landed with him in a heap on the cushioning earth.

Brion ended up on top, which was something Pelk hadn't planned. Brion pinned him down and stared at him like a stranger, then slowly lifted the ivory-and-threk hilted sword out of Pelk's harness.

From somewhere in the other onlookers there came a muffled gasp. Brion slid the sword out of the scabbard, watered steel catching the bright sunlight and throwing painfully bright reflections into Pelk's eyes.

Interesting, Pelk thought sourly. The sword of my dreams, and I'm going to end up on the wrong end of it.

"Let him go, Brion," Vurkanan Tyes said from where he still sat beside his daughter. He sounded tired, but there was unmistakable command in his voice. Brion seemed not to have heard. The edge lowered to touch Pelk's throat. "Brion — "

"I want to find my son," Brion whispered. His eyes were as mad as Kella's, suddenly, as he bent beneath a staggering weight of pain and anguish and fear. "Don't make me hurt you. I don't want to. I only want my son."

"I don't have him, my friend," Pelk answered shakily. Brion's eyes filled with tears. Pelk was stricken with the very real fear that Brion would kill him entirely by accident — the blade was that keen. No one dared moved, not even Daphine, but Brion finally put the blade aside and rolled away to lie weeping. Pelk raised himself on one arm, winced at a score of new bruises, and sheathed the blade with reverent care. He put it far out of Brion's reach — just in case.

"What's wrong with him?" Pelk asked Daphine as she sank down on Brion's other side. The Navigator shrugged.

"Brion has as much capacity for violence as any of us. He's shown extraordinary calm so far. I'm surprised it took this long." She raised her hand and trailed it over Brion's forehead gently. His eyes opened, briefly, then closed again. His breathing evened and quieted. "Were you tossed into an alien land and separated from those you love, I'd challenge you to act with as much restraint and intelligence, Pelk."

"Thank you," Pelk groaned, and flopped back down on his back. "I think I broke something."

"No, I don't think so," she answered, and got up to go back to Iarsang's side. The Navigator's eyes were closed, but he nodded at the touch of her hand on his cheek. Pelk winced at the look of fierce sorrow on her face, and threw an arm up to shade his eyes from the sunlight's glare.

One by one, they all fell asleep. The Changramai finally relaxed his vigilance enough to brace himself against a tree; even though he had never slept on watch in his life, he soon closed his eyes and fell into a dark, dreamless trance that trapped his body in a nightmarish stillness. The day waned. Twilight fell and tinted the sky pale purple and dark gold, and the birds fell silent, but still no one moved.

As the sun slipped under the hills in the west, Laurel Magen's simulacra opened her eyes.

She'd managed to keep the cleric from discovering her true nature by sly manipulation of Unlife, though the cleric had clearly detected something desperately wrong. Vurkanan Tyes, exhausted and drained by the encounter in Kelfour's Landing, had been easy to fool. Iarsang was no challenge. The Navigator Daphine had never even seen Laurel Magen, so only complete inner and outer stillness was necessary to convince her of harmlessness.

Only Pelk had been suspicious. Laurel Magen's lips parted in a wolfish grin, revealing razor-edged teeth. Pelk was the first, then. The others would sleep the bespelled sleep until she released them, one by one, into death.

The creature that had posed as Tyes' daughter levitated itself up on the wind, then stretched out as if flying level with the ground. It drifted ever so slowly to hang above Pelk's sleeping form, and the blue eyes (eyes that were turning to crimson) looked him over with critical, ravenous eyes. Too sharp of nose and chin to be more than mildly handsome, but young and vital — qualities she needed more than appreciated. The creature lowered herself down until she was touching Pelk's body. If he had opened his eyes, he would have been staring into hell.

He didn't open his eyes. Her devastating spells had already wound into his drugged sleep and begun wakening the responses she needed, so that suddenly she felt his skin flush with heat and his body tense under hers. His clothes were in the way, but she clawed them open with fingers that changed even as they moved into thin translucent claws. Beneath them, his body was dusted with a rush of golden hair, and his muscles were strong ridges under the skin. The demon hissed in amused satisfaction.

Pelk drew in a deep breath, but didn't wake. He was dreaming, now, and dreaming something utterly different than the red-eyed, clawed horror that hovered above him. His body temperature rose, and rose, until the demon could feel the sweet savor of it through her own skin. Almost ready, this one. A few more moments, and he would spill his energy into her along with his seed, and give her the strength to kill even the Loremaster.

It was all so easy. Her master would be pleased.

Brion woke as if a bucket of water had been dashed in his face. He'd been having a pleasantly vague dream, but menace had jabbed him as suddenly as a dagger. His eyes flashed open. For a moment he thought he was dreaming, because the thing that hung above Pelk was so fearsome and yet so beautiful that it could only have come out of nightmare. He stared at it in shock and amazement.

Then it turned its head, still absurdly adorned with Laurel Magen's curling golden hair, and looked at him with red eyes. Its mouth split in a grin like a shark's, and the teeth flashed silvery in the dim twilight. Brion scrambled backwards like a crab.

He screamed. No one else moved, not even the Changramai. The demon bent its head and nipped delicately at Pelk's throat. A thin bead of blood formed and ran down the side of his neck. Brion swore and ran to shake Ziv violently by the shoulder. The Changramai slid down to a sitting position. His head flopped helplessly forward.

"Tyes! Tyes, help!" Brion yelled, but without hope; he'd already guessed that the sleep was unnatural and had captured even the Loremaster. The creature was watching him, but it wasn't leaving Pelk. As he darted around to shake Iarsang and Daphine, it drew razor-edged claws down Pelk's ribs in a parody of a lover's caress. Pelk's back arched, and his breath caught. Brion swore and slapped Daphine across the face.

Her head lolled helplessly. He hit her again, and was rewarded with a faint fluttering of her eyelids. As much as he hated to, Brion slapped her for a third time, and then chafed her wrists until her eyes were open.

"What?" she whispered. Awake, but not really aware. Brion cursed in despair and spun away from her.

Pelk's sword was lying four feet away, about a foot away from where Pelk lay victim to the demon. Brion stared at it for a moment, sense arguing with need, then threw himself toward it. As his hand touched the hilt, the creature's head whipped around to stare at him, and one taloned hand grabbed the sheathed part of the blade. Brion yanked. It was like pulling at a stone.

Daphine was crawling to her feet, dazed but slowly recovering. Tyes was making subtle movements as the sleep lost its hold, but he wouldn't be awake in time to offer any help. Brion realized, quite clearly, that Pelk's life was resting in his incapable, uneducated hands — and in the sword.

Brion yanked as hard as his muscles would allow. The creature gave a hiss of anger as the steel slid out of the scabbard. She floated back from Pelk and stood up to face this new threat — not that he seemed much of a threat, from the uncertain way he held the sword. A child could have taken it from him. The demon laughed — a sound that made everyone, even those still sleeping, flinch — and struck out for his head with talons that dripped with dark poison.

Brion was too inexperienced to parry, but he ducked. The talons snagged a few loose strands of hair, but nothing else. He held the sword out at a shaky angle and tried to think about everything he'd seen Pelk do. It was all too complicated to learn in seconds. He realized in outright despair that there was no chance of him killing this creature, or even of protecting himself.

Daphine's hand fell on his shoulder. Brion glanced frantically back and found her standing there with alert, cold eyes. She held out her right hand in imperious demand. Brion gladly — if somewhat clumsily — surrendered the sword to her and backed out of the confrontation.

"Brion, stay away. She can still enchant you if she focuses her power on you instead of Pelk — she'll have to change forms to influence me." Daphine lifted the heavy blade as if it were nothing more than the Navigator's wand she had stuck haphazardly in her belt. Her lips thinned in angry contempt as she stared at the demon with luminous green eyes. "Come on, bitch. Or don't you have the stomach for steel?"

The demon shrieked and swung at her. Daphine countered with an effortlessly graceful sweep of Pelk's silver blade; it skidded along the creature's armored hand with a screeching protest. The demon drew back for another blow, but Daphine followed and allowed it no time to recover. Her arm never faltered as it struck with precise, controlled motions at the demon's head, neck, and body. She connected once, but the only result was a thin bloodless gash that sealed almost immediately. The demon hissed in something that might have been amusement and launched a slashing assault that Daphine was barely able to parry.

Under the cover of the assault, the demon began to alter its form again, from the seductively voluptuous female body it had chosen for its assault on Pelk to a more muscular, compact form. As the battle passed by Brion again, he recalled Daphine's words with a touch of fear.

The demon was, indeed, changing sexes. If becoming male would allow it to wield power over Daphine, it was already mostly there. Brion began looking desperately around for a weapon and ran across to the limp form of the Changramai warrior. Ziv was beginning to grope his way back to consciousness, but it wouldn't be soon enough to help anyone. Brion yanked his new sword free and turned back to look at the battle.

It was difficult to see the demon move and Daphine counter; they both moved quicker than anyone he'd ever seen, even Gerdar the Duelist, and for a minute he thought that Daphine was winning. She'd scored another hit, and this one ripped open the demon's outstretched arm with a sound like tearing cloth. The demon merely grinned with inward-curving razor teeth. Daphine took a step backward, and for the first time Brion realized that her face was pale and strained, and her hair damp and sticking in tendrils to her skin. She was tiring. The demon wasn't.

The demon completed its change to male form, and it was clearly having a toll on the Iylari woman; she hesitated in her parries, drawn in spite of herself by the creature's power, and Brion knew with a sinking feeling of doom that he could not cross the distance in time.

Daphine's attack went wide, and she tried to bring the sword back in line. Her muscles responded with nightmarish slowness as the creature's hideous influence descended on her. If only one of the others would wake, if only Tyes could summon up a spell —

But even though he was awake, he couldn't produce a spell in his weakened condition. Brion, crossing the clearing at a run, cried a desperate warning, but already the demon was bending over her. Talons closed over her skin, and all of her strength bled out of her in a rush. Daphine fell forward, trapped against the demon's body in a horribly parody of a lover's embrace. Her face was turned toward Brion as he crossed the distance, and he took in every aching detail: her face, blanched to the silver-white of moonlight; her eyes, huge and dark with pupil; her body slowly collapsing against her enemy's.

"No!" Iarsang screamed, and dragged himself to his knees. Too late. Even as he flung out his hands, even as he touched her desperate, reaching fingers, the demon bit down. Blood exploded in a dark sheet down her pale arms. Brion, horrified, watched the life drain out of Daphine's wide, anguished eyes.

Brion skidded to a halt and cut blindly at the demon. Ziv's sword bit deep into the arcane flesh and grated against some bonelike structure within, but the creature only dropped Daphine's bloody body and turned with an angry hiss. Brion slashed again without much skill but with a great deal of determination, and the demon gave ground. Brion followed, driven beyond fear, and when the demon raised a taloned hand to strike at him, he sliced wildly at it.

The watered steel encountered only a little resistance. When it swung past, five needle-like talons fell like a rain behind it. Brion stumbled under the force of his swing, and quickly drew his sword back into line to counter the attack that was sure to come.

He blinked in surprise several times, only to find that the demon had drawn away. The stubs of talons on the creature's right hand were bleeding a profuse stream of black. The demon retreated in sudden pain, and as it did, Brion took two steps forward and cut the remaining talons. He stepped back from the sudden jet of black blood that erupted, and the demon fell to its knees. It was struggling to change again, but it obviously lacked the strength; its flesh expanded and deflated like a sack.

Lifted its crimson eyes to the sky, the demon howled in despair and anger.

"The neck," Tyes rasped. The Loremaster got shakily to his feet, but there was no mistaking the certainty in his voice. Brion nodded, swung the sword back to the limit and cut with all his strength.

As the demon's head separated from its shoulders, the wailing stopped. So did the demon's existence. The two separated halves never reached the earth; they dissolved into greasy brown smoke and flakes of ash like the remnants of a fatal dream. The stench was overwhelming. Brion reeled backwards, coughing and heaving, and steadied himself with one hand on the tree.

"Daphine?" he asked hoarsely. No one answered him. Brion dropped the sword and returned to where she lay. The others were moving, but he reached her first — he and Iarsang.

Iarsang cradled her head on his knees. His right hand curled protectively over her neck. He was blank-eyed, hardly even aware, but as Brion reached out to touch the woman's face Iarsang lifted his head and hissed like a snake. His face was as pale and hard as exposed bone.

"My friend," Tyes whispered from behind Brion, and drew in a breath. Brion stared at Daphine, at her open, sightless eyes, and felt a scream welling up from the darkness of his heart.

"Astrid," he blurted instead, groping desperately for control. "Can Astrid help her?"

"No one can help her now," Tyes whispered. "Iarsang, I am sorry. So very sorry."

Iarsang moved his right hand to close Daphine's eyes, revealing the ruin of her ivory throat. Brion felt a surge of rage and loss so strong that it made him ill, but Iarsang seemed oblivious. The Navigator looked up at Tyes with blank eyes. He opened his lips to speak, but Iarsang slowly pulled himself back from whatever brink he stood upon.

"Not your fault," Iarsang whispered. It cost him a great deal.

Tyes shut his eyes for a moment, pain spasming across his face, and then bowed his head.

"I dragged her here. I should have sent her away," Iarsang moaned. "Vurkanan, I did love her, I did — "

"I know," Tyes whispered miserably. "Pelk knew. I should have listened to him. I should have known it wasn't Laurel, that it was a trap — "

"Enough!" Iarsang took a deep breath. Tyes looked up. "Enough. We both know whose fault it is. He has made me part of his evil. Do you understand? My compass made this possible. I will not rest until he is dead."

"I understand," Tyes carefully reached out to touch Daphine's warm hand. The skin would cool soon, but for now there was at least the illusion of life. He felt tears sting bitterly, but Iarsang's eyes stayed feverishly dry. There was a new feeling about him — not strength, because the loss of his Compass had slowly leached that away, but a terrible kind of obsession.

Lady Astrid, roused at last from the doomed sleep, flung herself breathlessly down next to Daphine's body and murmured half-heard invocations and spells. No one could find the strength to tell her it was useless: Astrid would not have listened. Iarsang stroked Daphine's hair with his one shaking hand. Tyes knelt beside him. After Astrid expended all of her spells in a futile, doomed attempt, the two Iylari wrapped the fallen Navigator in her cloak and laid her peacefully in the center of the clearing. The others wept or were grimly silent, according to their natures; Pelk was ashen as he finally recovered enough to get to his feet and realized the tragedy. Brion stood near him, answering his frantic questions in a low, unsteady voice. They fell silent as Tyes backed away from Daphine's body to stand with Iarsang.

The silence was terrible and unbearably long. Then Iarsang turned and walked away. Tyes stared after, gray eyes stricken and disbelieving.

"Iarsang?" the Loremaster asked.

When the Navigator paused with his outstretched hand braced against the bole of a tree. Iarsang didn't look back.

"I can't," he whispered, and his head fell forward to rest on the fevered skin of his arm. "Lords Above, no. It must not be so, not like this."

Tyes looked at his aide, and Pelk returned a sorrowful stare. That was all the communication they had, or needed. Pelk went to the Navigator's side.

Iarsang did not appear to even notice his presence.

"My friend, do you wish to take her to Nexus?" Tyes asked gently.

Iarsang's muscles tensed, then relaxed. "No," he finally whispered. "I would have to stay there, and then he would go free. No. I am all the family she had. Do — what you must."

Tyes looked at the still, lonely form of his friends, one living, one dead, and raised his hand.

"Walk the stars in peace, Daphine of Cypharia," he whispered, and a blinding flash of Essence ignited her body.

Iarsang, still facing away, cried aloud in pure agony and sank blindly to his knees. Pelk caught him and eased him down, but it was doubtful the Navigator even knew of his help. The tall Iylari sat there in trembling, agonized silence until the flames had consumed his love, and then got slowly to his feet.

"Do we rest?" Pelk finally asked, because no one seemed to want to break the silence.

Iarsang slowly swiveled to look at him. "We have rested enough," the Navigator said in a voice as cold and unyielding as steel. It went strangely with the tears in his eyes. "No more delays. You will find your son, Brion. I will find my enemy. One will live, one will die."

They gathered up their belongings in silence while Tyes searched for the strength to transport them.

They had agreed that, first and foremost, it would be Laurel's task to distract Walerin. Tiernan was plainly the only choice to overpower the man — Laurel's sorcery could not be counted on to disarm him, and the slightest hesitation would mean failure and their deaths. They'd talked about Evan, but neither Tiernan nor Laurel could countenance using the boy as a distraction. He seemed invulnerable to Walerin's powers, but —

Tiernan narrowed his eyes against the rising sun and concentrated on making his way through the sand. Walerin was cheating, he thought with grim, exhausted anger. The little weasel was using his powers to float just a fraction above the sand. It made for easier travel — but he wouldn't expend the power on his prisoners, so he wasted at least as much energy on impatience as he would have on slogging through the sand with them.

Tiernan was not a man who hated easily, but at this moment, he hated Walerin with every fiber of his being. He wished his father had caught and hung the little wretch after the stable fire. He wished Walerin had broken his feeble little neck, or that one of the maddened horses had stomped him, or — anything. If ever a little bastard deserved to die, this one did.

What practical use was there in being a prince of one of the mightiest kingdoms on Kulthea when he could only look at Evan's fear and Laurel's exhaustion and be heartsick?

"Faster," Walerin snapped. He was standing at the top of a monster of a hill. Tiernan glared up at him — there were, of course, no traces of his tracks going up the slope — and began doggedly toiling up toward him. Evan wasn't complaining, but his legs couldn't possibly keep Tiernan's pace, and even Tiernan couldn't keep the pace of their captor. Tiernan slowed.

"If you lag any more, prince, your pretty lady's head will roll — quite literally, I assure you. Carry the brat if you must have him." Walerin was bluffing — at least about the boy — but Tiernan surely didn't know it. The prince stooped without comment and picked the boy up. Laurel stumbled against him, and he steadied her.

"Now. It must be now, after we get to the top of the hill," she said urgently. Tiernan lifted Evan up atop his shoulders. The boy leaned over as if searching for a grip. What a clumsy bunch of conspirators, Tiernan thought in despair.

"What are you doing?" Evan asked urgently. Tiernan shook his head. "Please be careful, Tiernan. Please."

Tiernan nodded and toiled up the hill with his double burden. Walerin waited at the top, preening like a dusty peacock, arrogant and righteous and oh, so very dangerous. Tiernan looked down at his own feet again and tried not to think about the consequences, about his nonexistent chances for life, about Laurel's death. The top of the hill came far too quickly.

"Are you testing me?" Walerin asked him. The little weasel wasn't standing close enough. Tiernan lowered Evan to the sand again and tried to shoo him away, but the boy stayed fast beside him. There was a kind of sharp menace in the cleric's brown, malicious eyes, a hunger that Tiernan instinctively sensed wouldn't be satisfied with mere humiliation. He wanted blood today. Tiernan had a sinking suspicion whose it would be.

Even as he formed the thought, Walerin extended his hand to point at Laurel. She paused and looked at him with wide blue eyes, lank blond hair clinging to her damp face. She had never looked younger, nor more helpless. Tiernan felt a wrench of agony.

Walerin closed his hand. For a heart-stopping moment, the prince thought that the bastard had actually killed her, had carried out his horrible threat — but then, even as Laurel fell limply to the sand, he saw that the band was only constricting her breathing. It was surely torturous.

It wasn't yet fatal.

Tiernan's muscles tensed to spring. They were out of time. Even as he did so, Evan grabbed for his hand and pointed.

A man appeared coming up the dune just behind the cleric. Though Tiernan had never seen him — outside of his Navigator's costume — he knew instinctively who the dark-haired, amethyst-eyed young man was. Evan's panicked grip told him that.

"Andraax," Tiernan breathed. Walerin turned, startled, and gaped at the young man.

Andraax didn't do anything threatening, only stood there and looked. Walerin unconsciously relaxed his hand, and Laurel drew in a huge, gasping breath. Even Tiernan didn't look.

"Evan, this has gone on long enough," Andraax said, in the tone of a parent who's been about as patient as conscience will allow. He held out his hand to the boy, ignoring Walerin as he ignored everyone else. Evan clung tight to Tiernan.

"Who are you?" Walerin blurted. He might have been the wind speaking to the sand, for all the response he got. "Get away, man. You've no business here."

Andraax came a step closer. Walerin, abandoning his indecisive stance halfway between his prisoners and the stranger, wheeled around to stand firmly in his way. The cleric held out a threatening hand.

"Stop right there," Walerin warned him grimly. "Stop or I'll send your soul shrieking into the Pales!"

The threat got Andraax's attention. The former Loremaster fixed his eyes on the little brown-robed man and gave him a brief scowl. In no way did he seem cowed by the threat. He kept coming, and Walerin backed up.

"Are you mad?" Walerin howled, and lunged forward. A black nimbus formed around his hand, leaping hungrily for Andraax's exposed chest.

It never reached him. Andraax waved idly and dark force, hand, and cleric were all swept aside like bothersome motes of dust. Even as the cleric spat dirt and tried to struggle back to his feet, Andraax reached Tiernan's side and reached out for Evan's hand. Evan ducked behind Tiernan's bulk; the prince, white-faced but radiating determination, stayed still and faced Andraax firmly.

"Tiernan, Prince of Rhakhaan," Andraax said very softly, "you've played your part well. Now give me the boy."

"No," Tiernan said. Evan's hand tightened on his. "You're scaring him. What do you want?"

"I want the boy. I'm taking him to safety. Would you rather I left him out here to suffer and die with you?"

"Are we going to suffer and die?" Tiernan asked.

Andraax cocked his head to the side and looked at him from eyes so clear and hard they could have been carved from gems. "Your chances range from certain death to probable extermination. Certain death awaits if you do not remove yourself from my path and surrender the boy." Seeing that Tiernan wasn't going to be frightened out of his position, Andraax sighed and spread his six-fingered hands. "Evan, you know I am short of temper. Save your friend's life. Come with me."

"You didn't kill me before," Tiernan said softly. "That was you, wasn't it? The dragon?"

Andraax shrugged. "It wasn't convenient. You might have stuck in my throat, and if I'd eaten you it would have been a massive nuisance trying to change back to human form. I assure you, it wasn't goodwill. At the present time I don't have any." His eyes widened with alarming suddenness. "Evan! Give me your hand!"

The mental blast of power that accompanied the words gave Tiernan a ringing headache and sent him reeling. Evan stood there exposed and trembling; after a long, scared moment, he extended his hand toward Andraax.

"No!" Laurel gasped, and tried to lunge forward.

Andraax stopped her with a bare flick of his free fingers as his right hand took the boy's. "No, please, don't take him. Tiernan — "

Tiernan, using that rare good sense that occasionally resulted from his illustrious parentage, grabbed her by the shoulders and held her tightly out of the way as Andraax and Evan shot away over the sand at startling, unnerving speeds. The boy was arguing. Tiernan felt a sudden flash of amusement: Andraax didn't know what he'd let himself in for. Then he realized with a cold wrench that he and Laurel were alone, and the evil cleric Walerin was climbing to his feet.

Walerin was not in a good mood.

"When I tell you jump, you jump," Tiernan whispered in his lady's ear. She was trembling under the grip of his hands.

"Where?" she asked. He rolled his eyes.

"Anywhere but forward or back." Walerin was glaring at them with red murder in his eyes. In a second he would have his hands free, and Tiernan had no doubt what would happen then. "Jump!"

He accompanied the order with a shove that sent Laurel in a lunging sprawl to the right. Walerin's eyes inevitably followed the movement. Tiernan's long legs uncoiled like springs, and he was suddenly airborne and rushing down on Walerin's surprised, foolish face.

The cleric, grinning, closed his fist. Tiernan tumbled out of control and slammed into the Walerin, knocking the breath out of him; that was not much of a triumph, since Tiernan himself couldn't think of anything except the cold slick metal that was slicing through the skin of his neck and moving dangerously close to his pounding veins. It was pure instinct and desperation that made the prince grab Walerin's fist in his long fingers and wrench it open; he used a tad too much force in the process, and Walerin screamed as two of his fingers broke. The circlet around Tiernan's neck eased again. Walerin tried to clench his fist, but with his fingers pointing in crazily unhelpful directions he couldn't manage it. Still, Tiernan felt a touch of pressure around his neck.

The prince cold-bloodedly broke the remaining fingers. He took a shameful amount of pleasure in it, but remembered in time Laurel's danger as Walerin stopped flailing at him with his other hand and tried to clench it.

Five more crisp snapping sounds, and several agonized screams. Walerin was lying in a weeping, helpless heap on the sand. Tiernan stood and looked down on him with an absolute absence of expression; if there was any regret in him, it didn't show. His family and friends would have been astonished at the change in him.

Tiernan was more than a little astonished himself.

It was only as his whole body wavered that he became aware of the blood running down from his neck, and the cold blanket of shock that was numbing him. He turned on half-felt legs and walked over to where Laurel was scrambling to her feet in a shower of dust and curses. She froze on seeing him, and her blue eyes went wide and terrified.

"I'm all right," Tiernan tried to say, but nothing intelligible came out. His voice was a hoarse, aching croak. Laurel slowed his fall by throwing herself against him, but he still ended up on his knees with his head leaning on her shoulder.

"Oh, no, Tiernan, no! Lords of Orhan, let him be all right — " she was whispering in a frantic, continuous mumble as she moved his blood-matted hair away from his neck and saw the crimson streams still coming from under the necklet. "Not the veins, thank you powers and Lords — "

"I'm tired," Tiernan said distantly. At least that was what he tried to say. What actually came out sounded like the grunt of a mating hog. Laurel hardly noticed. She ripped at her gown and wiped at the blood with trembling fingers. Tiernan tried harder for intelligibility. "Laurel, careful; he isn't dead — "

Whether she understood any of that mumble or not, she looked over his shoulder to where he'd left Walerin crying and huddling over his ruined hands. Her eyes widened again, and she cursed with words Tiernan truly didn't know she knew, or could use with any fluency. He tried to tell her how surprised he was, but nothing came out; in the next instant he felt something enter his back with the cold caressing touch of steel.

Funny, it didn't hurt so much. It felt damned uncomfortable, especially since the steel didn't go away; Tiernan drew in a deep gasping breath and slumped forward. There was a feeling of cold spreading from the wound; it raced through his body and entered his head with capering glee.

His face felt odd, even by his own shock-altered senses. Laurel had wriggled out from under him, and as he rolled himself on his side he could see her standing there facing Walerin with an expression so fearsome even her illustrious father must have quailed before it. It all meant something, Tiernan felt certain. He couldn't quite bring himself to think what.

Laurel brought her hands up, and a glittering white shield formed between her and Walerin. The cleric looked in worse shape than Tiernan; his mouth was stretched in a white death's-head grin, and his hands were pitiful caricatures. In spite of that, there was venom and fire in his eyes, and strength.

The black force that he threw at Laurel shattered her shield with a sound like breaking hearts. She staggered backwards; the cleric approached her, chanting something that could be heard and yet not understood. It wasn't just Tiernan's shock. It was a spell, and a mighty one; Laurel tried to interrupt it, but without success. She backed away.

The insanely disarranged claws of Walerin's hands pointed at her, and he shrieked. Laurel staggered, but didn't fall. Walerin sank in on himself like a ruptured bladder, overcome with weakness, and Laurel jumped for him in a flash.

She couldn't kill him, Tiernan thought distantly. She didn't have the slightest idea how to do it. The prince, in spite of his distance and weakness, dragged himself to his hands and knees and began to weave unsteadily toward her and the fallen cleric.

Laurel finished rooting frantically in the man's clothing and came up with a dagger. Tiernan was still three or four feet away when she raised it in trembling hands and brought it down. She didn't falter, and she did not miss.

It was a far cleaner death than the man deserved.

The collars vanished from both of their necks, a weight that had been forgotten until it was gone. Tiernan abandoned his long effort and flopped face down in the sand. Laurel sat there for a frozen moment with the bloody dagger clenched in white-fingered hands, and then she flung it away and crawled over to Tiernan.

"Are you all right?" she whispered as she carefully touched his shoulder. He turned his head just enough to breathe and be understood.

"There's a knife in my back."

Laurel frowned and ran her hand lightly over his tattered, stained leather jerkin. There were no holes, no signs of blood, and most certainly no knives.

"There isn't," she told him with absolute confidence. He tried to laugh, but it hurt too much.

"You must be blind. I can feel it — " His arm moved laboriously to indicate the middle of his back. "Here. Gods, Laurel, this is no time for jokes."

"I'm not making one," she said unsteadily. "There's nothing there."

But she was thinking about what she knew of curses, and already she realized that the blade wasn't physical. The fact that she could not see it, or touch it, made it far more magical than she could deal with.

Magical blades didn't wound the flesh. They were a symbolic association to the curse itself, a physical manifestation of the pain caused by the working of the spell. Laurel had no idea what spell it was that Tiernan had fallen victim to —

And she wasn't about to confess that she herself had felt something cold pierce her from front to back, just as if she had been transfixed by a sword or spear. Instead, she rolled Tiernan over on his back and smoothed his long hair away from his face.

It was not Tiernan's face. Well — it was, and yet it wasn't — it was Tiernan's face if Tiernan had been a god, gifted with perfection that burned and hurt as much as pleased. Laurel froze with her gaze riveted to that face. There had never been any feeling like the one that ripped through her now. It stripped away every defense she'd ever erected, every lie she'd ever told herself. That face was everything she'd ever wanted in this life or any other, every joy she'd denied herself, every pleasure she'd wished for in the darkness. It was hers. It had to be hers. The alternative was — madness.

She stretched herself out full length on top of Tiernan's body and kissed those delicious lips, making sounds of terrible hunger and need, whimpering like a child. Tiernan's arms went around her, after a moment of utter surprise, and he kissed her in return. It wasn't enough. Laurel opened her mouth and welcomed the intrusion of his tongue; when it didn't come fast enough, she let her own wander in this new, unexplored territory and provoked a surge of surprise that hit him even through his shock.

"Laurel?" Tiernan asked breathless, utterly amazed, and held her back in spite of her determined struggles. "Laurel, are you — "

She wrenched her hands free and slipped them between her body and his own, tearing at the fabric of his shirt until she could slide her fingers along the smooth skin and hard ridges of muscle of his chest — then she lifted her hips and began tugging at the ties that held his breeches closed. Tiernan gasped and struggled with her, but she kissed him again, and his struggles became — distracted. She slipped her hands through the opening and began to deftly explore. Her entire body was afire.

"Laurel!" Tiernan shouted, and yanked her hands away. He rolled her over so that his weight pinned her on the sand and held her there with her hands stretched above her head. "Laurel, for Orhan's sake, what are you doing?"

"I must have you," she panted, and struggled to slip her hands out of his sweating grasp. "Have you or die. Have you or — "

At any other time, such a declaration would have been not just welcomed but actively encouraged — but Tiernan knew her better, and the sudden crazed strength in her made him afraid. The knife, he thought with sudden clarity. The knife in his back — that no longer hurt.

Tiernan, on a sudden surge of inspiration, covered Laurel's eyes with his hand and held her still until she stopped struggling. She lay there limp and breathing too fast, but the nervous trembles had subsided. He grunted softly and felt the stab of aches and pains he hadn't had time — or inclination — to feel before.

"This isn't you, Laurel," he whispered to her. "You'd never do this, not like this. Not with a man you killed lying two feet away and both of us bloody and exhausted. What is it? What's happening to you?"

"Your face," she said distantly. "I saw your face, and — I don't know. I just knew I had to have you. That I'd kill to have you."

Kill? A chilling thought. Was that why she'd killed Walerin, or had it been more mundane concerns? Tiernan pushed the thought aside, ignoring the aggrieved complaints of his body that wanted only too much to please Laurel's, and ignoring too the fear that gnawed at him. Was it a spell on Laurel or on him?

Dear Lords, would every woman he met feel this way? It was an appalling prospect, as humorous as it was terrible. No, he amended as Laurel began to weep silently under the mask of his hand. Not humorous at all, not when it stripped the will from those he loved.

"Shh," he begged her. "Keep your eyes closed, Laurel. Can you do that? Only for a moment."

She nodded convulsively, as revolted by her loss of control as he was afraid of it. Tiernan levered himself quickly off of her and used Walerin's bloody dagger to cut part of the dead cleric's robe away. It was none too clean (neither, he had to admit, was anything else on his body), but when wrapped around his head and secured with Walerin's rope belt, it was an adequate mask.

Hot as the demons, though.

Laurel, unable to resist, had opened her eyes, but fortunately all she saw was his back and the muffling swath of mask. She smiled slightly and dabbed at the tears still shining on her face.

"Handsome," she said. Her voice was almost steady. "I know what he's done to you, Tiernan. There's a spell — far above my abilities — called Beauty of Arraer. It curses the recipient to be the most desirable person in the world."

"Desirable enough to make women melt at my feet?" he asked in a tone of calculated interest. She didn't take the bait, only nodded.

"And men, if they were already inclined so, of course."

"Wonderful." Tiernan looked at his lady through the tiny gap he'd left in wrapping the mask and was suddenly glad the fabric hid his concern. She was too quiet, too acquiescent. He would have been more than happy to have her slap him again, if only to prove that she was still Laurel.

She smiled uncertainly at him when he held his hand out to her. Damn you, Tiernan thought fiercely at the corpse of the cleric as they went past it. Damn you, damn you, damn you.

The corpse stared at the sun with glazing brown eyes and seemed supremely indifferent. There was even a hint of a smile on his face.

Evan was reminded of the time when he'd gotten his hand caught in a jar full of coins, and couldn't get it free. That was how strong Andraax's grip was; he might as well have been pulling at the root of a tree for all the good it did. Andraax didn't even notice.

"Wait!" Evan shouted as his friends dwindled into a tiny dot in the distance behind them. The wind tore the words out of his mouth and lost them, but Andraax looked down at him with raised eyebrows.

"Why?" the Loremaster asked, mildly surprised.

Evan yanked at his grip again, without success. "You can't just leave them there! He'll kill them, I know he will, don't you understand that? It's up to us to help them!"

Andraax listened to him intently, head cocked to one side and lavender eyes narrowed. Even after the boy finished speaking, he remained that way, looking off into the distance with sober, absurd concentration.

"Andraax!" Evan yelled, and tugged violently at him. The mad Loremaster jerked as if catching himself falling and looked down at the boy again. "What?"

"Aren't you going to help them?" the boy demanded.

Andraax blinked. "Who?" he asked innocently.

It just wasn't a profitable conversation. Evan abandoned it and pulled violently at Andraax's restraining grip; his fingers slid just slightly. Encouraged by this sign of progress, Evan threw himself into the struggle with all of his energy.

He and Andraax hurtled abruptly out of the sky and tumbled end over end through the sand. Evan slid to a halt and coughed out some dust, then sat up and looked around. They had stopped at the crest of a hill; below there was some kind of oasis, green grass and scraggly trees kneeling around a shallow pond.

Andraax lunged to his feet, scattering sand in all directions like a dust devil with no sense of purpose. He had both hands clenched around his head as if it was going to come off. By this time, Evan was prepared to believe that — and now he turned to glare at the boy in childish resentment.

"Did you have to do that?" he demanded, and abruptly sat down again. "Oh, my head. You're a menace, boy, a genuine menace."

"I'm sorry," Evan apologized insincerely. "What happened?"

"You interfered in my control of the Essence!" Andraax abruptly stopped and stared at him with wide purple eyes. He kept holding his head, but the pain was apparently forgotten. "You interfered in my control of the Essence. You shouldn't be able to do that, boy. How did you do it?"

"I don't know," Evan answered truthfully, and shook sand out of his hair. "I just wanted you to stop, so I pulled — "

"You pulled on a great deal more than my hand. I was about to call you a fool — but perhaps I'm the fool." Andraax slowly began massaging his temples, wincing with pain. "You were brought here by a flow Storm. It's my experience that things caught up in flow Storms are usually charged with Essence already, so perhaps your arrival here was not so accidental as I thought. Perhaps you already control the Essence."

"I never even heard of Essence before I came here, and I'll be just as glad never to near of it again," Evan sighed morosely, and drew his knees up to his chest. "Tiernan and Laurel are more important. We have to go back and help them!"

"More important? You obviously don't realize what you've done, my friend. The last person to wrest control from me was Kirin Tethan, and that was so long ago my mind can barely recall it. And he did it by a trick!" Andraax shook his head experimentally and sighed. "The Thalan have the ability, of course, but they couldn't have done it so suddenly, or so completely. And not for long."

"Thalan?" Evan frowned. "You talked about Thalan before, when you were — "

"Less than myself?" Andraax supplied dryly. "It isn't quite precise to say that I'm mad. I'm actually quite sane most of the time, except when the Thalan are fighting for control of my mind. They do that periodically. They seem to have settled on me as being the most attractive host for their kind. It's most unfortunate."

"But what are they?"

"They don't have bodies, Evan, at least not now. They take whatever form comes to hand — a rock, a tree, an animal, a man. It only requires time and an unwary subject."

"Then how did they get you?"

A good question, Andraax thought; he frowned and searched through his memory. There were long blank spaces now, most annoying. "I'm not sure," he said slowly. "It must have been when I was resting. Or when I was truly mad."

"Were you really mad?" Evan wanted to know, dark eyes doubtful and steady. Andraax smiled slightly.

"Most certainly. Some say I still am — but not just at this moment." Andraax dug in his robes and brought out a smooth brown rock about the size of his palm. He tossed it carelessly in the air, then tossed it to Evan. "What do you think?"

"It think it's a rock," Evan said slowly, and tossed it back.

Andraax flipped it experimentally in his hand and nodded. "This particular rock holds a Thalan, my boy. It's dormant just now, resting from our last little confrontation, but it's most certainly there, and dangerous. I'm sane enough until it wakes; then I'm forced to devote myself to the struggle again. I'll try to get you to your father before that happens."

"Why don't you just throw it away, like the other one?" Evan asked, frowning.

Andraax looked at the stone and sighed. "I did. This is the same Thalan. It's most persistent. I keep the rock because at least I know where the Thalan is. I might truly lose my mind if I didn't know." Andraax shoved the stone back in his robes and stretched awkwardly. "Your friends have survived their encounter with evil, it seems; they're on their way to us. I fail to see why we should return if they're already heading this way, so perhaps we shall rest a while."

His eyes were closing even as he spoke, and in a few seconds he was fast asleep, sprawled like a child on the warm sand and looking as young and innocent as Evan.

Evan crawled carefully over and reached into his robes, recovering the brown rock. He retreated to hold it curiously up to the light.

"If you're really driving him crazy, then I'll hold onto you. Just in case." He shoved the stone into his pocket.

When he slept, lulled by the warmth and the peace, the sand seemed to whisper just under the edge of his hearing.

، CHAPTER FIVE ،

When Kella opened her eyes again, she was lying in a wide ruined stone hall. There were patches of clear sky showing overhead, and the stars shone brightly. She lay on a soft pallet of furs next to a low-burning fire, and her clothes were off. The hall was very quiet except for the furtive rustling of some night-foraging creature.

Jadel was lying next to her, his pale skin nearly a match for hers, his hand still curled over her hip. Sleeping, he looked absurdly young. His dark hair covered his pointed ears and half of his face. Kella felt an almost irresistible impulse to move the hair back, to gaze at his face without that dark veil, but she didn't do it. She'd already learned not to touch Jadel without his permission.

There was a livid bruise on her arm where he'd caught her in a grip too strong to be human. It still ached, especially the way she was lying on it. She shifted uncomfortably. Jadel's eyes snapped open.

It wasn't like watching any other man wake. Jadel was asleep — *flick* — he was awake. Like a machine, which this benighted planet could not imagine but Kella could. His eyes regarded her with complete knowledge and composure, and his hand caressed her hip in a smooth slide of skin on skin.

"Where are we?" she asked him. His fingers traced the curve of her hip. She felt them slip lower, tracing the line of her bones, and caught her breath. His eyes were unmoved, but faintly amused.

"A waystation, of sorts. Quellburn is a long jump, especially since this —" He held up his left wrist, which held the dark scintillating shape of Iarsang's Compass. " — resists my control to some extent. Journeys are tiring. I thought we deserved rest."

"I don't remember stopping," she protested. Her heart had begun pounding painfully fast. Jadel peeled back their top covering of furs and leaned sinuously over her as she pressed herself back into the pallet. "What happened? We were in Kelfour's Landing — "

"And by now the unfortunate Loremaster and his party — including your unworthy husband — has met a most pleasant death." Jadel smiled and touched the smooth inner stretch of her thigh. She gasped. He liked to hear her gasp, a pleasure alloyed by equal components of lust and cruelty, and just a touch of the heady flavor of affection. He had never felt affection before. It was interesting, in a clinical sort of way.

"How — " she whispered. He bent over and touched her lips with his, silencing her for a delirious moment, and then let her finish her question. "How did they die?"

"A Procreator," he said in quiet, almost childish delight. "A demon, one that drains the life and energy from its victims in a most — intimate — way. Not even Loremasters are immune to its power, if caught sleeping — and they will be. As I said, a most pleasant death, don't you think? I was merciful. It would have been much more entertaining to kill them slowly, but I am not stupid enough to sacrifice efficiency for aesthetics."

His mouth was just as compelling when not speaking, as it travelled down her neck and lingered on the sharp raised points of her collarbone. Kella ached to touch him, and dared not. She knew from the light in his face that an attempt would be ruthlessly stopped. This was Jadel's pleasure, and he was avid in its pursuit.

She gasped again as his mouth touched the circle of her breast. She forgot herself, for a few seconds, and wound her fingers in his hair.

Jadel jerked away from her with an oath and slapped her stingingly across the face. His handsome young face was briefly blazing with anger, and then it was camouflaged behind his customary expression of indifference. He raised one cautioning finger.

"I explained the rules to you, Kella. Do not forget them. I'll give you eternal pleasure if you do as I say."

Maybe it was because his blow had stunned and angered her, or maybe it was just the frustrated fire in her flesh, but for the first time she glared back at him.

"You also promised to give me my son. I'm not sure I believe anything you say."

"No?" Jadel asked, apparently calmly. He propped himself on one stiffened arm, hanging over her like a dark storm. The stars over his head were cold and indifferent. "Believe this, woman. You cannot defy me. And after this, you will not dare to try."

And like a storm falling, he fell. She screamed, but the empty stone walls echoed her without sympathy. After a time she met his rage and cruel demands with her own, twisting fiercely against him with something beyond mere desire. There was nothing of love in it, and nothing even of pleasure; he strove to hurt her, and she strove to hurt him, and it was a shock to both of them when their fierce battle brought them both to the release they needed. Jadel collapsed against her, his skin damp with sweat, and she closed her eyes against the burning bite of tears. After a moment of stuporous silence, Jadel raised his head and sought her lips with his.

The kiss was surprisingly soft. There were no demands in it, no sparks of anger or need. It shook Kella's composure into ruins. She burst into uncontrollable sobs and clung tightly to him, the one unmoving point in an ocean of strangeness, and hardly even cared that he would strike her for her temerity. The anguish in her soul wouldn't let her care.

Jadel submitted to the embrace without comment or struggle, dark eyes strangely lit and even more strangely soft. He lifted his hand to strike her, but it came down with inexplicable gentleness and traced the line of her cheek as she wept. He raised her chin.

"I will give you your son," he promised her. He meant it. As she gulped back her tears, he kissed her again. Her lips were trembling. "You may touch me when you wish, Kella. I will not strike you."

From Jadel, that was indeed a huge admission of affection. Kella understood it, and kissed him with sudden aching fierceness. The play grew serious again, though no less rough.

She awoke again barred across with morning sunshine, frightened into wakefulness to the accompaniment of curses and splintering wood. Kella sat up and drew the fur close up under her chin in instinctive modesty, but it was only Jadel. She breathed a sigh of relief.

Relief quickly disappeared as he swung around to face her. He'd gotten dressed without waking her; he wore his long dark robe and cloak, and he looked menacing even in the brilliant sunlight as he smashed another ruined chair against the far wall. It broke apart as if hurled from a catapult. His face was wild and utterly terrifying.

"Jadel?" she whispered. He hardly heard her. He stalked over to her and grabbed a handful of her hair, jerking her painfully erect. She didn't even dare to cry out. His eyes were dark and furious.

"Ruins. It's all in ruins. How dare they defy me like this?" He didn't expect an answer. He dropped her contemptuously on the furs. She whimpered but jammed her fingers in her mouth to stop the sound; Jadel was not in any mood to be sympathetic to her pain. He would explain when he was ready. Until then, the only sane thing to do was stay out of his way.

Jadel picked up an empty clay jar and smashed it into dust by pounding it violently against the floor. He should have looked childish. Instead, he looked like some terrifying natural force set loose in the too-small confines of the hall.

Just as suddenly as the fit had begun, though, it ended. Jadel froze, staring at the remains of the clay jug as if it held the secrets of the future, and then shrugged the black fabric of his robe back into its elegant lines around his shoulders. He turned slowly to look at Kella; she flinched under the burning, controlled rage of his gaze. He wore his customary expression, though, a mask of indifference.

"Forgive my outburst," he said with a stiff parody of a smile. "It seems my plans have suffered a setback. Your husband and his friends still live, for one thing; my demon was apparently not quite effective enough. Are you quite certain your husband is sexually capable? His performance tends to doubt it.

"To make matters worse, my assistant who was bringing your son to meet us has met with — misfortune. I warned the fool he was underestimating the prince of Rhakhaan and that sorcerous whore, and now he's disappointed me for the last time. My only regret is that he died quickly." Jadel grinned briefly, less a smile than a snarl. "Your son is in the company of Andraax the Mad again. It seems I shall have to deal with that meddler personally — and to do that I shall need more spells than I currently possess. Quellburn holds that power. We are going there now."

"Now?" she asked timidly. He crossed to her and yanked her up — by the arm this time. He scooped up her clothing from the floor and threw it at her.

"Now. Hurry."

Kella dragged the fabric over her head with trembling fingers and threw her cloak around her shoulders. As she was jamming her feet into her boots, Jadel grabbed her arm again and dragged her staggering into the center of a pool of yellow striped sunlight.

"Jadel?" she ventured as he looked down at his Compass. He didn't bother to answer. "Jadel, is my son in danger?"

"Probably," Jadel said sharply, bored, and wrenched them away from the waystation and on their way to Quellburn.

"Tell me," Brion panted, reaching for Pelk's hand, "do you do this often?"

Pelk heaved Brion up on the ledge beside him, careful of the crumbling limestone, caught his breath, and bent to help Astrid make the climb. She fought her way upward in grim, exhausted silence. Brion caught her other arm and lifted her up next to them, then offered a hand to the Changramai. Ziv ignored the aid and scrambled up without it. Brion leaned back against a sharp outcropping of rock and tried to catch his breath against the aching chill. The limestone dust they'd stirred in their ascent up the hill hung in the air and added a chalky taste to the brittle air.

"Often?" Pelk repeated, and drew in a deep breath. Coughed. "Well, not too often. Loremasters don't do a lot of this kind of work — but when they do it's usually this bad."

"And you like it?" Brion groaned. Pelk winked and grabbed Iarsang's proffered right arm.

"It's a living," the young thief shrugged. Iarsang vaulted up with only the slightest assistance. Tyes was next, and he scrambled up with energy that belied the strain he'd had to bear to get the party this far.

"Excellent," the Loremaster said with satisfaction, and peered around. "Have you looked ahead yet?"

"According to old tales, there are caves that begin here that go into the center of the city. It's supposed to be how Quellburn fell — at least how it fell so quickly." Pelk shrugged. "I'll need some magelight; it looks pretty dark in there."

"Open your hand," Tyes said. Pelk did it without question. A ball of light appeared on his hand, and he juggled it with grinning delight. "Don't play with it, Pelk, just move. And watch yourself, damn you."

Pelk waved jauntily and ducked into the dark embrace of the caves. Brion watched with a frown, but no one else seemed concerned; perhaps it was only the brooding height of the cliffs that towered above them, but Brion was in a worrying mood. The river that snaked below them had a nasty current, and the precarious distance to it made him faintly dizzy. Brion went a few steps toward the mouth of the cavern, but Tyes' quiet voice halted him.

"Pelk is an expert at ferreting out entrances, my friend. And he is better qualified than any of us — including you. Rest yourself until he returns. You can't do more than slow him down."

"What if he gets into trouble?" Brion asked.

Tyes smiled wearily. "Oh, I am positive that he will. He has never successfully avoided it."

Pelk reappeared without much fanfare. His face betrayed no haste and no alarm, but it didn't seem to hold much hope. He crouched down on the ledge while the others gathered around him.

"It's not an easy trip," he said without preamble. "I saw lots of side trails. We'll need a massive amount of luck to bring us through — and I'm certain there are hazards."

"What kind of hazards?" Iarsang asked.

Pelk shrugged. "The kind that rip you limb from limb and use your ribs as toothpicks. I didn't stop to ask for references. We seem to have enough sword arms to go around, though — " Pelk's eyes darted to Astrid and Brion, and he sighed. "I hope. For the rest — well, the tunnels weren't exactly stable a few thousand years ago. They're not in remarkably better shape now. We'll need to be roped together."

"Words of advice?" Tyes asked crisply.

Pelk gave him a perfectly bland look. "Don't trip. Don't talk. Don't breath."

"Jadel is in the city," Iarsang said suddenly, and his gaze lifted to meet Tyes'. "We're wasting time."

"Iarsang — " Tyes began, and then stopped. He sighed. "Yes. All right. Pelk, you're guide. Brion, Iarsang, Astrid, Ziv, and me. Keep your swords ready and your eyes open."

Pelk rose and pulled a long coil of thin rope out of his pack; he looked at it mournfully for a moment, then sighed and looped it around his waist.

"Is that thick enough?" the Changramai muttered distrustfully as Pelk tied the rope neatly off around Brion's waist and moved to secure Iarsang. The Navigator bore the contact without comment, but his brown eyes were both frighteningly far away and disturbingly bright. Pelk felt like an intruder on an intensely personal grief; he tied the rope with hurried, jerky moves and went on to Astrid.

"It's spelled," Pelk said belatedly, as the Changramai reached over to feel the thin satiny threads. "It'll hold ten times our combined weight without splitting."

"Handy," Ziv commented, and held his arms up to allow Pelk to rope him into the chain. "For sale?"

"Ah, well, everything's for sale—" Pelk began knowingly. "Here, master, you tie a passable knot. It's a good thing we're so few or we'd be short of rope—"

His voice trailed away as he stared blankly at the line, and he looked up to see Iarsang looking at him. Iarsang's eyes were sad and knowing.

"I'm sorry, sir," Pelk told him, meaning it.

Iarsang shook his head. "We are all sorry, I think. Come. She wouldn't want us to waste time on this." Iarsang blinked and looked away. Something passed over his face, rendering it as blank and distant as when he'd possessed his Compass. "I am pleased you remembered, Pelk."

Pelk knew he shouldn't have forgotten, even for a brief second, and said so as he handed the rope to Tyes and made his way back to the front of the party. He drew his sword, took a deep breath, and began picking their way through the Tunnels of Quellburn.

"Loremaster, what do you know of this place?" Astrid asked as the darkness closed over them. She was fighting back a surge of panic, suddenly thankful for the tall strength of Iarsang before her and her Changramai in back. Tyes added another ball of magelight to the one that burned faintly ahead, and threw the limestone walls of the tunnel into sudden shadowy relief.

"Quellburn was once the capital of this land. Refugees from the Wars of Dominion on Jaiman came here seeking refuge against the Unlife that ruled that land. They built the city that lies above us. That it fell at all is something of a wonder—it was reckoned unassailable."

"But these tunnels seem so wide!" Astrid marvelled—mostly to convince herself that the tunnels really were wide, and stable. Tyes grunted an assent.

"Unfortunately, one of the greatest sorcerers of the age—not a Loremaster, I point out— fell to the Unlife in a most spectacular fashion. It was he who betrayed Quellburn to the darkness. His magic carved out these tunnels so that Ice Kral and Trolls could assault the city."

"A mighty feat," Pelk commented, and grabbed hold of a projecting stalagmite. "It's starting to rise now. Watch your step, everyone."

"There's no one in the city, then?" Brion wanted to know.

Tyes' voice came softly out of the barely lessened darkness. "No one except ghosts, revenants, trolls, and other unsavory creatures." He fell silent a moment. "And Zenon, perhaps. When the Loremasters were informed of the disaster Malim Pelax came to survey the damage. He found a city where the streets were paved more with blood than stone—and he swears he saw the sorcerer Zenon alive and wandering the city."

"Well," Pelk drawled, a ghostly voice barely distorted by effort, "he'd be ancient by now—"

"So am I," Tyes finished wearily. It was his turn to begin the uphill pull, and every muscle in his body argued against it. He wished he'd dared to fly them into the city, but he wasn't strong enough to contest a two-year-old child, much less Jadel. He needed the respite — magically speaking. "In any case, if Zenon is alive, he'll be one more hazard to add to your list."

Brion slipped on the wet limestone and tumbled helplessly back into Iarsang; the Navigator braced him. Pelk turned and looped the rope around a handy stalagmite, then pulled the others up to the slight level patch of ground he'd reached.

Speaking of hazards, now — Pelk's sense of danger was as fine-tuned as his eye for gems, and he didn't question the sudden hammering of his heart. He whirled around with the magelight extended and peered ahead.

Nothing there, just limestone gleaming whitely. He held his breath for a few seconds, but it was difficult to pick up anything more than his own heartbeat and the shuffling noises of those with him.

"Quiet!" he hissed. They froze into as much of a semblance of silence as they were able. Pelk found himself looking at a particularly leprous patch of limestone. Strange that the stalactites there looked knife-sharp, while the others showed the effects of hundreds of years of erosion. There was something symmetrical about it, too —

They would have to pass directly by it, and that was what was raising the hackles on his neck.

"Go quietly," he told the others in a thief's whisper, and took extra caution in the way he put his feet among the loose rocks littering the tunnel. He gave an inward wince at the clumsiness of the others — excepting Iarsang and Tyes, Elven blood being what it was — and knew there wasn't any help for it. He could only hope that his instincts were wrong —

They weren't. The only thing that saved his life was that the creature lunged too quickly, perhaps overeager for fresh meat. Pelk tumbled back down the path and took the others with him in an untidy heap. The magelight was bright enough to reveal a nightmare edging out of the limestone spears. It was more than ten feet long, and as tall as Pelk's waist. The sharp limestone stalactites he'd noticed weren't rocks at all; they were the razor teeth of the thing. As Pelk watched, the teeth began to move. They rotated. The maze of stalactites and stalagmites didn't slow the creature; it simply sawed through them.

"A Tergon," Ziv named it evenly; even this monstrosity scarcely moved him.

Pelk made an effort to keep his knees steady. "What can we do?" Pelk asked breathlessly. He was on his feet again, not that that was much of an improvement, and the white worm was chewing its way through a forest of limestone on its way toward them. No one had any positive thoughts. "Ziv! How can we kill it?"

"Fire," the Changramai said shortly. "Chop it to bits. Not many other ways."

Helpful, Pelk thought despairingly, and felt Astrid press herself against his back as she caught her first look at the creature. Her breath stirred the hair around his ears. It was surprisingly distracting. He'd hardly even noticed her as female before.

"Maybe I can help," she offered. He shook his head. "No, Pelk, listen. My profession is Mentalist. I may be able to immobilize it."

"And you may not. No. Stay back, Astrid. Iarsang? Master?"

"My sword is at your disposal," Iarsang said with utter calm. "Unfortunately I have little else to offer just now."

"Master?" Pelk asked again, because Tyes didn't answer. The creature was chomping its way through rock at an appalling rate. He risked a look back and saw Iarsang turning as well.

Tyes lay unmoving against the massive base of a stalagmite. Astrid removed herself from Pelk and knelt beside the Loremaster.

"He's hit his head. He's unconscious."

When she looked up, Pelk was watching her. His eyes were dark and expressionless in the magelight. The sound of grinding rock was getting louder.

"How can I assist you, Benevolent Lady?" he asked with great politeness — and unhappiness. She forced herself to smile brightly and stepped up to stand shoulder to shoulder with Pelk, as she'd stood with another charming young thief. The comparison shook her, so she pushed it aside.

"Just stand ready. If I should fail, your swords will be our last defense," she said. Pelk nodded. Ziv was a warm, intimidating presence at her back. Brion stood empty-handed next to Iarsang, looking as frightened as she herself felt; she managed another smile for him, then closed her eyes and coaxed her power into full bloom.

It was easier this time than it had been on the dark path, so many lifetimes ago; she had power tingling through her every nerve and muscle, singing fiercely in time with her beating heart. The spell was at the very limit of her capacity, but she felt no special fear. Using that Essence her own body and mind produced, she began building an unseen fog around the creature. It was delicate work, but it went quickly; she opened her eyes and found Pelk looking at her in open concern.

"A spark," she commanded. "A flame. Something."

Pelk clawed out a spark wheel and a piece of cloth, almost fumbling in his haste. The wheel spun three times before the sparks caught hold on the dry cloth and began to burn.

"Throw it!" she shouted. The Tergon chewed noisily through the last of the limestone barriers and lunged. The little flaming bit of cloth danced across the intervening space and encountered the invisible fog Astrid had created around the creature.

Pure oxygen exploded into white-hot flame. The Tergon shrieked, a sound like rending rock, and began thrashing violently as it burned. Pelk tossed Astrid back without deference or hesitation and dove for cover himself.

Astrid ended up cushioned against Brion's body; he twisted to protect her as a blast of heat seared overhead, and the body of the burning Tergon slammed violently against the tunnel roof.

The Tergon collapsed, dead, impaling its repulsive white corpse on the broken stalactites with a liquidly ripping sound of puncture. The oxygen fire had burned out, but the corpse continued to blaze merrily. Pelk breathed a sigh of relief and raised his head from the rock-strewn floor.

As if it were mourning the death of a beloved child, the tunnel roof groaned. Pelk's gaze snapped up in time to see the crack spreading above them, and he had time for one breathless curse before covering his head with his bare arms.

The ceiling came down in a roar of outraged rock and water.

"Water!" Laurel croaked. Tiernan, hypnotized by the unending rhythm of his feet pushing through the sand, didn't react. She grabbed his chin and forced it up. "Look! There's water ahead!"

Tiernan blinked, then blinked again. Weakness was a constant irritation now, but thirst was worse; the air was warmer during the day, but no less dry. His wounds had given rise to a burning need for water. It was cruel of her to joke like this —

His eyes focused and steadied. There, in the distance, waved some stunted long-leafed trees, a scrawny-looking expanse of grass, and an equally unprepossessing little pool that reflected the empty blue of the sky.

It was the most blessed thing Tiernan had ever seen. He stopped dead in his tracks and stared as he waited for it to vanish — fate seemed to be permanently prejudiced against him — but the trees continued to wave, the water to ripple, and the grass to beckon. Tiernan swore softly.

"Come!" Laurel laughed breathlessly, running. He tried to match her, but he'd had taken more of a beating, and she soon pulled ahead. The sand sucked unpredictably at Tiernan's booted feet and threatened with each step to send him tumbling, but he staggered into the springy embrace of the grass without sprawling. Laurel whirled around. Her whole face was vivid with excitement.

"Water!" she shouted, and knelt down at the edge of the pool. She scooped up a handful and drank thirstily, then another; Tiernan sank down in an exhausted heap next to her and watched. She eyed him with a frown. "Why don't you drink? Surely you're thirsty."

Tiernan indicated the brown muffling mask he wore without comment. She raised the back of one dripping hand to her mouth in dismay, then smiled.

"I'll turn my back," she promised, and flung herself stomach-down on the cool grass with her face pointing out toward the desert. Tiernan sighed and unwound the horrible veiling wrap. The wind felt deliciously fresh — and the water tasted better than the finest wine ever served at his father's table. He drank thirstily, splashed it on his dusty face, and washed the bloody cicatrix at his neck. The depth of it made him shudder, but the wound had closed safely and without too much loss of blood.

He plunged his whole head into the pool and tossed his dripping black hair back over his shoulders with an animal sound of relief.

"Tiernan?"

He grabbed hastily for the brown robe and wrapped it over his face again, but she was still facing demurely away. At least, he thought it was demurely. Her voice was far too warm.

"I'm done," he said regretfully. She rolled over on her side and looked at him through huge blue eyes, the very match of the sky above her. He felt a breathless instant of desire, and forced it away. Damn you, he whispered silently, and not just to the dead cleric this time.

"No moons tonight," she observed. The change in subject left him behind. Laurel rolled her eyes in disgust. "The starlight will be too faint to see by. You can take your mask off. Are you sure — sure it was your face and not — "

"Not what?" Tiernan asked curiously. She blushed slightly, a charming exercise that sent his pulse pounding again. Damn the woman.

"Not the curse he put on me?"

The effect on Tiernan was galvanic. He had hardly had the strength to sit up at the water's edge, but suddenly he was on his feet and striding across to her. She hadn't even time to protest before he was kneeling beside her, eyes fierce and angry through the mask.

"What did he do?" Tiernan snarled. She put out a calming hand, and he caught it in both of his. "Gods, Laurel, tell me! What happened? Are you well?"

His fingers were trembling. His whole body was trembling. She stared at him in absolute astonishment, seeing what she'd never known or refused to recognize — that this young prince, the one she'd hurt so bitterly and tormented so unmercifully, this young prince loved her.

And loved her well beyond good sense.

It made her entire mind a blank.

"I'm well," she finally assured him incoherently. "I don't know what the curse was. Obviously it's gone astray. I feel no ill effects."

"If there's anything, anything, that feels amiss to you, you tell me at once, do you hear?" He touched her fingers to his lips, and they, too, trembled.

"There's probably nothing that can be done," she whispered. He shook his head angrily.

"I don't care. I want to know. Promise me." She did. He kissed her fingers again before releasing them. It took a real effort to pin his tattered self-control together, but he managed to sit back and look at her with something close to his usual composure. It held until she smiled at him again.

They both drank again, taking turns. The sun slowly sank below the horizon. They talked about moving on, but the inescapable fact that neither one knew anything about the area made the conversation a little ridiculous. Besides, it had been endless ages since they'd had a peaceful moment to stretch out and watch the stars. Laurel was right. The moons were dark, and as the last azure rays of the sun vanished into darkness Tiernan realized that he could barely see the outline of his own body in the dim starlight.

"You can take the mask off," Laurel said drowsily from a few feet away.

Tiernan sat up and unwrapped it. "I promise that if I feel the slightest twinge of desire I'll let out a scream."

"Very funny," he sighed, and rubbed at his face. "Do I look different, Laurel? Do I look — "

"Hideous? Oh, horrible. I was only kissing you to keep myself from retching, truly." Laurel's breathless laughter rang softly across the water. "You looked like yourself, only better."

"Better?" he asked, interested, and crossed his arms under his head as he studied the constellations.

Tiernan felt himself growing pleasantly drowsy. He was on the edge of sleep when he heard Laurel moving, heard the sound of cloth rustling. "Laurel? What's wrong?"

"Nothing's wrong." She stood. "I'm going to take a bath."

"Now?" he asked, interested.

She snorted. "It isn't as if you can see me, and I've gone too long with slavehold sweat and dust and blood all over me. I am going to be clean."

"The water's cold," he warned.

"I don't care — " Laurel's defiant declaration would have had more impact if she hadn't gasped as she stepped into the water. Tiernan shut his eyes, more to forestall his imagination than because he might see anything compromising. "Cold doesn't describe it. F — f — freezing."

"Then come out," he called. A ripple beached on the shore. His imagination, undaunted by his lack of vision, supplied an enchantingly graphic picture of Laurel wading into the water, and he sighed. Go to sleep, he told himself sternly. Dreams are almost always more accommodating than real life.

The ripples swelled; she began to hum as she scrubbed at herself with handfuls of rough sand. It really was intolerable.

"Laurel?" he asked, a little breathless now because he was stepping out over an abyss he'd never even measured. When he'd asked for her hand he'd received a blow that had crippled him, whether intended or not. His heart beat painfully fast.

"What?" she sighed. "The water isn't so bad once you get used to it."

"I need a bath too."

"Yes, you do," she agreed with unflattering candor. "Come in. The pool's big enough."

"You're sure — " he began. A handful of cold water flew out of the air and spattered him, jerking him upright. "You little — "

"Come in," she said softly. There was a sudden flush of gooseflesh along his back that had nothing to do with the chilling air; he stood there unmoving and fought against a sudden painful surge of pure lust. It hurt damnably.

"Lady Magen, you forget yourself," he told her with every bit of cold control he possessed. There was a silken splash of water, and ripples caressed the sandy edges of the pond. "Don't play. Not like this."

"I'm not playing," she told him, a patent falsehood. "I have never offered anything I wasn't prepared to give up."

Tiernan let out a deep, disgusted sigh and plumped himself rudely down on the grass. He couldn't see her except as a faint dark shadow — but was that the faintly lit line of her back, there, and the swell of breasts — no. Of course it wasn't..

"You," he said with precise and angry calm, "are impossible. This curse, this — Beauty of — "

"Arraer."

"Thank you. — Arraer, does it continue on even after you no longer see my face?"

"No," she replied serenely. "The water's quite warm, really, Tiernan. Try it."

The water wasn't the only thing of unnatural temperature. Tiernan realized that he was breathing too quickly and forced himself to slow, but that didn't help the sudden trembling all over his body, or the pressure growing uncomfortable in his breeches. Perhaps he did need a bath, a cold one, a frigid one.

"I fail to understand why you are so bent on ruining whatever self-respect I have left, Lady Magen. Do you want to see me beg? I've underestimated you. I thought you were merely thoughtless. Now I know you're actively cruel." Tiernan's voice was light, but the words stung nonetheless, and caused an agitated little storm in the center of the pond.

"Cruel!" she shouted, inadvertently swallowing water. After she was able to speak again, she found herself almost at a loss for words. "Damn you, you royal jackass — "

Tiernan jerked himself upright with an oath she hadn't ever heard from his lips, a sound that crackled with anger and a startling amount of pain. He yanked impatiently at the knots on his leather jerkin, pulled them open, and stripped the leather off. It hit the grass with a slap. He tore his shirt as he stripped it off, too, but that didn't matter, as ragged as he already was. He was suddenly, gloriously angry, and it felt good.

"I have put up with a great number of things from you, but don't you ever, ever call me a royal anything again, woman!" He cursed under his breath as the knots of his breeches resisted. The rough cloth finally slid down his legs and pooled at his feet — no, around his feet. He was still wearing his boots. Tiernan gave a sigh of utter rage and yanked one boot free, then the other.

"What?" Laurel taunted. He could see her, a faint silvery form that hovered quite near the shore. Tiernan took two long, catlike strides to the water's edge.

"You took away everything from me, Laurel. I offered you love, and you threw it back in my face like — like slop. I showed you my heart and you sat on it." He took a deep breath and let it out in a shout. "What do you want from me?"

For a second, only the ripples and echoes answered him. Her voice was so quiet that it was almost lost in that gentle watery rush; the sadness in it caught him painfully by surprise.

"Your forgiveness, your highness. I haven't the right to ask for anything else." And, after a second's breathless pause: "But if I may ask a favor, highness — "

"What?" he snarled. It was all just another elaborate, hurtful jest, he knew it. Lying, treacherous, deceitful little sorceress —

"I can't seem to feel my feet anymore. Can you help me out of the water?"

She sounded so pitifully small, so chastened, that Tiernan felt all of his anger melt away. He shifted a little in sudden embarrassment — he couldn't quite remember how he'd lost his clothes — but he bent over and held out his hand.

Her own fingers touched his gently, and he felt fire explode all through him. It was all he could do to hold still and show common courtesy — but she was being uncommonly courteous herself, and unusually quiet.

He should have known better. Those gentle, strong fingers closed over his wrist and pulled. Tiernan, already off balance, created a spectacular, freezing splash as he plunged forward. As he fought his way back breathless and gasping to the surface, the first sound he heard was her laughter.

"Blood of the Lords, I'm going to freeze!" he gagged, and shivered convulsively. The water dripped from his wet hair into his eyes and blinded him. "Laurel, where are you?"

"Here," she whispered, and suddenly there she was, a hot silken line of skin pressed against his back. As he stood there quite still, Tiernan could clearly feel every gentle curve of her body burning into his. "Cold?"

Indeed he was not. He was faintly surprised that the water wasn't boiling all around him. He wanted to turn, but he didn't dare; self-control was all well and good, but self-control wasn't worth a damn just now. Tiernan was wise enough to admit it without a struggle.

"Ah, don't play with me, Laurel," he whispered, not even knowing if she'd hear. "Some games go too deep. You've done enough."

"I don't think so," she answered him, her breath warm on the back of his neck. Tiernan shuddered in the grip of indescribable longings. "I meant what I said. Forgive me. I thought you wanted me because you'd had everyone else, and because your father wanted you wed — and because my father wanted me wed. I didn't believe you. You're a hard man to believe, you know."

Hard wasn't the word for it. Tiernan bit his lips to keep from laughing. Her hands slid up the smooth line of his hips and up the muscles of his back in a sensual glide, drawing all of his agonized senses with them.

"Don't do that," he begged her faintly. She let out a long sigh that trembled against his skin to shattering effect.

"No?" She sounded sad. "Then perhaps this — "

Her hands slipped in the opposite direction, measuring the narrow line of his hips and curving down and forward. Tiernan groaned and turned around to stand face-to-face with her, his hands holding her captured ones in grips that trembled.

"Why now?" he wanted to know. She let out her breath in another sigh, but this one was laden with disgust. Laurel was, it seemed, unaltered even in this extremity.

"Why do you have to question everything?" she shot back angrily. "Do I have to say I love you? That it was only when you left Jaiman that I knew you loved me too? That you've been driving me mad, damn you, running off like a witless royal fool and not even bothering to listen — "

"You love me?" he interrupted incredulously.

"Idiot," she hissed. "I don't stand around in ice water with every fool I meet, now do I?"

A valid point — but not nearly so convincing as the heat of their two bodies, so close to touching, so desperate to touch. Tiernan stood there for a few more seconds, then dropped her hands and turned back toward the edge of the pool.

"Where are you going?" she asked him, amazed and hurt. He reached back and recaptured one hand in his, then drew her out of the water without comment. "Tiernan! The wind — we'll catch — "

"No we won't," he told her briefly, and tripped her neatly onto the blanket she'd abandoned. She gave a protesting cry. He folded himself down comfortably next to her and began to gently wipe her body dry with a loose fold of the blanket, ignoring her comments and efforts to push him away.

After a few seconds, she didn't feel much like pushing. He was meticulous and gentle in mopping up all of the cold water, even toweling her hair dry. She sat up to let him rub her back dry, and smiled as she felt his body tremble. He handed her the blanket without comment.

"My turn?" she asked. He stretched out on the grass and let her do him the service, then reclaimed the blanket and spread it over both of their bodies.

She could just see his outline as he stared at hers, but she thought he was smiling, that lazy, infuriating smile that had always made her burn immodestly and say outrageously rude things to him. Laurel reached out and traced the line of that smile with impulsive fingers. Emboldened, she let her hands wander downward over the satiny skin of his chest and stomach, and smiled herself (a thoroughly wicked smile) as she caused him to lose his composure at last.

Tiernan pulled her over atop him and kissed her with long, unhurried passion. His tongue fenced delicately with hers as his hands slipped in to trace aimless circles on her back, all the way down the smooth swell of her hips. She moved those hips in pleasure, and felt his breathing catch.

"You'll kill me, Laurel," he warned her faintly, but he couldn't help the tensing of his muscles to meet hers, or the laughter that was bubbling up out of the incredible joy within him.

"My dear Prince, I hope not. I'm not nearly done with you yet," she returned, and her wandering hands touched him again in a way that made him wonder if he'd ever be able to draw breath again. He let out a breathless groan at the pleasure of it.

"I love you, Laurel." His voice was rough and uneven, and it made her shiver just as his touch made her burn. She answered him both in words and extravagant deeds.

On the crest of the hill above them, Andraax and Evan slept on, disturbed only by the whispering voices that might have been shifting sand, and might not.

After the roar of the cave-in, the silence was so total that every one of the party thought himself deaf. Tyes opened his eyes and coughed on the thick, dusty fog, and that broke the spell; Astrid eased out from under Brion and scrambled over chunks of stone to reach the fallen Loremaster.

"You'll live," she pronounced finally. He winced as she probed at the bump on his head. "Do you want to heal that, or shall I?"

"Be my guest," he told her faintly. The cavern was inky black. Tyes exerted a small amount of will and brought his magelight back into existence again; the bluish light conjured a frightening vision of Astrid, coated with white dust and seeming more revenant than living woman. But her touch was warm, and as Tyes waited he felt the equally warm glow of her healing mending the damage to his head. His intolerable headache faded to a faint annoyance. He smiled at her, and she smiled back.

"What happened?" he asked. "Is everyone in one piece?"

"Pelk killed the — "

"The Tergon," Ziv supplied dourly, climbing out from a huge block of stone. Astrid nodded to him.

"Yes, the Tergon — and the thing brought the ceiling down on us. I think we're all right — "

Her voice faded as she looked around; Brion was standing, looking as bad as she, and Ziv jumped down to join him. Iarsang was sitting not far away, in no worse shape than he'd been.

" Pelk — "

Pelk was missing.

Tyes realized it at the same moment she did. She put out a hand to restrain him, but it was like holding back the wind; he pushed her aside and jumped up without regard for his weariness or his injuries. He began a thorough, careful search of the piles of rubble.

"Where was he standing?" he demanded. Astrid glanced at Brion uncertainly.

"There, I think." She pointed to a nearby mound of rubble. Tyes looked at it with stricken eyes. "But, Loremaster — "

He ignored her and began digging. He'd only gone a little ways into the rubble before he uncovered a hand, as white as the limestone that covered it. Astrid sucked in a deep breath and ran to help Tyes sift away the wreckage; soon even Iarsang was digging one-handed beside her.

"Is he alive?" Brion gasped as he and Ziv levered the last chunk of rock away.

Astrid nodded. "I'll need your help, Loremaster — "

"Of course," Tyes whispered. The two of them bent silently to the work. Ziv turned away to look back up the path, blocked now by the charred bulk of the Tergon and treacherous falls of loose rock.

"It looks bad," Brion commented nervously, trying to keep his mind from Pelk.

The Changramai shook his head. "For trained warriors, it looks bad. For us — " Ziv's gesture encompassed Iarsang's weakness, Pelk's injury, Brion's lack of training, and Astrid's frailty. "For us it is impossible."

"Not impossible," Tyes corrected sharply from behind them. "I made a mistake trying to conserve power. We'll make it, don't doubt that. Have faith, Brion."

"I have faith that my wife is already here," the man replied softly. "And maybe she's already got my son. But I'm not going to give up. I can't."

Tyes looked at him, then nodded and returned his attention to Pelk, who was coming awake. Pelk's dusty blond head raised, then fell back.

"All right," he coughed weakly. "That was really not fair. Merciful Lords, what dragon stepped on my head?"

"Easy, my friend," Tyes interrupted, and helped him sit up. "Everything working?"

"Perfect," Pelk grunted. "Master?"

"Yes?"

"Is this an appropriate time to respectfully tell you that I resign?"

Tyes looked up the sharp slope of the path, and smiled. Pelk followed his gaze and groaned.

"You are insane," the thief sighed, and shook his head. "All right. If it weren't for my starving mother and six brothers and sisters, I'd quit your service now."

"You're an orphan, Pelk. Your brothers and sisters are all older than you and very well fed," Tyes told him, unimpressed, and gestured toward the path. As Pelk pushed by him to take the lead, Tyes put a hand on his shoulder.

"Be careful," Vurkanan Tyes warned him, deadly serious. "You're important to me, Pelk. Never forget that."

Pelk didn't turn to look at him, but nodded slightly, and moved on up the path. The others all fell into line behind him—exhausted, bruised, and filthy, but still determined. He shook his head and felt for his first foothold on the treacherous rock.

They encountered no more Tergon, though once Pelk heard the crushing roar of rotating teeth nearby; it was a good thing, since the ascent was backbreakingly difficult. It would have been mildly difficult for himself alone, but burdened with a party not used to such hazards it was murderous. Astrid almost plunged them all back down the path when her grip on a stalagmite caused the spire to shatter; only Pelk's stubborn strength held them in place. Brion slid a few minutes farther along, and broke Pelk loose from his hold, but this time Iarsang and Ziv managed to belay the slide. Stalactites were crashing down from the ceiling to the path with frightening regularity, but Tyes' magic managed to divert the ones that threatened the party, and even though the ascent took more than three hours, they reached the level space just below the city without major injuries.

No one took a vote; they all flung themselves down on the hard rocky path and gasped for breath. Pelk was surprised to find his muscles aching and weak from strain; he'd been concentrating too hard during the long pull to notice. Astrid dug a water flask out from her belongings and passed it around; the taste of the water, warm and leathery as it was, gave them all a sense of renewal.

"Up!" Pelk finally said hoarsely. Someone gave a groan of protest. "Up! If we sit any longer our muscles will stiffen and we'll be useless. Come, Benevolent Lady, give me your hand."

"There's the end," Iarsang said, and pointed toward the distant gray wall. Pelk squinted, then shook his head.

"I don't see anything."

"I do," Iarsang said with supreme certainty, and quickly untied himself from the climbing rope. "I'm going ahead."

"No!" Tyes protested. "No, I will not allow you to go alone. Stay with the party."

"We have no time to waste," Iarsang warned them, and turned toward the door. "If you're coming, hurry. Jadel is above, and he's close to what he's searching for. I will not lose him again."

They all followed him, even Tyes; Pelk darted from one to the other and untied the thin rope. He coiled it carefully and put it back in the concealed pocket of his cloak. There was a jagged hole at the far end of the tunnel; Pelk could just barely make it out as they got closer. There was nothing between them and the exit but a long, empty stretch of rock, warty limestone growths, and the occasional gleam of dripping water. The air was still, musty, and damp, underlaid faintly with a smell that might have been rot.

The smell made Pelk's neck ache again. He reached down and drew the sword he'd won in Kelfour's Landing; the blade was as warm and eager in his hand as a woman. He cast a look sideways at Ziv, who walked on the right side of his pretty young cleric; the Changramai looked oblivious, but Pelk noticed the gleam of a thin-bladed knife in his hand. None of the others seemed uneasy.

There wasn't a sound except for dripping water, the gritty slide of dirt under their boots, and their labored breathing. The air smelled musty, as if nothing had breathed it for years. They were slowly approaching the ragged hole torn into the rock at the end of the tunnel, and the darkness pressed close. Pelk shivered and tightened his grip on his sword.

He never knew what made him spin and bring his sword up, but it was the difference between life and death; a repulsively shapeless thing spitted itself on the blade, howled, and dragged itself up the shaft toward Pelk. He shouted and yanked the blade free as the darkness exploded into movement around them. The thing that had attacked him — a horribly decaying thing that only vaguely resembled a human form, and yet undeniably was — crouched on the stone and rubbed its torn flesh. Pieces of it fell away, but the zombie was oblivious. It clambered to its feet again and lunged. Pelk swung and felt a slight resistance as his sword passed through rotting flesh and brittle bone; the creature's claw-tipped right arm dropped off to flop on the floor.

The thing scarcely noticed.

"Pelk! Pelk, get back!" Tyes shouted. Pelk gave ground, and the zombie followed him greedily. The Benevolent Lady Astrid was incanting something in a breathless, trembling voice. The Undead creature turned its sagging fungus-like face toward the sound of her voice.

Pelk lifted his sword and cut it cleanly through the neck. The head toppled from the decaying shoulders and struck the rock with a sickening damp splash. The black holes of its eyes stared unblinkingly back as Pelk gaped — and the body continued to shamble forward.

"I can't banish it!" Astrid warned. "Something stronger is controlling it. Run!"

"I'm afraid we can't," Iarsang said calmly. He held his own sword in his good hand, and he was facing the tunnel's end. As the others looked, more Undead poured out of the shadows in front of them, cutting them off from advance. "We must fight, it seems."

Pelk chopped his opponent's left arm off. It kept coming. The stench of the thing filled him with nausea, but as he cast a frantic look over his shoulder he saw more creatures approaching from the other side, and something glimmering faintly in the dimness behind Astrid —

"Changramai! Behind you!" he called.

Ziv spun. For a second he saw nothing, but a ripple in the air betrayed the thing. It was taller than Iarsang, and the black robes that clothed it were both real and phantom, just as it was. Only the red eyes were real, and inimical.

"A wraith," Astrid breathed in horror. "No, Ziv: there's no fighting it!"

The wraith, barely seen, moved forward and raised one spectral, skeletal hand. It held a knife that glittered blood red and obsidian black, and shimmered in and out of reality just as the hand that held it. Ziv bared his teeth and threw his own knife; it passed harmlessly through the apparition and landed with a metallic clink against a stalagmite. The wraith ignored him, advancing on Astrid, who backed hastily away. The others were engaged in battling off zombies — even Brion, who was using his plain steel sword with awkward, desperate strokes. The zombies made a horrible, ululating wail that echoed continuously around the rock walls.

One by one, they burst into ravening flame, even the fallen, writhing pieces. That was Tyes' doing, as he dropped his guard and spent his store of power in a reckless pyrotechnic display. He staggered, and Pelk caught him.

"Go!" Tyes yelled, pushing his assistant toward the unguarded doorway. Pelk ran, then turned back at the entrance. Brion was coming, and Iarsang — Astrid and Ziv seemed frozen where they were. Tyes started towards them, the but wraith lunged with sudden, bitter speed.

It seemed impossible that anyone could move faster than the apparition, but Ziv twisted himself into the thing's path. The knife slid easily into his shoulder; the Changramai's returning cut went harmlessly through the creature's robes. Ziv staggered backwards; the knife was still pulsing strangely in his shoulder, and he reached up to tear it out. The hilt came away in his hand, but the red-and-black blade was gone.

His wound did not bleed.

Tyes grabbed Astrid and flung her toward the entrance, then turned back for Ziv. The Changramai was already retreating, facing the bitter knowledge that he could not win this fight, not even with Tyes next to him. The Loremaster evidently reached the same conclusion, for he grabbed Ziv's arm and pulled him toward the others.

Ziv made it to the entrance, but he sagged against the rock, his breath coming fast and uneven. His face was contorted with silent pain.

"Brion, help him!" Tyes gestured to Pelk to continue. Pelk hesitated a few seconds, then nodded and led the way.

The watery flare of sunlight ahead took them all by surprise; somehow, Pelk hadn't expected to come out in the open. After the darkness of the cave even weak light was painful: Pelk narrowed his eyes to slits to peer out.

They stood at the bottom of a long, sloping ramp that led up into the city. Pelk looked at the others, then shrugged and ran lightly up the ramp to stick his head outside.

They faced a huge smooth stone wall of smooth granite, engraved with arcane symbols. Pelk whistled soundlessly. The wall was more than seventy feet high — and there were skeletons clearly visible all around the base of it.

"We've found it," he called, turning to look out over his shoulder. He didn't whistle, this time. The destruction he looked on was too total to evoke any levity. "Now all we need is a way to get inside."

The city of Quellburn had been smashed like a child's toy. As far as he could see, shops, houses, and monuments lay smashed into rubble. Scattered bones lay everywhere. The distant far wall of the city was still standing, but everything else in the city except for a few of the larger, more massively built buildings had been reduced to dust and kindling.

"What is this?" Astrid asked breathlessly from behind Pelk. He glanced back at her. She was staring raptly at the huge polished wall.

"The Citadel of Wizards," Iarsang said as he pushed his way around Pelk and up. "If it hadn't been for Zenon's treachery, no one could have breached it."

"Is Jadel inside?" Pelk asked.

Iarsang nodded. He looked skeletal in the cold sunlight, all pale skin stretched over bones. His eyes were dark and violent.

"I was afraid of that. Master?" Pelk asked.

"A moment," Tyes said, distracted. He knelt by Ziv, who had collapsed at the foot of the ramp even with Brion's help. "Your shoulder. Let me see it."

"Nothing to see," Ziv whispered. Tyes unlaced the warrior's black leather armor and pulled it away. On his pale skin there was a cold blue stain, and a black center pulsing beneath the skin. Tyes touched it.

The Changramai tensed in agony. "Leave it. I'll manage."

"You know what it is?" Tyes asked as calmly as he could.

Ziv nodded. "A slay-knife. There's nothing to be done."

"You know what it will do to you." It was more than half a question.

Ziv blinked. "It will kill me," he said bluntly.

Tyes nodded, gray eyes never leaving the Changramai's ravaged face. "It will make you his. Death will not free you, not if you die by its poison. I cannot save you. The blade is pure Unlife. Do you understand me?"

"I'll become like him — a wraith. A slave to the Unlife." His voice was still calm, even though his hands were trembling. The darkness in his shoulder pulsed and spread. Ziv caught his breath. "I will not end so. Tell the lady — remember her promise. I served her as well as I would any other Scribe. Tell her — remember."

Tyes promised.

Ziv nodded convulsively, throat working, and flexed his hand. A knife appeared in it, seemingly from nowhere. He hesitated.

"Go. This is private, Loremaster."

"So it is," Tyes agreed, gray eyes anguished. "You honor your calling, warrior. May your rest be easy."

"May your road be long," the Changramai whispered, nodding to Brion as Tyes drew him away up the ramp.

Ziv looked contemplatively at the silver flash of his knife, estimating how long he had yet to live.

Not long, he thought. It was better so. He loosened his leather armor the rest of the way, until he knelt bare-headed and clad only in his black leather breeches and thin white shirt, and set the knife to his stomach.

The wraith was watching him with malignant triumph from the shadows below. Ziv gave it a humorless, victorious smile and plunged the knife in, jerking it savagely to the left and up.

The end was quick and painful; the last sound he heard was the wraith's impotent, angry wail as he escaped it forever.

"Where's Ziv?" Astrid demanded.

Tyes and Brion climbed out of the hole to stand beside them. Brion looked down, but Tyes didn't. His gray eyes were steady and compassionate.

"Dead," he said baldly. "It was his choice. He said to remind you of your promise, Benevolent Lady."

Astrid stood there in silence for a few seconds, eyes bright with unshed tears. Then she blinked them away and lifted her chin. She reached for Brion's offered hand, taking comfort and strength from the warmth.

"I have never forgotten my promise," she declared. "The only thing that will keep me from fulfilling it is my own death. I owe that to him."

"I never doubted you." Tyes turned to look at the wall that faced them, then made a slow circular survey of the ruined city around them. His face betrayed horror and a deep sadness. "So much death here. I am not surprised to find a Dyar Elf crouching in the middle of it."

"Tarsang says he is in the Wizard's Citadel." Pelk indicated the smooth walls. "Over the walls?"

"No. The spells are still very much in place." Tyes indicated the skeletons strewn around the base. "Unwise to try it. We walk around until we find the gates."

"And if the gates are locked?" Pelk asked.

Tyes shot him a look. "I have faith in you, my friend. Did you not open the doors of Kalim Heket's harem — and further, get out again without being exposed — ah, detected?"

Pelk glared at him. "I didn't know you knew," he said, chagrined. Tyes raised his eyebrows.

"It was a challenge — he said they were impenetrable — "

"And so they were." Tyes smiled slightly. "And so are these, apparently."

Pelk shrugged, pleased, and led the way. The walls stretched off into the distance, and they had a long walk to get around them.

"Nothing!" Jadel snarled, sweeping the scrolls from the elegant table. There was a finely crafted chess set sitting on the corner, and he lashed out at that, too, sending white and black pieces flying to the stone floor. Kella froze at the bookcases, where she'd just gathered a new armload of scrolls. The Dyar's black eyes blazed at her. "Basic Sorcerer's spells. Children's rhymes! I need more! I need Zenon's secret spells, the ones that crushed this city and its circle of mighty wizards. Find them!"

"Where?" she demanded, then bit her lip.

He slammed his hand down on the table, splintering the wood. "Have you a brain, or are you as mindless as all the rest?"

"I thought you were pleased with me." She carefully put the scrolls down and smoothed the faded ribbons, binding them with something like reverence. "I summoned those creatures, didn't I? And the wraith — "

"Failures!" Jadel sneered. "You failed again to kill them. Is this how you repay me?"

"I did my best!" she shouted, red spots high in her cheeks. "Why don't you kill them yourself? Why don't you face them directly? You're always trying to get at them from someone else. Are you afraid?"

"Afraid?" Jadel asked softly, standing very close to her. She had to bend her neck painfully back to look up at him, but she set her jaw and did it. His smooth, cool hands rose to hold her face, to trace the slender line of her neck. "Yes, I'm afraid. Without Zenon's spells I have little chance of besting Vurkanan Tyes face to face, and I cannot control your husband."

"Brion? But he's — nothing."

"Oh, no, my dear, he's quite something. Your Brion is a natural force, a vessel for Essence, if he ever learns to control it. He cannot be harmed directly by any magical agency using the power of Unlife. Thus, he's the most dangerous of all to me."

"And me? What am I?" she challenged.

Jadel smiled, a beautiful, hurtful smile that brought tears of pain and longing to her eyes. "Look in your own soul and see. You're his opposite, my love. Your spirit longs for darkness. Your whole body aches for its touch. You are a vessel — for Unlife." Jadel's eyes grew distant. "Sadly, your son resembles his father, not his mother. He will grow bothersome."

"What do you mean?" Kella whispered.

Jadel bent and kissed her, wiping out all thought, all fear, in a wash of unclean, agonizing need. She clung to him, her prince of darkness, and forgot.

"Enough," Jadel finally said, and thrust her back against the bookcase. A few scrolls toppled out; he kicked them carelessly out of the way. "Search Zenon's other chambers, then. I'll continue to examine these scrolls, but I doubt he'd store his hidden knowledge so openly."

Kella sucked in a deep, steadying breath and nodded as she walked to the door. Jadel watched her go, then yanked another scroll out of those neatly pigeonholed in the bookshelves. It was useless. He crumpled it carelessly and tossed it in the corner.

Kella looked at the other doors, then opened one at random. A storeroom. She poked cautiously around, seeing nothing of interest, then went on to the next room. This one was obviously a bedchamber, elegantly furnished and retaining some vestige of faded glory. She went to the massive oak desk that stood in the corner; it was covered with pages of scribbling, apparently aimless nonsense. The drawers were all empty. A ring lay forgotten in a circle of dust, but she was distracted by the sight of the bed. A faint sigh escaped her; a massive wooden bed, sumptuously covered in musty velvet and silk. She raised the silk to peer under the bed, but there wasn't anything — except dust.

The temptation was simply too much. Kella crawled up on the massive bed and stretched out in guilty, hungry pleasure. Her aching muscles shouted relief. Perhaps she should shut her eyes for just a minute —

She woke to find someone holding her hand. The skin was as cold as ice, as cold as Jadel's, and she murmured sleepily and turned to look at him.

The man who sat there with her hand captured in his wasn't Jadel, was nothing like him. He was older, with cruel lines cut around his mouth and eyes. His hair was dark and chopped short, shot through with streaks of silver.

His eyes were of a pure, cold, lightless purple, like the absence of warmth. His voice was deep and commanding.

"It's been a long time since I found a pretty woman in my bed," Zenon noted with cool, acid humor. "You didn't come alone, my lady. Arise. We shall see your lover. If he wants my power so much, I think he should pay the price for it."

Kella shivered and tried to protest, but nothing came out. There was power around this man, power that dwarfed the menace of Jadel. A frown from him could stop her heart. She slid docilely off of his bed and followed him, a mute, frozen, terrified doll, and prayed that Jadel was gone.

He wasn't, of course; the sound of his destructive search was clear down the hall. Zenon pulled his captive along with only the lightest of pressures until they stood in the doorway of the library; Jadel, oblivious, flung a torn scroll aside and yanked out another. The scroll rolled unevenly across the stone floor and bumped against Zenon's boots.

The silence was profound. Jadel's shoulders tensed: Kella could feel his aura intensifying in response, but he didn't turn.

"Looking for something?" Zenon asked, too softly. The menace in his voice was surgically sharp. "Do you think you are great enough to wield it once you find it, puppy? Master of Unlife! You would have been my master of chamberpots!"

Jadel didn't respond to the contempt. He didn't turn. The sense of doom in the library grew even more oppressive, laden with the ravening dark hunger of Unlife that consumed both men. Kella bit her lip and tried again to speak, but something held her still despite her struggles.

"Turn around," Zenon whispered. Jadel slowly obeyed. "Dyar, you've developed a fatal ambition. Fatal for you, at least. No man treats me so lightly and lives."

Jadel looked at him, this strangely terrible figure, and then past him at Kella's white, terrified face. Something stirred in the cold cauldron of his heart, some alien feeling that ate disturbingly at his instinct for survival. He strangled it ruthlessly.

"I thought you dead, Master Zenon. My error, most certainly," Jadel finally said with silken grace. "Your pardon for my intrusion."

"Prettily said," Zenon said. "But not enough."

"What do I have that you could want, Master?" Jadel asked bluntly. Zenon's black brows rose in slow, grim contemplation. "You are far mightier than I. There is no spell I know that you have not mastered. Your ability in the Unlife is far deeper than mine. So what can I offer you?"

Zenon raised Kella's hand slowly, brows stilled raised. Jadel's smile faltered, briefly, then hardened.

"If you wish," he finally said indifferently. "Take her. There are more like her, certainly."

Kella made a faint sound of horrified betrayal, but he didn't even look at her. Zenon lowered her hand and shook his head.

"If I wanted her, I could easily have her. No, Dyar, you are not so poor as all that. You hold something that I do not, something that will free me from this decaying grave of a city and bring me the world. The Compass. I want it."

Jadel's eyes blazed: he hissed a denial. Zenon gestured, and the Dyar looked down to see the Compass burn a brilliant, luminous purple. Jadel bared his teeth and turned it back to darkness.

"Don't defy me. Give me the Compass and serve me, and I will let you live." Zenon smiled without humor. "Perhaps I'll give you something for your trouble. Will this pitiful continent suffice?"

"No!" Jadel snarled.

Zenon's smile, humorless as it was, disappeared altogether. "It is a better bargain than I have any reason to grant you, fool. Take it, or I will shatter you like glass. Any land you wish."

Jadel stared at him for a moment, the ruins of his plans rising up in misty ghosts in his mind. He slowly pulled the Compass off of his wrist and held it out to the sorcerer.

"Jaiman," he specified quietly. The Compass tugged itself free of his grip and floated slowly across to the Master Sorcerer of Quellburn, where it slid onto his hand like a living thing. As soon as it touched his cold skin, it blazed a violent, hurtful purple that flashed like lightning in the room.

Jadel cried out in agony and fell to his knees.

"Down!" Zenon shrieked, raising the Compass. Jadel shivered like a leaf in a storm. "Down on your face, Dyar, or die like the fool you are!"

Jadel resisted for a few heartbeats, then collapsed to hug the cold stone floor in widespread arms. His face burned hot with rage, but he couldn't make a sound. He crawled forward to grovel at his new master's feet, hating himself, hating Zenon — hating Kella, who witnessed this utter betrayal and made it painfully real.

Kella flinched so badly when Zenon's eyes fell on her that she actually began to sink to her knees, but his cold hand held her up with unnatural strength. She was terrified beyond tears. Zenon smiled slightly.

"A choice, pretty one. Your lover has no place left in his heart for you, assuming he had one at all; stand with me, or crawl with him. You decide."

Kella stared at him from dead, dark eyes and knew there wasn't a choice, not really. She slowly drew her hand out of his and prostrated herself beside Jadel on the cold stone. The Dyar's presence was a fevered hating pressure next to her, but he didn't look at her, nor she at him.

Zenon snarled in contempt and turned his back on them.

Tiernan woke to the light of dawn warming his face, feeling both worse and better than he thought possible. Worse, because every muscle in his body ached, and he hadn't had an ounce's worth of sleep, and better because —

The reason was coiled together with him in an intimate tangle of limbs under the warm shelter of the blanket. He eased himself up on an elbow, winced at the strain on his shoulder, and looked at her. She was, as the morning sun gilded her, the most beautiful thing he'd ever seen. Skin of pure satin, hair of purer gold, just a hint of freckles dotting the sunburned nose, blue, blue eyes the color of the sea at twilight —

Eyes? He had a vague memory of why that was dangerous, but it was lost as her body pressed closer to his. Laurel didn't say anything, only leaned forward to kiss him a gentle good morning.

It wasn't very gentle. She all but sucked his tongue down her throat. Tiernan tried to gently push her away, but she clung to him like a limpet. It was then that he remembered the curse, and the mask — and then it was a real struggle to free himself from her tenacious assault and wrap the cloth around his face again. For good measure, he got out of the blankets and stood uncertainly a few feet away while she watched.

"Better?" he asked her.

She rubbed at her forehead in confusion. "I apologize. I thought perhaps the spell would have worn off."

"Apparently not. I thought you were going to eat me alive."

"An interesting proposition," Laurel smiled, and her smile turned into a full-scale laugh. "Really, Tiernan, for a man so bold in the darkness you do blush in the most interesting places. Do you know how silly you look standing there stark naked with a rag around your face? How do you feel?"

"I feel stupid standing here naked with a rag around my face," he snapped back, and came back to the comfort of the blanket. "There. At least now I'm warm and stupid."

"Ah, normal," she said knowingly, and pushed him away. "Not so fast, Tiernan. We must move on."

"Why?" he asked wistfully. She rolled her eyes and shoved him out in the cold morning air. He sighed and began hunting for his clothes. When he was dressed, he turned and saw that she was industriously rolling up the blanket and already fully clothed. It was most disappointing. He still hadn't — well — seen her.

Though, he cheerfully admitted, it was probably a silly thing to be harping at. Tired or not, sore or not, he hadn't felt so good in months. Years.

"Never," he decided aloud, and she looked at him as if his brains had leaked during the night. They probably had. He was grinning like a fool under the mask, and it was just as well she couldn't see it. She'd certainly never let him forget it.

"There's someone coming," Laurel said, shading her eyes against the glare of the sun. Tiernan stopped grinning and turned to look himself. There certainly was, a full score of them, mounted on horses. They were riding for the oasis.

"We can't get away in time. Perhaps they can help us." Laurel's tone wasn't encouraging; they certainly hadn't encountered an overpowering amount of helping hands so far in their journey, and neither of them was optimistic this time. Tiernan wished he'd kept Walerin's knife. He felt more naked now than when he'd been a slave. At least he'd had chains to swing then.

The riders drew up at a cautious distance. They were fierce-featured, dark people, men and women alike, heavily robed and cloaked against the desert chill. Tiernan said nothing. One of the riders, a big-shouldered man with a splash of gray in his black beard, inclined his head.

"You are trespassing," he said, his words barely decipherable beneath a thick gargling accent. It wasn't a hospitable beginning.

"We did not know," Laurel said with great respect, and bowed. "Forgive our ignorance. We're travellers. We lost our guide — "

"Heading for the city, ah?" the man asked, cutting her off. She nodded, at a loss but determined to stay with him. "Fools. Always fools head for the city. Some idiot sells them a tattered old map for a silver piece and they come to make their fortune. Buh!"

He spat on the sand at Tiernan's feet. The prince didn't move.

"What's wrong with you, man?" the man asked, and edged his horse closer. "You have it wrong, eh? The women veil, the men do not. Unless you are a woman?"

Tiernan tensed his sore muscles. Laurel's voice cut incisively through the laughter of the man's companions.

"He's a leper," she said clearly. The laughter stopped. The man backed his horse, then backed it a pace further for good measure. "We won't trouble you further."

"Lepers. Lepers at the oasis," the man whispered, and bared his teeth. "You foul the water. Water is life here. No, you go nowhere. We post your bones as a warning sign."

"No! We did nothing — " Laurel began, alarmed, but the man drew his sword and spurred his horse into a sudden gallop. Tiernan ducked under the slash and grabbed the man's arm as he passed. The rider was catapulted off his mount and into the pool with a splash. He fought for the shore with a breathless scream. Laurel was closest; she kicked sand in his eyes and grabbed up his sword when he dropped it to claw at his face.

A terrible look came over her face when she felt the weight of the blade in her hand. It was half terror, and half completion, and her eyes fixed on Tiernan's unprotected back.

Five more were coming, now, shouting and spurring to the attack. Tiernan swore under his breath, ducking under another slash from the first rider as he stripped his sword away. He moved just in time to block the second blow aimed at him, then dropped and rolled to come up after the third. He killed the fourth. He didn't dare to look to see if Laurel had been hurt; he had to trust her to hold her own, because his own skill was being strained to the very limits just staying alive. The fifth nomad pulled up and began to fence with him in earnest, but he wasn't good enough, not nearly, not against a prince who'd taken to the sword at the age of six. Tiernan exchanged three passes with him and then ran him through.

When the coldness pierced his back, his first disoriented thought was that one of the riders had slipped up behind him, but as he staggered around to strike he saw Laurel's contorted, desperate face. He was so surprised that he couldn't move — and before he could cry out, she lunged again. The steel entered his belly and slid in and through, tenting the torn fabric of his shirt in the back and letting in a flow of agony. He did cry out, suddenly, and grabbed for her. She staggered backwards with tears glittering in her wild, bemused eyes.

"Laurel!" he gasped, utterly betrayed, and tasted blood. The sword was still in him. He grabbed for it in clumsy, numb fingers, and tried to draw it out. He couldn't do it. He tried to ask her why she'd done it, but all that came out of his mouth was blood; he hardly even felt it when he toppled over to lie on his side in the cold sand. His life was running out. There was no heat anywhere; even Laurel's brilliant hair was going gray.

He would sleep a little, he decided, and shut his eyes. The day would look better after he'd had a little rest.

The riders didn't bother to kill the madwoman; they gathered up their fallen, muttered curses, and went back into the desert the way they'd come. Laurel stood there, oblivious, with her hands stained with Tiernan O'Locklir's blood, and slowly began to come back to herself.

When sanity struck, it struck hard. She flung herself down in the sand and tried to hold him, but the blood, oh, the blood was everywhere, and she couldn't bear to touch the sword. She held him close and felt his breathing falter, and her heart faltered with it.

A shadow fell over her. She raised a face marked with tears and blood and saw a spectacularly beautiful young man with long dark hair and huge purple eyes staring down at her. Andraax, she recalled with a strange kind of apathy. A pale-faced Evan hung back, weeping.

"What have you done?" Andraax asked coldly. Laurel opened her mouth, but she couldn't get the words free. "Daughter of a Loremaster, how could you fail to know the sorcerer had cursed you with Friendslayer? Even a fool should have known that steel in your hand, cursed as they were, would mean the death of your closest friend."

Her only defense sounded too thin even to her inner ears, so she only looked back down at Tiernan's face. He was still breathing, but it was shallow and uneven. His skin was an awful grayish color, so transparent that she could almost see hard bone underneath.

"He is dying," Andraax whispered. She made a sound of protest. "It is as I foresaw. The Prince of Rhakhaan had no chance to survive this journey."

"Liar," she said just as softly. "You might have saved him. You still could. Evan wants you to, don't you, Evan — or is that just like every other promise you've made to him, just another whim to be cast away at will?"

Andraax continued to look at her for a long, long time while she stared at her lover's ebbing life. He then reached out and tilted her chin up with his pale hand so that her tear-filled, defiant eyes were focused on him.

"It is the destiny of Tiernan O'Locklir to die. Further, it is not my place as Loremaster to interfere in every trouble that inflicts itself on the unfortunate. You had as much of a chance of avoiding this as I did, Loremaster's daughter. This you know to be true." Andraax shook his head. "You and the prince served my purposes admirably. You kept the boy safe from harm, you taught him much about good and evil. I would have seen you happy, if it were allowed."

He let Laurel go, but her hand whipped out and fastened around his wrist, stained as it was with Tiernan's blood, and clung with surprising strength. More surprising still was the fury blazing in her blue eyes.

"You can save him, damn you. You have the power. Do something."

"No," he simply said, and pulled. She added her other hand, pulling back. He frowned in annoyance.

"Yes. You brought us here. You put us in the middle of the desert with a man who you knew was beyond my power to best magically, and you abandoned us when you had what you wanted! This is your fault, Andraax, and even madmen must pay their debts!"

She was shouting, and in the ringing echo of her shout she heard that one, faint sound that she had dreaded with all of her heart.

Tiernan's breathing faltered and stopped.

Andraax's luminous purple eyes softened as the knowledge hit her. Her grip on him became less of tenacious rage than of need, and she opened her mouth. Nothing came out but a terribly thin keening cry. The mad Loremaster gently freed himself and shook his head.

"Tiernan!" Evan shouted, and pushed by Andraax even as the man reached down to stop him. He flung himself down next to Laurel and looked helplessly at her, at Tiernan. "He isn't dead. He can't be dead. Andraax!"

"I saw his destiny before your arrival, Evan; the prince was fated never to survive his journey. This was the kindest of deaths he could have suffered. I did what I could." Andraax held out his hand. "Evan, come away."

"I'm not going anywhere!" Evan screamed in a sudden fury. He was crying the tears that Laurel couldn't, dusty tracks on his too-red face, but his voice was clear and enraged. "You — liar! You said you'd help them, and all you did was watch him — you dragged me here — I hate you! I'm not going anywhere with you, I'd rather be dead!"

"Don't say that," Andraax whispered, stricken.

Evan wiped at his tears with angry fists. "Go away or do something for once. I'm sick of you and your excuses. What's wrong with you? She needs your help!"

"I cannot help!" Andraax reached up to hold his head in trembling, white-knuckled hands. "The Thalan is waking, he's trying to pry into my head again, and if I waste power helping them I will lose this battle, don't you understand? What is he? A minor prince of an insignificant land! What do I care about his death?"

The wind whipped a handful of sand up and cast it in Evan's face, but he didn't blink, didn't turn away. He'd stopped crying, and his face was the same young/old mask that Andraax wore.

"I care," he whispered. He drew in a deep breath. "Help him, Andraax. You have to, or you're not anything at all. You said you were a Loremaster. You said it like it meant something. Don't turn your back on him now."

"You do not know what you're asking," Andraax whispered faintly, shutting his eyes. He squeezed at his temples as if trying to force his precarious sanity back inside, then straightened and nodded. His eyes opened, nearly all pupil in the rising sun's glare. "Will you come with me when it's done?"

"I'll do anything you want," Evan answered miserably.

Andraax looked at him a moment. "Move away from him," the Loremaster said, reaching to take Tiernan's body out of Laurel's protective arms. She didn't want to give him up, but Evan persuaded her. Her skin was freezing cold with shock. He wrapped the blanket around her and held her hand as Andraax bent over the prince.

"Easy," Andraax advised, taking hold of the sword that protruded from Tiernan's stomach. Before Laurel could cry out, he pulled it smoothly free. Andraax clamped one hand over the wound and stripped Tiernan's ragged mask away with the other. He faltered a little when he saw the prince's face, but then he slid his other hand over the still-warm skin of Tiernan's forehead.

"What are you doing?" Laurel asked. Her voice seemed to come from a great, aching distance.

Andraax didn't look up. "Being a great fool," he murmured. "Silence, both of you. This is not a task I assume lightly."

There was nothing to see, but there was a buzzing, strangely insistent sound in Evan's head. The air seemed heavy, suddenly, and hung over them like a cold glaring enemy. He shivered and felt Laurel's body echo him. Andraax's whole body moved in a painful flinch, but the Loremaster hung on despite the pale set of his face, the undeniably panicked look in his eyes.

The Thalan were awake, seeking entrance.

Andraax poured his power recklessly down into the body under his hands, knitting impossible wounds, forcing life back into lifeless tissue. Breathe, he begged silently, unnerved, as the whispers of the Thalan drew into sharp, terrible focus. Madness seemed so much easier than such an obscene invasion —

Tiernan pulled in a deep, gasping breath and coughed up a mouthful of blood. His eyes flew open to stare blindly at the sun. He curled convulsively on his side and coughed again, bringing up more blood. Evan felt the pressure ease, but there was something left in its place — a chaotic, swirling void that frightened him.

Andraax sat back and rested his head on his clenched fists. Tiernan's convulsive twist had left him facing toward Evan and Laurel, and now the prince blinked at them and forced himself sit up in spite of his pain.

"You're the first," he whispered. Laurel stared at him with tear-filled, shining eyes.

"What?"

"You're the first woman who's ever been this dissatisfied." And he smiled, a warm, half-betrayed smile that forced her to break into joyous, heart-rending sobs and to throw herself into his arms.

There were no explanations given, and none required; all that mattered was the touch of her body, and the living warmth of his. They forgot about the others for the moment.

"Thank you," Evan whispered.

Andraax raised his head to look at the boy with empty purple eyes.

"Come," he said softly. Evan hesitated. "Come. No more delays."

Evan's fingers brushed the brown surface of a stone in his pocket, and the whispering, chaotic storm that had been swirling around his head was suddenly inside, confusing and frightening. He stiffened and backed away from Andraax's reaching hand.

"I don't want to go with you," Evan heard himself say. His hand closed over the rock in a convulsive spasm. "Go away, Andraax. I don't need you."

Andraax sat there on his knees in the dust, dark hair stirred a little by the desert breeze, and stared at him. The Loremaster said nothing. Evan felt a surge of white anger that pushed the boy to his feet.

He didn't want to stand, but he did it anyway.

"Don't, boy," Andraax warned. His eyes were strangely distant and yet intent. "You don't understand what's happening. Hold fast."

"To what? You lied to me, Andraax! You chased me all over the place and you tricked me! I'm not going anywhere with you."

Andraax reached for him with something like anger kindling in his amethyst eyes, but Evan darted back and threw his arms around Tiernan's shoulders. The prince looked surprised, but didn't flinch as the Loremaster came closer.

"We've already had this debate, Loremaster. If the boy doesn't want to go with you, he doesn't have to." Tiernan's face was still too pale, his eyes too distant, but he meant what he said. Laurel held to him with fierce strength and nodded.

"As you say, Prince Tiernan, we've already had this debate," Andraax acknowledged gravely. "Yet you lost before, and you will lose now. I've given you back your life. Would you throw it away like this?"

A short, painful pause, while Laurel bit her lip and Tiernan held the Loremaster's gaze. Tiernan smiled a old wild smile, and Andraax felt his lips twitch in response.

"If I have to," Tiernan said evenly, and slid one hand protectively around Evan's shoulders. "He stays with us, Loremaster. If you want to take him somewhere, you take us all."

Andraax was hard put to keep the amusement off of his face; he raised his eyebrows and looked from Tiernan to his lady. He'd expected better sense of the woman, somehow, but she looked as defiant (and as frightened) as the prince himself. Well, then.

"It appears it is not worth the effort," he said

The cold calculating portion of his mind measured his remaining strength against the likelihood of attack by Thalan, and quailed at the possibilities. Each use of power drained him that much more, left him open and vulnerable and increasingly distant from sanity.

An interesting problem. Theoretically.

"Very well, then. I shall charge you Navigator's rates for such an expedition." Andraax felt a distant shove at his mind, and frowned slightly. When he remembered his companions, they were looking at him oddly. Tiernan was already on his feet, held there by the combined efforts of his lady and the boy, and they were plainly awaiting something. Andraax's face smiled, undirected by his conscious mind, and he stared blankly past them.

"Sir?" Laurel finally asked hesitantly. He said nothing. She waved a hand in front of his eyes. "Sir, are you — "

"Mad," Tiernan hissed in disgust, and bent over in a sudden spasm of pain. "I'm mad myself to want to go with him. It's like sticking your hand in a wolf's mouth."

"He can't help it," Evan whispered, and felt the voices in his head again, stronger now. He clung to Tiernan even more fiercely. "Andraax? Can we go?"

"Go where?" Andraax echoed.

"Remember? You wanted to take me to my father. Can we go now?"

Andraax doubled over in silent pain, hands clawing the dirt

"Quellburn," Andraax said, a note of warning in his voice. "There are Thalan near. I've lost the one, but there are more. Be careful."

Tiernan and Laurel looked at each other in incomprehension, then down at Evan. He shrugged, one hand still wrapped tightly around the stone in his pocket. Laurel made a meaningful if unflattering gesture at her forehead, and Tiernan nodded.

"No need to worry, I'll look out for them," Laurel promised. Andraax seemed satisfied; he held his hands out, one to Evan and one to Tiernan. Laurel completed the circle without being instructed, and Andraax lifted them up on an Essence Flow. The sight was just as Evan remembered; a gray nothing, featureless and unmoving. Andraax stared off into the distance.

"Down," Andraax murmured, just as Evan was preparing to ask where they were going. The landing wasn't as good as before; Evan felt only air under his feet, and fell hard to the cobbled street. He winced and got up; Tiernan was standing, but just barely, and Laurel was just climbing to her feet. Andraax was already striding across the street.

Street? Well, it had been a street, once, but the houses that lined it were all burnt and toppled, and the street itself was buckled and ripped as if the earth had moved under it. Evan turned in a jerky, disbelieving circle, and saw only destruction and decay. There was a wildly overgrown place to their right that looked like it had once been a park, from the shattered marble statues that still rose up out of the gnarled shrubs and grasses. Andraax was heading straight for it.

"Hey! Andraax! Where are we going?" Evan yelled, sprinting after him. Andraax paused with his foot in the grass and looked back at him.

"Shortcut," he said bluntly, and looked at Tiernan and Laurel, who were picking their way across the rubble after him. "Follow, if you wish."

"Maybe we should stay here," Laurel said with a tired frown at the overgrowth.

Andraax shrugged. "As you like. Wights and Ghouls inhabit the houses, but they will not trouble you until dark, or until you stumble on them. Of course, then they will rip your bodies apart and drink your blood."

Laurel swallowed, shot him a murderous look, and tightened her grip on Tiernan's arm. He looked almost his old self, except for the darkness in his eyes, and the white set of his lips.

"Can you make it?" she asked him breathlessly. He shrugged, a mirrored copy of Andraax, and she cursed him before she kissed him.

"Incredible," Andraax sighed. It was Tiernan's turn to shoot him a grim look. "You realize, of course, that Laurel Magen remains unaffected by your curse?"

"Perhaps it's broken," Tiernan said hopefully. Andraax smiled and shook his head.

"No. I can feel it. Lady Magen is a stronger person than I would have believed, or else there is something in her feelings for you that allows her to ignore the curse."

"Well," Tiernan told him with a perfectly straight face, "love is blind, isn't it?"

Andraax stared at him for a few seconds, sighed, and turned back to begin pushing a way through the overgrown park.

"Excuse me," Laurel panted, some minutes later, "but wouldn't it be easier to just fly over all this?"

"Much," Andraax agreed pleasantly. "Evan, have you seen my rock? I seem to have misplaced it."

The boy shook his head sullenly, not at all like the boy Andraax remembered. The Loremaster felt cold settle around his heart. If, as he'd suspected from the moment Evan had backed away from him, the Thalan had the boy, the damage they could do with such wild, untamed power was incalculable.

It was going to require a great deal too much effort to handle such a problem.

"Very well," Andraax murmured. "The answer to your question, Lady Magen, is that I have just drained myself to the dregs in order to restore health to your lover, and to transport you out of danger beyond your wildest imagination. Therefore I have no power left to fly us over this tangle, and you should be grateful for the favors you've gotten rather than counting the ones you haven't." Andraax sounded uncommonly on edge.

Laurel slapped at a hovering insect and touched the Loremaster on the sleeve with a tentative hand. "Loremaster? Forgive me. I failed to even thank you for what you did for us. Will you accept my apology, and my gratitude?" She delivered him a courtesy that was far too elegant and graceful for her garb and their situation, but he smiled and nodded. Driven as much by mischief as good manners, Laurel rose and kissed him.

Andraax was a surprisingly good kisser, as he demonstrated. Laurel finally fought politely free, only to find him smiling at her with mischievous delight, and to find Tiernan frowning. She squeezed the prince's hand and mollified him.

"I envy you your good fortune, Prince Tiernan," Andraax said mildly, and his eyebrows rose. "Duck."

"What?" Laurel asked.

Andraax kept smiling. "Duck," he said again, throwing himself flat. The others stared at him in confusion, and then Tiernan grabbed Laurel and threw her down. Something whistled over their heads and embedded itself with a metallic singing sound in a twisted tree.

"What in the hells was that?" Tiernan yelled, and twisted to look. He wished he hadn't.

A headless man stood there, arm still outstretched from the throw that had almost decapitated them. Tiernan gaped and shook his hair back out of his eyes as creature dug another round, sharp disc out of a pouch at its belt and flung it. It made a buzzing sound as it flashed just above Tiernan's head, slicing off several wayward strands of hair on the way.

"Andraax!" Tiernan yelled. The Loremaster was slowly getting to his feet, his eyes on the headless ghost.

"Evan, give me the rock," he said imperatively, and held out his hand. Evan actually took it out of his pocket, then shook his head and shoved it back in.

"I don't have it," he said mutinously.

Andraax spared him a searing glance. "You're a worse liar than I am. Give me the rock!" Andraax gestured again. Evan buried his face in the grass as another blade zinged over his head. "Infuriating boy! Very well. I shall have to do without it."

The ghost's blade was in its hand as Andraax climbed to his feet. The Loremaster watched the steel circle as the ghost tensed for the throw, and then said a single unpronounceable word. The steel exploded into red gas.

"Now then," Andraax said, and stepped up to the ghost. "Veernon, isn't it? You were a merchant; I remember you. Our heads will not restore yours. Rest now."

Andraax clapped his hands once, sharply, and the ghost exploded soundlessly into smoky vapor and was gone. He smiled sadly at the empty space and then reached down to offer Laurel Magen a polite hand up.

"Poor man," Andraax said quietly, still looking back. "So many dead, for no purpose. So much evil left behind."

"Are there a lot of ghosts here?" Tiernan wanted to know.

Andraax glanced at him, amused. "Prince, Quellburn is a city of ghosts. Some of them even still breathe."

He was, Evan felt suddenly sure, talking as much about himself as anything native to Quellburn.

"Well?" Pelk asked, and wiped at his forehead with the back of a dusty hand. "It looks simple enough. The gates are open — "

"Mmm," Tyes agreed doubtfully. "I've never been here. I have no idea how many traps the Citadel of Wizards may contain, but I'd be willing to bet that there's at least one on the gate."

"I've been here," Iarsang volunteered. "But I was always expected, and announced. There used to be a gatekeeper who stood in the alcove inside."

"Lots of bones," Pelk sighed. "Not all of them date back to the fall of the Citadel. Bad sign."

No one had any argument with that. Tyes shrugged and began walking toward the gates that loomed open and mocking in the intimidating walls.

"Master!" Pelk protested, and ran to catch up. "Master, don't. Let me."

"Not this time. Stay back, Pelk."

"Master — "

"It isn't open to debate, Pelk. Go back." Tyes waited until his aide had reluctantly backed away, then shook his chameleon cloak back over his shoulders and strode in. As he passed the threshold, Tyes felt the distinctive cold sensation of a spell activating.

He instantly flung up his arm, a blue-green bracelet glittering in the pale sun. Something flashed brighter than the sun, something that struck Tyes and, in spite of the spell shield that the bracelet threw around him, nearly knocked him down. The light faded, and Tyes stumbled through the threshold and into the entrance hall of the Citadel of Wizards.

The warding bracelet was hot. Tyes shook his hand in a vain attempt to cool it, blinked away afterimages and waved to the others who stood clustered on the other side.

"Are you all right?" Pelk shouted.

Tyes shrugged. "Not the most elegant method for entering the hall, but it will serve. Now, the rest of you."

"I hate to point it out, master, but we'll be baked to a crisp if we try it," Pelk called back.

Tyes shook his head and smiled. "Iarsang, what did you say about how you entered the hall?"

"I was always — announced." Iarsang gave Tyes a rare, bitter smile. "Very good, Loremaster. Very well. Announce me."

"Iarsang of the Guild of Navigators," Tyes called, and Iarsang walked calmly over the threshold.

Nothing happened. Iarsang stopped next to Tyes. The Loremaster raised his eyebrows.

"You weren't sure that would work," Iarsang said in surprise.

"Not entirely, no. But it was the best possible answer. Pelk of Karilôn!"

Pelk didn't linger. Tyes announced Astrid and Brion, and sighed in relief as he turned back to face the Citadel.

The silence was complete and ominous.

"Where is he?" Tyes asked. Iarsang didn't need to ask who he meant.

"Far back in the Citadel. Come. This way."

"Careful!" Pelk said anxiously. "This entire place is one trap after another. They were terrified even before the attack, apparently."

"I'll be careful," Iarsang replied, and gave him a humorless look. "Besides, of all of you I have the least to live for. It seems good that I should lead the way."

"She wouldn't want you to die foolishly," Tyes snapped back.

Iarsang lifted his eyebrows, dreamy brown eyes far away and unmoved. "I know that you are doing me a vast favor, Loremaster, but it would be a great kindness if you would keep your opinions to yourself," the Navigator said with insulting patience. Tyes shook his head angrily and gestured him on ahead with exaggerated politeness.

Iarsang ignored it and started down the black marbled hall.

Zenon was sitting in silent contemplation of a ruined, battered room that still bore the scars of terrible battle. He drew in a deep, slow breath and stepped forward into the arms of cold memory.

"It was here I was — defeated," he said softly, words falling like chunks of black ice on the dead air. Something rattled against his foot; he shoved it out into the open and smiled slightly. A shattered bit of white bone, bleached and dry. Zenon bent and picked it up, then reached further to heft an unbroken thigh bone. He held it lightly in between his palms and turned to look at his new acolytes.

The Dyar's face was bland and innocent, but his eyes were dark doorways into madness. He hated, that one, hated with an intensity all out of proportion to sanity. Jadel was the kind of man who could bear no master, and Zenon knew that as masters went, he was not the easiest. It pleased him, the pain he caused.

It was all the feeling that was left to him, after all these years of the corrosive touch of Unlife.

The woman, now — pale, weak, and flawed but still curiously compelling. She had surprised him by showing loyalty. She was not the loyal kind, that one.

The power in her was far weaker than the dark elf's, but growing. She would be useful.

"This," Zenon said aloud, and lifted the thigh bone, "was Alladyre, Ruler of Quellburn and Master Mystic. A woman of unparalleled accomplishment, and a fool. She set herself against me. Against me! You can see how well she succeeded; I live and she — is dust."

Zenon snapped the bone in half. The fragments clattered harshly to the broken stone floor. Kella flinched, but said nothing; Jadel's face was as intent as a hunting predator's.

"Her curse held me powerless for a long, long time — but now it is over, and I walk. She will never walk again." Zenon stamped down on the bones, grinding them into gritty powder. "My demons tore her limb from limb. Soon my demons will do the same to anyone who opposes me. You, my servants, will take care of the intruders I feel in my city; they are nothing that requires my own attention. Kill them all, and do it swiftly. If you succeed, I shall let you both live.

"If you fail, the fate that befell Alladyre will seem the benediction of the gods."

Kella flinched again as those hot purple eyes raked her, but Jadel smiled, bloodthirst rising to bank the fires of hate. Time enough for Zenon's doom when his own dishonor was slaked by the defeat of others.

Besides, he could sense the identity of those others who approached, even at this distance. It would give him a gratifying pleasure to see Iarsang plead for death, and as for Vurkanan Tyes — the Loremaster deserved something innovative.

Kella, without a word being spoken, understood that the others were hers — including Brion.

"When I get back to court," Tiernan panted as he pushed aside another spiky, thorn-laden branch and ducked underneath, "I am never, never leaving again. I'm going to take that hereditary stonepile of an estate that my father was kind enough to give me, and I'm going to marry and get fat and old and have lots of children. But I am never leaving again."

"Liar." Laurel tried to push her sweat-streaked hair back from her face. The air was still and close, and none of them could forget the dangerously narrow escape they'd had from the headless ghost of Veernon. "You'd spend a month poking around the place, then you'd get bored and organize some sort of mad entertainment like fighting wolves with your bare hands or wrestling Trolls — "

"Yes, my lady," he answered meekly, and swore as he freed his long hair from a thorned branch. "I swear that this place is trying to strangle me."

"See? You'd never hold your own in wrestling Trolls, then, so you'd better not make any rash promises. The Lords of Orhan may not be paying attention — "

"But then again," Andraax interrupted, "they may. They frequently are, at the most inopportune moments. Quiet. This is the end of the park, and from here on we will face many unpleasant things. Stay close."

"Is that our only option?" Tiernan whispered in Laurel's ear. She choked on laughter and pushed through the last reluctant set of bushes to emerge on a wide stone thoroughfare.

Rising above the devastation like diamonds above coal dust were the huge unbroken walls of the Citadel of Wizards.

"Lords above and Demons Beyond!" Evan whispered, Thalan whispers temporarily silenced. No one disputed him.

"Let me guess," Laurel said, shaking her hair free of clinging bits of leaves and bark, "that's our destination."

"Yes," Andraax said softly, and smiled. "Yes, you might say so. The end of your quest, Evan."

"My parents are there?" Evan asked. He obviously doubted the answer, even before he got it.

"Indeed they are. But I would not like you to be surprised, Evan, so I will tell you this: your parents are not the people you knew, just as you are not the child they remember. Their anger has changed to something much more dangerous. Do you understand?"

"They used to fight," Evan said slowly. "Are you saying it's gotten worse?"

"I'm saying that each is a vessel for energy, just as you are. Your mother was drawn to the Unlife by the rage and anger within her. Your father is just as powerfully susceptible to the power of Essence. They are two halves of a single thing, but they are opposed. Light and dark, night and day—do you see?" Andraax was obviously trying hard to sound rational, as if it were something deadly important for the boy to understand. Laurel and Tiernan exchanged glances, and Laurel raised her finger to touch her temple. Tiernan nodded.

"You mean my mother can't be trusted?" Evan asked slowly, struggling to understand.

Andraax hesitated. "She is weak. She has submitted to evil, and it is very difficult to return from such a thing. In truth, I don't think she wants to." The Loremaster shook his head slightly. "Believe me, Evan, what she is, she has chosen. I can offer you no comfort other than that."

Because Andraax was looking down at the boy, he didn't see the shadow slip from the trees behind him, but Tiernan did. Even as the huge creature tensed and sprang, the prince lunged forward and knocked Andraax and Evan flat.

It was a bold move. Unfortunately, it left Tiernan standing flat-footed and off balance in their places as the huge gray wolf completed its jump and bowled him end-over-end down the street.

"Tiernan!" Laurel screamed. Andraax struggled to a sitting position and evaluated the situation in a single glance. The wolf was an enormous specimen, as tall as a tall man as it stretched itself atop Tiernan and snapped for his throat. The prince was struggling to keep the massive jaws from clashing shut on his throat, but that battle was destined to be short; Tiernan was still recovering from his brush with death, and the wolf was starving and desperate. Andraax freed his sword and slid it across the street to lie next to the struggling young man.

It wasn't a lot of help, Tiernan thought desperately, to have a sword digging painfully into your ribs while you breathed in the rancid stench of a starving wolf and it dripped saliva on your throat. He snarled as fiercely as a wolf himself as the beast's claws dug at his legs in a struggle to disembowel him. Tiernan found the strength to unbalance the animal and roll away. His dexterity hadn't failed him, at least; he was able to scoop up the sword on the roll and bring it up as the wolf scrambled to its feet among the rubble and lunged again. It avoided the blade and sunk its teeth in his shoulder. Tiernan shouted wordlessly and tossed the sword to his free hand; he put all of his strength into the thrust; the sword took the wolf just under the right foreleg and angled in. The animal's enraged snarling turned to yelps of agony, and it released him. Tiernan rolled away again and stabbed down three more times until the wolf was still.

"Tiernan!" Laurel cried, and skidded to a breathless stop next to him. He grinned at her in sheer terrified exhilaration as she looked at his shoulder. The wound was bloody but shallow. She sagged against him in relief. "Tiernan, you jackass. You might have been killed — again."

"If I am expected to wrestle wolves and Trolls — " Tiernan gestured vaguely at the animal's corpse and felt a sudden surge of pure terror now that he saw how big the thing really was. Laurel, heedless of his wound, slapped him painfully on the shoulder.

"You — idiot! I swear to you, that's it. I wouldn't marry you if you were the last — "

"Have I asked you?"

"Children!" Andraax interrupted, reaching over Laurel's shoulder to recapture his sword. He frowned vaguely at the blood on it, then gestured at the blade. The liquid ran to the tip and pooled on the ground, leaving the blade clean. "Shall we go?"

"Talk about gratitude." Tiernan winced as Laurel grabbed him and pushed him in the direction of the others.

There was something about the city that made travellers hurry, even in sunlight; the houses were so silent, so devastated, and everywhere they looked skulls looked back. A half-shattered skull under a bench. A whole skull, perched rakishly atop a leaning pole. A whole skeleton sprawled awkwardly half-over a crumbling wall.

Laurel shuddered as she stepped carefully over the skeleton of an adult curled protectively around the skeleton of a child, and felt the miasma that hovered over the whole city strike at her.

"It's still full of hate, isn't it?" she whispered softly. Andraax turned to glance at her and nodded. His usually impassive, perfect face was marked with dirt and sweat, and he seemed to be straining to maintain his control. She cast another glance at Tiernan, but he was looking across the street. She followed his gaze, and shuddered again.

"Horrible," she whispered. Someone, Trolls had fashioned a crematorium in the alleyway. Charred bones were jammed in between the stone walls to a depth as high as Tiernan's shoulders. The prince pulled in a deep breath and put his unwounded arm around Laurel's shoulders, pulling her closer; she didn't object. "How much further?"

"See?" Andraax pointed to the end of the street, where the walls loomed. "There are the gates to the Citadel of Wizards."

"Not soon enough for me," Laurel sighed. Tiernan's fingers caressed the side of her face. She shivered and turned to touch her lips to them. "Did everyone die, Loremaster? No one survived?"

"Some escaped, to die in the wilderness or to live on as little better than animals. A few survivors fled far enough to found the Shrine of Hraask." Andraax was silent a moment, then rubbed at his forehead. It glittered with sweat. "Only one lived here in the ruins."

"One?" Tiernan was stunned. "But the city — it's huge. It must have held thousands."

"Tens of thousands. Yet they perished for Master Sorcerer Zenon's ambition. He wanted to rule over Quellburn. So he does." Andraax frowned. "Ruler of a city of the dead."

"He's still alive? The one who caused this? Even the Lords of Orhan should have stepped in to exact some kind of justice for this." Tiernan cast a look back at the alley. Its contents were mercifully hidden now, but his imagination supplied them, clothed in flesh and hideously betrayed.

"Perhaps they are stepping in," Andraax suggested morosely, and slowed to a halt as they approached the open brass gates. "Someone's already inside."

"How can you tell?" Evan asked. Andraax pointed wordlessly at a red-robed skeleton that lay across the threshold. It was soot-stained and still smoking.

"Look!" Laurel pointed. In the distance, at the end of the hallway beyond the gates, a group of people were pushing open heavy bronze doors. She squinted her eyes against the glare of the sun. "My father. I think that's my father!"

"Wonderful," Tiernan sighed.

Laurel ignored him.

"We are out of time," Andraax said, his hands on his hips. "Here, we part company. Evan, you come with me."

"We can't split up now!" Evan protested. "Hey! That's my father!"

"No," Andraax took Evan's hand. He was trembling with strain, and sweat dripped from his face to stain the robe at his neck. Still, his eyes glittered with power. "Don't cross the threshold until someone calls to you."

"Andraax! Wait!" Laurel cried. Andraax held up a single admonitory finger, and then he and the boy shot straight up, levitating upward so fast that they were lost to sight after only seconds. "Wait! Come back!"

It was too late. They were gone. Laurel ran to the gates, remembering in time Andraax's warning, and shouted for help. Tiernan joined her, after a slight hesitation; he wasn't at all eager to see Laurel's father, not after dragging the man's daughter through dangers he would have hesitated to subject his worst enemy to — but he needn't have worried.

Vurkanan Tyes, after a brief, unworthy pause, called him into the Citadel of Wizards.

"Let go of me!" Evan screamed, trying to wrench loose. Andraax's grip on his shoulders was like iron. They touched lightly down in an overgrown area that nearly hid a weirdly shaped little building to the north. "That was my father, you told me you'd take me to him, you promised — "

"Not yet! Not yet, boy. Be still." Andraax looked around, frowning, and Evan realized that his face was too pale, too strained. He was still sweating, and now it was running down his face like rain. "Not yet, I am not done yet. You took the rock from me, Evan, that was a foolish thing to do. Give me it to me while you still can, boy."

"No, you said — "

"Fool!" Andraax clenched his trembling hands. "I'm expending all of my power to hold them back from you. Give it up while you still can! If I fall they'll take you and never give you up!"

"No," Evan's lips said. He realized with cold fear that the blessed quiet in his mind was slowly fragmenting up into snatches of speech, howling calls, and screams of rage. The Thalan were back —

And they were angry. The stone burned in his hand as he pulled it out in the open. Andraax winced and doubled over in agony.

"Ours, Loremaster," Evan's voice said, but it wasn't Evan talking. Andraax gave a breathless cry and summoned up a final surge of Essence. He wielded it like a precision tool, sweeping the Thalan screaming out of Evan's mind and back into the rock, imprisoning it there in spite of its terrible, costly attacks.

Evan staggered as he was released, and he looked at the rock dazedly. The Loremaster straightened. Andraax's eyes opened wide. His lips twisted back from his teeth in a silent vicious snarl. When his voice came, it was almost a howl.

"Give me the stone! Now!"

There was so much menace in him, so much madness, that Evan handed it over. Andraax stood quite still, looking at it, and then slowly raised his head.

He looked straight into the eyes of a huge wolf, twin to the one that had attacked Tiernan and so nearly killed him. This one was too close for Andraax to even move for his sword, and far too close to Evan, who stood frozen in terror. Andraax reached for Essence, but nothing came. For a second neither one of them blinked. The wolf lunged.

Andraax threw the stone with perfect accuracy, catching the wolf in the skull just between the eyes. The rock hit with an audible crunch, and the wolf crashed down, lifeless, at their feet. The rock rolled free and bumped against Andraax's feet.

"Now that," Andraax said, taking in a deep, shuddering breath, "is the most useful thing a Thalan's ever done. Do you hear me, you worthless body-stealing—"

Andraax suddenly stopped talking, bent down, and picked up the stone. He rubbed it between his palms, rather as if he was petting it, and then he thrust it back into his pocket. Without a word to Evan, he turned and walked away.

He kept walking even when the boy cried out, because his mind had retreated far, far beyond a mere mortal's call.

"Wait!" Evan shouted. The mad Loremaster didn't turn, didn't pause; he disappeared behind a tree. Evan ran after him, but there was nothing on the other side of the tree except overgrown thorn bushes dotted with fragrant wild roses and knee-high, sweet-smelling grass. There was no one anywhere in sight or hearing.

He was alone again.

"Quiet!" Jadel hissed, pulling Kella down beside him. They were hidden by the huge shadows behind the dais, but there were eyes sharp enough to pierce that cover, and he wasn't yet ready to be discovered. The woman fell painfully to her hands and knees and fought back a whimper, knowing that he would not understand or forgive it. Her hands were bleeding, long crosscuts from the thickets of thorns they'd pushed aside to reach this place; she wiped at them absently and watched the scratches fill again. One, deeper than the rest, spilled over and drew a thin crimson line along the white curve of her wrist. Kella watched it, hypnotized, until Jadel's grasp on her arm brought her back to reality.

"Let's go," she suddenly said, grabbing his arm with unexpected strength. "Jadel, let's go, let's get out of this cursed place. We could go somewhere, anywhere—forget about Zenon—"

"Forget?" Jadel hissed, and bared his teeth. "Forget that he made me crawl on my belly like a slave? Forget that he stole what was mine? Do you think I can forget anything?"

"We have to try!" she cried softly. He put his hand over her mouth in unmistakable command. She swallowed and nodded. Jadel gave her one more warning look and let her go. "Jadel, we'll die here. You'll kill us both."

"No," he said, indicating the great bronze doors at the end of the hall. "When those open, be ready. When I am finished with these meddlers I intend to take back what's mine. I came for power, Kella. I intend to get it."

Kella stared at him, unconvinced, but he was blind to her doubt. There were visions in his head that occupied his attention: Iarsang, crippled and dying; Vurkanan Tyes, choking on his own blood; Kella's husband Brion, kneeling at his feet and begging for mercy.

Another new feeling, as he savored that image. He couldn't identify it, having never known it before, but it disturbed him. There was something obscurely satisfying in destroying a man who had once lain with Kella in his place. Jadel kept his burning eyes on the door, and when Kella's hand touched his shoulder he didn't turn, didn't slap her aside.

There was an obscure alien comfort in that, too. But he longed for the more familiar comforts of death and pain, and he knew, as she knew, that no gentler emotion could ever replace those longings. Perhaps it was the same for her.

He could not, even now, bring himself to care.

Vurkanan Tyes was not a demonstrative man, but seeing his child in the dead city of Quellburn — especially when she looked more dead than alive herself, streaked as she was with half-dried blood and covered with dirt and bruises — would have made a more reserved man than Tyes a weeping mortal. Before Laurel or Tiernan could blurt out half a word of explanation, Tyes swept his daughter up in a strong embrace and held her. Her whole body was shaking, but after a few seconds she relaxed and put her arms around his neck.

"Father," she whispered. Tyes held her even tighter in response. "What are you doing here?"

"A long story. Is yours shorter?"

"Not much. Oh, father, it's good to see you! Are you all right?"

"What a question, coming from my bloodstained daughter — "

"It isn't mine, it's Tiernan's. I — " Laurel's voice faltered, and she shivered again, convulsively. "I killed him, father. Andraax restored him."

Tyes pushed his child back at arms length, staring at her, and slowly shook his head.

"I can see catching me up on your adventures is going to take several hours, Laurel, so you may leave the details for later. Is Andraax here in Quellburn?"

"I think so. He left us there at the gates and went off on his own." Laurel grabbed hold of her father's hands and squeezed them in distress. "He's got a little boy with him. I'm very worried for him. Andraax seems sane just now, but I remember — "

"Yes, so do I. This little boy — " Before Tyes could even phrase the question, Brion pushed past Astrid's restraining hands and grabbed Laurel's shoulder.

"Evan? Is she talking about Evan?" he asked. Laurel nodded. "He's here, in this city? Enough of this, Tyes. I want to find my son, now."

"Please be patient — " Astrid begged, but Brion turned on her with fury in his eyes, and she stepped away. She bumped into Tiernan, who was standing in the shadows, and turned to apologize. The words froze in her throat as the light fell on his terrible, beautiful, enchanted face, and she felt all of her will drain out of her and congeal into a single hard purpose.

"Are you all right?" Tiernan asked, frowning, and then gasped as the young woman flung herself on him and sent him toppling backwards against the cold stone wall. "Hey! Wait!"

"Damn you," Laurel sighed, and it wasn't clear just who she was cursing. Astrid was struggling with Tiernan like a woman possessed; Pelk stepped in to try to pull her away, and she clawed at him like a wild thing. He released her and retreated, shaking a nail-raked hand.

"Beauty of Arraer," Tyes identified, "and well-cast, too. Your trip must have been very interesting, Laurel."

"It had its moments. Father, if you would — "

"Oh, I don't know," Tyes said, cocking his head to the side and watching as Tiernan struggled to keep Astrid's hands away from his breeches. "This looks like just what an arrogant young man needs."

"Father!"

"Oh, all right, Laurel, of course," Tyes sighed, and removed the curse. Tiernan's body convulsed briefly as the spell rearranged itself, and he looked up at them from his old, chagrined, perfectly suitable face.

Astrid laid there a moment in frozen astonishment, then climbed slowly to her feet and brushed at her clothes in agitated embarrassment. She looked bewildered as well as horrified, but she courteously offered Tiernan a hand up. He took it with a relieved, mischievous smile that made her blush furiously.

"Perhaps you'd like to properly introduce us, Father," Laurel said in a voice too smooth and courteous to be real.

Tyes cleared his throat. "My daughter, Laurel Magen, this is the Benevolent Lady Astrid of the Order of Eissa. This is Brion, whose son you have been concerned about. I believe you remember Pelk — "

Pelk grinned, and Laurel's grin exactly matched it.

Tyes sighed, thinking again that he had left the thief alone with the girl far too many times.

"And you remember Navigator Iarsang."

Laurel's impudent grin disappeared, and she bowed to the tall Navigator. He smiled slightly at her in return, but said nothing.

"The tall young man who just afforded us such entertainment is Prince Tiernan of the kingdom of Rhakhaan in Jaiman, my daughter's former suitor," Tyes finished blandly.

Tiernan raised one eyebrow in mocking imitation of Tyes' own manner. "Former?" he asked with great dignity. "I think we have something to discuss, Loremaster Tyes."

"Later!" Laurel snapped, and looked at Brion. "Your son was well, when last we saw him. He's a brave boy. You should be proud of him. He saved our lives, probably more than once. If you want to find him, I'll go with you."

"You're not going anywhere, daughter of mine; we have enough trouble without worrying about you meddling up more. Brion — "

"No more excuses, Tyes," Brion gritted. "I mean it. I want to find my son, now, and if you won't then I will go myself. Am I making myself clear?"

"Perfectly." Tyes cast a look at Iarsang, who was leaning against the stone wall and staring blankly off into space. "Navigator?"

"It appears we now have a difference of opinion," Iarsang said simply. "I am going to find Jadel. The rest of you, do as you wish."

Iarsang turned and began to walk away. Pelk cast a helpless look at Tyes, who jerked his head imperiously at the Navigator; Pelk followed him. Tyes looked back at Brion, whose dark eyes held no hint of weakness.

"All right, Brion. I've got my child. It seems only right that you should find yours. Come, then."

If only, Laurel prayed, it would be so easy.

There were huge bronze doors at the end of the long black-tiled hall; Iarsang strode toward them like an unstoppable force. Laurel caught up with her father as he turned to follow, but he shook his head and waved her back. She saw the sense in that, at least; she was her father's daughter, but not in sheer power. Tyes was the only one of them who could stand against any magical assaults they might come against, since Andraax's defection. Laurel fell back and found herself next to the dark-haired man. Brion.

Stormriders

Evan's father. There was a certain resemblance, but it was subtle. Brion's face was marked with lines of strain and sorrow, though he wasn't much older than Pelk, and he had none of his son's spontaneous charm.

Or maybe, Laurel amended as she looked at him, he'd had it burned out of him.

"You were with my son?" Brion asked her suddenly, surprising her. She nodded. "What's happened to him? He hasn't been hurt, has he?"

"Hurt?" Laurel managed a smile. It wasn't easy; there was a kind of sad fury in this man that wiped humor away. "No, I think Andraax is quite devoted to him, in his own way. He's a wonderful child, Master Brion. You should be proud."

"I am proud," Brion said, quietly certain of it. "He's always been old for his age. I guess he has had to be. It's been hard for him, even before — this."

Brion gestured helplessly around, including the dark dusty confines of the hall, the alien world, his equally alien companions — and she herself, as alien as the rest. Laurel smiled a little.

"He holds himself well. He'll be all right, Brion, I truly believe that."

"She's not often wrong," Tiernan put in. His arm went around her, a warm pressure that made her shiver in remembrance of a long, passionate, starlit night and a mercilessly cruel morning. His long fingers fit around her waist as if made for it. She opened her mouth, but nothing came out. Tiernan smiled down at her, only his own human smile, but the one that had always made her go beyond herself to reach for more.

"Thank you," she heard herself say, and he stared at her with wide, soft eyes until she blushed. He blinked, then, and looked away with a deliberate cooling of his expression. The sight of her lingered like the afterimages of a brilliant sun.

"Marry me," he said. It came out in a commonplace voice, the one he used for commenting on neutral subjects and matters far from his heart. He didn't dare put any more emotion into it than that. Laurel missed a step, caught herself, and looked at him in utter astonishment.

"What?" she stuttered, and then held up her hand when he opened his mouth to reply. "Never mind. I heard you, I only doubted my sanity. Now? You want an answer now?"

"I don't see why not." Tiernan's blue eyes met Brion's frankly amused ones over the top of Laurel's head, and in spite of his preoccupation Brion had to smile. Tiernan was struck by the resemblance between father and son, and smiled in return. Laurel glared at them each in turn.

"You would have to do this to me, wouldn't you? Asking me in the presence of witnesses again, as if you could shame me into saying yes — "

"I would have asked this morning, but you didn't give me a chance," Tiernan broke in, a little cruelly. She stopped, open-mouthed and furious.

"Unfair, Tier," she finally managed, and looked away. Her eyes filled up with sudden tears. "I would have turned the blade on myself before I'd have hurt you, if I'd known what I was doing. Surely you must know that."

"It isn't the first time you've stabbed, or the first time the wound went deep," Tiernan answered her cryptically, but he was still smiling. "Is that a yes, then?"

"No," she whispered, and laced her fingers together to still them. His arm stiffened around her waist. Oh, don't do this, some soft voice whispered in her heart, but she armored herself against it and went on. "I can't say yes, Tiernan."

"Why not?" he asked. It was still his commonplace voice, the same one he'd used to devastating effect that day when she'd first refused him. You could've heard every breath taken in the Court, that day; no one had believed her nerve, or her cruelty — or his apparent unconcern. She looked sidelong at him, and saw that same infuriating mask she remembered so painfully.

"I'm not ready to say yes," she finally said.

His jaw tightened, and loosened with a deliberate effort. "You were ready last night."

It was unfair, and so deliberately hurtful that Laurel gasped, but instantly he was looking down at her with that open, wounded expression she knew like her own heart. She'd seen that look as he'd fallen to his knees with her sword in his body, as he'd struggled to understand the impossible.

And, in spite of every bit of good sense she possessed, she finally bowed to the inevitable.

"All right," she said then, offhandedly, and smiled slightly. "If you get us both back to Rhakhaan alive."

"Oh, I will, my lady," Tiernan promised, eyes bright and fierce. "I swear that with my heart's blood."

Laurel rubbed her bloodstained hands together in a sudden convulsive shiver.

The bronze doors swung open and Pelk and Iarsang moved inside. Tyes cursed softly under his breath and ran after them; Tiernan let go of Laurel's waist and followed him. Brion, Laurel, and Astrid were slower, but they all crossed the threshold of the Council Audience Chamber before Iarsang was more than halfway through it.

The audience chamber was dominated by the four thrones of the Council that sat on a raised stone dais, but there was a brooding, unhealthy feeling about the room, as if some huge creature slept and waited for a sign to wake. The air smelled of cold stone and mold; Laurel found herself shivering, and touched Tiernan's arm to caution him. He nodded, personal hurts and joys forgotten, as Iarsang reached the midpoint of the long row of six stone columns that led to the dais and wished that Andraax hadn't been so quick to reclaim his sword.

When the form took shape in the darkness and moved, Laurel thought it was another phantom; it was ghostly enough, black robes and white flesh, but it lived. It glided up to an angle just the other side of the dais and stood there, hands mockingly outstretched.

Jadel threw his head back and laughed, a wild, mad laugh that echoed in the dark room like a scream. Iarsang froze, head snapping up, and his brown eyes went flat and dead. Before anyone could move to stop him, he drew his sword and leaped for the dais, for the mocking figure who'd cost him so much and who had so much to answer for.

As his foot touched the dais, the six stone columns moved. They flowed like molten iron, becoming live things that still had the toughness of stone but the fluidity of flesh. Their rough, molten heads turned blindly toward the dais, and they lunged for the intruder who'd set foot on the thrones.

Pelk was closest, and the quickest; he intercepted the nearest, giving Iarsang time to roll aside before the golem could hammer him into the floor. The golem's blow shattered a piece of stone flagging and crushed a skeletal corpse dressed in wrinkled leather armor. Pelk shouted and attacked. His sword met stoneflesh and rang like a bell; only the incredible quality of the steel allowed it to withstand the blow, and he scored a thin, bloodless cut on the golem. The creature, undeterred, turned with its fellows and blindly pursued the only intruder they cared about —

Iarsang.

Jadel laughed again and came out from behind the shadows, exulting in the sight of his Iylar enemy so pursued. Vurkanan Tyes was summoning up a spell; Jadel drew Unlife out of the very corruption of the city and unraveled it before it was complete, then wove one of his own, a seamless black net that he cast toward the Loremaster. Tyes lost valuable time and energy in countering. In the interim Jadel grabbed for a shield and found one — a fragile shield of flesh and blood, barely taller than a half-grown child. Tyes froze in the act of casting a spell, and Jadel smiled grimly.

"This time, my friend, this really is your child," he said, one hand wrapped around Laurel's throat. "Go ahead, Loremaster. Cast your spell. She suffers before me."

Tyes lowered his hand, ignoring the fury in his daughter's eyes. Only Tiernan saw, and tensed; when Laurel's elbow snapped back into Jadel's ribs, only he was ready to move. Jadel gagged at the pain and loosened his grip on her. Tiernan was there in a second, pulling her free and knocking the Dyar Elf back with a blow that might have killed him, and should have, if anger had been any measure.

Jadel sat up and spat blood, then crouched there like a venomous spider. As Tyes advanced to take him, another dark shadow ran forward to pull him back, and this one brought Brion's troubles painfully close.

Kella looked terrible, pallid and bruised and sick, but there was still fire in her eyes as she caught sight of him, and rage. Brion flinched a little at that, wondering again helplessly what he'd done to make her hate him. Jadel shoved her away with brutal indifference and staggered to his feet.

"If you want me, Tyes, come for me," he taunted, and he and Kella ran for the far door. Tyes swore and began to follow, then turned back to look for Iarsang.

The Navigator had retreated behind the dais. He and Pelk were fighting a losing battle against impossible odds; the golems couldn't be hurt, but each dodge the Iylar and thief made was another step toward death. They were going to be cornered. Two golems were closing in from the far end of the dais, and soon they'd be caught in between merciless walls of moving stone.

"Up here!" Tiernan shouted. The others looked at him in surprise; he was standing up on the dais studying the thrones. "There must be a control here. Something to stop them!"

Brion, the closest, bounded up to join him. As he did, Tiernan stabbed at a raised button on the left arm of the closest throne.

"No!" Tyes shouted, but it was too late. Three steps between the dais and where the rest of them stood, a Wall of Force shimmered into being. Tyes advanced to try to bridge it, but he was thrown back like an impudent child.

"Oops," Tiernan murmured absently.

Brion hit the right-hand button. The golems, who'd finished surrounding Iarsang and Pelk, ground to a sudden halt and turned their blind faces toward him. Brion gaped at them, looking almost as blind.

"Say something!" Tiernan prompted him urgently.

"What?"

"Anything! Tell them to — to stay where they are."

Brion shivered, feeling a sudden unpleasant sensation of power wash over him. He looked at the golems, and they looked back in utter stillness.

"Take me to my son," he commanded them. They turned, all six of them, and began moving for the side door. Brion exchanged a startled look with Prince Tiernan and jumped down from the dais to follow.

"Wait!" Tyes called from the other side of the barrier. He pounded on it ineffectually. "Brion, no! Don't go alone!"

"Tiernan, go with him! Hurry!" Laurel shouted. Tiernan looked at her in indecision, then nodded and ran after the golems and their new master.

Iarsang and Pelk, forgotten, leaned panting against the wall and wiped sweat from their faces. Iarsang took up Jadel's trail again. He didn't so much as glance at the others, still trapped behind the Force Wall; his face was set in an expression that left no room for anything but his own obsession.

Tyes swore and gestured for Pelk to follow him. The thief gave a helpless shrug and went, vanishing with the Navigator into the darkness.

The Force Wall shimmered on, oblivious. Laurel sagged against it and stared at her father and the cleric Astrid.

"What now?" she wanted to know. Her father gave her a grim, unhappy look.

"Now we wait," he said.

She didn't much like the answer.

A storm had crept up with startling suddenness. When Jadel and Kella burst out into the open air, they were met with a bone-chilling gust of wind and a slashing curtain of rain. Within seconds, they were shivering and soaked to the skin.

"Call the trolls!" Jadel shouted over the crash of thunder. Kella stared blankly at him, illuminated by a vivid actinic flash. He reached out to slap her and found himself holding her face between his hands instead. "Kella! You remember how! I taught you how! Call them, now! Otherwise we will never separate them!"

Kella's eyes suddenly cleared, and she reached up to cover his hands with her own. "No, Jadel, let's go, let's get out of here, please — "

"Do as I say. Do it!"

He released her and stepped away, but she only shook her head. He felt a surge of pure terror shake him; if they failed Zenon, if they didn't manage the deaths of these intruders —

Zenon would carry out his threats.

"Do you want us to die, Kella?" he asked her softly, raising his hand. A dark glow formed around it. "Do it, or I will kill you. I must save myself from Zenon's wrath. Do it, now."

"Jadel, I thought you — loved me — " she whispered, and backed further away. Her feet caught in a snare of grass. The tough roots resisted her attempts to pull free, but it wasn't merely a whim of nature; the grasses pulled tighter, moving like dry snakes over her legs. She cried out and looked up at Jadel. He was watching with a distant, almost-sad smile on his rain-streaked face.

"In my own way, I do love you," he said quietly. "And yet you have repaid my love with weakness, with failure, and with impudence. How can I continue to love you, Kella? You failed in the simplest of tasks. You constantly oppose me even when you must see that I am right. What more can I do?"

"I'm sorry," she whispered. The grass tightened painfully. "I'm sorry! Oh, Jadel, please don't do this. I love you. I'll obey you. I'll do anything you say!"

"Anything?" he asked. She nodded convulsively, dark hair pressed lankly around her pale face by the force of the pouring rain. He smiled again, that smile that had first bewitched and then terrified her — and, still, bewitched her. "All right. One final chance, then, my love. One last opportunity for you to prove yourself worthy of what I've given you, and what I can still teach you. Call the trolls, and I'll give you one more chance to kill your husband."

"Here?" Kella looked wildly around, as if she expected to see the man bearing down on them.

"He's coming. I will take care of Iarsang. I trust you can manage something so simple."

"I have no weapon," she told him. He pulled a jagged-edged dagger from his belt and tossed it to her. He turned away before she had even picked it awkwardly up from the grass. "Jadel! Free me!"

"Free yourself, woman. You must learn how to wield the Unlife sooner or later. If you fail, you still have the knife." He kept his face expressionless even against the imploring desperation of her tears, and turned away.

Kella stared down at the grass, and the stems cutting into her flesh, and began to feel the dark power of the Unlife flowing through her veins like the storm writhing above.

Evan pulled himself farther into the shelter of a ruined doorway and shivered with chill; he was angry and tired and hungry, and Andraax hadn't wandered back around to help him at all. Things were not looking so great; he couldn't even decide which direction he'd been in when he'd seen his father for that one, uncertain moment, and he certainly couldn't figure out how to start to get back.

Anyway, Andraax would show up again—sometime. He'd have to, wouldn't he? Unless he'd really gone crazy after all —

It wasn't a comforting thought. Evan hugged himself harder and flinched from a loud crash of thunder. He counted under his breath, but the next crash was even sooner. The center of the storm was drawing closer.

When he looked up, lightning flashed whitely, illuminating a tall man walking toward him. Evan froze for a second, then stood up with a glad cry. The man stopped a few feet away and put his hands on his hips.

"Andraax, you — " Evan's voice trailed off uncertainly. It looked like Andraax, certainly; dark, silver-streaked hair, strange purple eyes, even six fingers on the long, graceful hands. But where Andraax had radiated warmth and ease—and occasionally menace — this stranger had nothing about him except coldness.

It was a kind of chill that froze Evan's heart into fearful stillness.

"Andraax?" the stranger said, cocking his head. He looked at the boy like some interesting new specimen of insect discovered in a garden. "I thought I sensed someone of more power than these others. He is sadly diminished since last we met, if he is here; he would have made a ripple in the Essence like a tidal wave when Quellburn still stood. Well, then. If you know Andraax, boy, take me to him."

"Who are you?" Evan asked, pretty reasonably he thought.

The stranger's face went cold, as cold as his aura. "Death," he whispered, and smiled slightly. It was a frozen smile, the kind the dead find themselves smiling. "To all intents and purposes, yours. Up, boy. Let us find this friend of yours. I've been longing to see my relatives for more than two hundred years."

Evan didn't have any choice but to go with him. The moment his flesh touched Zenon's, though, he felt a shiver go through him like the touch of raw lightning. Andraax knew. He sensed the danger, and he was coming.

Evan hoped he was at least partly sane.

The Force Wall flickered, and died; Tyes and Astrid were only steps behind Laurel in their run for the door, but there was nothing to see but slicing ribbons of rain and gray stormclouds scraping the ruins.

Iarsang and Pelk had disappeared; so had Brion and Tiernan. Tyes shook his head and wiped rain out of his eyes.

"There!" Laurel shouted, setting out at a foundering, muddy pace for the distantly glimpsed figures moving north. The cold and rain couldn't deter her, not for a moment. She hadn't said everything she intended to her prince — he couldn't die yet, damn him.

Not that he would ask her opinion, naturally.

The golems were stalking off through the woods, crushing underbrush and splintering trees. It was crude, but certainly effective; Brion was following them in spite of the difficult pace they set. Tiernan paused and looked back to see his lady racing toward him, and his traitorous heart gave an undeniable leap.

Damned woman, he thought, but he thought it in near desperation.

"Where are you going?" she shouted as she reached him. Tiernan shrugged. Laurel's father and the other young woman drew up behind her, looking as comfortable as drowning cats under the continuing assault of the rain.

"You said to follow!" he shouted back. She looked at Brion and frowned.

"What's that?"

"Where?"

Tiernan automatically reached for Laurel's hand, but she was moving away from him, shouting something that was lost in a crash of thunder. Tiernan wiped rain from his eyes and saw a huge black shape loom up out of the downpour. It was only one of several that were appearing from the trees around them. Tiernan swore and threw himself out and toward the one closest to Laurel. As he did, the shape became clear in a flash of lightning.

The gods had certainly been listening in the park; first wolves, and now Trolls. This one stood nearly a head taller than Tiernan, and was four times as broad. It grinned and snarled something in Trollish that sounded like steel grating on rock, and swung a rusty short sword at the man who blocked its path. Vurkanan Tyes, acting quicker than thought, drew his sword and tossed it to Tiernan, who stood helpless.

Tiernan plucked it gracefully out of the air, stepped back to let the blade whistle by, then closed to thrust. The troll twisted like a cat, faster than a creature of its bulk should have been able to move. Tiernan only barely recovered and parried. The blow shattered the troll's sword where the rust had weakened it, but the creature only grinned and tossed the haft away. Before Tiernan could bring his blade back into line, the troll crashed bodily into him, lifted him in the air, and slammed him down with skull-rattling force to the wet ground.

Fortunate, Tiernan decided dazedly, that it was wet ground. Otherwise he'd have shattered bones instead of general agony. The prince rolled away as the troll threw itself down toward him, and managed to get out from under the huge bulk before it slammed into the mud.

Tiernan rolled, sword raised, and stabbed it through the back. The troll convulsed and died, still face down in the mud.

"Laurel!" he shouted, and lunged to his feet just barely in time to parry a blow meant for Laurel's back, striking over her shoulder to do it. The troll snarled and tried again, but Tiernan's sword was everywhere, fueled by rage and fear. When the troll lunged for a third time, Tiernan caught it deftly through the heart and skipped aside as the body crashed down, dead.

Tyes, weaponless but wielding Essence like a living ally, was nevertheless being backed even farther away from Tiernan and Laurel. He had the cleric with him, at least; she was contributing what strength she could to the magical battle, but something was countering his spells just as quickly as he spun them.

"Scatter!" he shouted when Tiernan paused to look at him.

Tiernan grabbed Laurel's hand and looked around for Brion.

Brion was gone, vanished along with his golems.

The golems had gone ahead, crushing attacking trolls as if oblivious to their blows. Brion wasn't so lucky; he tried to follow and was cut off. While Tiernan battled for his life, Brion was forced into a tangle of brambles and through to the other side, rolling free with a mass of tiny, bloody cuts. A troll stomped furiously on the opposite side and reached through after him.

Brion scuttled back out of reach, slipping on mud and wet grass; the oversized groping hand flailed blindly, grabbing only loose sticks and dead leaves. Brion sat there in relief as the troll shambled away and drew in deep breaths. He had to catch up to the golems, somehow. He had to find his son; to stop now, when he was so close —

A hand fell on his shoulder, a hand scored as his was with red bleeding scratches. Brion exploded into startled movement and paused when he realized who it was who stood behind him.

Kella lowered her hand slowly to her side.

"Where is he?" she asked softly. Brion cocked his head to the side and looked back at her, seeing the wretched fear in her and not understanding it. "Oh, Brion, please tell me: is Evan all right?"

"They say he is," Brion said, unable to lie even to comfort her. She desperately needed comfort; he could feel that need burning off of her like fever. "I'll find him soon. You can come with me, Kella. I know you've been — ill — "

She laughed. It was a terrible laugh, like Jadel's, all empty noise and wild challenge. Her eyes glittered with tears.

"Ill? Ill! I've never felt better, oh, God, that's the truth." She bit back a sob. "I don't want to be like this, Brion, truly. Can't you believe that?"

He nodded, more because she wanted him to than because he really did.

"Jadel's good to me," she whispered. Brion felt a sudden ugly rush of anger and jealousy, frightening because it was so utterly unexpected. He couldn't still love her. He couldn't. "He understands. You never could. You always wanted different things."

"I want Evan," Brion said bluntly. Her dreamy expression disappeared, leaving a dead, quiet mask.

"You can't have him," she promised, and drew in a deep breath. Her hands were clenched in her pocket. " I can finally get what I want, and nothing you say or do can stop me."

Brion thought, with a surge of enlightened pity, that he hardly needed to. Kella was tottering on the brink of self-destruction, a living tornado of emotion spinning more and more out of balance with each breath she took. In a way, it hurt to watch it. He slowly came to his feet, wary of how her eyes followed him, and held his hands out to her.

"Kella, you are sick, can you understand that? I didn't understand it before, but I do now. Let me help you. I've learned so much here, I know that someone can help you — "

Kella stood there in utter stillness for a few seconds, looking at him, and then as if someone had thrown a hidden switch her face lit up and she smiled. It was a beautiful smile, full of need and hope, and Brion sighed as she reached forward to take his hand.

Her other hand came out, too fast to see. She drove the blade in hard.

Brion cried out in disbelief, eyes still locked on hers, and she stabbed him again. "No, Kel," he whispered, and she pushed him away. He felt nothing else except a sudden terrifying slide into darkness.

She felt a weak, hot surge of relief and horror wash over her as she looked at him. The blade was still in her hand, running red but washing clean now in the rain. She lifted her heated face to the cold touch and shivered, then tried to shove the dagger into her wide pocket.

Something clinked musically against the steel. She pulled it out and stared at the tiny glass bottle of poison that she'd brought so far, to so little purpose, and laughed aloud.

She looked up as the Unlife that pulsed through her cried a warning, and saw Pelk's set, white face watching her from across the little clearing. Iarsang stood next to him, expressionless but burning with revulsion and anger.

Pelk had a knife in his hand, ready to throw.

Kella spread her empty hands and turned to go. Pelk wouldn't throw; he couldn't stand to have the death of an unarmed woman on his conscience, not even one he'd seen murder a friend. Kella prided herself on her judgements of people, and she'd known him from the first moment she'd looked in his eyes so many ages ago.

He couldn't kill her. He almost loved her.

It was an utter, horrifying shock when she heard the knife whistle end over end through the rain, doubly a shock when it slid in between her ribs and grated on bone. All of the strength drained out of her body in one gush, and she fell clumsily forward, cutting her hands on thorns as she did. She lay there senseless for a second, then began to claw her way back to her feet. Even as Pelk readied a second knife, as remorseless as an executioner, she staggered into the trees and was gone.

Pelk stood there in silence a moment, controlling an overwhelming need to weep, and then went to Brion.

His friend was treacherously, tragically, mortally wounded — but he was not yet dead.

Kella staggered on, holding to the rain-slick branches and boles of trees, crawling after she reached the end of the garden. Numbness was growing, and the knife in her back was a hot wedge of agony. Every breath she drew was a horrifying trial. But Jadel would help her, if she could make it to his side —

She pulled herself over the threshold with the last of her strength and collapsed in a pool of blood and rain in the hall, her face pressed against the moldering fabric and dust clogging her lungs. She coughed, but the spasm left her gasping for air as her lungs slowly filled up with warm blood.

A shadow fell over her, and warm hands touched her face, then slid under her body and lifted her up. She clung to Jadel and wept from agony and fright, and he took her to Zenon's bedroom.

"I can't," Astrid protested, looking down at Brion with tear-filled eyes. She looked up at Iarsang and Pelk, both wearing identical hard expressions, and buried her fingers in the wet grass of the clearing. Brion was barely breathing now, lungs filling with blood with each heartbeat. "You don't understand what you're asking. It isn't something anyone can do lightly, and in this place it's a terrible risk. I can't do it."

"Astrid, you must," Pelk begged. Tyes was a dark, silent shadow at his back. "Please. Only you can do this. Are you not a senior cleric? Don't you know the Life Mastery spells?"

"It isn't that simple!" she cried, and wiped at her eyes. The rain was slackening, but her tears were not. "The wounds are mortal. It requires a great spell, and I haven't even acted as a cleric since before I came on this journey! I was leaving the Order. I was going to join the Scribes of Nomikos. I don't want to make these kinds of choices any more!"

"Listen to me," Pelk hissed, and grabbed her wrist. "I just made a choice that will haunt me until the day I die. I killed a woman. You'll forgive me if I feel less than sympathetic about your hard choices, Benevolent Lady!"

Astrid jerked free and looked at Brion with agonized eyes, then nodded. She drew in a deep breath.

"It will not be easy. If Eissa will not grant me the power, then I will fail — and in failing, I may die. Stay clear, and say nothing." She bowed her head. Pelk looked around at his friend, who fought for breath through grayed lips flecked with blood.

"Try," he begged again, softly.

Iarsang, unnoticed, slipped away through the trees.

The doors to the Theatre flew open at Zenon's touch. The Master Sorcerer strode inside, dragging his prisoner with him. The gloom should have been impenetrable, but instead there were flames burning merrily in the torch sconces at the edge of the stage: magical flames, surely, because several of them had no sconces left to sit in. Zenon remembered well the destruction of the Theatre, and he smiled a little as he pushed a pile of rags and bones out of his way. The place was a mass of wrecked seats and dismembered bones. The majestic red curtains were shredded and faded, splotched here and there with huge splashes of ancient blood; the entire room stank of fear and death. Zenon had never bothered to count how many had died here in this terrible place, but he rather enjoyed speculating.

He was enjoying even more the prospect of adding to that count — by two, at least. The boy, who was strong enough to resist every spell of Unlife he'd been able to devise against him so far, and —

His anticipation quickly faded as a scarecrow of a figure stepped out on the stage. It was laughable, smothered in layers of moldering costume and paint — but the purple eyes were familiar and unmistakable.

"Hello, cousin," Zenon said, and clapped politely. "Very pretty. Were you intending to be anything in particular? You seem to be wearing beggar's robes and king's furs, a lady's gown — is that a crown under the jester's hat? Very funny. Shall I see how it all burns?"

Zenon lifted his hands, dark glow forming between them, but Andraax began to dance. It was a slow, graceful waltz, curiously moving, and he bent and scooped up a skull that lay half-smashed at the foot of the stage. His purple eyes caught the magelight for one instant, wide and strange.

Zenon lowered his hands, fascinated and bemused.

"Her name," Andraax said in his clear, beautiful voice as he held the skull up and continued to dance, "was Kala. She was seventeen, the daughter of the Master Healer, and she'd come here to watch the players enact the founding of Quellburn."

Suddenly, the skull was gone, and a pale, insubstantial young woman with bright russet hair danced in Andraax's arms. She opened her mouth to speak, but nothing came out. Andraax smiled at her kindly and spun her around in a graceful, exact circle.

"What is this foolishness?" Zenon asked coldly. "What do I care for the Healer's brat?"

"Nothing," Andraax said sadly. "That's exactly the point, my cousin. You survived the Interregnum, just as I did; you and I, we are the last of the old blood, the Lords of Essence. You lived as human. You learned, as I learned, to master the ways of Essence instead of technology, and what have you to show for it? A city of the dead. A girl who will never see her eighteenth birthday. Treachery, deceit, and horror. But I will forgive it all if you will release the boy and let us go in peace."

"This is idiocy," Zenon scoffed, and raised his hands again. Andraax bent his head forward and touched his lips to the insubstantial ones of Kala the Healer's daughter, and opened his arms. She stepped back, bowed to him, and flew shrieking at Zenon with all the fury of a demon from the Pales.

Zenon was startled, but not panicked; he banished the ghost without much effort, though the shadow creature drew a little of his power away with its passing.

A half-smashed skull toppled out of the air before him and broke apart on the stained flagstones. Evan drew back as far as Zenon's grip would let him. As he did, the sleeve came up on Zenon's robe, baring his left wrist.

Iarsang's Compass gleamed on his skin, flashing like a jewel. Andraax's eyes touched it briefly, then moved to Evan.

The distance made contact indistinct and difficult, but Andraax held to it anyway until he felt Evan's mind open cautiously to his.

The bracelet. Take it from his arm when I tell you.

"You're a fool, in addition to being mad, Andraax," Zenon said. "But then you've been mad for far longer than I was, so I'm sure you're much better at it. Still talking to rocks, cousin?"

"Not at the moment. I'm talking to the dead." Andraax looked away from Evan, forced himself to forget the boy's danger. He began to dance again, speaking in a slow, dreamy voice. "The city is full of the dead, Zenon. They all know you. They all have waited for you, all these years. They have quite a lot to tell me."

"You're going to die here, cousin," Zenon taunted him gleefully. "Perhaps you'll haunt me, too?"

"Perhaps we will be ghosts together — cousin." Andraax's self-control broke, just for a moment, and his rage shone through, diamond-bright. "Leave the boy out of this. I've let too much happen in my selfishness, and so have you. I'm as guilty as you, Zenon — in intent, if not in scale. Let's die together, and finish this."

"I don't intend to die at all," Zenon said with a derisive laugh. Andraax extended his arms, holding an imaginary partner, and began to dance again. His voice was far away.

"Perhaps you don't," he agreed. Zenon whirled as the doors slammed shut behind him, and locked with a metallic click. "But I hardly think it matters, my cousin. Release the boy, or die."

With a dry rattle of bone, every skeleton in the theatre rose and began to dance, taking on flesh and substance as Zenon gaped.

Kella opened her eyes and blinked back stinging rivulets of sweat. She felt unnaturally hot. The wound in her back was agonizingly evident, though the knife was out, and when she gasped for breath she could draw in only a tiny bit of air. Her lungs were drowning in blood. She coughed, and a river of blood poured down her chin. She wiped it away.

Jadel was sitting on a chair, watching her. He played with the Pelk's dagger, tossing it up and catching it. When he heard her cough he bent forward.

"Are you awake?" he asked gently. She nodded. "You failed me, worthless bitch. Brion lives. He thrives under the care of a cleric. You are dying far faster than he is. You've cost me my life for this failure."

"No," she whispered, and struggled to sit up. Her wound sapped her strength. She felt a fresh spurt of blood warm the sheets beneath her. "No, I killed him, I did —"

"You stabbed him, but you failed to kill him. I had such hopes for you, Kella. I'd even planned to let you bear my children."

"Jadel — "

"Quiet. Save your strength. You'll need it, because you'll take a long time to die, lying here, drowning in your own blood. I have no further use for you, woman, and neither does Zenon. Die, if that is your destiny."

Her eyes felt hot, but not with tears; if she could have wept tears of fire, she would have. She ached suddenly with a spasm of rage so hot it felt as if it would consume her whole body. She'd never hated anyone so much as this slim, elegant, handsome man who sat and mocked her as she died for him. Not even Brion.

Not even herself.

She felt another spasm of coughing approaching; as she rolled on her side in convulsive shaking, she clawed the bottle of poison out of her pocket and pried the rubber stopper loose. As she wiped the blood from her lips, she poured the liquid into her mouth and swallowed.

The taste was lost in the salty flavor of her own blood.

When she rolled back strengthlessly to stare at Jadel, he was still sitting and smiling at her. She smiled, too, faintly, and let a little of the poison dribble out over her lips. She coated her lips with it, then swallowed the rest.

"Jadel," she whispered. "I am sorry I failed you. I loved you, I did. Please forgive me this one time. I'm dying for love of you. Can you at least give me one last kiss?"

He caught the dagger and stared at her, eyes narrowed, then smiled a little sadly. Fool, she thought fiercely, hating him, hating herself. Come. Come and die.

"In my own way I tried to love you, woman. You must be content with that." Jadel leaned forward and pushed sweat-streaked hair back from her pale face, then covered her lips with his. She smiled at the pressure, and then he stood up. She was still smiling, a strange, serene smile.

"Good-bye, Kella," he said, and turned away. She watched him walk to the door of Zenon's bedroom, and felt the poison leeching the last of her life away. It was more painful than she'd thought — but assuredly less painful than the death he'd planned for her.

"See you in hell, Jadel," she whispered, and closed her eyes.

It was only a few more moments, and the pain was forever gone.

Iarsang was, like all of them, at the raw end of his strength. Jadel's hold over the Compass had been painful, but now that Zenon's power ruled it every move an exercise in agony. Iarsang had felt the terrible wrench as Zenon had claimed his bracelet, but he hadn't dared to tell anyone, not even Tyes. Tyes would have insisted on going back, reporting it to the Navigators, wasting precious time and robbing

Iarsang of what he needed. The Navigator continued to walk toward the hexagonal building near the far corner of the wall, and wasn't surprised when he saw Jadel emerge from the house.

The ruin of his left hand had given a huge throb of agony as warning.

The Dyar was momentarily surprised, perhaps because he'd never believed that Iarsang would survive so long, but surprise didn't deter him for long; he walked up to within a few feet of the Iylar Navigator. He looked worn and less than perfect, as if the Compass was sucking life from him as well. He didn't fare well in the newly breaking sunlight, like a creature of darkness melting in the direct glare of noon.

"Come to beg for death? As it happens, Navigator, I am in a mood to grant favors just now. Look what I found in the Citadel's museum: they captured it from the army of Unlife they fought in order to found this pitiful place. A sword made to slay Elves. Isn't that lucky for you?"

Jadel reached behind his head and pulled the blade free: an enormous thing, cruelly serrated and covered with runes of vile origin. It was designed to strike fear into those who looked on it, but Iarsang didn't flinch; he raised his chin and looked past it at the Dyar who held it, and smiled faintly.

"You took something precious from me," Iarsang said softly. "Something no one should have to lose. You shall pay for that."

"Not to reclaim it? I don't even have it anymore, Iylari fool. Surely you knew that."

"Not the Compass," Iarsang said, and took a step forward. "You took something I loved. You took a woman I cared for more than my own life, and whether I ever am a Navigator again, that I can never reclaim. I came for her."

"You came on a fool's errand," Jadel told him just as softly. "I have no pity for you. I have no regret. I have no mercy."

He would have said more, but then he shrugged and lifted the sword. Its edges glittered in the dying sunlight, blood-red. Behind them, Jadel's dark eyes were wide and fixed.

Iarsang drew his own sword and knew that no matter how determined he was, how enraged, he had no strength for this fight. His muscles would barely support the weight of the blade. Yet he could not come so far and fail, he would not — not after Daphine —

Jadel moved like tarnished quicksilver, and Iarsang's arm moved of its own volition to parry. The Dyar's killer-sword hit Iarsang's broadsword with a sound like glass shrieking, and the broadsword shattered into a thousand metallic fragments.

It was just as well, Iarsang thought with one cold logical part of his mind as he threw the useless hilt aside. He hadn't the strength left to even raise the sword again. He could only do his best now, whatever little that best might be.

He flung himself at Jadel like a madman, empty-handed against a slay-sword and certainly dead if the steel so much as touched his flesh. He waited for the cold bite of it as he closed, but Jadel's face had gone pale and strangely distracted, and as Iarsang's hands closed weakly over his throat Jadel choked of his own volition and dropped the sword.

"No," he whispered in stunned disbelief. "No, Kella, you bitch, no — "

His legs went numb, unable to support his weight, and Jadel fell to his hands and knees. He stayed there. The poison wasn't concentrated enough to kill him outright, but he couldn't force his muscles or his magic to obey him. His arms collapsed, sending him face down into the mud.

Iarsang stepped forward and picked up the sword. Jadel's left hand was extended, whether to attack or to plead for help was not clear. The Dyar was in no shape to answer even such a simple question.

"You forgot one thing," Iarsang said very, very gently, and lifted the sword. "A sword designed to kill Elves will kill any kind of Elf. Iylari, Erlini — or Dyari."

He brought the sword down.

The Theatre was full to bursting and resembled a festive convention of ghosts. Andraax still danced on the stage, now with this woman, now with that; the ones on the floor crowded around Zenon and clawed at him. As each one advanced, he dispelled it. A huge mound of bones lay around him, but still they came, and each one sapped part of his power. Already his strength was nearly gone, and still they came, oozing out of the warped, shattered walls, coming up from the floor, coming in response to Andraax's call from everywhere in the ruined city. Most of them Zenon knew. Some had even been his friends.

Thus far, Andraax's power had kept Evan safe from them, but the ghosts knew no politics; they drew life from any living thing, good or bad, innocent or evil. Andraax was failing as quickly as Zenon.

"Evan," Andraax called from the stage. The boy looked up from where he sat huddled, still trapped by Zenon's hold on him. The Loremaster's purple eyes caught his, commanding.

Ready? Andraax asked him crisply. Evan nodded.

Now.

Evan yanked at Zenon's wrist with all of his strength. Andraax took the last dregs of his power and sent them arrowing for his enemy-cousin, breaking Zenon's hold and opening the secret clasp of the Compass in the same second. Evan stumbled backwards with the Compass held in his hands, even as Zenon spun to grab for him.

Run Andraax whispered into the boy's mind. The doors unbarred behind him. *Go, Evan! Find your father!*

"What about you?" Evan shouted, even as he reached the doorway. Andraax smiled faintly at him and shook his head. The door swung shut too quickly to allow Evan to duck back inside. Evan heard the bar fall back in place with a thud.

He cradled the Compass close to his chest and sat with his back stubbornly to the doors, waiting.

The last of Zenon's power flashed through the air in a spiteful, malicious strike at the boy; Evan's own natural defenses deflected it back into the theatre. The ghosts lapped up the power and strengthened, attacking from all sides, touching Zenon with cold cloying fingers and begging him with mute dark eyes for restored life. He pushed at them in a panic, but more came, and more, and his store of power was limited —

As he dispelled the last of his power, he fell to his knees and cried out. Andraax, dancing with the ghost of the last Ruler of Quellburn, Alladyre, smiled a faint, sad smile, and stepped out of her embrace.

She clung to him, drawn by the pulse of life. He had no more power left than Zenon, whose life was ebbing away as the ghosts stole more and more of his very soul; Andraax felt the first weakness beginning, and reckoned it a fair bargain. He'd abandoned Evan when the boy had needed him most, and he could not live with such on his conscience, never, better to die in the arms of a beautiful ghost —

Alladyre stepped back from him, smiling with transparent lips, and nodded her respect.

"The boy needs you, Loremaster," she whispered from a great distance. "More than that, this world needs you. Your game was dangerous, but you played it perfectly. My thanks for putting the city to rest."

"You call this rest?" Andraax laughed, and looked at the surging tides of ghosts, at the scrap of flesh that was withering away in the midst of them as Zenon's life dissolved. "I call it chaos."

Alladyre spoke gently. "Go now, Loremaster, before my people turn on you. You were always the best of your kind."

He bowed to her wearily and jumped down from the stage, stripping off bits of costume as he went. The ghosts parted to let him pass. Zenon lay in the floor, a withered, wizened old man, breathing his last as the ghost of Kala Healer's-daughter bent over him with a smile.

Andraax shook his head and went out the doors. They slammed and locked behind him, and the ghosts continued to feast.

· CHAPTER SIX ·

Brion could make no sense of the conversation swirling over him. There were two voices, only slightly familiar; they argued as quietly as possible. One was male, one was female, and he while he could swear he'd heard them before he had no idea where —

"And I tell you, Prince, that that is the stupidest idea I've ever heard in my entire life! I am not going to make a public announcement. I wish I'd never said yes!"

"But you did! I have witnesses!" the man said, a low, mischievous rumble.

The woman sighed. "No. Tiernan — "

"There is such a thing as bowing to inevitability. You will marry me, you know. And it will be with all of the ceremony my father's going to want."

"Shh," another voice said urgently. "This is the third time you've had this stupid fight today. You're going to wake him up!"

The third voice Brion knew. His eyes flew open, and he raised his head a quarter-inch, enough to see to the foot of the bed.

Evan sat there, nestled comfortably on the lap of the tall, handsome young man Brion vaguely remembered as having been introduced as prince of something-or-other. At the first sign of wakefulness, Evan writhed free and threw himself down on the side of the bed.

"Evan," Brion whispered. His throat felt dry and hot. Evan swallowed and threw his arms around his father's neck, and Brion hugged him back as hard as his weakness would allow.

"I'm all right," Evan said, when he was able to speak. "Tiernan and Laurel, they took care of me. They wanted to sit with me, and they promised to be quiet but they woke you up anyway — "

"Sorry," Tiernan said, not very remorsefully.

Brion smiled. "Thanks for looking after him. I was — "

"Yes, we know," Laurel put in, leaning forward with a cup of water. Brion drank thirstily. "Slowly, now. You've been quite ill."

"I'm surprised I'm not quite dead." Brion froze in the act of handing the cup back. "Kella — "

Laurel shook her head slightly and put the cup back on the table next to her. Evan sat up and looked at Laurel, but she didn't volunteer anything further. Neither did Tiernan.

"She's dead," Evan finally said softly. "She tried to kill you, and Pelk hurt her, so she took poison."

Brion stared at him, appalled by how calmly his son took such ghastly news.

"Your son's been very brave, Master Brion. He's sat with you for three days now — ever since we brought you here."

"Where's here?"

"Kelfour's Landing," Tiernan supplied promptly. "Evan, why don't you tell the others your father's awake?"

Evan jumped down and ran to do it. As soon as the door was shut, Tiernan rose and began pacing around the room like a huge, black-maned lion.

"From your reaction I see you wished Evan not to know what happened. I'm sorry for that; Andraax made the decision in your absence, and no one argues with Andraax. It seems to have been the right decision; Evan was sad, but it seems he — understands. Just as you surely do."

"Oh, I understand. Poor Kella." Brion shut his eyes. Laurel and Tiernan traded long looks.

"Yes," Tiernan said, still looking at his lover. "Poor Kella. From what I heard, she would have killed you, Brion; she would have killed anyone who stood in her way. You owe your life to Lady Astrid's skill, not to any mercy given to you by your wife."

"I know," Brion said, and opened his eyes. "It's strange that Evan seems so — old — "

"He's seen a lot. Maybe more than you have. You might consider that without him Laurel and I would both likely be dead now."

Laurel Magen had been uncommonly silent throughout this exchange; she rose and went to the door as someone knocked. It opened to admit a tall, dark-haired man with luminous purple eyes. Evan was riding on his shoulders, and bent low to avoid the doorframe.

"You are well, Brion?" Andraax asked, swinging Evan down. Brion nodded. "I am Andraax, affectionately known as the Mad by my friends. I hope that you will be my friend, even though I have done you injustices beyond measure. I should never have taken your son into such danger. In reparation for that, I would ask you to allow me to instruct Evan for a time in the workings of Essence."

"Instruct him?" Brion asked, bewildered. "He's only ten years old!"

"Almost eleven," Evan put in solemnly.

Andraax smile down at him with real affection. "Are you ready for the Thalan yet?" Andraax asked, apparently at random. Evan shook his head. "So. Your son is very gifted, Brion, as you are yourself, but he has a few things to learn. I expect he could learn them from me as well as anyone else. I can't promise to teach him with any regularity — my life isn't structured so — but I will promise to finish what I start."

"It's common practice for the children of Loremasters to be tutored by others," Laurel contributed helpfully; Brion blinked at her uncertainly.

"I'm not a Loremaster," he pointed out.

She smiled. "That is the other half of the offer, of course. Oh, not that you would be a Loremaster — at least not right away — but that you attend the school on Karilôn. I think it would be good for you, Master Brion. And keep you out of trouble." She laughed aloud. "You seem to have a talent for trouble, like some others I could name."

"Not fair," Tiernan murmured. "Besides, I have no talent whatsoever for magecraft. Well, you don't have to decide just now."

"If I let these two chattering birds know, they'd tell him before I had the chance," Vurkanan Tyes said as he pushed in past Andraax. The two Loremasters looked at each other a little warily, and then Andraax bowed his head. Tyes returned the gesture. "Lady Astrid's also asked you to visit the Library at Nomikos. She left this morning to begin her apprenticeship as a Scribe, just as she promised Ziv. I doubt they'll turn her away, considering the piles of scrolls she's bringing them from the ruins of Quellburn."

"Where's Iarsang — and Pelk?" Brion asked.

Tyes looked at him a moment. "Iarsang is well; he's gone back to his guild to report the recovery of his Compass — and Daphine's death. He's coming back to take my wayward children back to Jaiman — where they will stay." Tyes stared down Laurel's defiant objection, and smiled slightly. "Pelk is waiting outside. He wants to speak to you alone."

"Please," Brion nodded. Andraax took Evan's hand and led the boy out; the others filed out, even Laurel, who looked as if she'd taken the permanent job as Brion's guard and nurse.

Tyes paused at the door. "You should take Andraax's offer to tutor your son. There are not two Loremasters living today who can lay such a claim. No harm will come to him, and no one else could teach him half so well."

"I'll think about it," Brion promised.

Tyes ducked outside and Pelk entered. The young thief stood there by the doorway, hands twisting uncomfortably in his belt, and Brion smiled.

"You've stolen some new clothes," he commented. Pelk was indeed well dressed in new leathers and a shining white shirt of silk. The handle of his sword was a gleaming ornament at his side. A short cape of red wool completed the picture — but Pelk looked miserable, and looked worse at Brion's attempt at humor. For once, he didn't want to trade insults.

"I killed your wife, Brion," he said softly, as if the words were a bitter geyser he couldn't keep bottled up any more. "When I saw her strike you, and when you fell — I threw at her, and I didn't miss. She would have bled to death if she hadn't taken the poison."

Brion nodded.

"You want me to hate you for that?" he asked quietly. Pelk said nothing. "Kella was mad. In my world she would have been confined, treated, perhaps healed — but here she could only do harm to herself and others, and I guess there wasn't any other end for it. She understood that. So do I."

Pelk drew in a deep breath and crossed to Brion's side. His blue eyes were blurred with tears.

"Then perhaps I will have to forgive myself, my friend. I think perhaps I loved your wife, at least a little."

"Then you lost more than I did. I couldn't even lie to her, at the end. I couldn't even pretend to love her." Brion shook his head and held out his hand. "Thank you, Pelk. No one said so, but I'll bet I owe you my life."

Pelk shook his head, turned away, and wiped at his eyes. When he turned back he was smiling — it was a strained attempt, but Brion smiled back.

"Believe it or not, I didn't steal my clothes — but I did steal yours. Here." Pelk unslung a bundle of cloth from his shoulder and laid it on the foot of the bed. "Don't wear them around the mayor of this fleabitten town, and there won't be any trouble. Oh — and come back to Karilôn. I'd like that."

"I'd like it too," Brion said, and held out his hand again.

This time, Pelk took it.

Iarsang stood in the circle of white light, facing the representatives of the Navigator Guilds. He was done talking, finally, and now he waited in silence as they thought over his words. Porel of the Pathmasters of Hulgan shifted uncomfortably in his seat and looked at the others, then cleared his throat.

"Perhaps you would care to explain why you failed to report the loss of your Compass at the time it occurred, Navigator?" the old man asked, not unkindly.

Iarsang looked off into the distance and didn't change expression. "A matter of honor. It was necessary to make it clear to the minions of Unlife that Navigators would not allow Compasses to be taken with impunity. I felt that since I had a connection to the Compass, I could best serve my guild by tracking the thief myself."

"And Daphine? How do you justify endangering and causing the death of one of the Order of Cypharia?" challenged Arone, representative of that guild. Iarsang said nothing. "You failed to report her death as was proper. Perhaps you can explain that failing, Iarsang. I cannot, upon my life!"

Iarsang stood like a statue, barely breathing, and then he closed his eyes. His voice came from a great distance.

"I have no explanation," he finally said. The others looked at each other, plainly baffled and worried, and the representative from Iarsang's own guild stood up.

"I believe we've taken enough time for this matter," the tall Elf said, looking at the Guild representatives with eyes that dared them to say otherwise. "I call for a vote."

One by one, the representatives cast their votes for Iarsang's reinstatement—even, at the end, Arone of Cypharia. Iarsang said nothing, only turned and walked to the window that overlooked the pounding sea below. Arone followed him, her white gown billowing in the fresh sea air, and laid a hand on his shoulder.

"What is it?" he asked shortly.

She stepped back cautiously. "You stated that the Dyar thief is dead, Navigator. I only wished to be sure that he paid for my sister's death before he died."

Iarsang turned to look at her, tears shimmering in his brown eyes and spilling over to run down his impassive face, and shook his head.

"No, Mistress Arone. If he had suffered a thousand years, if he had died a thousand times, it would not have been enough to pay for Daphine's death." Iarsang looked down at his Compass, glowing on his restored left hand. There were only faint scars now, and those were fading. "But he paid as much as he could pay. You may well believe that."

"I do," Arone said, studying his face with something like fear in her eyes. She bowed slightly before turning to go. The others were already gone, Jumped back to their Guilds. She paused as she lifted her Compass, and looked at his stiff, unyielding back. "Do you need assistance, Navigator?"

"If I do," Iarsang whispered, "it will pass. Such things do."

But he greatly feared that it never truly would.

After a few more moments he Jumped back to Kelfour's Landing, where his newest customers waited.

Tyes had somehow arranged a temporary truce, because the inn was silent when Iarsang appeared. Pelk was sitting at the bar with Tyes; they waved to the Navigator and offered him a mug of ale. He accepted it.

"An easy bit of travel ahead," Tyes sighed, and rubbed his temples. "Jump them all the way to Jaiman, my friend. I'll find the money to pay the bill. I can't take the chance of either one of them falling into trouble along the way."

"You underestimate them," Iarsang said gently. Tyes shook his head vehemently.

"No. I do not. That's what's so frightening."

"Where are they?" Iarsang asked, frowning. Tyes pointed to a booth in the back, where Laurel's golden head could be seen, and the shadowy form of her prince. Iarsang walked over to the table, then walked back. His face was sober and impassive, but there was a light in his eyes that hadn't been there since Daphine's death.

"What is it?" Tyes asked wearily. Iarsang beckoned to him, and the Loremaster slid off of his bench to follow.

The woman who looked up at him was the innkeeper's scullery woman. Her best feature was her cloud of yellow hair, teased out in curls to hide her face from casual observers. The man impersonating Tiernan was the stableboy, a tall, gangly youth who gulped when faced with Tyes' cold glare.

"Where," Tyes asked carefully, "did they go?"

"She left a note, sir," the scullery woman said helpfully, and slid it across the table. The stableboy was eating his soup hurriedly, as if fearing it was about to be taken away from him. Tyes unfolded the note and read it, then passed it to Iarsang with a sigh.

Father, please extend our apologies to the Navigator for this ruse. We have decided to discuss our future on a long sea voyage. The Royal Swallow *is setting sail now; by the time you read this we will be well on our way. Please forgive us, but I have decided to bow to the inevitable; Tiernan says to tell you that we will work out the terms of my marriage settlement on the way, and send word to you after we reach an acceptable figure.*

I personally intend to take him for everything a prince is worth.

Tyes stood there in stunned amazement as Iarsang read it. Iarsang raised his eyebrows.

"Do you think they're actually on the Swallow?" the Navigator asked.

Tyes shook his head. "Of course not. My daughter is far too intelligent to make it that easy. Lords above, what am I going to do?"

"May I suggest?" Iarsang asked, and led him back to the bench.

Tyes sat down and stared morosely down at his cup. "What?" the Loremaster snapped.

Iarsang held up his own cup, eyes steady and warm. "To love!" he said.

"To love," the Loremaster agreed, and drank. Suddenly, his eyes lit up, and he laughed, a slow infectious chuckle that made Iarsang cock his head in inquiry. "If Laurel thinks she's avoiding trouble, she's sadly mistaken. As I recall, I last saw her mother Isseline heading for Jaiman. Marriage— whether her own or her daughter's — has never agreed with Isseline — "

"Indeed not. A formidable woman, your wife. I may make the Jump to Rhakhaan in any case, Tyes, just to study the look on Prince Tiernan's face when he sees her!" Iarsang lifted his glass again. "Then — to bowing to the inevitable."

Tyes raised his glass and drank deeply. The wine was sweet but had a bite to it. "To the inevitable!"

THE END

If you enjoyed reading *Stormriders*, imagine living in the Shadow World of Kulthea. You can! Iron Crown Enterprises also publishes fantasy role playing books and games that transport you and your friends into the muck and magic of Kulthea, the Shadow World. Like acting or "getting under the skin" of a character **you** create, fantasy role playing brings friends together to act out a living, breathing novel; everything you do changes the adventure you're playing. Better yet, ICE offers two game systems, *Rolemaster* ™ and *Fantasy Hero*™. *Rolemaster* is easily the most realistic — yet playable — fantasy role playing system (for fighting, casting spells, locating and using healing herbs, etc.) in existence. *Fantasy Hero* is more action-oriented and quicker to use. Whichever system you and your friends decide to play with, enjoy yourselves and let us know what's happening, okay?

In case you want to know more about *Shadow World*, read on!

ABOUT
SHADOW WORLD

The *Shadow World* is the planet *Kulthea* — a cauldron of mystical forces. The *Unlife*, an unspeakable horror from the Void, feeds upon the vast energies it has found here. Standing against the Unlife are the scattered servants of a noble race and the valiant few who can be gathered to combat this monstrous evil.

Shadow World products are designed to be used with the *Rolemaster* and *Fantasy Hero* role playing systems.

The following pages provide information about how to use and connect the fantasy role playing books currently available as adventure and resource guidebooks in the Shadow World series.

While most are already located near or on the continents of Jaiman or Emer, those that could be 'moved' by the GM include suggestions on how best to do so. Other books cover large or immobile lands; ideas for "linking" these realms to the overall plot line of Shadow World are included.

• SHADOW WORLD MASTER ATLAS

This boxed product is the cornerstone of the series. It includes a large 3 ft. x 4 ft. poster/map of Kulthea's western hemisphere, the *World Guide* containing explanatory maps and general information (as well as weather patterns and a history of the *Shadow World*), and the *Inhabitants Guide*, covering the races, beasts and plants of Kulthea. Read more about the Loremasters, Navigators, Dragonlords, and other denizens of the Shadow World.

• EMER, THE GREAT CONTINENT

Emer is a new, giant boxed set, complementing the Master Atlas and enriching the Shadow World Legacy.

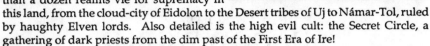

Gathered in a boxed set are color maps of Emer and her primary cities, as well as strategic maps, and two books, each nearly 100 pages long and packed with material.

One is devoted to an overview of Emer itself, the greatest continent on Kulthea. More than a dozen realms vie for supremacy in this land, from the cloud-city of Eidolon to the Desert tribes of Uj to Námar-Tol, ruled by haughty Elven lords. Also detailed is the high evil cult: the Secret Circle, a gathering of dark priests from the dim past of the First Era of Ire!

The other book is an *Atlas Addendum*, supplementing the general information in the original *Atlas*. A greatly expanded timeline is just the beginning. Also included are complete sections of Dark Gods, more demons, ancient technology, magic artifacts, and a random encounter system

Access Suggestion: *Primarily source material, Emer is invaluable as a general resource for GMs running a campaign in the Shadow World. The Emer book is an excellent reference to the continent, with adventure ideas and background on the world's most powerful evil cult. The Atlas Addendum reveals the secrets of the demons, the Dark Gods, and lesser deities. There is a massive encounter matrix, artifacts, technology and more!*

• QUELLBOURNE, LAND OF THE SILVER MIST

Set in NW Jaiman, Quellbourne offers a variety of low and mid-level scenarios intended for small parties in search of stand-alone adventures. Battle the ragged Destroyers of Galtoth, who seek to annihilate all forms of life on their isle. Overcome the evil clerics who worship Hraask, the Spider Goddess.

Read about the lands where *Stormriders* takes place!

• JOURNEY TO THE MAGIC ISLE

An island east of the continent of Thuul, the *Magic Isle* — not surprisingly — is focused on spells and spell learning. The adventures are very specific and channeled. This is an ideal location for fledgling magicians, but warriors will be bored.

Access Suggestion: *The Magic Isle is isolated and so can be shifted rather easily to almost any location. It could even be a hidden isle, not appearing on maps, with no 'fixed' location.*

System Note: *Fantasy Hero players should probably stay away; system information is spotty because of the lack of spell support for FH at the time Magic Isle was published.*

• DEMONS OF THE BURNING NIGHT

This scenario takes place on the isle of Aranmor, southwest of Jaiman. It is an offbeat, eerie setting involving high-level ancient evils and powerful demonic forces. Not for the squeamish (or a non-magical party of fighters).

• TALES OF THE LOREMASTERS, BOOK I

Set on the exotic Shinh Archipelago — a rugged string of tropical islands west of central Emer — adventurers battle outcasts, bandits, vampires and dragons in this series of stand-alone adventures ideal for FH gamers and RM warriors alike.

• STAR CROWN EMPIRE AND THE SEA OF FATES

The Star Crown Empire is located on the continent of Govon, far to the southeast of Emer. This book is mostly historical and cultural material for the GM wishing to begin a campaign or send his characters to a new land. Heavy on history and background; light on adventures but of special interest to FH gamers.

Access Suggestion: *Since it would require considerable work to move the Star Crown Empire or graft it onto a land adjacent to Jaiman or Emer, I suggest that the players either must go there as part of an extended quest, pass through a Portal and arrive there, or are forced there by a freak Essence storm. If the players go intentionally, they could brave the seas on their own, hire a ship with experienced crew, and/or hire a Navigator. Note that there will not be any normal trading voyages to a place as far away as Govon. Even from SE Emer it is a perilous journey across 1500 miles of treacherous open sea.*

• KINGDOM OF THE DESERT JEWEL

Like Star Crown Empire, Desert Jewel is largely a background piece, providing an overview of a large arid land in NW Thuul. Not unlike ancient Egypt on our earth, Gethrya has a long history rich in religion and ritual. *Desert Jewel* has considerable background and layout material but adventures are covered only briefly.

Access Suggestion: *Gethrya is far from Emer or Jaiman, travel there is perilous without a Navigator. I suggest that a GM wishing to send his characters there have them encounter a strange, temple-like structure set in a cliffside. It bears the symbols of Gethrya (though the PCs wouldn't recognize them), and inside lies a gate. This temple in fact exists in two places; it is a spacial link between Gethrya and another location of the GM's choosing. When the PCs emerge from the temple, they are in the Kingdom of the Desert Jewel, and might require some special item to return.*

· TALES OF THE LOREMASTERS, BOOK II

A book with ten stand-alone adventures, "Tales II" provides an array of unique settings to help GMs fill in gaps in their campaign. Of special interest to FH gamers.

Access Suggestion: *While set in various locales across Jaiman, these adventures are easily moved to wherever they are convenient.*

· CYCLOPS VALE & OTHER TALES

This features a series of nine linked, low-level but easily made stand-alone adventures set in the Peaks of Pelegris, in the south of Tai-emer, on the continent of Emer. Of special interest to *FH* gamers.

Access Suggestion: *Because of the isolated nature of the peaks and context in these adventures, they can easily be moved to any mountainous area.*

· JAIMAN, LAND OF TWILIGHT

This book provides an overview of the entire continent of Jaiman: its cultures, races and long, tangled history. Eight medium to high-level adventures take players from the ancient tombs of forgotten kings to the treacherous citadels of Priests of the Unlife! Four adventures can be linked to form a mighty quest affecting the fate of all Jaiman.

Also included: details about Nomikos: the Scribes and their library; the Dragonlord Sulthon Ni'shaang, and the secret Gryphon College.

Access Suggestion: *This large book contains several 'high-powered' adventures. It is best used in concert with other books set in Jaiman (such as 'Tales II') as part of a Quest, employing the other adventures to advance the characters towards the large, sweeping adventures found in Jaiman.*

· ISLANDS OF THE ORACLE

This supplement is set on the Abarquan Islands, 3200 miles east of Emer. Three low to medium-level adventure scenarios include a visit with the fabled Oracle, a battle at sea with ruthless Pirates, and a mission to uncover the source of the Unlife's power in the region. Of special interest to FH gamers.

Access Suggestion: *While in fact rather far from Emer or Jaiman, the GM could move the Isles closer or even force the players there by utilizing a flowstorm at sea. Acting like a huge, random Portal, a sailing ship could be swept by a storm through a shimmering curtain and transported thousands of miles (to just off the coast of the Islands of the Oracle!).*

• SKY GIANTS OF THE BRASS STAIR

This campaign module is set on the continent of Jaiman, in the region known as Wuliris. Seven low to medium-level adventures set in and around the realm of the Sky Giants and four detailed cities/strongholds are provided.

Access Suggestion: *Since this book is set in a relatively isolated area, it could be moved to any region adjacent to high mountains.*

• NOMADS OF THE NINE NATIONS

Explore the vast grasslands of southwest Thuul, home to the people of the Jengada Allied Nations. Primarily a background book, *Nomads* has seven briefly detailed adventures.

Access Suggestion: Nomads *is set near the Kingdom of the Desert Jewel, and GMs may wish to tie these two together. Otherwise, the only expedient way to get PCs here is via Portal or a Navigator-directed Teleport.*

• NOREK, CITY-STATE OF JAIMAN

Set in a coastal trade city in southern Jaiman, *Norek* is packed with nine low to medium-level adventures set both in the city and in the surrounding countryside. Of special interest to FH gamers.

Access Suggestion: *While linked to the Jaiman political situation,* Norek *could be moved without too much difficulty to another temperate coastal area.*

· THE JOURNALS OF KALEN AVANIR ·

Editor's Note: To clarify the connection between the Shadow World books currently available, we present the following tale. By adding his own touches to the books, a GM may create a single thread which binds the entire theme of the Shadow World together.

With Kalen's Journals, one all-encompassing vision of the Shadow World is partially revealed. More will be told in future books, but the GM may wish to use the ideas here as a springboard for his own campaign. Also — the route described here by Kalen does not mean the books must be used in this order!

This is a series of brief excerpts from the travel journals of the young nobleman and adventurer Kalen Avanir. A youth of particular insight, he has voyaged to many lands on Kulthea in search of a single directing force behind the creeping evil which seems to be slowly covering the world in Darkness.

More from the diaries of this singular youth shall be forthcoming as events in the Shadow World Warrant.

THE TALE

My name is Kalen Avanir, heir to the Duchy of Prevan. Perhaps you have heard of the Rhakhaan Empire in Jaiman, of which Prevan is a part? No matter! The story which I must tell you tonight leaves Prevan far behind, dwindling in the greater picture of a darkening world. An evil grows; the thralls of the Unlife ascend in strength, feeding on some new power. This was a journey I dreaded, yet it had to be made. The Loremaster Randæ Terisonen, as enigmatic of any of his kind, had placed this burden upon me and me alone. I sought lore regarding the Shadowstone: the heart of Darkness, the bane of Kulthea.

My travelling party was small: I invited my friends Keela and Taluk; also my squire Jad Hurok, and two house guards. I determined to hire a Navigator for the journey and had sufficient funding for a few direct Jumps, so decided to begin my journey without delay.

A touch on the Navigator Obelisk in the Rhakhaan capital of Haalkitaine summoned a member of the Guides of Vurn-Kye. I knew as much by his aloof demeanor as by his black garments and glittering Compass-device.

"Tar-esiir, at your service." He bowed.

"I would like to be transported by Jump to the town of Forvers," I replied. He named his exorbitant price, and after a brief preparation, we were there.

NORTHERN LU'NAK[1]

In the Northern hills of Lu'nak I sought a meteorite which fell in the area long ago. Its nature might lead me to other clues of ancient origin — and of things beyond the world. Our search for the stone was a convoluted one, involving several adventures which I will not tire you with, except to say: beware the glance of the Basilisk and the sharp tongue of the Sphinx!

For days we marched across an icy plain. My anxiety grew; Jad caught cold. At last I found the great rock from the sky. Its origins were as I feared: from beyond the Void. An analysis of the pitted mass of grey ore provided me with an image — and a new direction. The trail led us westward through the ancient Blue Forest to Quellbourne.

IN QUELLBOURNE²

Far to the Northwest, in the cold reaches of Jaiman, lies a bay surrounding a mountainous isle. On the shore of the bay lie the ruins of the city of Quellburn. Here my search continued, where the High Priest of Athimurl once laid waste to a civilization. Only the wind moans through the empty towers of Quellburn, yet among the city's bones I uncovered another hint from the deep past.

Clues I found — as well as trouble, brought by the insidious Destroyers of Galtoth. An ancient trail pointed south to a hint about the origins of the ancient Lords of Essænce.

ON TO ARANMOR³

We took ship out of Kelfour's Landing, sailing along the western coast of Jaiman without incident (Navigators are expensive, but worth it) until we approached the Isle of Plasidar. Dyari pirate ships skimmed the coast, but seemed content to observe us from afar.

The ruined city of Tarek Nev was my goal, there to find the legendary Helm of Kadæna, Empress of the Lords of Essænce. As we approached Aranmor, the seas began to steam, then to boil — heated by volcanic activity deep beneath the ocean surface. Only by Tar-esiir's spells and Taluk's seamanship did we make it safely to shore.

Through the Weyr Forest we trekked, until we came to the vast black ruin of Tarek Nev. Terror gripped our hearts in this city of ancient power. More I will not tell; my small powers of sorcery were enough so that I learned what I needed to know. Yes, the Helm is there; I left it for another to solve the riddle of that hideous place — at his peril.

NOMIKOS AND THE CATACOMBS⁴

We took ship again and sailed into the port of Ormian, on the isle which was the cradle of all lore on the Shadow World: the library of Nomikos. Many days I spent buried in books and scrolls (Tar-esiir advised me to call when I needed him again). But I found what I wanted: a map to an ancient tomb.

We then sailed into the Bay of Urulan, docking at a coastal village of Tanara. Tales spun in Prevan inns say that Tanara is home to a race of assassins with blond giants for slaves. Well, we saw none of those (only shy Sea-elves live along the coast), but my map proved true: we found the Catacombs of Ûr. Filled with secrets they are, and priceless knowledge — and traps. The trail led north to Wuliris, within the lands controlled by the Dragonlord. There would lie a Dwarven-city, abandoned but for a pair of reptilian residents.

CONSULTATION WITH DRAGONS[5]

After an arduous journey and a climb up the legendary Brass Stair, I held council with two of the most regal beings I have yet to encounter. True Drakes, they had wisdom and knowledge spanning the ages. Little could they tell me however, except to say only: "The Eyes of Utha guard the Earth, and when they close, all will perish. One has blinked." Cryptic words indeed, but they advised me to seek the truth west of Emer on a coastal Isle. A Temple holds a key...

THE ISLES WEST OF EMER[6]

Another Jump carried us many hundreds of leagues (and nearly emptied my money-purse). We arrived on one of a cluster of tropical isles west of Emer. It was a welcome change but I was soon frustrated by the effects of this beautiful climate. All traces of the structure I sought had been obliterated in the seasonal storms. I was forced to take a path I feared more than Aranmor: into the jungles of southern Emer.

Heading east, we wandered for weeks in a unending jungle. Many times I doubted my direction, fearing that I had misread the clues. And many times I regretted bringing my friends on this perilous journey. Taluk died in the Rulaash forest, taking the deadly needles of a dartspore plant intended to kill me. There are riches there: emeralds uncut lie glittering at the foot of the black mountains. But no treasure will buy back dead friends.

THE PELEGRIS MOUNTAINS[7]

On the north coast of Rulaash, Tar-esiir spoke to me. "I must leave you at this time. My replacement is a capable Navigator, of the Guild which bears the name 'The Navigators'. He will grant a free Jump anywhere on Emer to compensate for the inconvenience." Without so much as a farewell, he shimmered and was gone.

An instant later, a tall Elf in grey leather blinked into existence, bathed in a rainbow of light. On his wrist was a metal band set with a brilliant opalescent stone.

"I am Iarsang." He smiled crookedly. "It will be my pleasure to serve you."

"He's already nicer than Tar-esiir," Jad whispered.

Our new guide transported us to the Pelegris Mountains in southern Tai-emer. There I sought a great obelisk, to understand its links to a being long past. Isolated in the windswept mountains of Pelegris we encountered a race of winged men and a golden pool guarded by a fell giant. We found the obelisk, and I learned what I needed from among its many secrets. I must seek lore regarding the mystical items known as the Eyes of Utha — and a dark cult whose name hearkens to a time before my race walked the earth... the Jerak Ahrenreth. I had heard of an Oracle far to the east of Emer. With emeralds from Rulaash (harshly undervalued; it would seem that all Navigators are the same after all), I paid Iarsang to take us to a cluster of isles far away.

THE ORACLE OF TATHAM[8]

We arrived only to encounter a most bizarre people: lizard-men! Though strange, this was a civilized race, and they agreed, after some discussion to allow me to speak to the Oracle. Standing in that vast chamber I learned many things about the order known as the Jerak Ahrenreth — the Secret Circle. But the Oracle could not tell me much of the Eyes of Utha, for they are of the First Era, and the Oracle was born in the late Second Era. It did warn me that others of less virtuous purpose sought the Eyes — and advised me to flee the Isles with all speed.

A LOST CITY IN THE DESERT[9]

Another costly Jump took us to the deep deserts of western Thuul and the land of Gethrya. An ancient tomb in the lost city of Thri-Zirakan was said to hold glyphs telling of Utha and the Eyes.

Fortunately, we met none of the denizens of this arid land, and the tomb contained just the hints I sought: at the end of the First Era, Utha placed two items of the greatest power — 'eyes' — at the poles of the world to shield it from outside powers. Only the Lords of Orhan could pass through the barrier; the dark forces of the Unlife were barred.

SOUTH TO THE JAN[10]

The Jan are tribes of nomadic warriors, virtuous yet barbaric. They fought against an evil empire which followed the teachings of the Dark God Scalu. It was from those of the Cult of Scalu that I required information. We were not to achieve our goal, however, for a freak Essænce storm swept across the snowy plains. Before Iarsang could get us away, we were caught up like dry leaves in a rush of wind. An eternity of wrenching moments later, we tumbled to earth in a lush, blue-green forest.

THE JUNGLES OF GOVON[11]

Iarsang rose and dusted himself off, then began to take bearings. "We appear to be in Govon; quite a Jump! I'm afraid we are stuck here for a few days; my powers have been thoroughly drained."

We ended up staying quite a bit longer than that. Captured by Lizard-men, we became embroiled in a complex political situation which delayed us for more than a month. On the brink of execution by Dwarves, Iarsang managed to work our escape.

THE ARCH-MAGE[12]

Upon the Isle of Uman is a secret school of magic; it was here that I hoped my journey would end. I gained an audience with the Arch-mage of the Magic Isle, a woman! She had some knowledge of what I sought, speaking of the Eight Secrets of the ancient cult of Ahrenreth. She said that the wearer of the Shadowstone could only be defeated by one who could wield the Soulsword from the First Era. She knew not where it lay, but counselled me to seek Andraax the Insane.

But that is another tale.

FOOTNOTES TO THE LOCATIONS BY BOOK NAMES

1. Tales of the Loremasters II.
2. Quellbourne, Land of the Silver Mist.
3. Demons of the Burning Night.
4. Jaiman, Land of Twilight
5. Sky-Giants of the Brass Stair
6. Tales of the Loremasters I
7. Cyclops Vale
8. Islands of the Oracle
9. Kingdom of the Desert Jewel
10. Nomads of the Nine Nations
11. Star Crown Empire
12. The Magic Isle

THE ADVANCED FANTASY ROLE PLAYING SYSTEM!

Rolemaster is the most advanced, realistic, and sophisticated FRP rules system available. Reformatted and reorganized in a second edition, the flexibility of its three competent rulebooks allow it to be used wholly or separately to improve the realism of most major FRP systems! It is the next step up for players of *Middle-earth Role Playing*™ and similar basic/intermediate role playing systems.

A complete FRP system boxed with three component books: *Arms Law & Claw Law*®, *Character Law and Campaign Law*™, and *Spell Law*® totalling some 400 pages of sophisticated lore. These books may be purchased separately, allowing GMs to upgrade the weaker aspects of their existing fantasy role playing system at an affordable pace. This state-of-the-art system adds realism and depth to your campaign without sacrificing playability. Experience the ultimate in role playing!

PRODUCT SUMMARY

Title	Setting	Stk #	Price
Shadow World Products			
Shadow World Master Atlas	*	6000	$20.00
Emer, the Great Continent	Emer*	6100	$30.00
Quellbourne	Jaiman	6001	$12.00
The Magic Isle	†	6002	$9.00
Demons of the Burning Night	Jaiman	6003	$12.00
Tales of the Loremasters, Book I	Emer	6004	$6.00
Star Crown Empire	†	6005	$12.00
Kingdom of the Desert Jewel	†	6007	$12.00
Tales of the Loremaster, Book II	Jaiman	6008	$6.00
Cyclops Vale & Other Tales	Emer	6009	$6.00
Jaiman, Land of Twilight	Jaiman	6010	$15.00
Islands of the Oracle	†	6011	$9.00
Sky Giants of the Brass Stair	Jaiman	6012	$12.00
Nomads of the Nine Nations	†	6013	$12.00
Norek, City-state of Jaiman	Jaiman	6014	$12.00
Rolemaster Products			
Rolemaster	—	1000	$38.00
Arms Law & Claw Law	—	1100	$14.00
Spell Law	—	1200	$14.00
Character Law & Campaign Law	—	1300	$14.00
Creatures & Treasures	—	1400	$12.00
Creatures & Treasures	—	1410	$12.00

* Sourcebook
† Not set on Emer or Jaiman; requires difficult travel; or GM can 'transplant' it.
‡ Not included in the Rolemaster Boxed Set.

These products are available at book and games stores, or contact
Iron Crown Enterprises
P.O. Box 1605
Charlottesville, VA 22901
1.800.325.0479

ABOUT ICE'S ROLEMASTER PRODUCTS

In order to role play in the Shadow World you need the *Shadow World Master Atlas* boxed set and a fantasy role playing system. We highly recommend *Rolemaster* as your best choice for an advanced fantasy role playing sytem.

Rolemaster boxed set   **$38.00**

A complete advanced FRP system boxed with three component books: *Character Law & Campaign Law*, *Spell Law*, and *Arms Law & Claw Law*. Now reformatted and reorganized, this state-of-the-art system adds realism and depth to your campaign without sacrificing playability. Experience the ultimate in role playing! Polysided dice must be purchased separately.

Arms Law & Claw Law — combat system for *Rolemaster*   **$12.00**

A combat system that improves any game and serves as one of the three cornerstones of the *Rolemaster* system. Fast-paced and realistic, it resolves most attacks in only two die rolls. Contents include 30 weapon attack tables, ten critical strike tables, a dozen animal and martial arts attack tables, and a variety of optional rules.

Spell Law — magic system for *Rolemaster*   **$14.00**

Spell Law is a mighty tome that can add realism and depth to your campaign without sacrificing playability. This magic system includes over 2000 spell descriptions, individual spell attack tables, critical strike tables, a power point system, detailed alchemy rules, and a variety of optional rules.

Character Law & Campaign Law™
— character development system for *Rolemaster*
                                                             $14.00

Character Law & Campaign Law is a complete character development system that includes extensive campaign and Gamemaster guidelines. It improves any game and serves as the core of ICE's highly acclaimed FRP system, *Rolemaster.*

War Law™ boxed set
$30.00

Mass combat comes to *Rolemaster*! Perfect for *Rolemaster* Gamemasters whether their priorities are ease-of-use or realism. *War Law* is a complete mass combat system that includes extensive guidelines for situations involving large numbers of combatants and serves as a key supplement for *Rolemaster*. Now conflicts between fantasy armies are handled within your existing fantasy role playing campaign and regular *Rolemaster* combat resolution is simplified and resolved in a speedier fashion.

In *War Law*, a GM makes numerous detailed decisions for every aspect of battles that can have anywhere from two to thousands of participants. In addition, a simplified boardgame, usable by any GM, is provided for resolving mass combat. However, this simplified version does not require a GM as it makes standard decisions for many of the key battle system aspects.

War Law covers morale rules, maneuver rules, ferocity rules, leaders, formations, fortifications, development of units and their skills using the *RM* development point cost system, plus historical and tactical considerations. *War Law* is a boxed product containing rules, a hexagonal playing surface, hundreds of counters, and dice.

Rolemaster Combat Screen™
$6.00

A collection of useful charts and tables designed to provide Gamemasters with a screen and table summary for greater ease-of-play.

Rolemaster Character Records™
$12.00

This 144 page book contains a set of tailor-made, individualized, blank character records for each *Rolemaster* profession in Character *Law* and the *Rolemaster Companions I-IV*. Each set of character records has the exact Development Point costs and level bonuses for all of the skills from *Character Law* and the *Rolemaster Companions*. Players no longer have to laboriously copy the Development Point costs for all skills of their chosen profession — just photocopy a couple of pages and you are ready to go!

Creatures & Treasures™
$12.00

Provides complete descriptions and game stats for over 500 animals, races, and fantastic beasts, including: Demons, Elementals, Dragons, Undead and Giants! Tables help generate unusual treasures and a wide variety of random encounters. Spice up your game with monsters and magic!

Creatures & Treasures II™
$13.00

The second in a series of best-selling monster and artifact compendiums provides gamemasters greater flexibility when designing role playing encounters. This 112 page compilation of new monsters and treasures for *Rolemaster* includes fantasy animals, artificial beings, composite monsters, demons, undead, entities from other planes and from deep space! Treasures are grouped into their power categories, and there are plenty of charts to create encounters and hazards.

Rolemaster Heroes & Rogues™ $16.00

Rolemaster Heroes & Rogues is a complete 160 page collection of characters that can be used an NPCs or pre-generated high level PCs for *Rolemaster* campaigns. This compendium covers all of the 20 *Character Law* professions: Fighter, Rogue, Magician, Animist, Mentalists, Mystic, Bard, etc. For each profession, a detailed background and *RM* statistics are provided for 1st, 3rd, 5th, 10th, 15th, and 20th levels. Put away your pencils, pads, and calculators — *Rolemaster Heroes & Rogues* is the fast and easy way to introduce new characters into your campaigns and adventures.

Rolemaster Companion™ $12.00

Expands this classic system with optional rules and guidelines. Provides 32 new spell lists and numerous high-level spells. It also gives 8 new professions and a variety of new races, creatures, and secondary skills. The optional rules also include an abbreviated combat system and numerous game aids to help in running a smooth campaign.

Rolemaster Companion II™ $12.00

Something for every *Rolemaster* GM and player! Thirteen new professions, 65 new spell lists, over 100 new optional skills! This supplement also provides comprehensive 'Master Tables' and descriptions for all the skills and professions in *Rolemaster*!

Rolemaster Companion III™ $12.00

The tradition of superbly detailed optional support for *Rolemaster* continues! Twenty-one variant professions, more than 40 new spell lists, 7 new critical tables, 4 spell attack tables, and optional rules. Add a Companion to your *Rolemaster* campaign!

Rolemaster Companion IV™ $13.00

Rolemaster Companion IV (ROCO IV) expands ICE's *Rolemaster* fantasy role playing system with a variety of optional rules, spell lists, and guidelines. In addition, this 96 page supplement provides a complete index of all *Rolemaster* spells and spell lists, along with a complete Checklist/Index of all optional rules, professions, and spell lists in *Rolemaster*, *Elemental Companion*, and the *Rolemaster Companions I-IV*. Summon your sages, get our your spells books, and sharpen your quill-pens — your campaign is about to be enriched by *Rolemaster Companion IV*.

Elemental Companion™ $15.00

The sourcebook for elemental power in a FRP environment includes extensive campaign and Gamemaster guidelines for situations involving elementals and elemental spells in combat. Included are new spell lists, new variant elemental professions, new elemental creatures, complete coverage of the elemental planes, and a detailed history of the development of elemental magic.

Dark Space™ $16.00

Dark Space is a **Rolemaster** 96 page genre book that fully details a sci fi/fantasy/ horror setting. Magic and technology coexist and evil alien horrors plot the downfall of mankind. *Dark Space* includes new professions, new spell/psion lists, twenty detailed worlds and the specifics of the society which binds them. It also includes ready to run scenarios, tons of information on the Elder Worms, their servants, motivations and tactics, and hundreds of new high tech items based around Softech, the science of biological engineering. Usable as a campaign on its own or it will fit into your existing campaign—whether it's fantasy or science fiction!